The Cottage on Plum Island

Cobble Beach Romance — Book 2

AMY RAFFERTY

AMY RAFFERTY VIP READERS

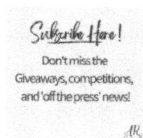

Don't want to miss out on my giveaways, competitions,

and 'hot off the press' news?

Subscribe to my email list.

It is FREE!

Click Here!

CONNECT WITH AMY RAFFERTY

Not only can you check out the latest news and deals there,

you can also get an email alert each time I release my next book.

Follow me on BookBub

I always love to hear from you and get your feedback.

Email me at ~ books@amyraffertyauthor.com

Follow on Amazon ~ Amy Rafferty

Sign up for my newsletter and free gift, Here

Join my 'Amy's Friends' group on Facebook

AMY RAFFERTY VIP READERS

Don't want to miss out on my giveaways, competitions,

and 'hot off the press' news?

Subscribe to my email list.

It is FREE!

Click Here!

CONNECT WITH AMY RAFFERTY

Not only can you check out the latest news and deals there,

you can also get an email alert each time I release my next book.

Follow me on BookBub

I always love to hear from you and get your feedback.

Email me at ~ books@amyraffertyauthor.com

Follow on Amazon ~ Amy Rafferty

Sign up for my newsletter and free gift, Here

Join my 'Amy's Friends' group on Facebook

TABLE OF CONTENTS

CHAPTER 1

J ennifer Gains's head throbbed from the five-hour Los Ange-
les-to-Boston flight. The idea of checking into a hotel for the
night crossed her mind, but her aunt needed her. She adjusted the
rental car's mirror and watched Boston fade into the distance.

Jennifer wasn't due back in Plum Island for another two weeks, as
she was supposed to fly from Los Angeles to New York to pack up her
life before moving home to Plum Island. But her aunt Betty had fallen
off a ladder and broken her leg. Jennifer's older brother, Liam, had
been with her for the past six days while Betty was in the hospital. But
Liam was taking his daughter and some of her friends to Disneyland
for a week and had left early that morning. Jennifer knew the kids had

1

been excited about going, so she'd moved her timeframe up to help out her aunt so Liam could go.

Luckily, Sam Donovan, a key figure on Plum Island and one of Betty's oldest friends, had come to her rescue. Sam's goddaughter, Doctor Daniella Thornton, ran a small clinic on Plum Island. Sam had taken Aunt Betty to Daniella, and she'd gotten Betty transferred to Newbury Port Hospital. That was two days ago, and Aunt Betty was ready to be released. Jennifer was going to fetch her on the way through.

Jennifer was still unclear as to why her aunt would be trying to climb onto the roof. She had forbidden Betty to attempt to clean out the gutters two years ago after Betty's last fall. She sighed and put her hand over her mouth as she yawned.

The past week in Los Angeles had been a whirlwind of meetings with various celebrities, courtesy of her new friend, Harriet Joyce. Jennifer had found herself at countless functions and parties with her new friend. For a woman who didn't like to socialize much, Harriet had dragged Jennifer to their fair share of social gatherings.

Although they were select functions, the parties were tasteful garden or yacht parties. They also only stayed at a party for a short time. A smile touched Jennifer's lips as she thought about Harriet's mantra:

You just need to show your face, mingle for a while, and then discreetly leave, and don't forget to grab a bottle of champagne on the way out.

Jennifer yawned once again and glanced at the dashboard clock. She'd been traveling for forty minutes. Jennifer didn't have much farther to go. As she yawned again, Jennifer decided she needed water to refresh and rehydrate. She'd read somewhere that sometimes fatigue meant you could be dehydrated. Jennifer reached into the cup holder in the door to get her bottle of water, and as Jennifer opened the lid, it took a nosedive to the floor.

"Shoot!" Jennifer cursed, glancing down to see where the runaway cap had gone.

She spotted the white lid next to her foot. Jennifer managed to maneuver the lid back to where she could reach down to grab it. She placed the opened water bottle in the dashboard cup holder and bent down to grab the lid. A terrible crunching noise resonated through the vehicle as her fingers closed around the little troublemaker.

"Darn it!" Jennifer exclaimed as the clatter-clatter noise mimicked the sound of a flat tire. "That's all I need!"

Wondering what she could've hit that would give her a flat, she glanced in the mirror. As her eyes were drawn back to the road ahead, they widened as a man appeared in front of her, flapping his arms widely in the air. Instinct kicked in, sending pinprick shockwaves zapping through her nerve endings, and she swerved sharply to avoid him. As she turned the wheel to right the car, water and the other items on the passenger seat flew everywhere.

As she pulled to the side of the road, Jennifer barely heard the clatter-clatter noise still coming from the front of the car as a whooshing noise echoed through her ears. Shaken, Jennifer sat for a few seconds staring ahead, unblinking, with her hands attached to the wheel in a death grip.

Her chest rose and fell as her heart hammered against her ribcage. She nearly jumped out of her skin when the crazy man, who'd been flapping his arms in the middle of the road, banged on her window.

Jennifer turned to see a handsome man with stormy aquamarine eyes glaring at her accusingly.

"You nearly killed me!" The man was so close to the window that his breath misted a spot on the window. "Are you crazy, lady?"

The shock faded and was replaced by instant, boiling rage at being called insane by a man flapping around in the middle of the road. *Did he just call me crazy?*

"*I'm* crazy?" Jennifer seethed. Her eyes narrowed as she shoved her door open with a force that sent the man stumbling backward. She pushed herself out of the car.

"What the—" The man stared at her in disbelief, holding his chest where the door had hit it.

His eyes widened as Jennifer advanced on him, enraged. Index finger at the ready, she pointed at him accusingly and hissed, "Who jumps around in the middle of the road on a *bend?*"

"It's a slight curve, and you can see around it." The man's shock eased, and he retaliated, giving as good as he got. "For *your* information, I wasn't in the middle of the road. I was on the curb, which is where *you* were driving!"

"It's natural to go slightly into the curb when taking a *bend!*" Jennifer exclaimed, her voice raising slightly. "Why on earth would you be jumping around on the side of the road?"

"Oh, I don't know!" The man said sarcastically. "Why do people usually try to flag people down from the *side* of the road?" He turned to glance at his blue pickup parked on the grassy verge with its hood up. "I was trying to get help."

"What century are you from?" Jennifer sneered. "Because in this one, we have cell phones to use that don't require us to jump out in front of moving vehicles."

"I *didn't* jump out in front of you," the man said through gritted teeth. "And my phone has died. That's why I was trying to flag down the only car I've seen in an hour. I didn't expect to nearly get killed by a crazy person swerving all over the road."

"I swerved to avoid the idiot standing in the middle of the road flapping his arms around like Peter Pan trying to fly!" Jennifer was seething. "And anyone with any *road sense* would've put an emergency triangle out to warn vehicles!"

"I did have one out!" The man snarled, storming to the front of Jennifer's car, and crouching down.

Alarmed, Jennifer moved to see what he was doing, and her eyes widened as she watched the man untangle something from between the tire and fender of her car. He stood with a mangled piece of orange plastic in his hand and held it up for her to see.

"Here's my triangle!" he exclaimed. "You killed it!"

Oh! That's what I drove over! Jennifer realized. *Oops!* She had to bite her lip not to laugh at the crunched-up triangle and cleared her throat.

"Again!" She pointed at the mangled mess in his hands and arced her index finger through the air. "It needs to be placed on the—" She leaned forward, saying forcefully, "*SIDE OF THE ROAD!*"

"Here's a little tip for you, *sweetheart.*" The man's eyes narrowed. "That mirror attached to the windshield is for *glancing* behind you, *not* staring at yourself or putting on lipstick. And those signs with the numbers on the side of the road indicate the speed limit, which is the law and not a suggestion of what speed you should be doing."

Jennifer's chest rose as fury exploded inside her. *Who does this arrogant jerk think he is?* She was about to give him a piece of her mind, but she'd already wasted enough time with him.

Jennifer raised both her hands. "You know what? I don't have time to stand here and argue with a crazy stranger. I have to get to Newbury Port Hospital."

She pushed past him and was about to climb into her car when he called from behind her.

"You may want to change your skirt before going to the hospital!" He laughed. "I think you may have wet yourself when you nearly killed me."

Jennifer glanced down at her navy skirt, and her cheeks burned with humiliation as she saw a large wet patch strategically placed on it.

She raised her chin, her eyes narrowing dangerously, as she turned to him. "Here's a bit of advice for you, *sweetheart!*" She mimicked his tone. "Always ensure you have a phone charger in your car and a fully charged phone while driving on—" She glanced around the quiet road. "Quiet country roads." She gave him a smug smile as she slid into the car and closed her door. She started her engine and lowered her window. "Good luck with the *next* vehicle."

With that, she pulled off, leaving the man staring after her. Jennifer's humiliation and anger melted into a delightful feeling of satisfaction as she watched him fade into the distance.

"Take that you, rude, arrogant, insufferable," *a gorgeously handsome* voice whispered in her head, but she pushed it aside, "jerk. I hope you're stranded there for hours and hours."

Five minutes later, Jennifer's conscience got the better of her, and she called the roadside rescue service.

"I didn't do that for him," Jennifer said, speaking to no one in particular as she hung up. "I did it because it was the right thing to do. My aunt didn't raise me to be petty. And besides, I wouldn't want to live with it on my conscience if I read about a man dying on the side of the road."

Two hours later, Jennifer was pulling away from Newbury Port Hospital with her aunt propped up on the back seat and heading to Cobble Cove on Plum Island.

"Are you okay in the back, Aunt Betty?" Jennifer glanced at her aunt as they made their way to Plum Island.

"I'm fine, honey," Aunt Betty assured her. "I feel awful that I've put you out like this. You didn't have to interrupt your plans to babysit me."

"It's not babysitting, Aunt Betty." Jennifer slowed down as they neared Plum Island town center. "I can get to New York any time." She glanced at the library as they drove past it. "It's hard to believe that just ten months ago Caroline was still the head librarian there."

"Yes, we miss her at the library," Betty told her. "Although we do like Daniella as well."

"I'm surprised Daniella has the time to run the library and the clinic," Jennifer commented as they turned onto Cobble Cove Road.

"She's a remarkable woman," Betty remarked. "Sam said she'd had a hard time of it before moving to Plum Island with her daughter."

"Oh?" Jennifer looked at her aunt in the mirror. "Daniella doesn't speak much about her past."

"Not many of us do, dear," Aunt Betty pointed out. "When is Liam getting back from his cruise?"

As they drove past, Jennifer turned to see the Summer Inn, the hotel her brother owned.

"I'm not sure." Jennifer frowned. "I think he said he wasn't due home for another two weeks."

"He needs a break." Betty nodded. "Oh, Jen, honey, I nearly forgot to tell you. I've invited Sam to dinner tonight. He's going to quote on the work that needs to be done on the cottage."

9

"Aunt Betty, I told you I'd take care of the repairs when I was back in town," Jennifer reminded her. "Sam can't possibly handle the amount of work that needs to be done on his own."

"Don't worry about it, Jen. Sam has help," Betty told her as they turned onto Middle Point Road, which led to Beach Plum Cottage's driveway. "His nephew Harley, a wonderful man, helps him out now." She paused. "Harley will be at dinner too." She gave Jennifer a look.

"Seriously, Aunt Betty, I know that look, and I'm not going to tell you again," Jennifer warned her. "I don't like being set up."

"I'm not getting any younger, Jen." Betty started with the guilt trip. "I want great-nieces or nephews."

"You have a great-niece," Jennifer reminded her. "With compliments of Liam."

"It was such a joy raising you and your brother." Betty sighed, her eyes misting with crocodile tears, making Jennifer roll her eyes as she glanced at her in the mirror.

"Oh, look at that! We're home!" Jennifer breathed a sigh of relief.

As they pulled up to the cottage, Jennifer frowned, noting a blue pickup parked beneath the old plum tree where she usually parked, sparking a spurt of irritation.

What is it with blue pickups today?

"Oh, Sam's here already," Betty said. "Be a dear and ask him to help you get me inside."

"I can get you inside, Aunt Betty," Jennifer assured her, unbuckling her seatbelt. "Let me ask Sam to move his pickup, and we'll have clear access to the front door."

She looked around as she pushed her door open, glancing at her aunt and asking, "Where is he?"

"He must be assessing what needs to be done to the house," Betty guessed.

"Wait here. I'll be right back." Jennifer climbed out of the car.

"I'm not going anywhere!" Betty pointed at her leg in a thick plaster cast.

She walked around the side of the house, calling, "Sam?" She craned her head and saw two figures disappear around the other side of the house. "Great!" She sighed, looking at her two-inch pumps. "These shoes are not meant for walking in the dirt."

Jennifer hurried after them.

"Sam!" Jennifer called.

As she rounded the corner, Jennifer skidded in the dirt and flew into a solid wall of muscle. Strong arms clamped around her as she plowed into him like a bowling ball. He flew backward, taking her with him as they landed in the dirt.

11

"Oh, my word!" Sam said, rushing to help untangle Jennifer from the man she'd plowed down. "Jen, are you okay?"

Sam helped her up as she dusted off her skirt.

"I'm so —" Jennifer turned to apologize to the man, and the apology froze on her lips.

"*YOU*!" The man and Jennifer hissed in unison.

He rose like a bear unfolding itself to tower over her. Aquamarine eyes bore into her.

"Do you two know each other?" Sam looked from one to the other.

"Yes, she tried to run me over earlier!" The man dusted off his clothes.

Jennifer gaped at the man, frozen in disbelief. *Was he this tall before?* She couldn't remember.

"Jen?" Sam's voice broke through her shock. "Are you okay?"

"I'm sure she is!" The man grunted. "She finally finished what she started on the road."

"Excuse me?" Sam's brow furrowed in confusion.

"She's the crazy lady that—." The man started to talk at the same time Jennifer said, "He's the crazy man that—"

"Whoa!" Sam stepped between them and raised his hands. "I'm sure this is just a misunderstanding."

"Misunderstanding?" The man snorted. "Uncle Sam, she nearly rode me over on the side of the road a couple of hours ago and then left me stranded."

"I called a tow truck," Jennifer told Sam as the man's words sank into her head. "Did you say Uncle Sam?"

"Yes!" Sam nodded. "Jennifer, this is my nephew, Harley." He looked at Harley. "Harley, this is Betty's niece, Jennifer."

"No way!" Jennifer and Harley growled in unison.

CHAPTER 2

H arley glanced at his alarm clock—*5:02 am*. He pulled a pillow over his head and tried to force himself to get back to sleep, but he'd not slept well for the past two nights. As he thought of his uncle in the hospital with a back injury, he was overcome with guilt and anger.

Harley pulled the pillow off his face and slapped it on the bed beside him. Uncle Sam wouldn't be in the hospital right now if it weren't for Jennifer Gains and her control freak ways. The woman was a menace and determined to sabotage the Beach Plum Cottage job for Harley and his uncle. She'd only been back in town for seven days, and they'd already had more than a dozen run-ins.

When Jennifer saw Harley's assessment and suggestion for the roof tiles, she insisted she wanted another opinion. While Harley and Jennifer were locked in a heated debate about his work's accuracy, Uncle Sam climbed onto the roof to check Harley's work. The tiles Harley *had correctly assessed* had given way, and Uncle Sam had crash-landed in the same hedge that Betty had landed in a week earlier.

Betty and Uncle Sam were *not* happy with either of them, which Harley didn't think was fair as it wasn't him being antagonistic—it was Jennifer Gains. Harley was sure she went out of her way to make him uncomfortable and rile him whenever he went to Beach Plum Cottage.

"And I have to keep going back there for the next six months or so!" Harley grumbled to his room. "I wish Miss Jennifer Gains had found another contractor to do the work. Then my uncle wouldn't be in the hospital."

Deciding to go for a run, Harley swung his legs over the bed and got up. After changing into his running clothes, he set off toward Cobble Beach. Harley lived in the guest cottage attached to Sam's house, and Cobble Beach was only a mile down the road from his uncle's house.

Harley found that going for an early morning run always helped to clear his mind. The beach was deserted as he set out at his usual pace, lulled by the gentle sound of waves crashing against the shore. As the sun slowly rose over the horizon, it stretched out its golden rays that reflected in the sky and over the land in hues of pink and orange.

As he ran, the steady rhythm of his footfalls echoed the cadence of his thoughts. The cool sea breeze tousled his hair, and the salty scent filled his lungs, gradually easing the tension that had built up in him. The steady motion of his body helped him find a semblance of peace amidst the chaos in his mind.

Reaching the end of the beach, Harley slowed to a walk, taking a moment to savor the tranquility. The horizon stretched before him, a vast expanse of possibilities and uncertainties. The sun was inching its way up, and its shadow looked like a golden globe floating over the sea. Harley took a deep breath, allowing the sea air to fill his lungs.

Deciding to head back, he retraced his steps along the shoreline. As he approached Cobble Beach, the familiar sight of the Beach Hut came into view. The quaint cafe, with its vibrant blue and yellow decor, sat overlooking the water. It was a popular spot for early-morning enthusiasts, offering a variety of refreshing drinks.

Harley's throat was parched, and the thought of an organic smoothie from the Beach Hut appealed to him. He picked up his pace, anticipating the hydrating and energizing blend. The Beach Hut was known for opening early to cater to joggers, surfers, and sea lovers who frequented the beach at the break of dawn.

As Harley neared the cafe, he spotted Finn emerging from the waves, surfboard in hand. Finn, the owner of the Beach Hut, was a friend who shared Harley's love for the sea. Harley waved at Finn, and the two exchanged nods of acknowledgment as Harley neared the cafe entrance.

As he turned to walk inside, he collided with a patron walking out of the Beach Hut. Harley's breath caught in his throat as the shock of the freezing liquid sent a shiver down his spine, and he stood staring at his soaking shirt.

"What the—?" Harley exclaimed.

At the same time, they said, "Oh, I'm so—" pausing and sucking in a breath. "You *again!*"

Harley's head shot up, and his gaze locked onto Jennifer, her expression a mix of surprise and annoyance sparking his ire as his eyes traveled to her now empty cup and the phone in her hands.

"I see your walking skills are on par with your flagging a person down on the road skills!" Jennifer sneered, shaking smoothie goop from her hand and phone. "Luckily, I had a wetsuit on!"

His eyes immediately glanced over her attire. Jennifer was in a salmon and black wetsuit. Her hair was scraped back into a pigtail and wet. A brightly colored beach towel was hooked around her neck.

"You surf?" Harley asked her in amazement.

17

"No!" Jennifer's voice dripped with sarcasm. "I wander around in a wetsuit to blend in and look cool." Her eyes flashed with disdain before she ducked to the side and dumped the smoothie cup in a trash can.

"No need to be rude!" Harley glared at her. "You caught me by surprise. You just don't seem to be the surfing type."

"Oh!" Jennifer wiped her phone and hands on the towel. "And just what *type* do you think I am?" Her eyes narrowed dangerously.

Uh-oh! Harley was not going to answer that question. It was a trap masking a bottomless hole.

"Of course you'd surf!" Harley tried to skirt around the slippery edges of the trap. "Your brother and his best friend are legendary surfers. I apologize for the comment."

Jennifer's eyebrows shot up as she looked at him in shock. "Are you apologizing?" She placed the back of her hand dramatically against her forehead at his nod. "I think I'm going to swoon!" She fanned her face and batted her eyelids. "So, pigs really do fly!"

Harley's anger stirred once again as she threw the words he'd used the other day when Uncle Sam and Betty tried to get him to apologize for his cutting remark to Jennifer about her being a snooty New Yorker who knew as much about carpentry as he did ballet.

The conversation flashed through his mind.

"Harley, that's not a nice thing to say. Jennifer has been studying what needs to be done with the cabinets. Apologize to her," Uncle Sam ordered.

Harley raised an eyebrow and turned his gaze to Jennifer as he replied, *"Sure."* A smug smile curled his lips as he finished, *"When pigs fly!"*

"I was being *polite*," Harley stated. "But obviously, your personality hasn't adjusted from rude New Yorker to polite New Englander yet!"

"I'm not the one who rushed into the cafe like a kid in a candy store!" Jennifer shot back.

Her eyes turned a deeper shade of blue that Harley had seen happen a lot in the past three days. He'd come to think of the color as a dangerous blue. It meant her anger gauge had hit the top of the red, reminding him of the high striker machine at a fair, and Harley seemed to be the one that always struck the jackpot. Only there was no ding or a parade of flashing lights, but a spitting mad Jennifer with a tongue as sharp as a razor blade.

For some reason, Harley's mind shifted out of gear, and he couldn't stop himself from giving as good as he got. The woman just pushed all his wrong buttons and made him crazy! Harley had never met anyone as infuriating, stubborn, and unyielding as Jennifer Gains.

"Oh, don't act like the victim here!" Harley sneered. *Oh no! Just let it go!* His subconscious pleaded, but he was again ensnared in a verbal battle with Jennifer and determined not to allow her to have the final word. He glanced pointedly at her phone. "You weren't paying attention to where you were going either!"

Jennifer's eyes narrowed some more, and she was about to say something when Finn's voice came from behind Harley.

"Not that the two of you aren't very entertaining!" Finn popped his head around Harley. "But you're blocking the door and scaring my customers."

"What customers?" Harley and Jennifer said in unison, looking around the cafe.

"The ones that climbed out the window rather than get between whatever the two of you are standing off about." Finn pushed past Harley and grinned. "I have a gym with a boxing ring out back if you two want to finish this up there."

"Funny!" Jennifer pulled a face at Finn and then looked at her watch. "I have to get going." She gave Harley a scathing look. "I have to get in some *real* work before overseeing the contractor renovating Beach Plum Cottage."

With that, she pushed past Harley, not bothering to say goodbye.

"How rude!" Harley turned, staring after Jennifer in disbelief, before turning to Finn and pointing his thumb over his shoulder. "Can you believe her?" He shook his head. "She didn't even apologize for ruining my favorite shirt." He flicked tiny black seeds off his shirt. "What is this?" He eyed the purply red stain on his shirt.

"Hmmm." Finn tilted his head, examining the stain. "I'd say that is a Raspy Blueberry ice smoothie!"

Harley's eyes shot up in surprise. "Seriously? You can tell what smoothie it is just by the stain."

"Nope!" Finn shook his head, his grin widening. "It's Jennifer's go-to smoothie after an early morning surf." He patted Harley on the back. "How about I buy you a smoothie and a clean shirt?"

"I'd appreciate that," Harley told him, following Finn to the counter.

Finn reached beneath the counter and pulled out a t-shirt with a cartoon picture of the Beach Hut logo. "One t-shirt, as promised." Finn put the menu in front of Harley. "Now, which delicious smoothie can I get you?"

"I think I'm going to try the one that killed my shirt!" Harley pushed the menu back toward Finn.

He pulled off his shirt and put the clean one on, feeling a lot less sticky and wet.

"That's an excellent choice," Finn agreed. "I'm going to join you."

Harley watched Finn make the smoothies.

"Is Jennifer always like that?" Harley couldn't stop himself from asking.

Finn chuckled as he divided the smoothie from the blender into two glasses. "Jen has always had a short fuse and is a force to be reckoned with." He put the beaker behind the counter. "And it seems you've stirred up the force!"

Harley rolled his eyes, suppressing a smile. "Yay, lucky me." He took a sip of smoothie and looked at it with raised brows. "Wow! That is delicious."

"Uh-huh!" Finn nodded, savoring his smoothie.

"I think this has just become my new favorite smoothie." Harley took another sip.

"I'll let the creator of it know!" Finn raised his glass toward Harley.

"Oh, yes, please give your chef my praise." Harley wanted to get the recipe to make it at home.

"Oh, my chef didn't design this delicious concoction." Finn looked at the glass.

"Oh?" Harley looked at him curiously. "May I ask who came up with this delectable drink?"

"I'll give you a hint," Finn teased. "We were going to call the smoothie JG, but the creator doesn't like being in the limelight and came up with Raspy Blueberry Ice."

Harley frowned as the initials bounced around his brain before his eyes widened in realization. "Jennifer created this smoothie?"

Finn's grin widened, and his eyes filled with amusement as he nodded in confirmation.

"Oh great!" Harley muttered. "I can't even enjoy a delicious smoothie without her spoiling it for me."

"Wow, my friend!" Finn put the glass on the counter and casually leaned against it. "You have it bad, and I don't think you even realize it."

"What are you talking about?" Harley's brows creased in a tight frown.

"I think you're falling for Jennifer!" Finn looked at him knowingly.

"Don't be absurd!" Harley harrumphed. "I can't stand to be in the same room as the woman. She's like a burr that's managed to burrow under my skin and irritates me every opportunity it gets. And we've only just had the displeasure of meeting seven days ago." He shook his head emphatically. "No, I'm sorry, but you've read the situation wrong. Jennifer and I are like mortal enemies." He looked at Finn. "We're nemeses."

"Okay!" Finn shrugged. "You're nemeses!" He held up his hands. "My mistake."

But Harley could see Finn was only humoring him and rewarded the man with a glare. Harley finished his smoothie and stood.

"Thank you for the smoothie and t-shirt," Harley said. "But I'd better get going. I have a busy day, especially with Uncle Sam in the hospital."

"How is Sam?" Finn asked.

"In pain and unhappy. He has to wear a back brace and hates all the tests and X-rays he's gone through," Harley answered.

"I can imagine," Finn sympathized. "Sam doesn't like feeling helpless."

"No, he doesn't," Harley agreed before saying goodbye and leaving.

He walked home, forcing thoughts of Jennifer Gains from his mind. Harley needed a few more hours of peace without her annoying presence before having to face her again.

Three hours later, Harley pulled into Beach Plum Cottage's driveway. He'd just exited his pickup when Betty hobbled out of the cottage awkwardly, trying to maneuver her crutches.

"Betty, be careful!" Harley rushed to help her, but she brushed him away.

"Thank you, young man, but I need to learn how to use these things on my own!" Betty huffed.

"Okay, sorry." Harley stepped back, keeping within arm's reach in case she toppled over. "But at least let me walk with you wherever you go. My uncle would demand it."

"Sure." Betty nodded.

"Where are you going?" Harley frowned, noting Betty was heading toward his pickup truck.

"*We're* going to visit Sam," Betty informed him. "Now come along. Visiting hours start soon."

Harley glanced toward the closed front door and looked around the parking area. Jennifer's car wasn't there.

"Does Jennifer know you're going?" Harley asked, helping Betty into the passenger seat and putting her crutches in the back before walking to the driver's side.

"What am I? Ten?" Betty looked at him indignantly. "I don't have to log my every move with my niece, young man!"

"Of course." Harley apologized and started the vehicle. "I apologize."

"I'm just pulling your leg." Betty's eyes sparkled with mirth. "Don't worry about Jenny. My whereabouts have been noted."

Harley's frown deepened as he turned around the driveway and headed back toward Cobble Cove Road. Half an hour later, they were sitting in the waiting room of Newbury Port General, waiting to see Harley's uncle.

"Are you sure you should be here, Betty?" Harley looked at her worriedly.

Her face was pale and strained, as if the exertion of walking across the busy parking lot of the hospital had exhausted her.

"I'm fit as a fiddle!" Betty assured him and was saved from saying more when a nurse told them they could see Sam.

Harley knew her words weren't true when Betty let him help her to Sam's room and help her into the chair, he positioned beside Sam's bed with another one to put her leg on.

"How are you doing, Uncle Sam?" Harley asked, feeling like the third wheel in the room.

"Impatient!" Sam grumbled. "I want to get out of here and sleep in my own bed where I'm not bothered every few minutes the entire night." He shook his head. "No wonder people don't get better in hospitals. They don't allow us to rest!"

Wow, Uncle Sam really is hating it here. Harley watched his uncle. "I'll talk to the doctor," he promised. "The only other time I saw you so grumpy was when you broke your hip."

"Bruised!" Sam corrected him. "I kept telling everyone it was just a bruise, but the next thing I knew, they were replacing my hip with some plastic metal thing." He scowled. "Maybe it's good that the nurses and doctors wake me every few hours. At least I can ensure I don't wake up with a metal spine, halfway to becoming Robo-Cop!"

Harley bit his lip, trying not to laugh at his uncle's outrage at a picture of the tall, still-fit-for-his-age man as Robo-Cop.

"Oh, come now, Sam!" Betty tutted. "You're getting the best care here." She reached over and squeezed his hand. "Besides, if they make you into a cyborg, at least you can fix my roof without fear of getting hurt."

Betty's grin was Harley's undoing and he laughed. Not even his uncle's stern stare could stop him.

"When you're done having a laugh over my predicament," Sam said, crossing his arms over his chest, "would you be so kind as to find a doctor to get me out of here?"

Harley quickly cleared his throat and got his humor under control. "Sure." He nodded. "Can I get you a coffee or something from the cafeteria while I'm out?" He looked at Betty.

"I could drink a coffee," Betty told him.

"How about a whisky?" Sam said.

"Sure, Uncle Sam, I'll get right on that!" Harley said, walking to the door, where he stopped and looked at Sam. "Do you want your coffee with or without milk?"

"With milk today," Sam told him.

Harley nodded and left the room, walking toward the cafeteria. While he was waiting in line, his phone rang. Harley pulled it out of his pocket, frowning when he saw it was his ex-wife, Angela's mother, Margaret Wesley.

What has Angela done now? Harley sighed and toyed with the idea of ignoring the call, but his conscience got the better of him. "Hello, Margaret."

"Hello, Harley." Margaret's clipped tone warned him what she was about to say would not bode well with him. "Where are you?"

"Why are my whereabouts any of your concern?" Harley asked her.

"Because Angela has escaped and left a note for the nurses at the facility telling them she's gone to visit Sam in the hospital!" Margaret's words sent shock waves down his spine. "What's wrong with Sam?"

"He fell and hurt his back," Harley told her, rubbing his eyes, and sighed. "I'll find her."

"See that you do." Margaret hung up.

Harley stepped out of the queue and was about to go back to Sam's ward when he heard his name being called from the hospital gardens.

He turned and saw Angela walk toward him with an arm full of flowers she'd picked from it.

"I have flowers for Sam!" Angela smiled, holding them out to Harley. She was dressed in pink scrubs she must've stolen from the nurse's station at the institute and was not wearing any shoes. "I remembered he loved wildflowers."

"Thank you, Angie." Harley's voice softened, and he took the flowers. "How did you get here?"

He started guiding her out of the cafeteria.

"I walked," Angela told him, her eyes going toward the treats. "Oooh, can I get a pie?" She looked at him pleadingly. "They won't give me pie at home."

Harley's heart squeezed as she called the mental health facility she was in home.

"Sure." He nodded. "Let's get you some pie."

"Can I still see Sam?" Angela asked, placing her hand on the glass case as she checked out the pies like a child looking into a candy shop window. "Look, Lee, they have my favorite." Her eyes lit up, and she glanced at him excitedly. "Cherry. I want cherry. Please."

"Okay." Harley hooked the flowers into the crook of his arm and ordered a pie and some coffee. "Do you want some tea?"

"No, thank you." Angela made a gagging face. "You know I hate that stuff." She shuddered. "Can I have a grape soda, please, Lee?"

"Angie, you know you can only have pie or soda," Harley reminded her.

"Fine!" Angela rolled her eyes and sighed, reminding him of a teenager not getting their own way. "I'll have some water and pie."

"Good choice," Harley said, smiling.

They were walking to Sam's room, with Angela digging into her pie while Harley balanced the coffee, her water, and the flowers, when Harley's phone rang. He pulled it out and saw it was Margaret, again.

"Hello, Margaret. I've found Angela," he told her.

"Oh, good. I was calling back to say, call me when you find my daughter," Margaret said. "Can I speak to her?"

Harley looked at Angela, enjoying her pie. "Angie, your mothers on the phone and wants to speak to you."

Angela's head shot up. Her eyes widened and darkened as she dropped the plate that clattered to the ground and shattered around her bare feet.

"NO!" Angela's words were laced with fear. "No!" She pointed at the phone, shaking her head, her eyes filling with panic as she grabbed her stomach.

"I have to go!" Harley hung up and pocketed his phone. Holding up his hands toward her as he saw she was about to have a panic attack. "It's okay, Ange." He glanced at her bare feet as they inched nearer the broken plate. "She's not here anymore."

"No!" Angela shook her head and wrapped her arms around herself, starting to sway.

"Nurse!" Harley called as loud as he could without startling Angela as he cautiously approached her. "Ange, don't move. You're going to cut your feet."

"Home!" Angela's breathing became labored, and her rocking motion started getting faster. "I want to go home!" Panic had her gasping for breath.

"Nurse!" Harley bellowed, dropping what he had in his hand on a bench next to him and lunging forward.

He heard someone ask what was wrong from behind him as he grabbed Angela, and she started freaking out, screaming, clawing, and trying to shake him off. But Harley held on, lifting her as gently as he could off the floor. He saw a nurse and doctor rush toward him. He barely heard what they asked him as Angela's agitation grew.

"Can she take Lorazepam?" the doctor asked him again, preparing a needle already filled with the substance.

"Yes!" Harley nodded.

He held Angela as steady as he could. At the same time, the doctor administered the sedative, and within seconds, Angela's body went limp in his arms. Harley scooped her up.

"What happened?" the doctor asked.

Harley explained how Angela escaped the mental health facility a few blocks down the road.

"I'll call them," the nurse offered.

"Ask for Annie Garmen," Harley advised. "She's head of the ward that Angela is in."

The nurse nodded and started walking. "Follow me. We can take her to exam room five."

"Thank you," Harley said, following the nurse with the doctor walking beside him.

"Has your wife always suffered with mental health?" the doctor asked Harley.

"No!" Harley shook his head. "After a traumatic event, she had a breakdown."

They walked into the room. Harley laid Angela on the bed, and the nurse started to take over.

"I see." The doctor nodded and took his tablet from the nurse.

"She was in a mental health facility in Boston and was doing well until—" He cleared his throat. "Until she tried to kill her sister, who was visiting her."

CHAPTER 3

J ennifer drove to the lighthouse, taking her best friend Caroline Shaw's pets home to wait for her and her family, who were returning from their vacation in half an hour. The German Shepherd, Sandy, sat in the back of Jennifer's SUV with her head out the window, enjoying the wind blowing against her face. The large ginger-striped tabby, Melton, slept beside Sandy, enjoying the ride.

"Too fast! Too Fast!" Blue Beard, a large blue and red Macaw, squawked from his seatbelt-secured cage beside Melton. "Slow down. Bad driver! Bad driver." There was a flapping of wings. "We're going to die. We're going to die."

"Stop it, Blue Beard!" Jennifer glanced at the offensive bird in the mirror. "Or I'm going to include parrot on my menu tonight."

"Where's the parrot?" Blue Beard squawked back. "Where's the parrot?"

"I meant Macaw," Jennifer said impatiently. "You rude bird!"

"Bad driver! Bad driver!" Blue Beard shouted back.

"Good grief!" Jennifer shook her head. "Talk about a backseat driver." She looked at Blue Beard, who was hanging onto the side of his cage by his claws and beak. "Wow! You are such a drama queen."

She breathed a sigh of relief when she pulled into the driveway of the Cobble Cove Lighthouse and drew to a stop. Jennifer let Sandy and Melton out of the car first before walking around to the other side and taking Blue Beard's cage.

"Come on, nervous Nelly, let's get you inside." Jennifer fidgeted in her purse to find the key to Caroline's house.

She unlocked the back door and quickly stood aside, knowing how excited Sandy and Melton got when they got home after being away from it for some time. And they'd been staying with Caroline's brother, Finn, for over three weeks. Sandy and Melton shot into the house like bullets, running all over like crazy animals.

Jennifer shook her head. She had just stepped inside when Blue Beard let himself out of his cage to join his furry friends in the fun. She hung his cage on the hook beside the living room window, admiring the view of the cliff dropping off into the ocean.

"The bird has the best view," Jennifer mumbled.

She walked into the kitchen to the far side, set up for the animals to eat, and poured them some fresh water.

"Caroline or Jules can give them something to eat," Jennifer said, putting Melton's water bowl beside Sandy's. She stood up and dusted her hands together. "Okay, now to order some takeout from the Cobble Cove Restaurant for Caroline and her family for lunch."

Ten minutes later, Jennifer sat on the front porch, sipping a glass of iced tea, when Sandy started barking excitedly and rushing toward the back door. Jennifer stood and followed the excited dog, almost being knocked over as Melton rushed past her. She skillfully ducked, knowing Blue Beard wouldn't be far behind, and he perched himself on Sandy's back.

Crazy animals! Jennifer pulled open the back door and waited for the dash outside before walking after them. A smile curled her lips when she saw Caroline and Jules pile out of the car. Jennifer was so happy that her best friend was home at last. She stepped outside, and Jules, Caroline's fifteen-year-old daughter, threw herself into Jennifer's arms.

"Hello, Aunt Jen. It's so good to see you!" Jules gave Jennifer a tight squeeze before turning her attention to her pets. "Hey, there's my amazing trio!"

"Hi, Jen," Caroline called from the car.

"Hi, you!" Jennifer stepped around the reunion and greeted Caroline, who walked to the car trunk and popped it open. "It's so good to see you."

She embraced Caroline before helping her with the luggage.

"Jules," Caroline called her daughter. "Come help us, please."

"On my way," Jules called back, jumping to her feet and walking toward her.

Jules's faithful trio plodded along beside her. As usual, Blue Beard, the lazy bird, was perched on Sandy's back.

"How has Sandy not gotten bald spots where that bird perches on her back?" Jennifer shook her head in amazement.

"Sometimes he leaves welts, but we treat them and put a harness on her back where Blue Beard rests," Caroline explained. "But Sandy hates the thing and tries to bite it off."

"Oh, yes, I've seen it," Jennifer remembered as they entered the house. "I've ordered lunch for you and Jules. Although I ordered a lot because I thought Brad and Connor would be joining you."

"They'll be here later," Caroline told her. "And thank you. That was thoughtful of you, as I'm starved and too exhausted to go to the store to get groceries."

"Let me help you get your bags upstairs, and I'll put the kettle on for coffee," Jennifer offered, lugging the bags into the hall and up the stairs to Caroline's bedroom. "I'll go put on the coffee." She looked at her wristwatch. "The food should be here any minute."

"You're an angel." Caroline sighed. "I'm going to leave the unpacking for later and shower."

"You do that," Jennifer said, leaving Caroline and going downstairs to the kitchen.

She had just put the kettle on the stove when the food arrived from Cobble Cove Restaurant.

"Hello, Reef," Jennifer greeted him.

Reef was Carly Donovan's son. Carly owned the Cobble Cove restaurant.

"Hello, Miss Gains." Reef greeted her respectfully, handing her the bag of food. "Is Jules home?" He glanced at Caroline's car.

"Yes, they arrived a few minutes ago," Jennifer told him, suppressing a smile as she gave him a nice tip. "Here you go."

"Wow!" Reef's eyes widened, holding up the dollar bills. "This is too much."

"No, you're off to college soon," Jennifer commented. "You're going to need every cent."

"Thank you, Miss Gains," Reef said politely, stuffing the bills into the pocket of his jeans. "Will you tell Jules I said hi, and I'm looking forward to seeing her at the restaurant tomorrow, please?"

"I will do that," Jennifer promised, biting back another smile, knowing Caroline would not be pleased to hear that!

"Enjoy the meal," Reef said, turning to go. "Bye."

"Thank you, Reef." Jennifer waved him off. "Bye."

As he pulled away in the restaurant van, Jules flew into the kitchen.

"Did I hear Reef?" Jules's eyes were wide with excitement.

"You just missed him." Jennifer turned, smiling knowingly, as she took the food items from the bag and placed them on a tray.

"Oh no!" Jules's voice was laced with disappointment. "I wanted to say hi."

Jennifer turned and looked at her. "Reef asked me to tell you he said hi and is looking forward to seeing you at the restaurant tomorrow."

"He's working tomorrow?" Jule's eyes lit up once again. "Great!"

She walked over to the tray and started going through the tubs. "Are you feeding an army, Aunt Jen?"

"I thought Brad and Connor were going to be with you," Jennifer told her.

"Oh, yeah, they're coming here later." Jules turned to look at Jennifer. "Maybe Mom will let us have some friends over later this afternoon."

"I don't know, sweetie." Jennifer pulled a few plates from the cupboard to place on the tray. "Your mother is exhausted, and I think you all just need a quiet night to recuperate."

"You're right!" Jules nodded, stealing a few fries. "Lila is home tomorrow and is coming to spend the night. So tomorrow would be better."

"That's right," Jennifer confirmed, saying that her brother, Liam, and his teenage daughter, who was the same age as Jules, would be home the next day. "I think that's a great plan."

"Yes, and I can ask Tucker to come over." Jules took a few more fries as she plotted. "Mom is always more at ease when my cousin Tucker is around."

"That's because he's like your big brother, and your mother knows he'll look out for you," Jennifer agreed. "You'll see Reef when you work your shift at the restaurant tomorrow morning."

"We're just friends!" Jules shrugged, her cheeks pinkening slightly. "Now that I'm older and Tucker doesn't mind having Lila and me around, we're like a group of friends."

Jennifer smiled at the beautiful teenage girl. "It's so nice to see you happy again, Jules."

"I just feel bad for how I treated my mother up until a year ago." Jules's eyes darkened with sorrow. "You were right. I was a brat and unfair to my mom." She shook her head. "I feel bad for my dad too, though." Her eyes held Jennifer's. "It can't be easy for him, having had to uproot his life and move to Newbury Port. Not to mention having a newborn baby and a wife who's in a mental health institute."

"But he has you and your cousins to help him," Jennifer pointed out. "Plus, he and your mom are getting along now, too, so you all support him."

"It's just sad that it took a divorce and the horrible ordeal his wife put us all through last year to bring my family together." Jules sighed. "Well, not together, together. But get along, you know?"

Jennifer nodded in understanding as she took the whistling kettle from the stove, the shrill sound temporarily filling the kitchen. The steam rose gracefully as she poured hot water into the mugs she'd carefully arranged earlier. The aromatic fragrance of coffee wafted through the air, creating an inviting atmosphere.

Glancing over at Jules, who was picking fries from the food, Jennifer shook her head and sighed, eyeing the instant coffee with distaste.

41

"Why won't your mother get a coffee maker?" she inquired, her tone carrying a playful note.

Jules smiled. Leaning back against the kitchen counter. "Mom doesn't like the taste of it," she confessed. "She says it's too strong and sludgy."

Jennifer raised an amused eyebrow. "That's because your mother doesn't make it correctly," she declared with a grin, her eyes sparkling. "When she was in New York with me last year, I had to ban her from using my machine. It was a coffee catastrophe waiting to happen."

Jules laughed, a light and melodious sound that filled the kitchen. "I can imagine," she agreed, picturing her mom attempting to navigate the intricacies of a coffee maker. "She prefers the quick, instant way."

Jennifer finished preparing the coffee. "Well, we'll have to get her a coffee machine, ban instant coffee from her kitchen, and teach her how to use it the proper way."

"Ooh, can we get her one of those mini barista machines that can make lattes and fancy coffees?" Jules's eyes widened with excitement.

"Since when have you drunk coffee?" Jennifer's brows rose as she looked at Jules questioningly.

Jules grinned, taking a few more fries. "Don't you know? They have coffee vendors around the high school now selling fancy brews."

"Mm!" Jennifer shook her head. "We didn't drink coffee until we went to college."

Jennifer put two steaming mugs of coffee on the tray with the food.

"I buy tea as I'm not too fond of the taste of coffee," Jules admitted. "Although I do like a few of the lattes, especially the chai ones."

Jules picked up the crockery and cutlery, following Jennifer into the dining room that was bursting with sunlight pouring in from the side window and reflecting from the living room, where you could see the ocean. Jules laid out the plates and cutlery, while Jennifer set out the food bowls.

"This is just for you and your mom," Jennifer told Jules. "I put the other half of the takeout in the oven for Connor and Brad when they arrive."

"Thank you, Jennifer," Caroline said gratefully as she walked into the living room, fresh from her shower and a clean change of clothes.

"You look nice and fresh," Jennifer commented, pulling out one of the chairs at the table and sitting down next to Jules, who was already dishing up some food. Jennifer laughed. "You'd better come to get some food before your daughter devours it." She picked up her coffee. "Didn't you feed her while you were on Long Island?"

"You know Jules has always had a healthy appetite!" Caroline sighed, shaking her head as she sat in front of a place setting and watched her daughter.

"I'm starving!" Jules looked at her mother and Jennifer. "I'm a growing girl, and I need nourishment. Especially as Connor and I are going to do the hike up to Lookout Point this afternoon."

"Are you two still going to do that?" Caroline dished up some food.

"Yes." Jules nodded, adding some ketchup to her plate for her fries.

"Why don't you wait for when Lila and Tucker are back home tomorrow?" Caroline suggested.

"I agree with your mother," Jennifer told Jules. "That hike is best done in a group." She gave Jules a knowing smile. "Maybe you could ask Reef and Emily, Daniella's daughter, to go too."

"That's a great idea," Jules agreed with Jennifer.

"I guess," Caroline said, eyeing Jules worriedly.

Jennifer knew that Caroline was concerned about the budding teen romance between Reef and Jules.

"With Reef and Tucker on the hike, you'll be able to breathe a little easier," Jennifer told Caroline. "They are both volunteers in the Plum Island search and rescue who have been trained on how to handle various situations."

"And they can both do first aid," Jules added.

"Of course," Caroline stated, sipping her coffee. "I'd feel better about you going on the hike tomorrow when your cousin is home and can go with you."

"Okay," Jules agreed, pushing her chair back. "Excuse me, I'm going to get some juice."

"Can you bring a few bottles of water, too, honey?" Caroline asked as Jules went into the kitchen.

"I was hoping that this Reef crush would die down while we were visiting Brad's parents," Caroline admitted.

"Oh, come on, Caro," Jennifer said as she leaned her elbows on the table, cradling her coffee mug. "It's Jules's first crush. Rather be supportive and keep an open flow of communication than have her sneak around with the guy."

"You're right," Caroline agreed.

"Reef's a decent guy," Jennifer commented. "Right up until Jules showed an interest in him, you liked the guy."

The gentle sea breeze tenderly brushed against Jennifer and Caroline as they sat on the front porch swing, gazing out over the endless expanse of the ocean. Their second cup of coffee was cradled in their hands, the rhythmic lull of the waves providing a soothing backdrop. Caroline and Jules had already wrapped up their early lunch, leaving the two friends to share a quiet moment before the anticipated arrival of Brad and his son, Connor.

Underneath the afternoon sun, its golden rays turned the water into a mesmerizing tapestry of sparkling jewels. Jennifer, enveloped in the comforting creaks of the swing, delved into recounting the day's events: Aunt Betty, the unexpected encounter with Harley on the roadside, Sam's unfortunate fall, and the lingering irritation sparked by Harley's presence. However, her narrative was abruptly halted by the jarring ring of her phone—a call from a Newbury Port furniture store—breaking the tranquility.

"Sorry, Caroline, I have to take this; I'm waiting for a bed to be delivered." Jennifer's voice softened as she answered. "Hello?"

"Is that Miss Gains?" inquired a voice on the other end.

"Yes, it is," Jennifer replied, hope and frustration mingling. "Please tell me you're not canceling the delivery again today."

"No, ma'am," reassured the man on the line. "We're here at Beach Plum Cottage, but no one is home."

"Are you sure?" Jennifer's brows knit tightly together. Aunt Betty was there when she left, and Harley was about to arrive. "My aunt and a contractor, Mr. Donovan, should be there."

"There's no one here, Miss Gains," the man assured her. "We've been here for nearly ten minutes and have walked around the cottage."

"Is there a pickup in the driveway?" Jennifer asked him, her worry escalating.

"No, there's only a blue sedan," the man told her.

"That's my aunt's car." Jennifer's frown deepened as her heartbeat picked up speed. "Give me ten minutes; I'm on my way." She hung up and readied herself to leave.

Caroline's concern deepened as she listened. "What's happening? Is it Aunt Betty?" she inquired.

Her brow furrowed. Jennifer shook her head and replied, "Aunt Betty's new bed I ordered for her has arrived. But Harley and Aunt Betty aren't there."

The revelation cast a shadow over the sunny porch. Jennifer's worry intensified when she checked her phone for missed messages or calls. She attempted to call her aunt, only to be met with a voicemail. A futile attempt to reach Harley yielded the same result.

"I'm sorry, Caro, but I'm going to have to go home," Jennifer announced, the weight of uncertainty tainting her words.

"I'm coming with you," Caroline declared, echoing Jennifer's concern.

As the two friends headed towards the house, Caroline called out to Jules, who had been drawn to the commotion. A brief exchange ensued, with Jules agreeing to stay behind and await the arrival of Brad and Connor, accompanied by her trio of furry companions.

Navigating the winding road away from the lighthouse, Jennifer's car carried them toward Midpoint, leaving the coastal beacon in their wake. Silence hung heavy in the air, accompanied by a sense of foreboding that grew stronger with each passing moment.

"Maybe Aunt Betty asked Harley to take her into town for something," Caroline suggested, attempting to dispel the uneasy atmosphere.

Jennifer nodded, though uncertainty lingered in her eyes. "Yeah, that could be it. But Aunt Betty rarely goes out without telling me. Especially now with a broken leg."

Approaching the fork in the road leading to Lookout Point or Beach Plum Cottage, Jennifer slowed down and took the turn off. The bumpy journey down the familiar road felt unusually prolonged before the car finally pulled into the driveway.

The delivery van stood conspicuously near the front door of the cottage. As Jennifer parked beneath the old beach plum tree, she and Caroline stepped out to greet the delivery men. Their unease over the missing Betty was palpable in the soft rustling of the leaves overhead.

Jennifer signed for the bed and unlocked the silent cottage, guiding the delivery men to place the bed in the living room. She intended to handle the arrangement later, considering the need to sort out Betty's room and remove the old bed. Despite the men's offer to assist, Jennifer graciously declined, knowing her aunt preferred rearranging the room herself.

While Jennifer saw the men off, Caroline ventured into the kitchen. As the delivery truck drove away, Caroline abruptly interrupted Jennifer's troubled thoughts by handing her a note found on the refrigerator door.

Gone out!

Aunt B.

"Gone out!" Jennifer hissed in frustration. "Where on earth would she go?" Her hands shot up in exasperation. "And why didn't she call to let me know?" She shot an irritated glare at the note. "Aunt Betty knew I was at the lighthouse for most of the day."

Before Caroline could respond, the rumble of Harley's pickup truck echoed in the driveway. Seated beside him was Aunt Betty.

"Oh, they're home," Caroline remarked, slipping past her irate friend to welcome them.

Jennifer's fury flared. A wildfire fed by dry, gasoline-soaked grass. Her rage intensified as she closed in on Harley, who'd just exchanged pleasantries with Caroline, and strolled toward the passenger side of his truck.

"How dare you?" Jennifer hissed, her fists clenched, as she confronted Harley, dismissing her aunt's cheerful greeting from inside the pickup.

"Can you be more specific?" Harley drawled, raising his eyebrows and calmly meeting her enraged gaze. "There's so much you've accused me of—sabotage, negligence, and incompetence," he added, his tone laced with amusement.

"How dare you just take my aunt out without letting me know?" Jennifer didn't think she could get angrier than she already was, but somehow, he managed to escalate it.

"Your aunt left you a note." Harley tilted his head casually, a smile lifting the corner of his mouth.

"This is the twenty-first century, Mr. Neanderthal," Jennifer said through gritted teeth. "We have these devices called mobile phones that people use to let others know when they're taking their loved ones on a joy ride!" Her voice raised a few decibels.

"My phone battery died!" Harley shrugged. "And Betty left her phone at home."

"Well, that makes it all okay, then!" Jennifer's voice shook with sarcasm and rage. "And it makes me feel so much better about you traveling on the roads with my aunt!"

Harley shrugged. "Betty needed a lift, and I took her where she wanted to go." His cool eyes held hers. There was no apology as he stared at Jennifer with a small smile tugging at his lips. "It's not my fault you can't keep track of your aunt." He looked at her innocently. "Maybe you should hire a guard to keep track of her movements for you." He snapped his fingers. "Oh, or get one of those spy cameras you can attach to a pendant for her. That way, you'll know everything Betty's doing."

Jennifer glared at him, her anger and frustration nearing the point of no return. "You know what?" she sneered. "I may not be able to keep track of my aunt's every moment, but what I can do is remove bad influences from her life." She glared at him. "You're fired. Get your tools you have scattered all over this property, and go!"

That got a rise out of him. A look of stunned disbelief shot into his eyes, sparking a flash of anger as he raised his hands. "Fine by me," he growled. "It will be such a relief not to have to come here each day and find ways to avoid you!" His eyes narrowed. "I can actually start to look forward to each day again without schooling myself for whatever nitpicking problem you've dreamt up about my work."

"Nitpicking?" Jennifer had never wanted to slap a smug look off someone's face as badly as she did right then, and she commended herself on her restraint, especially as she was so angry.

51

"Jennifer and Harley!" Betty's voice cracked like a whip over them. "That's enough!" She looked at Harley. "You're not going anywhere." She looked at Jennifer. "I asked Harley to take me to visit Sam."

They spun to see that Caroline had helped Betty from the pickup, and she'd hobbled over to them on her crutches.

"I'm sorry, Aunt Betty, but he has to go!" Jennifer gestured with her hands. "He is insufferable, disregards anyone else's opinions, and has absolutely no respect for other people's feelings."

"I'm insufferable?" Harley gave a disbelieving laugh. "Lady, you may as well be talking about yourself. If it weren't for you having to triple-check everything I do, my uncle wouldn't be lying in the hospital right now. Betty wouldn't have had to sneak out to see him because you have her under house arrest!"

"I think you should leave!" Jennifer's anger raised her voice. "Before you get me into trouble for punching you!"

"Oh, so now you're threatening me?" Harley raised his eyebrows as the two of them went head-to-head. "And do you really believe a tiny slip of a woman like you can cause me bodily harm?"

"Should we find out?" Jennifer took a step closer.

"No, thank you," Harley taunted back. "I don't want to go to jail for defending myself and accidentally hurting you in the process."

"Am I talking to myself here?" Betty's voice hardly registered with Jennifer and Harley. "Caroline, you hear me, right?"

"I've got this, Aunt Betty," Caroline said, stepping in between Jennifer and Harley. "Okay, this is going a bit too far."

"She started it," Harley said, stepping back and giving Jennifer an angry sideways glance.

"She started it," Jennifer mocked in a silly voice before squinting at him in disgust. "What are you? Twelve?"

"Unbelievable!" Caroline raised her mom's voice. "Both of you are acting like you're five." She narrowed her eyes and gave them the no-nonsense stare she used with unruly children. "Harley, please help Aunt Betty inside. She'd like you to help her with her new bed." She turned to Jennifer. "You need time to cool off, so you'll walk me home."

"We don't need help with the bed. Liam can do it." Jennifer and Harley didn't take their angry eyes off each other.

"Liam isn't here, and I want to try out my new bed tonight," Betty said as she stepped into the ring. She addressed Harley. "I would like your help sorting out my room, moving my old bed out, and setting up the new one, if you don't mind."

"Of course, I'll help you, Betty." Harley smiled at Betty, and all anger disappeared from his eyes when he addressed her.

"Aunt Betty—" Jennifer started to object, but Caroline stopped her.

"Go cool that hot head of yours off," Betty snapped, not looking at Jennifer. "Don't come back here until it has."

"Might I suggest a dip in the ocean?" Harley gave her a smug smile.

"If you don't stop tormenting my niece, I'll push you into the ocean myself," Betty warned him. "Now break it up, you two." She started hopping toward the cottage on her crutches. "Come along, Harley."

"Yes, ma'am." Harley shot Jennifer one more glare, and she had to suppress the urge to pull a tongue at him before he rushed after Betty to help her inside.

As they disappeared into the cottage, they heard Betty say, "Why do you have to rile her up like that?"

"See!" Jennifer looked at Caroline and pointed toward the empty doorway of the cottage. "Even my aunt agrees that he deliberately torments me."

"I don't think that's what she meant," Caroline told her, suppressing a smile before slipping her arm through Jennifer and maneuvering her toward the cove. "Instead of driving me home, I think a walk to the lighthouse and back is just what you need to cool down."

"Never seeing that arrogant, smug face or having to deal with the man again will alleviate all the stress and irritation I've been living with over the past week," Jennifer told her as they navigated the stone stairs into the cove.

The sound of the sea washing onto the shore and the tangy, salty breeze flowed over her, draining away her tension. Jennifer and Caroline slipped off their shoes and walked along the water's edge as they made their way toward the lighthouse side of the cove. They walked in companionable silence, each lost in their thoughts, until they neared the stairs leading to the lighthouse and Caroline's house.

"Do you want to come to my house and stay for some warmed-up takeout?" Caroline smiled at Jennifer.

"No, thanks, Caro," Jennifer sighed. "I think I'm just going to sit in our secret spot for a while and clear my mind and nerves." She shook her head. "I hope Aunt Betty isn't unfiring him."

"You know she's already done that," Caroline commented. "So, I think you and Harley will have to learn to get along for everyone's sake around you." She grinned at the glare Jennifer pinned her with. "At least for the next six months or so until the cottage is finished."

"I'm going to find another contractor and then go into town to pay Harley a visit to let him know his services are no longer required," Jennifer plotted. "By the time Aunt Betty realizes we've switched contractors, it will be too late."

"Or—" Caroline pointed with her index finger. "And hear me out now." Her smile broadened. "You and Harley look beyond the reason all those sparks fly whenever you're around each other."

"What's that supposed to mean?" Jennifer had a fair idea where her friend was going with this.

"You know that old adage: wherever there's sparks, there's fire!" Caroline reminded her. "If you and Harley don't contain those sparks soon, you'll both get badly burned."

"Are you implying that I'm attracted to the man?" Jennifer looked at Caroline incredulously. "Because you'd be way off the storyline." She gestured with her hand, arcing it. "You're not even on the same page; you're in a different book—like some soppy love story while I'm trapped in a comedy of errors."

"I like the writing analogy," Caroline told her, her eyes sparkling with mirth. "Very apt considering our professions." She patted Jennifer's shoulder. "But my dear, dear friend, I'm afraid you've met your match with Harley, and deep down, you know it. That's why your heart and mind are warring."

"He is not my type!" Jennifer huffed.

"Oh, I think he is. That's what makes you so angry because instead of fleeing when you try to push him away, Harley stands his ground and pushes back." Caroline raised her eyebrows. "And you're terrified that he's going to break through that fortress you've constructed around your heart, and when he does, you won't be able to scare him off like you have all your other relationships."

CHAPTER 4

H arley strolled into the grand entrance of the Summer Inn, admiring the polished floors that shone under the soft lighting. He was always impressed by the hotel's magnificence, and tonight was no exception.

He made his way through the brightly lit foyer, marveling at Alex Blackwell's persuasive power to get people to do things they ordinarily wouldn't do, like attending an impromptu dinner party on a superyacht.

Harley liked to think he'd only caved because of the day he'd had going head-to-head with the obnoxious Jennifer Gains—the huge thorn currently twisting in his side.

But it wasn't only Jennifer Gains who drove him to the party. It was Alex's superyacht! Or, as Harley referred to it, Alex's super-su-peryacht, which the man had custom-designed. At the end of shooting the second season of The Cobble Cove Mysteries, Harley, Finn, Liam, Brad, and Alex were setting sail for a high-seas adventure on the su-per-superyacht called Black Ocean. And Harley was looking forward to that.

He walked toward the lavish glass-fronted hotel lounge with its magnificent three-sixty-degree sea view. Harley considered turning back. Still, he encountered Dawn Vanderbilt, the screenwriter for the series, and Harriet Joyce, who used to be Brad's executive assistant.

"Good evening, Harley," Harriet greeted him and introduced him to Dawn. "I don't think you've met Dawn."

"No, we've only seen each other in passing," Harley answered, holding his hand out to Dawn, who took it with a firm grip.

"It's nice to meet you, Harley." Dawn smiled. "I've heard so much about you from your Uncle Sam."

"Uh-oh!" Harley joked.

"Oh, come now," Harried laughed. "You know how proud your uncle is of you and the rest of your family on Plum Island."

"Yes, Sam bursts with pride every time he mentions the five of you," Dawn told Harley.

Feeling uncomfortable with the line of conversation, Harley shifted it as he noted the ladies' evening attire. "You ladies are looking stunning," he complimented them. "Am I to assume you're on your way to Alex's party?"

"Yup!" Harriet sighed resignedly. "We tried to decline, but Alex has this way of twisting your arm until you succumb to his will."

"I was going to curl up with Caroline's latest book in the Cobble Cove Mysteries," Dawn admitted. "That was until I ran into Alex when I got back to the hotel after my run earlier."

"Yeah, I also ran into Alex," Harley said, pulling a face. "In my driveway when I got home this afternoon. He was there waiting for me and stuck around until I agreed to come to his dinner party."

"We'd better not keep him waiting," Dawn warned. "Or he'll just have another dinner party and rope us all into going again."

"Why would he do that?" Harley asked, opening the door for the ladies that led out of the hotel and to the dock.

"Because he's Alex Blackwell, and he can!" Harriet said sarcastically.

As they stepped out into the crisp night air, the distant sounds of music, laughter, and the scent of the ocean filled the air. With the warm lights of the Summer Inn guiding them, the trio walked toward the yacht dock, where the superyacht gently bobbed, rocked by the sway of the sea.

"If you dislike Alex, why do you attend his parties and hang out with him?" Harley asked as the lively sounds of the party on the yacht reached them when they got closer to the dock.

"Our families are friends, and that makes me obliged to." Harriet blew out a breath. "And I'm best friends with his brother."

Harley's shoulders tensed at the mention of Ethan Blackwell, Alex's reclusive brother. The man was lucky that he kept to himself and was hardly seen except on the movie set. Harley was not a fan of Ethan Blackwell, and for a good reason—the man had all but ruined his sister's life. Harley shook off thoughts of Ethan. He'd had enough contention for one day. It was time to relax and enjoy himself with good company, food, and music. Plus, he loved Alex's superyacht.

Harley's eyes drifted to the boat. A sleek design and luxury marvel stretched an impressive 200 meters in length as it gently swayed on the inky waters. The exterior, painted in a deep, glossy black, perfectly complemented the yacht's moniker, "Dark Ocean." Soft LED lighting illuminated the sleek structure, creating a romantic atmosphere topped by a curtain of gleaming stars.

While Harley was not much of a party person, especially one packed with A-listers and hosted by a billionaire, a world he did not belong in, as evidenced by his failed marriage to a socialite, a party on that yacht was well worth the effort.

"Do you drink champagne?" Harriet asked.

They stopped at the bottom of the gangplank, which wasn't so much of a plank as it was a set of stairs engineered to fit the side of the boat without too much sway. As an engineer, Harley could appreciate the small things, like the stairs, and what went into designing them. He doubted that any of the people at this party even noticed the stairs. They just took it for granted that they'd be there for their convenience as they boarded the boat.

"Harley!" Harriet's voice snapped him from his thoughts.

"Sorry," Harley said, looking at her. "I'll drink it, but it's not my beverage of choice."

"Good!" Harriet's eyes opened and were filled with mischief.

"Harry!" Dawn rolled her eyes and shook her head as she turned to Harley. "You're about to get roped into stealing a bottle of champagne before you leave tonight for her."

"Can't you just order yourself a bottle from the hotel?" Harley asked, frowning. "I believe Liam has quite an expensive collection for his guests."

"Yes, but he doesn't have Krug Clos d'Ambonnay." Harriet's pronunciation was perfect. "Alex always has buckets of it lying around."

"Wait!" Harley's brows rose. "Isn't that like over three thousand dollars a bottle?"

"Uh-huh!" Dawn nodded. "Harriet is collecting bottles of it from Alex's party."

"Why are you collecting it?" Harley looked at Harriet curiously, and her mischievous grin spread. "Are you planning on having the most expensive champagne party?"

"That's actually not a bad idea!" Harriet said thoughtfully. "But no, I want to have an expensive champagne bath." She grinned at Harley's expression. "It's one of my to-dos before I'm fifty."

"She still needs about two dozen bottles of champagne to fill her bathtub," Dawn explained, rolling her eyes again.

"Oh!" Harley didn't understand rich people. They were so weird. "Why don't you buy your own? Then you'd be able to take your bath a lot sooner than steal a few bottles from Alex's parties."

"It's this thing between the two of them," Dawn told Harley. "And she gets the rest of us to steal a bottle each at the end of the night because Harriet has a one-bottle theft maximum policy."

"So you're an expensive champagne thief with a moral code." Harley laughed.

"Oh, the policy isn't mine," Harriet told him. "It's Alex's."

"Ah!" Harley nodded in understanding. "So, Alex knows you steal champagne at all his parties?"

"That's why he buys that particular label," Dawn explained. "It's Harriet's favorite."

"Is there something romantic between you and Alex?" Harley asked Harriet.

"Nooo!" Harriet pulled a disgusted face. "He and I are frenemies."

"Trust me, that's all that they are," Dawn backed up Harriet's statement. "And I should know. I grew up with Harriet, the Blackwells, and—" She was interrupted by a deep voice behind them.

"And me." They turned to see Brad Danes walking toward them. "Good evening. It's nice to see you all here. I thought it was going to be one of those boring evenings when I had to mingle with Alex's latest band of groupies and business associates."

"There you all are!" Alex called from the yacht. "I've been waiting for you, and for a few moments, I thought you weren't coming."

The four greeted Alex and made their way onto the deck.

"I'm sure you would've had ample people to keep you amused for the night," Harriet drawled.

"Yes, but who'd steal the excess bottles of champagne I had brought in especially for you, Harry?" Alex kissed her cheek affectionately and was rewarded with a shove from Harriet.

"I'm sure your girlfriend of the week would've helped you finish it," Harriet told him, taking a glass of bubble from a tray one of the servers brought them.

"Where is your beautiful fiancée?" Alex glanced toward the hotel. "I thought you were bringing Caroline with you. A few people are dying to meet the latest mystery writer sensation."

"You know Caroline hates it when you parade her around all your entertainment connections." Brad's eyes narrowed as he looked warningly at Alex. "We've just gotten back from Long Island and want to have a nice night out together."

"Of course," Alex said with a grin. "I understand, but..." He stopped talking. "Well, I can't say why. But as the shooting of series one of Cobble Cove finished, Caroline and I were chatting."

"So, Caroline finally forgave you for comparing her to a nag?" Harriet looked at him in amazement. "As you couldn't have won her over with your obnoxious charm, I assume you bought her forgiveness."

"Ah, Harry." Alex sighed, holding his heart. "You say the nicest things to me." He grinned as she shot him a black look. "But no, I apologized to sweet Caroline and was her Ethan translator during the filming because you know how he is. We became friends."

"Wow!" Harriet said with raised eyebrows. "You actually apologized to someone." She glanced up at the clear night sky, scattered

65

with sparkling stars. "It is amazing that we were not blown away by a monsoon."

"We still could be," Harley warned Harriet. "We get some violent hurricanes and are in the Atlantic hurricane season."

"That's just great, Alex." Harriet swatted him on the head. "You're tempting nature to throw a hurricane at us."

"Ow!" Alex groaned. "You make it seem like I never apologize."

"You don't!" Harriet, Dawn, and Brad said all at once.

"Geez, thanks, *pals!*" Alex shook his head at the three of them before being interrupted by Caroline and Harley's cousin, Doctor Daniella Thornton.

Caroline seemed surprised to see Harley. After greeting the two women, Alex was about to lead them to the entertainment deck of the four-deck yacht when Caroline stopped them.

"Wait," Caroline said. "We're just waiting for—"

"I'm here!" Jennifer's voice made Harley's spine stiffen, and his heart sank.

Great! Harley fumed inwardly. *Of course, Jennifer Gains has to appear and ruin my evening on a superyacht.*

"Sorry, I had to take that call." Jennifer carefully climbed onto the deck. She had yet to see Harley, who tried to hide behind Alex. She looked at Harriet. "It was Brody Craft."

"Brody Craft?" Harriet, Alex, Brad, and even Dawn spluttered.

"The Brody Craft?" Alex asked stupidly. "The latest teenage star that shot to fame overnight and is not only a huge teenage heartthrob but also one of the greatest actors we've seen in a long time?"

"Yes, *that* Brody Craft." Jennifer's eyes narrowed as she tilted her head to look behind Alex.

Harley looked over Alex's shoulder, and his and Jennifer's eyes met. Her brow creased, and her eyes clouded over.

"What did Brody want?" Harriet's question distracted Jennifer, and she turned her attention away from Harley.

He felt strangely deflated for a few seconds but shook the feeling away as Finn's words flitted through his mind: *You're falling for Jennifer.* Harley was certainly not falling for Jennifer; they weren't even frenemies like Alex and Harriet. They were nemeses and verbal-sparring partners.

"You're kidding me?" Harriet's words sliced through Harley's thoughts, drawing his attention back to the conversation that he'd missed the first part of.

"Nope." Jennifer shook her head, delight sparkling in her eyes. "And he's agreed to play the part of the long-lost nephew in Cobble Mysteries. He's coming to Cobble Cove next week and wants to meet with you and me, Harriet, to discuss being his manager."

"Congratulations, Jen!" Caroline was happy for her friend.

"This calls for a champagne celebration," Dawn stated. "My niece will be delighted that Brody's going to be here, as she's arriving to spend the summer with me in a week's time."

"I think all the teen girls on Plum Island are going to be glad that Brody's going to be here," Brad commented.

With that, Alex took them to the entertainment deck of the four-deck craft.

The entertainment deck sprawled before them as they ascended. A vibrant display of opulence unfolded—soft ambient lights adorned the perimeter, casting a warm glow over the glossy deck. Plush seating areas with comfortable cushions invited guests to relax, and a sleek bar beckoned with an array of top-shelf spirits. The atmosphere buzzed with animated conversations, laughter, and the occasional clink of crystal glasses.

In the center, a sumptuous spread awaited, a feast for the eyes and palate. Tables adorned with crisp white linens showcased an array of gourmet dishes—delectable appetizers, succulent main courses, and an enticing array of desserts. Alex had spared no expense, ensuring a culinary experience worthy of his superyacht's grandeur.

The aroma of grilled delicacies filled the air as skilled attendants manned the barbecue, adding a touch of smokiness to the sea breeze.

The chilled champagne bottles that nestled in silver buckets of ice glistened with condensation. After the recent conversation with Harriet, Harley could only imagine the price of each one and smiled at the thought of their champagne heist later that evening.

A live band on a raised platform captivated the audience with a melody that blended seamlessly with the rhythm of the waves. Couples twirled on the improvised dance floor, lost in the music, their laughter harmonizing with the melodies.

The night sky, adorned with stars, provided a celestial backdrop to the festivities. The distant lights of Plum Island twinkled like a constellation, mirroring the luminosity of the yacht's LED accents.

Alex led the group to an elegantly arranged seating area with an unobstructed view of the seascape. The cushy chairs offered comfort, and a low table displayed an assortment of delicacies. Caroline, Daniella, Jennifer, and the others settled in, their eyes flickering with a mixture of appreciation and anticipation.

Harley found himself between Dawn and Harriet, with a prime view of the entertainment unfolding.

"Impressive, isn't it?" Dawn commented, her eyes scanning the surroundings.

"Alex certainly knows how to throw a party," Harley acknowledged, taking in the scene.

"His flair for the dramatic extends beyond the movie set," Harriet added, her eyes glinting mischievously as she picked a bottle of her favorite champagne from an ice bucket beside her. "Oh, look what I found."

"It's a bit early to be stealing champagne, Harry," Brad, sitting on the other side of Harriet, teased, taking the bottle from her. "What say we open this one and drink it at our table?"

"Okay, but remember, I expect each of you to take a bottle as you leave," Harriet reminded them.

"Yes, we know!" Brad, Dawn, Caroline, Jennifer, and even Daniella chorused.

"Daniella, has Harriet dragged you into her life of champagne crime?" Harley laughed.

"As long as Harriet keeps donating to the clinic," Daniella said, raising her glass to Harriet, "I don't mind stealing the odd bottle of champagne that costs more than some people make."

As the night went on, the group enjoyed each other's company as their laughter echoed through the cabin, mingling with the lively sounds of the band playing tunes across the decades. Harley started to relax as he soaked up the atmosphere—the tension and disagreements of the day momentarily floating away into the ocean on the gentle breeze that blew in through the open doors.

As they tucked into the meal, Harley joined in the camaraderie of his friends, and while their eyes clashed during various table conversations, Harley and Jennifer managed to avoid direct conversation, opting to speak around each other rather than reigniting the sparks of temper that always seemed to flare up between them. Harley couldn't remember ever having a conversation with Jennifer that didn't end in a heated argument and where one of them, usually her, stormed off in a huff.

Finn arrived late, as usual, and took center stage in the group. Within an hour, Finn had everyone heading for the dance floor as he got the band to play his favorite medley of dance songs. Harley started to feel awkward once again as everyone at the table began partnering off for a dance until only he, Jennifer, and Harriet were left.

Harley breathed an inward sigh of relief as he couldn't possibly dance with two women, and, even though they were nemeses, it would be rude to leave Jennifer sitting alone. He was about to offer to go to the bar and get the ladies a drink when an old friend of Harriet's ambled over to their table and asked her to dance.

Drat! Harley thought, eyeing the bar. *If I ask Jennifer if I can get her a drink, it will avoid the pressure of asking her to dance as I escape to the bar, where I'll take my time.*

Harley was about to carry out his plan when Harriet trapped him like a rat in a glass cage with nowhere to hide.

"Come on, you two!" Harriet said. "On the dance floor, or you'll have Alex over here dragging you there."

"I don't dance," Harley said. At the same time, Jennifer said, "I can't dance in these heels."

They stopped and looked at each other, wide-eyed. They couldn't help snorting as they realized they were making excuses to avoid dancing together.

"No excuses," Harriet said, refusing to leave until they joined her on the dance floor.

Knowing Harriet wouldn't let up, Harley asked Jennifer, "Would you have this dance with me?"

"Sure," Jennifer said, mumbling as they stood up. "At least this moment of awkwardness will take my mind off my aching feet."

"And you may get the added bonus of stomping on my foot with one of those lethal spikes," Harley whispered.

"Now there's a thought." Jennifer surprised him by grinning, which softened her features and made his breath catch in his throat.

"You could always take them off," Harley told her. "These deck floors are gleaming like diamonds. They are so clean."

"Believe me, I've had my shoes off up until now," Jennifer admitted as they walked onto the dance floor and faced each other.

They stood, trying to figure out how to approach each other, until Brad and Caroline danced over to them.

"Oh, for goodness' sake, you two," Caroline said for their ears only. "Getting up close and personal for one dance won't kill you."

"It might," Harley said, his eyes meeting Jennifer's and then pointing to her shoes. "Have you seen those heels?"

He was struck by the mirth that highlighted the silver flecks that glistened like crystals in her deep blue eyes. Jennifer had beautiful eyes. There was no doubt that she was a gorgeous woman with a lithe figure and a natural grace. Harley swallowed as his throat suddenly felt dry, and Finn's words at the Beach Hut flashed again through his mind.

Harley shook them off and made himself remember how infuriating she was with her red-hot temper. Jennifer was also judgmental and mistrustful. She was what Harley considered a high-maintenance career woman who expected everyone to conform to her ridiculously high standards and get in line behind her work for her attention.

"I can assure you, Jennifer will not throw a shoe at you." Caroline glared at her friend. "*Right, Jennifer?*"

"What if I stand on his foot?" Jennifer looked at Caroline sweetly. "You know how clumsy I can be?"

"No foot stomping either!" Caroline pointed her finger warningly at her friend before turning to Harley. "And no tormenting Jennifer."

"I'll try!" Harley answered Caroline, grinning at Jennifer as they stepped toward each other. They took the dance pose but held each other stiffly at arm's length. "I can't make any promises, though, just in case Jennifer stomps on my foot or kicks me in the shin."

"I wouldn't give Jennifer any ideas, Harley," Brad warned. "Now, please, can you two start dancing instead of standing there like you're posing for a portrait painting so I can continue enjoying dancing with my fiancée?"

"Good grief!" Caroline rolled her eyes, stepped away from Brad, and approached Jennifer and Harley. "There you go." She shoved them closer together. "See, now all you have to do is sway around the floor."

As Jennifer's warm body collided with Harley's, her perfume tantalized his senses, and his heart thudded in his chest as if trying to reach and embrace her. He cleared his throat, readied himself to start dancing, and nearly tripped over her foot as their feet weren't yet in sync.

"Sorry," Harley mumbled.

"No, it was me," Jennifer said, stifling a giggle at their clumsy dancing attempt. "It's these stupid shoes."

"Do you want to take them off?" Harley asked her again as they found their rhythm after the third or fourth stumble. "I don't mind if you want to stand on my feet." He teased. "Daniella's daughter, Emily, used to do it when she was young."

"Don't tease me about that," Jennifer replied jovially. "I may just take you up on that offer. My feet sting like crazy. I can't wear these shoes like I did when I was younger."

"Why did you wear them then?" Harley felt himself relax as they swayed around the floor. "I can assure you, your legs would've looked just as gorgeous in lower heels." He glanced at her H-line, gently forming a little black dress that ended just above her knee. "While I'm not a fashion expert, my ex-wife always said that her little black dress could make any size heel work."

Jennifer leaned back slightly to look at him in disbelief. "Did you just compliment me and give me fashion advice all in one go?"

Harley thought about it before pursing his lips and nodding. "I believe I did."

"Well, thank you for complimenting my legs and for the tip about my dress," Jennifer said. "I wore these heels because Harriet bought them for me when we first arrived in Los Angeles a month ago, and their price tag was as high as the heels."

"Ah!" Harley nodded in understanding. "You're obligated to wear something because of what it costs and who gave it to you, dilemma."

"Yes, exactly," Jennifer concurred, her eyes sparkling with mischief. "Like that ugly sweater, a family member buys or makes for you."

"Oh, I hate that peer pressure," Harley agreed, slightly shuddering and enjoying their light banter. "Especially if it's given to you by someone younger."

"Or an older person on their deathbed!" Jennifer prompted.

"I've found that the shrinking in the washing machine routine always works," Harley advised. "Especially if I wash it." His eyes widened, and he gave his head a slight shake. "Laundry is not one of my handyman strengths."

"Do you think if I give you these shoes, you can do something about them?" Jennifer joked.

"You could always break the heel and then *forget* to have it fixed," Harley suggested. "Or give them to me to wash for you. I could perhaps turn them into Barbie shoes."

They both laughed at the thought of Harley shrinking Jennifer's shoes down to a tiny size. They were transitioning into their second dance when his pocket started to buzz.

"Either your pacemaker is going crazy or your phone is ringing," Jennifer told him, staring at the vibration from his shirt pocket.

"Phone!" Harley assured her, reluctantly letting her go as they walked to the edge of the dance floor.

"I hope it's not Sam." Jennifer's eyes widened with concern as she looked at her wristwatch. "It's almost eleven-thirty."

That thought had flashed through Harley's mind as he pulled the phone out of his pocket, frowning when it clicked off and he saw the name on the screen.

Harley's frown deepened as he looked at Jennifer. "It was Betty!"

Jennifer's eyes widened with a flash of panic. "Why is she calling you?"

They turned and rushed to the table, where Jennifer pulled out her phone and Harley dialed Betty's number. It rang with no answer and eventually went over to voicemail.

"She's not picking up." Harley's voice echoed his worry.

"That's so strange," Jennifer said, scrolling through her phone. "There are no missed calls or messages from my aunt on my phone for this evening."

"We'd better get over there just in case," Harley advised, grabbing his jacket and scanning the dance floor as he asked. "Do you have your car here?"

"No, I came with Caroline and Brad," Jennifer answered, putting on her coat and grabbing her purse.

"I have my pickup," Harley offered. "Let's go."

"I'll message Caroline that I've gone home on the way," Jennifer said as they slipped unnoticed off the boat and headed toward Harley's pickup.

The ten-minute drive to Beach Plum Cottage felt like an hour's drive as the tension hung heavy in the vehicle.

"She's still not picking up," Jennifer told Harley while trying to ring Betty for about the tenth time since they'd left the hotel.

When they arrived at the cottage, no lights were on, which worried them even more, and they were nearly frantic by the time they got inside the house. The hallway light was on, and a soft light glowed from Betty's room.

They rushed toward the room and found Betty lying curled up on the floor beside her bed, holding her arm in pain.

"Betty!" Harley yelled at the same time Jennifer did.

They rushed to her side, where she was curled up in a ball, hugging her wrist, and moaning in pain.

CHAPTER 5

J ennifer woke up from a restless sleep, her face cushioned against a warm pillow with a heartbeat. The subtle, musky scent of cologne tickled her senses as the world came into view through the haze of sleep.

"Morning!" Harley's deep voice vibrated through her pillow.

His words cleared whatever leftover remnants of sleep still clouded her foggy brain as she realized her pillow was Harley's chest. They were at the Plum Island Library Clinic. They'd slept on the chairs in the clinic as they waited for news about Betty.

Jennifer sat straight, ignoring the pain slicing through her cramped legs. She slammed onto the ground, her bare feet hitting the cold tiled floors, and Harley's jacket slid from her shoulders. She glanced at the chair beside her where her torturous high-heeled shoes were perched and remembered kicking them off as she curled onto the chair.

"Morning," Jennifer croaked, feeling mortified that she must've been sleeping with her mouth open as her throat was dry.

She glanced toward his shirt and pursed her lips. She noticed the small wet patch where her mouth had been. *Oh no! I sleep drooled on his shirt.*

Harley rubbed the sleep from his eyes and looked at Jennifer, who perched his jacket over his shoulder, hiding her drool. The aroma of coffee drew her attention, and she glanced at the coffee machine stationed on the small cabinet across from them.

"Do you think that coffee is the same pot percolating throughout the night?" Jennifer pointed to the pot and looked at Harley.

Jennifer noticed him stifling a groan as he rotated the shoulder on the side of his body she'd slept on.

"Sorry!" Jennifer's brow creased apologetically. "I ruined your shirt and made your arm lame." *Uh-oh! Did I just admit I drooled on him? That's not going to go down well. I can imagine that coming back to bite me.*

"No, it's an old hockey injury," Harley assured her. "My shoulder is always stiff when I wake up in the mornings."

Jennifer's brows knitted together a little more tightly as she eyed him strangely. *Is he being nice to me?* She glanced at her wristwatch—it was five past six in the morning.

"Wow! We've been here for six hours!" Jennifer exclaimed.

"Morning, Jennifer," Daniella seemingly appeared out of nowhere, dressed in her doctor's coat and holding a tablet as she greeted Jennifer before turning to Harley. Her brows creased. "Is your shoulder giving you problems again?"

"No more than usual." Harley gave Daniella a tight smile and stopped massaging his shoulder. "How's Betty?"

Daniella scrolled through her tablet. "Betty is going to be fine." She looked at both of them. "I had to put a new cast on her leg, but the x-rays show she didn't damage it again. She has a sprained wrist. I've put a compression bandage on it, and she must keep it in a sling for at least a week." She gave a reassuring smile. "Currently, she's resting comfortably. I'd like to keep her here until lunchtime, and then you can take her home."

"Thank you, Daniella," Jennifer felt relieved now that she knew that Aunt Betty was going to be alright. That was quite the tumble she took off the bed. I'll have to go to the cottage and show you how to set it up for Betty to avoid future tumbles." She glanced at the tablet.

"I'd appreciate that," Jennifer told her.

"Sure, I'll pop around sometime during the day," Daniella told them. She pulled an envelope from her doctor's coat pocket and handed it to Jennifer. "This is a prescription for a few supplements as her blood work showed some deficiencies, and pain meds should Betty require them."

"Can we see her?" Jennifer took the envelope.

"You're welcome to check in on her," Daniella replied. "But she's finally sleeping peacefully and needs to rest, so please don't wake her."

"Don't worry, I won't." Jennifer stood and stretched the kinks from her body.

"My doctor's orders for the two of you—" Daniella put the tablet under her arm. "Go home, get something to eat, shower, and get at least four hours of sleep." She smiled. "More if you can. Betty will need a lot more help with her wrist in a sling, and I don't want her putting any pressure on her injured leg, which means complete bed rest for at least three days."

"I plan to do just that." Jennifer gave her a weary smile.

"Good, I don't want to see either of you here after having an accident because you were sleep-deprived," Daniella warned them. "And on that note. I have to go home and see my teenage daughter."

"Give Em a hug and kiss from me," Harley told Daniella.

"Will do." Daniella nodded, adding before she left. "Oh, and I wouldn't drink that coffee. It's been there for two days." She waved goodbye and walked off toward the nurse's station.

After checking on Betty, Jennifer and Harley returned to Beach Plum Cottage, where he'd left his car.

"Thank you, Harley," Jennifer saw the surprise in his eyes as she walked him to his pickup truck. "I don't know what I would've done if you hadn't been there last night."

"Of course," Harley said, opening his vehicle and sliding into the driver's seat. "You can call me anytime."

Jennifer nodded, pushing the door closed as he started the engine and slid the window down. "I'll stop by the clinic later to see Betty if that's okay with you?"

"Yes," Jennifer said, a twang of guilt for the way she'd attacked him for taking her aunt out yesterday sliced through her. Harley really did care about her aunt. "Please take the day off and relax. It's been a stressful night."

"I hope you'll take Daniella's advice and get some rest yourself?" Harley said.

"Yup!" Jennifer nodded, stepping back as Harley put the pickup in reverse. "I'm headed to my bed as soon as I've had a shower and something to eat."

"Sweet dreams, Jennifer!" Harley's voice was low and husky, sending a warm shiver through her.

"You too!" Jennifer squeaked, feeling flustered as she waved Harley on his way. *What was that? An impression of Alvin the chipmunk?* She cleared her throat. Glad he couldn't see the embarrassed heat creep through her cheeks.

Later that afternoon, Jennifer was at the lighthouse visiting Caroline and waiting for Liam to arrive and drop the kids off. Jennifer was perched on a kitchen stool on the dining room side of the kitchen counters, watching Caroline make cookies for all the teens staying at her place that night.

"Where is Aunt Betty now?" Caroline asked Jennifer.

"Harley helped me fetch her from the clinic and get her home," Jennifer explained. "Daniella met us back at Beach Plum Cottage, and she and Harley fixed Aunt Betty's home hospital bed." She sipped her coffee. "It's now the perfect height, and Daniella fixed the side rails, so Aunt Betty has something to hang onto getting in and out of bed."

"I told you to get her the normal one and not the height-adjustable one," Caroline pointed out.

"I bought that one as Aunt Betty isn't getting any younger, and I don't know when she's going to need all the added bits that go with the bed, including being able to make it go higher and lower." Jennifer defended her choice of bed.

"One shiny beacon of light to come from Aunt Betty's fall is you and Harley seem to be getting along much better," Caroline commented.

Jennifer's heart gave an unexpected lurch. *Traitor*! Her eyes narrowed in on Caroline, who casually went on rolling out cookie dough as she threw that into their conversation.

"I guess." Jennifer shrugged, deciding to play it cool. "He's been very helpful with Aunt Betty."

"Uh-huh!" Caroline looked at Jennifer with a sly smile. "You seemed to enjoy each other's company at the dinner party *before* Aunt Betty's fall."

"We were trying not to cause a scene among the people *you* have to work with on The Cobble Cove Mysteries." Jennifer took another sip of her rapidly cooling coffee. She was about to move the conversation onto Jules and Reef when Jules flew into the kitchen, followed by her animal possie.

"They're here at last!" Jules's voice was laced with excitement as she yanked open the back door and disappeared outside.

"Looks like my brother's arrived." Jennifer smiled.

Sliding off the stool, Jennifer headed toward the back door, silently breathing a sigh of relief. Although she knew Caroline would pick up the topic at a later point. The next few minutes were a whirlwind of greetings and gifts from Disneyland.

The house quietened down again when Jules and Lila left the kitchen followed by the animal trio.

"Are you sure you're going to be okay having a bunch of teenagers staying over?" Liam accepted the cup of coffee Jennifer made for him and stole a choc-chip cookie from the cooling rack.

"It won't be a problem. Brad will be here and is staying in one of the guest bedrooms," Caroline told them. "The teens want to put up the tent out front."

"Like we used to do." Liam smiled, leaning against the kitchen counter as he dunked his cookie in his coffee.

"Yes." Caroline nodded, grinning. "Brad and I will discuss it later when he brings Emily, Tucker, and Reef."

"They're going to do the Cobble Point hike together tomorrow," Jennifer informed her brother.

"Lila told me." Liam ate his cookie, pausing for a few moments while he chewed. "I'm glad that Tucker and Reef will be with them, being part of the island's volunteer search and rescue."

"Yes, that's what we said," Caroline told him. "Carly is going to have a picnic lunch ready for them when they reach the top."

"Sounds like they're going to have a great time," Liam commented. "Makes me nostalgic for when we were young and did those things."

"You can still go camping and do the hike," Jennifer pointed out. "Besides, you've just turned fifty, not a hundred."

"Didn't your great-grandfather, who was nearly a hundred, do that hike?" Caroline reminded them.

"That old man was a cyborg or something." Liam laughed. "Aunt Betty told us stories about how he was still chopping down trees and making furniture until the day before he died."

"I think Aunt Betty was exaggerating a little bit." Jennifer shook her head and thought that was the perfect moment to tell him about Aunt Betty's fall. "Speaking of Aunt Betty, I didn't want to stress you out on your trip home, but Aunt Betty had another fall last night."

"She fell out of the fancy new home hospital bed Jen bought her," Caroline added, grinning at the black look Jennifer gave her.

"She didn't fall out of it," Jennifer corrected Caroline. "She tried to get back into the bed and was trying to lift her broken leg onto the bed. The heavy plaster cast made her slide off it."

"So basically, it was what Caroline said!" Liam's eyes were wide with worry. "Aunt Betty slid off that costly bed you bought her."

"You're all going to be pleased she has it when the time comes, and she needs it!" Jennifer said impatiently. "Besides, it was Harley who set it up." She glared at Caroline. "If you remember, I told Aunt Betty to let me help her set it up."

"I do remember that conversation." Caroline nodded, putting the next batch of cookies into the oven and adding to the already warm, sweet smell of baking. "Vividly, as I was the one who had to break up the argument between Harley and you."

"Ah!" Liam nodded in understanding. "I see you're still using Harley as your verbal sparring bag, little sister."

"What's this?" Jennifer looked from her best friend to her older brother. "Gang up on Jennifer day?"

"No!" Liam patted her shoulder. "It's just that when you dislike a person, you tend to have these blinkers on that won't let you see past their perceived flaws."

"To be fair," Caroline started cleaning the kitchen, "Harley was rude and obnoxious to Jennifer when she stopped at the side of the road to help him when they first—" She stopped and grinned at Jennifer. "*Ran* into each other."

"Side of the road?" Liam's brow creased, and he looked at Jennifer questioningly.

Jennifer sighed and rolled her eyes at Caroline before telling Liam how she and Harley first met. After she finished, Liam burst out laughing.

"You mangled his emergency triangle?" Liam shook his head and put an arm around Jennifer's shoulders. "Oh, my beautiful sister. You do get yourself into the most awkward of situations."

"It wasn't awkward," Jennifer told him. "Well, not until I turned to get back into my car and leave Harley stranded on the side of the road and he pointed out my skirt was wet in the most inconvenient of places."

"Hilarious," Liam teased. "You and Harley had a heated coincidental meeting and then found out you were the niece and nephew of two old friends." He laughed. "Classic." He looked at Caroline. "You could write a love story about them."

"That's what I thought," Caroline agreed, giving Jennifer a sly look. "But Jen is adamant that there is nothing between them and that Harley is not her type."

"Let's just say he and I didn't see eye to eye after that," Jennifer told her brother.

"And while Jennifer was hounding Harley about his work on the cottage, he was riling Jennifer up and baiting her whenever he could," Caroline explained to Liam. "It wasn't only your sister causing the friction between them. Harley was just as much to blame for the constant battle of wills the two of them have been in since they met."

"I believe you've finally met a man who doesn't back down from you?" Liam pursed his lips thoughtfully. "And I missed it all."

"No, he's still here, and Aunt Betty rehired him," Jennifer pointed out. "I'm sure you're bound to see us in one of our heated arguments when our silent truce wears off. Now, can we discuss Aunt Betty?" Jennifer looked from Caroline to Liam.

Jennifer's phone rang before they could discuss Aunt Betty's current medical needs. It was Aunt Betty.

"Can you put it on speaker so I can say hello?" Liam asked Jennifer, who nodded and hit the speaker as she answered.

"Hello, Aunt Betty. I have you on speaker phone," Jennifer warned before Aunt Betty started speaking. "Liam and Caroline are here with me."

"Hi, Caroline," Betty greeted Caroline first.

"Hello, Aunt Betty," Caroline called. "I'm glad you're okay after last night."

"Thank you, sweetheart," Betty replied before greeting her nephew. "Hello, Liam." Her voice perked up as she spoke to Liam. "How was your trip?"

"Great," Liam told her. "I hear you had another fall?"

"Yes, but I'm fine," Betty assured him before pausing for a few seconds and lowering her voice. "I'm glad you're there with Jennifer, Liam. It saves me having to make another phone call."

"Is everything okay, Aunt Betty?" Jennifer's brow furrowed worriedly at the sudden urgency in her aunt's voice.

"Can you and Liam come home urgently?" Betty asked in hushed tones.

"Have you hurt yourself again, Aunt Betty?" Liam asked, his eyes widening with concern.

"No, no," Betty said. "But we need to discuss something, so please come home now."

"Okay!" Liam said and looked at Jennifer curiously. "We'll be there in fifteen minutes."

"Thank you," Aunt Betty said. "Bye, Caroline. I hope you stop by for a visit soon."

"I will, Aunt Betty," Caroline promised before Jennifer hung up. "I wonder what's going on?"

"I guess we're going to find out in the ten to fifteen minutes it takes to get to Beach Plum cottage," Jennifer said, collecting her purse and turning to Liam. "You're going to have to drive us there as I walked here."

"Let's go," Liam said, turning to Caroline. "If Lila needs anything, just give me a call."

"I will," Caroline told him, waving them off.

Jennifer's heart raced as they headed toward Beach Plum Cottage. "I hope Aunt Betty didn't get some terrible news about any tests she may have had done at the clinic last night."

"Don't even go there," Liam warned her, slowing down to turn onto the road that led to the cottage. "Aunt Betty is as fit as a fiddle, and I'm sure she's going to live to over a hundred."

"Let's hope so," Jennifer said, her voice throaty with emotion.

As they pulled into the drive, they saw a car they didn't recognize in the driveway.

"Do you know anyone who drives a Jaguar XJ?" Liam asked Jennifer as he parked and switched off the car's engine.

"Nope!" Jennifer shook her head. "I don't think I've ever seen a Jaguar on Plum Island!"

"Yeah, it's not the typical car you see on the island," Liam agreed, sliding out of his SUV and glancing at the pickup. "I see Harley's here."

"Yes, he's working on the roof, and that's why I left Aunt Betty to go to Caroline as he was here with her," Jennifer explained. "Daniella was here earlier when I left, too."

Liam nodded and followed Jennifer inside.

"Aunt Betty?" Jennifer called, walking into the house.

No one was in the sitting room, and they walked through to Aunt Betty's bedroom at the end of the hallway. The door was open, and voices were coming from it. Liam and Jennifer frowned at each other before walking into the room and freezing at the person sitting beside Aunt Betty's bed.

"There you two are," Betty greeted them as the man stood.

He looked the same except for the streaks of gray in his hair and a few age lines. He stood on the opposite side of Betty's bed to them, looking at them with uncertainty in his blue eyes. Eyes that her mother always said were so much like Jennifer's.

"Hello, Jennifer. Liam." His voice was deep and had a slight husky sound to it.

Jennifer's mind spun, and she couldn't find any words as she gaped at the man before them. The shock of seeing him wore off, replaced by years of pent-up hurt and anger.

"What are you doing here?" Liam's voice was low. His eyes narrowed and flashed with the same emotions burning inside Jennifer.

"Liam!" Betty raised her brows as she looked at her nephew. "Please don't be rude to your father."

"We don't have a father!" Jennifer and Liam said in unison.

Betty was about to say something to them when Andrew Gains stopped her. "It's okay, Betty. I deserved that."

"Is this why you wanted us home so urgently?" Jennifer's words were back and tumbling through her lips before she could stop them. "Because *he* suddenly showed up thirty-nine years too late?"

"Jennifer!" Betty hissed. "That's enough."

"I'm out of here," Jennifer said, holding up her hands. "I just remembered I have to be anywhere else but here right now."

She turned to leave.

"I'm coming with you to wherever it is we need to be beside here," Liam said, following Jennifer to the bedroom door.

Betty's voice rang sternly through the room, stopping them as they were about to exit through the door.

"You two *will* come back here right now and listen to what your *father* has to say," Betty ordered. "I did not raise the two of you to be rude and turn your back on someone who needs your help." She glanced at Andrew. "No matter who they are!" Her eyes narrowed further.

Jennifer and Liam stood at the door, staring at their aunt before looking at each other and nodding as a silent agreement passed between them.

"Fine," Liam became their spokesperson, and they returned to the room. "You have ten minutes, and then we have a thing."

"What thing?" Betty looked at them suspiciously.

"We just told you," Jennifer reminded her aunt. "An anywhere but here with *him,* thing."

"Look, I know I don't deserve to even ask for your help," Andrew told them.

Jennifer looked at him more closely and saw the dark emotion in his eyes. He looked tired, drawn, and haunted by sadness. Jennifer almost felt sorry for him as he was obviously going through a hard time.

"No, you don't," Liam agreed with him.

"Maybe you two should take a seat?" Betty suggested.

"No, we're good," Liam refused. "Can we move this along?"

Andrew took a breath. "I remarried seventeen years ago." While she tried to remain aloof and emotionless, his words still felt like a dagger to Jennifer's heart.

"Congratulations!" Liam said sarcastically. "So what?" His brow furrowed, and he shrugged. "Did you come here to ask us to give you our blessing?"

"At least he's only seventeen years late this time," Jennifer commented, she and Liam exchanging glances.

95

"Thank you for sharing that," Liam told him. "But I think I speak for Jennifer and me when I say *we don't care who or when you got married.*"

"Yeah, we actually thought you were dead," Jennifer said nastily. She wasn't a vindictive person, but she couldn't stop the anger mingled with all the hurt he'd caused her from fueling her tongue with acidic barbs.

"Jennifer!" Betty looked at her in disbelief. "What an awful thing to say. Apologize."

"No, Betty, she doesn't have to apologize," Andrew said. "How would Jennifer and Liam have known whether I was alive or dead after disappearing without a trace from their lives." He looked at Jennifer and Liam. "I didn't come here for your blessings or to disrupt your lives, although I would like to say how incredibly proud I am of both of you."

"Don't give them openings like that to throw barbs at you, Andrew," Betty warned him. "They both had a big shock seeing you again. Your words won't mean anything now."

"Aunt Betty's right," Jennifer said before Liam could. "We really don't care what you think of us. If you didn't come here to rub your seventeen-year-old marriage in our faces, what did you come here for?"

Andrew took his wallet from his pocket and pulled out a few small photographs the size of a credit card. He slipped three back into his wallet and extended the third toward Jennifer and Liam, who took it. It was a photo of a dark-haired teenage girl with eyes the same color and shape as Jennifer's. The teenager bore a striking resemblance to Jennifer.

"Is she your granddaughter?" Jennifer asked.

"That's your sister, Molly," Andrew's words had Liam and Jennifer's eyes widening in disbelief. "She's just turned fifteen."

"Don't you think she looks like you did at fifteen, Jen?" Betty tried to ease the tension, which had suddenly wound much tighter in the room.

"Aren't you too old to have children?" Again, the angry, hurtful words spilled from Jennifer's mouth before she could stop them.

"I was sixty when Molly was born," Andrew admitted. "Georgia, my wife, is fifteen years younger than me."

"Look at that," Liam raised his brows and looked at Jennifer. "Seems it's not too late for you if you still want to have kids."

"Oh, heck no!" Jennifer gave him a disgusted look. "I don't want to end up looking like my child's grandparent."

They both snorted and turned back to Andrew. The flash of pain did not escape Jennifer's notice, and though she felt a pang of guilt for her sharp barbs, she quickly pushed it away. She reminded herself of how he'd kissed her goodbye one morning and never returned and how Jennifer had waited for him to come home for months after. She refused to believe her father would abandon them and had waited for nearly a year, never giving up hope before she started to believe Liam that their father was never coming back.

Liam handed the photo back. "She looks like a lovely child. Again, congratulations on having a daughter the same age as *my* daughter."

Andrew ignored Liam's dig at him and continued, "Molly is the reason I'm here." His voice dropped and wobbled with emotion. "I'm not sure if you remember, but my mother was a doctor, and she gave me your medical records."

"Whoa!" Jennifer stopped him. "You pulled our medical records?"

"No," Andrew denied with a shake of his head. "She had your medical records from when you were babies."

"Okay!" Liam said. "What's this got to do with Mandy?"

"Molly!" Andrew corrected. "You and Jennifer are a good match to help her."

Jennifer suddenly didn't like where this conversation was going. "Like with a kidney or something?"

"No, not a kidney," Andrew said. "Bone marrow. Molly has leukemia."

CHAPTER 6

H arley felt awful as he listened to what was happening inside Betty's room. He didn't mean to eavesdrop, but he was stuck in that attic until one of the room's occupants walked down the hallway. The entrance to the attic was close to Betty's room, where he was sitting and waiting for someone to hand him his ladder, which had fallen on the floor.

Harley was surprised none of them had heard the loud bang it had made when he accidentally knocked it over. Betty wanted to turn it into an entertainment area, and Harley had climbed into it to measure it. He'd been in the attic for a few minutes when he realized that Jennifer and Liam were discussing a private family matter in Betty's room.

One thing Harley had learned, besides Andrew Gains having deserted his kids over thirty years ago, was that the attic needed to be soundproofed if Betty wanted it as an entertainment room. Harley could hear their conversation as if he was in the room with them. As soon as Harley realized what was happening, he tried to scramble out of the attic but kicked the ladder over in haste.

Here he sat—stuck and unwittingly eavesdropping on the Gains family. Harley was sure this would come back to bite him as Jennifer would not be pleased to hear he was listening in on them, which was a pity because Harley and Jennifer had just started to get along. Or at least they hadn't argued in the past fourteen hours. He couldn't even message or phone anyone because his phone was in Betty's living room.

A gap in the floorboards gave him a peek into the room where he saw the tall, distinguished-looking man he'd answered the door to. He was on the window side of Betty's bed while Liam and Jennifer stood on the side nearest the door. Betty was the mediator between the two warring parties.

"No!" Liam's voice traveled up to the attic. "Why should we help you?"

"Liam!" Betty stated, shocked by her nephew's vehemence.

"He's right, Aunt Betty," Jennifer backed her older brother. "Why should we help him? He deserted his old family thirty-three years ago."

"Exactly!" Liam picked up from his sister, his eyes narrowing at their father, Andrew. "Where were you when our mother, your wife, was dying?"

"We tried to reach you!" Jennifer's voice filled with bitterness. "Mom needed you. She needed your help."

"You left us to deal with it." Liam's voice grew hoarse with the memory of their loss. "Aunt Betty had us and her sister to look after. She struggled to make ends meet, pay for Mom's medical bills, and keep us fed!"

"I was eight, and Liam was eleven," Jennifer sneered at Andrew. "While all the other kids got to do sports after school and play with their friends, Liam and I came home each day to help Aunt Betty take care of Mom."

"Do you know what that's like for children of that age?" Liam's voice wobbled with emotion. "Each day, we watched Mom slip a little further away from us." He swallowed, and Harley saw Liam struggling to control his emotions. "Each day we tried to will the pieces of life we could see she was losing back into her."

"The first thing I'd do when I got back from school each day was check the mailbox to see if there was *any* news from *you!*" Jennifer pointed at him accusingly. "Even though you'd been gone for nearly two years, while my mind had given up on you, my heart was sure my dad, my hero, would ride in and save the day."

"You broke Mom's heart so badly that it couldn't be fixed," Liam told Andrew. His voice dropped and became flat. "And ours. So, I ask you, why would you ever think we'd help you?"

"Now you get to feel what it's like to have family turn their back on you!" Jennifer raised her chin defiantly.

"It's not a good feeling, feeling helpless and alone." Liam's tone of voice matched his sisters with an added touch of malice. "To have the last glimmer of hope extinguished as you reach the end of a very dark tunnel."

Harley watched from the crack in the attic floor, unsure of what had caused this heated argument. He could feel the tension and resentment in the air and wondered what Andrew had asked for that had warranted that kind of reaction from Liam and Jennifer.

"Come on, Liam, let's get out of here," Jennifer said.

Harley was about to stand and rush to the attic opening when he saw Jennifer and Liam turn to leave Betty's room. But Betty stopped them, and Harley remained crouched as he continued spying on them.

"Stop right there!" Betty's voice boomed, making Jennifer and Liam stop and turn toward her. "I didn't raise the two of you like this. We help others in need, no matter who they are."

"Not when they're *him*!" Liam looked at Andrew Gains as if he was something nasty Liam had stepped in. "He doesn't deserve our help and had some nerve coming here asking for it."

"He didn't come here asking for help for himself," Betty snapped, looking at her niece and nephew she raised in disappointment. "He came here asking for an innocent fifteen-year-old girl who has done nothing to either of you."

"Yes, but—" Jennifer began, but Betty cut her off angrily.

"Did I say you could speak?" Betty glared at Jennifer. "I'm not done." She pushed herself into a more comfortable position in the bed. "How can the two of you walk out here so coldly without a thought to Molly?" She shook her head. "Especially you, Liam. As a father to a fifteen-year-old daughter, I thought you'd understand. What if it was Lila who needed help?" She hit a nerve with Liam. "I bet if you had to, you'd put that pride in your pocket and go wherever you could to save her."

"Betty's right," Andrew said. "I would never want to disrupt your lives. I know I have no right to ask for your help. But I'm asking anyway. Molly is only fifteen. She deserves a chance to live her life and go to college." He rubbed his tired eyes before looking at Jennifer and Liam pleadingly. "And I'll do anything to get her the help she needs. Including begging the two of you to help her to fight the leukemia."

Andrew's words sent Harley's mind reeling at the mention of his teenage daughter with leukemia. He swallowed as the room whirled around him, and he was suddenly transported back ten years to another time, another place, and another fight against leukemia.

·♥·♥·♥·♥·♥·

Boston Ten Years Ago

Harley hadn't had time to change out of his Navy SEALs uniform. When the military plane landed at the base near Boston, he'd hopped in the town car the military had arranged for him and headed to Boston General.

On the way, he played Angela's message that had come for him a week ago, but he was on assignment repeatedly.

Harley, you have to get here as soon as you can. Daniel's condition is worsening. Your bloodwork finally came back, and you're a match. Please, your son needs you now more than ever.

The town car had barely stopped outside the hospital, and Harley was out of the car and rushing to find what room his son was in. The nurse pointed him in the direction and hadn't even finished speaking when Harley's boots pounded down the corridors to find Daniel.

Harley burst through the door of Daniel's room, his heart pounding in his chest. His eyes immediately landed on the small figure lying in the hospital bed, hooked up to various machines. Daniel's face was pale, his features drawn with pain. He barely registered his ex-wife sitting in the chair next to their son's bed.

"Daniel," Harley breathed, rushing to his son's side. "I'm here."

Daniel's eyes fluttered open, and a weak smile spread across his face. "Dad," he whispered.

Harley took Daniel's hand, trying to hold back tears. "I'm so sorry it took me so long to get here," he said, his voice choked with emotions that he gulped back. "I promise I won't leave your side again."

Daniel squeezed his father's hand, his grip weak but filled with love. "I know you didn't want to leave," he said softly. "But I'm glad you're here now."

"Harley, at last!" Angela interrupted the tender father-son reunion. "We've been waiting for you."

She stood up from the chair, her eyes glazed with a mix of desperation and hope. Harley tore his gaze away from Daniel to look at Angela, taking in her disheveled appearance and the haunted look in her eyes.

"I'm sorry I only got your message yesterday," Harley told her and looked at his son, who had drifted off to sleep.

"Doctor Ainsley told me to get her as soon as you arrived," Angela told him. Her voice was a hushed whisper so as not to wake Daniel. "She's eager to get the bone marrow extraction procedure done as soon as possible."

Harley nodded. He stood up from Daniel's bed, reluctantly letting his son's hand go. They'd been waiting for nearly a month to find out if Harley was a match for Daniel. He'd been astounded that finding that information out would take that long. Especially when a twelve-year-old's life depended on it, but the doctors had assured them Daniel would be okay.

Not fine, Harley realized as he followed Angela down the sterile halls, just okay. Daniel had gotten sick at the beginning of the year, three months after his diagnosis. Angela, most of her family, Harley's family, and he got tested to find a match for Daniel. That was four months ago. It had taken eight weeks for the lab to return without a match, and Harley had to be retested as his DNA sample had been corrupted.

For some reason, Harley's DNA had to be taken three times before they got a decent sample of his DNA. While the lab was doing its test, Daniel's condition worsened. Harley hadn't wanted to go on this last assignment, but Angela, the doctors, and Daniel had convinced him to go. The lab would take another three weeks to get the results, and Daniel was responding to the chemo treatments.

While Harley had known the odds when the doctors had diagnosed Daniel with leukemia in his mind, he never imagined it would come to this. The weight of guilt settled heavily on Harley's shoulders as he thought about his time away from his son.

The time he spent defending his country to ensure it was a safe place for Daniel to grow up in all suddenly felt like it had been for nothing. The real enemy lies inside a person. Harley swallowed the burning lump stinging his eyes as Angela stopped before a door labeled Doctor Jessica Ainsley - Oncologist.

A twelve-year-old kid shouldn't need an oncologist! Angela knocked on the door and walked in without being invited.

The doctor was a petite redhead with cool eyes. She stood when they entered, and Angela introduced her to Harley.

"I'm so glad you could get here so quickly, Mr. Donovan," Doctor Ainsley's voice was as cool as her eyes.

Harley understood her reserve. Like him, she was also a type of soldier fighting a war against a silent enemy that no military could defend the nation against. Her war was with cancer.

"Can you explain the procedure to us?" Angela asked the doctor as they sat in front of her desk.

Harley was consumed by guilt and worry, and his mind couldn't think of anything else. He couldn't help but blame himself for Daniel's condition, for being away on his assignments while his son suffered. The weight of his choices and their consequences on his family pressed heavily on his shoulders.

As Doctor Ainsley continued to explain the bone marrow extraction procedure, Angela nodded along, her eyes filled with desperation. But Harley couldn't focus on the details. Instead, memories of the past flooded his thoughts—the times he had missed, the birthdays and holidays he hadn't been there for.

His mind kept drifting back to Daniel lying in that hospital bed. The guilt gnawed at him, consuming his thoughts. He couldn't shake the feeling that he had failed his son by not being there when he needed him the most. As the doctor continued to explain the bone marrow extraction procedure, Harley found it increasingly difficult to concentrate.

"Mr. Donovan, are you listening?" Doctor Ainsley's voice broke through his thoughts.

Harley snapped back to attention and nodded, forcing a smile. "I apologize, doctor. It's just that my mind is preoccupied with my son's condition."

Doctor Ainsley gave him a sympathetic look. "I understand, Mr. Donovan. This is a difficult time for you and your family."

Angela reached across the desk and took Harley's hand, offering and drawing comfort. "We'll get through this together," she said softly.

Harley squeezed her hand in return, grateful for her support. While he and Angela had barely been able to be in the same room before their divorce, the one they were always united with was Daniel. They ensured their son was their first priority—at least Angela did. Harley was off fighting for his country. He knew there was honor in that as a patriot, but as a father with a sick son, it somehow felt like desertion.

"We can do the procedure as soon as you're ready, Mr. Donovan." Doctor Ainsley's words cut into his thoughts.

Harley blinked at her for a few seconds before realizing they were waiting for his answer.

"I'm ready now," Harley told them.

"You'll need to fill out these forms." Doctor Ainsley put a sheet before him and handed him a pen. "When last did you have anything to eat or drink?"

Harley looked at her and frowned as he tried to remember. "Yesterday, when I returned to Los Angeles from an assignment."

"What time of day was it, Harley?" Angela asked for verification. "You're not supposed to have anything to eat or drink since midnight."

"Then that's not a problem," Harley informed them, filling out the form, signing it, and handing it back to the doctor.

The next couple of hours were a blur as Harley's bone marrow was extracted, and he insisted on recovering in his son's room.

Six torturous weeks later, Daniel's blood count was going up. While celebrating that small victory, Harley and Angela knew Daniel's immune system was still fragile, and he wasn't out of danger yet. Daniel was still in the hospital during the seventh week as his immune system was still weak. Before anyone entered Daniel's room they had to put on a mask, gloves, booties, and a disposable sterile gown. The doctor had stressed that if anyone had a slight sniff or headache they were *not* to go into Daniel's room.

As a Navy SEAL, Harley was vaccinated once a year against influenza and he made sure he took vitamins to ensure he didn't contract anything while Daniel was so sick. Not that it had mattered on that day. Harley was visiting Daniel and they were going through the latest Superman comic book Harley had bought him, discussing his son's superheroes.

Daniel was an excellent artist and wanted to write his own comic books. He'd started drawing his own at the age of seven. They had been discussing colleges Daniel would like to attend one day when he suddenly began coughing. Within a couple of hours, Daniel was running a high fever. The doctors tried to control the fever, but his system couldn't fight it.

Twenty-four hours later, Daniel was gone—lost to them forever! Angela and Harley were still in shock when Angela's family arrived.

"Angela, Harley." Clair, Angela's twin sister, rushed toward them. Her voice sounded weird. Gruff and throaty. "What happened?"

Harley didn't know why he'd even noticed it, as he never had time for Clair and rarely noticed anything about her. She was a spoiled, pampered rich girl who'd gotten in with the wrong crowd to spite her parents. Clair had been in and out of drug rehab facilities since her rebellious teenage years. She may have cleaned up her act, but Harley still didn't trust or like the woman.

On the other hand, Angela was the more responsible twin—the one her parents had groomed to take over the Wesley clothing manufacturing empire. However, Harley had sensed over the past couple of years since Clair had come back into the family fold that Clair was gunning to take over the business.

He shook off thoughts of Clair. Harley's mind was just spinning, trying to find whatever it could focus on—anything but the painful truth of the reality surrounding him.

"We thought Daniel was doing much better." Margaret Wesley, Angela's mother, embraced them both. Her eyes were wet with tears.

"He was." Harley cleared his throat, thankful for the numbness of shock keeping him going. "He got the flu." He shut his eyes and swallowed, pausing for a second. "After all those precautions Daniel still got the flu."

"His body was too weak to fight it," Angela's voice broke as the bubble of shock that had surrounded her burst.

She collapsed in Harley's arms, and they managed to fall into the line of chairs against the corridor hall as he held her. He felt each sob that wracked through his ex-wife's body. Harley didn't know how long they sat there or where her family went. He didn't even know when his uncle, sister, and cousin arrived. Nor did he feel or realize the violent sobs racking Angela's body weren't only hers.

They were coming from him, too. The weight of grief and guilt crushed Harley's chest, making it difficult to breathe. He had failed Daniel, just as he had failed Angela. He had promised to protect and be there for them, yet he had been absent when they needed him the most.

As the tears streamed down his face, Harley clung to Angela, their shared grief merging into one solemn moment of despair. The hospital corridor was filled with a haunting silence, broken only by their stifled sobs echoing through the empty hallways.

Harley's mind drifted back to that fateful day when he had received the call from Angela informing him of Daniel's diagnosis. He remembered the anger and frustration he felt at himself for not being there sooner, for not being able to prevent this tragedy from unfolding.

The following year, Harley felt like he had moved through fragmented pockets of time. One minute, he was lost in thought; the next, he'd find himself pushing through a mission. He'd thrown himself into whatever he could to keep his mind from having any downtime to think or feel.

But no matter how hard he tried, the guilt and grief always found a way to catch up with him. The weight on his shoulders grew heavier with each passing day, and there were times when Harley felt like he was drowning in an ocean of regret, guilt, and grief. They lingered like dark shadows in the back of his mind. It was a constant presence, always there, reminding him of his failures as a father.

Harley had stormed courageously into battle, yet it had taken over a year to find the courage to go through Daniel's room at his house and sort out his son's things. That day, Harley stumbled upon a journal hidden under his son's bed. Curiosity overcame him as he opened the book. It was filled with pages of Daniel's thoughts, dreams, and aspirations. It was like peering into his son's soul.

As Harley read through the entries, he discovered something that broke his heart—Daniel had written about his fear of being forgotten, of disappearing into oblivion without leaving a lasting impact on the world. Daniel had compared himself to Harley—a hero who fought to keep them safe and how his father had made a silent impact on the world—an unsung hero.

Harley had already lost his heart for the military and served his country for another two years after Daniel passed away before he took a job in Boston, putting his engineering degree to use. It also meant he was only a few hours away from his Uncle Sam, who wasn't getting any younger, and he was in Boston to help his ex-wife. Angela had fallen apart after Daniel's death. She'd had a breakdown that landed her in a mental health facility in Cambridge.

She'd lost her second husband, who was having an affair with Angela's twin sister. As for Angela's parents, they downplayed Angela's mental health because it didn't sit right with their social standing. While anything romantic between Angela and Harley was long dead, they still considered each other family. Where Harley came from, family always took care of family, and that is what he intended to do—take care of Angela.

Not ready to let go of any of Daniel's things, Angela had asked Harley to rent a storage locker to pack the contents of their son's room in the house she'd shared with her soon-to-be second ex-husband, Wallis Hanover. Every item Harley packed into the storage locker was filled with a memory of Daniel. But by the time the locker was packed, Harley's t-shirt was wet from the tears that flooded his cheeks.

It didn't seem right to be packing his son's whole life into a small container when Daniel should've been living a big life.

· ♥ · ♥ · ♥ · ♥ · ♥ ·

Present Day

A noise from Betty's room snapped Harley back to the present, and he felt his cheeks were wet. He wiped away the tears of the past with his t-shirt and moved to the attic's entrance.

"We need to think about it," Liam spoke for himself and Jennifer.

"I'm staying at your hotel," Andrew told Liam. "I'll be there until tomorrow, waiting for your decision. Here's my number when you've made up your mind."

Harley was already sitting on the edge of the attic's opening when Liam and Jennifer left Betty's room.

"Liam, Aunt Betty's right," Jennifer told her brother. "Molly isn't the one we're mad at."

"I know, Jen," Liam's voice was soft and filled with doubt. "Come to the hotel for dinner later, and we can discuss this."

"Okay," Jennifer agreed as they started to walk down the hallway.

"Um..." Harley called. "Hi down there."

Jennifer and Liam stopped, turned, and looked up at Harley.

"Harley?" Jennifer's brows furrowed. "What on earth are you doing up there?"

"I bet Aunt Betty is finally going ahead with her plan to make the attic into an entertainment room?" Liam rolled his eyes and shook his head.

"Yes, she wanted me to look into what needs to be done to make an entertainment area up here," Harley confirmed his suspicions. "Could you put the ladder back up so I can get down?"

Liam got the ladder and positioned it so Harley could climb down.

"Thank you." Harley sighed, relieved to be back on the ground. "Are you two leaving?"

"I'm heading home," Liam told him. "I can't stay here. This place has become rather stifling."

"While my aunt's *visitor* is here," Jennifer said, "I don't want to be here either."

117

"Want to join me at my house?" Liam offered.

"No, thank you, big brother." Jennifer kissed Liam's cheek. "I think I'm going to go to the cove and clear my head."

"You're going to come for dinner tonight, though?" Liam looked at her for confirmation.

"Yes, I'll be there." Her eyes widened. "Oh, wait, I can't. What about Aunt Betty?"

"I can stay here and watch her until you get home," Harley offered. "All I have to do is visit Sam later this afternoon, but I'll be back by seven."

"You'd do that?" Jennifer looked at him in surprise.

"Of course," Harley said, nodding.

"Thanks, Harley, you're a king!" Liam slapped Harley on the shoulder and glanced at his aunt's bedroom as they heard footsteps heading their way. "That's my cue to leave."

Liam said his goodbyes and slipped through the front door before Andrew popped out of Betty's bedroom.

"Jennifer," Andrew called, reaching out a hand. "Do you think we could talk?" He glanced at Harley. "In private?"

"Now's not a good time," Jennifer's voice dripped with ice, and her shoulders stiffened.

"I was hoping we could catch up." Andrew's eyes flashed with emotion as he gave Jennifer a tight smile. "But I understand."

"Good!" Jennifer said, giving him a cold look. "At least now I won't have to waste more time talking to you to explain why I have no intention of *catching up* with you—*ever*!" She looked at Harley. "Sorry to do this to you again. But would you mind keeping an eye on Betty for another..." She glanced at her watch. "Hour. I need a walk."

"Of course," Harley said, nodding. "Take your time."

Jennifer's eyes narrowed as she turned toward Andrew. "Don't be here when I get back. And don't try to contact us again. Liam will call you when we've made our decision."

Jennifer turned and flounced out of the house, leaving Harley standing in awkward silence with Andrew Gains.

"I should go after her," Andrew said, his voice laced with sorrow.

"No, I will." Harley sighed.

"Thank you," Andrew said. "I'll stay with Betty until you're back and leave before my daughter returns."

As Harley made his way to where he knew Jennifer would be, he felt torn. After overhearing the situation, Harley understood Jennifer's and Liam's anger towards Andrew for leaving them to deal with their dying mother alone.

But on the other hand, he couldn't ignore the desperation in Andrew's voice as he pleaded for help for his innocent daughter, who was caught in the crossfire of their family drama.

Harley may never have met Molly, but the mention of her leukemia struck a chord. And he knew what Andrew was going through. He understood that desperation soaked in helplessness as you stood and watched your child suffer. Grasping for any tiny thread of hope to find that one lifeline. Only the threads slipped through your grasp like streams of dust in sunlight, teasing you with empty-handed hope.

Harley didn't want to get caught in the middle of this conflict. Both sides had their pain steeped in heartbreaking loss. Andrew deeply hurt his family, forcing Jennifer and Liam to grow up too quickly. But he was also a father driven to walk into the line of heartbreaking fire to plead for help for his youngest child.

Molly was the one who was caught in the middle. A fifteen-year-old girl who deserved the chance to fulfill her dreams, suddenly Harley knew—he was meant to overhear what he had. His heart swelled, and a smile touched his lips as he knew the path he'd been on since Daniel's death had led to this moment. This was his penance and a chance to make a difference in another teen's life.

"I won't let you down this time, son," Harley said to the gentle breeze that seemed to pick up from nowhere and push him toward his destination.

As he stepped around the rock, he sucked in a breath, and his heart squeezed when he saw Jennifer sitting with her knees drawn to her chest and tears streaming down her cheeks.

I like her, Dad! The wind whispered in his ear, and as he made his way toward Jennifer, he thought he caught a shadowy glimpse of Daniel waving to him beside her.

CHAPTER 7

Jennifer sat alone in her secret spot, nestled between the jagged rocks that overlooked the crashing waves of Cobble Cove. Tears streamed down her face, a mix of anger and sorrow that she couldn't control. Jennifer had always prided herself on being strong, never shedding a tear since the day her mother died. But today, all the emotions she had suppressed came rushing back to the surface.

They hadn't seen Andrew Gains in forty years! Jennifer swiped at the tears and wiped her nose with her shredded tissue. She knew that because he'd walked out on them two days after her seventh birthday. It seemed poetic that he showed up a few days before her forty-seventh birthday.

When Jennifer first saw him in Aunt Betty's room, her heart had jolted, and the little girl who'd waited for him every day since he'd left resurfaced. Her heart had jolted, and she'd wanted to rush into his arms. But the memory of her mother's face as she took her final painful breath had flashed through her mind along with the feeling of suddenly being orphaned.

It shouldn't have been surprising to discover that Andrew showing up had nothing to do with him finally coming to give them closure and explain himself. He was only there because he wanted something from them—their DNA. Jennifer and Liam weren't even his first choice to get help from—they were his *last* hope.

She breathed deeply as she stared over the lazy ocean sparkling in the afternoon sun. Jennifer had never understood how her mother or Aunt Betty had always seemed to stick up for him or harbored no ill toward him for deserting them. Instead, they always told Jennifer and Liam that one day they'd understand.

"Understand what?" Jennifer muttered bitterly through her tears. "That our father despised us so much that he turned his back on us." She picked up a small pebble and threw it into the ocean as if trying to hide her pain. "He couldn't even come to our mother's funeral or check on his children."

Fresh tears spilled down her cheeks, and Jennifer breathed in a shaky breath as the past washed over her and pulled her into the painful memories of her childhood.

·♥·♥·♥·♥·♥·

Thirty-Nine Years Ago

"Your mother wants to see both of you today." Aunt Betty's smile was strained.

"Have they found her a new heart?" Eight-year-old Jennifer looked at her aunt questioningly.

"Well, the doctors haven't had any luck so far in finding a special heart for your mother." Aunt Betty's words were laced with sadness and frustration. "But, remember, we never give up hope. Miracles happen every day."

"Mommy said I have a special heart," Jennifer frowned at her aunt. "Why can't Mommy have mine?"

Aunt Betty's eyes filled with tears at her words. "Yes, you do have a special heart, my dear. But I'm afraid your heart has to stay special for you."

As they arrived at the hospital, Jennifer's heart sank at the sight of her mother lying in the bed, pale and weak. But she was still smiling, that same loving smile that always made Jennifer feel safe. She sat up to greet them, but it was clear that something was very wrong, and in her young heart, Jennifer suddenly understood they were there to say goodbye.

Jennifer and Liam rushed to their mother's side, their small bodies clinging onto hers as if trying to hold on for dear life. Tears streamed down their faces as their mother mustered all her strength to speak to them.

"My darlings, I need you to know how much I love you both," she said, her voice trembling with a hint of urgency.

Jennifer's mother brushed away their tears and held them tightly with shaking hands. "We love you too, Mommy," they whispered in unison.

"I need you to promise me something," she pleaded, her eyes searching theirs desperately. "Promise me that no matter what happens, you will always protect each other. That you'll always be there for each other."

Jennifer's heart clenched as she looked over at Liam's tear-stained face, and they nodded vigorously in agreement.

Her mother's grip tightened around them.

"Please don't go," Liam begged through his sobs. "Don't give up hope."

But hope was fading fast as Jennifer felt her mother's body weaken beneath her embrace. "Please stay with us," she pleaded, holding onto her mother and trying to force some life into her. "Please hang on, Mommy. Aunt Betty said miracles happen every day."

But this time, the miracle didn't come. And that was the day everything changed for Jennifer and Liam. They were left alone without their mother but lucky to have Aunt Betty to lean on. She became their rock, organizing the funeral and trying to make sense of it all for them.

Three years went by without a word from their father. Liam and Jennifer came to accept that he had moved on and didn't care about his children anymore. And one day, they decided to bury any remaining hope of their father ever returning.

Jennifer and Liam gathered mementos and memories of their father, placing them in a shoebox, which they set ablaze on the edge of a cliff overlooking the vast Atlantic Ocean. As the flames consumed the box, they scooped up handfuls of ash, symbolically saying goodbye to Andrew Gains.

"Goodbye, Daddy," Jennifer's voice was cold and hollow as she released her handful into the wind.

Liam followed suit. They stood, siblings holding hands, each one's heart hardening even more as they watched the ashes drift away—memories lost in the wind.

Liam and Jennifer stood side by side, their hands tightly grasped in a silent pact.

"As of today, our father is dead," Liam declared, his voice cold and emotionless. "The man we once knew as Dad is now Andrew Gains, who is nothing more than a stranger to us."

"We've buried him here, in this place that was so special to our family," Jennifer added, her eyes glistening with tears. "His memory has been scattered across the ocean, where the wind and waves will wash it away."

Suddenly, Aunt Betty appeared on the scene, her face filled with concern as she took in the fire and the two siblings standing together. "What on earth are you two doing?" she asked.

"We're saying goodbye to our father," Liam replied, his tone cutting.

"We'll never speak of him again," Jennifer promised fiercely, standing by their promise.

Aunt Betty's expression softened as she stepped between them and wrapped an arm around each of their shoulders. "May your memories of your father rest in peace," she said gently, kissing their cheeks. "I'm

127

proud of you for letting go of your anger and resentment towards your father. And I hope that someday, when the time comes, you'll be able to forgive him."

Jennifer shook her head sadly. "Our father died the day he walked out of Beach Plum Cottage without looking back."

"If we ever do come across Andrew Gains," Liam interjected, "we'll pass him by without even acknowledging him."

Liam and Jennifer turned away from their father's final resting place and walked hand in hand back to Beach Plum Cottage. As they passed beneath the oldest Beach Plum tree on the property, Liam plucked two plums that hung from the lowest branches.

"These were Mom's favorite," he said, handing one to Jennifer. "It feels somehow fitting that we each have one today."

Jennifer wiped the plum on her shirt and took a cautious bite. The sourness made her mouth water, but she forced herself to eat the entire fruit in honor of their mother. She always found sweetness and light through the most bitter and dark times. Eating the sour plum was a small gesture, but it felt like a final goodbye to the past and a step toward healing for the future.

·♥·♥·♥·♥·♥·

Present Day

A shadow fell over Jennifer, pulling her from her memories. She looked up, surprised to see Harley standing over her.

"Hey," Harley said, his voice gentle but laced with concern. "Are you okay?"

Jennifer blinked, her tear-stained eyes meeting Harley's concerned gaze. She hastily wiped away the remaining tears, suddenly self-conscious of her vulnerability. "Yeah, I'm fine," she murmured, avoiding his gaze as she fumbled for a clean tissue in her pocket.

"Here." Harley handed her a paper towel roll as he sat on the rock beside her. "I grabbed it from the kitchen on my way to find you."

Jennifer laughed, knowing how protective Aunt Betty was of her paper towels. *You don't need to use the whole roll all at once*, Aunt Betty would say.

"Aunt Betty's going to be mad at you," Jennifer warned, taking the paper towels.

"I'll buy her a new roll," Harley promised. "Besides, if we don't tell her, she won't know, as she is stuck in bed for the next two weeks."

"Good idea." Jennifer gave a shaky laugh as she wiped her eyes and nose before turning to look at him suspiciously. "How long were you stuck in the attic?"

"Long enough!" Harley admitted. "I'm sorry," He shifted on the rock, trying to find a more comfortable position. "I didn't mean to

129

eavesdrop. I didn't realize who Andrew was when I let him in." He dusted the sand from his hands. "When I heard how you and Liam greeted him, I tried to leave but knocked the ladder over, and my phone was in the living room."

"It's okay!" Jennifer sniffed and looked out at the sparkling ocean drifting lazily past them. "That attic's not very sound-proof."

"I know, right!" Harley smiled. "Betty will have to soundproof it if she wants to use it as a television lounge and games room."

"Aunt Betty's been talking about doing that to the attic for years," Jennifer told him before they fell into a companionable silence for a few moments.

Harley's voice was soft as he said, "I can't pretend to know what you've been through, but I can offer a listening ear if you ever want to talk."

Jennifer studied him for a moment, searching for any signs of his usual arrogance or judgment in his eyes. But all she saw was sincerity, understanding, and a haunting sorrow.

Jennifer's voice trembled as she fought back the tears that threatened to spill down her cheeks. "Thank you," she managed to choke out, her throat tight with emotion. "But I think you heard everything there is to say."

Harley's gaze bore into her, searching for something in her soul. "Are you sure about that?" His voice was low and gentle, but his eyes were piercing. "What about your decision to help Molly?"

Surprise flickered across Jennifer's face, not just because he had overheard their conversation but also because of the pain that laced his words when he mentioned Molly. It was as if he knew her intimately. Her brow furrowed as she noticed the familiar look of sorrow that haunted Harley's features.

"I know she's just a kid," Jennifer began, her voice trembling. "And..." She struggled to find the right words as memories flooded her mind, memories of her own mother's struggle with heart disease. "I..." She closed her eyes, trying to silence the tumultuous emotions inside her.

"But you understand what it's like," Harley said softly. "To watch someone suffer and feel helpless to save them." He cleared his throat before continuing. "My parents died in a boating accident when my sister, Carly, and I were young."

Jennifer's eyes widened in sympathy, and she turned to face him fully. Is that where the pain in his eyes comes from? "I'm so sorry."

"It was a long time ago," Harley replied with a grateful smile for her genuine condolences. "Like you, we lived with our uncle after our parents passed." He chuckled lightly. "Although you lived with your aunt instead of your uncle."

"I understood what you meant," Jennifer assured him, struck by their similar experiences. "That explains why you and Sam are so close."

"We were close even before that," Harley explained. "My cousin, Daniella's parents, and mine traveled often. Her mother was my father's youngest sister. The three of us grew up together with our uncle whenever our parents were away."

"Sam is an incredible man," Jennifer murmured.

"Just like Betty is an incredible woman," Harley said, a hint of admiration in his voice. "They put their own lives on hold to care for their siblings' children. They loved us as if we were their own."

"I can't argue with that," Jennifer sniffed, wiping away a stray tear.

"I'm sorry if I seem like I'm meddling where I shouldn't," Harley said, holding up a hand to stop Jennifer from interrupting. "But I feel like I have to say this." He took a deep breath. "This isn't about your father... about Andrew. It's about Molly." The shadow of sorrow in his eyes darkened. "If there's even the slightest chance that you or Liam can help her, I implore you to do so."

Harley looked at Jennifer with pain and tears glistening in his eyes. "While Andrew may be seen as a villain in your eyes, he's also a father to your half-sister. One who will do anything to save her. He'll grasp at any lifeline he can." He swallowed hard and wiped his eyes. "As someone who has been in his shoes, I know what he's going through."

Jennifer's heart dropped, and she instinctively took Harley's hand. "I had no idea, Harley."

He squeezed her hand tightly for support as he told her the heart-breaking story of his twelve-year-old son Daniel's battle with leukemia. A struggle that Daniel ultimately lost. By the time he finished re-counting the devastating story of how he and his ex-wife Angela had lost their only child, fresh tears streamed down Jennifer's face.

"Of course, I'll help Molly," Jennifer's voice was hoarse with emo-tion. "And I know Liam will as well. He just needs to get over the shock of seeing Andrew again."

"Did your mother and father get a divorce?" Harley's question came out of the blue when they were discussing Molly.

"No," Jennifer was so taken off guard by his question that the words just tumbled from her mouth. "When I was four, I got ill, and a world-renowned cardiothoracic surgeon that my parents knew discovered that I had an ICC, the same condition my mother had suffered with her entire life."

He gave her hand a comforting squeeze, drawing Jennifer's eyes to their still clasped hands. What surprised her was that she didn't want to let go of his hand. Jennifer was finding the warmth and firmness of his grasp comforting, as if she was drawing strength from it.

"What is an ICC?" Harley asked, concern flashing in his eyes.

"Inherited cardiac condition," Jennifer explained. "Luckily, the surgeon who caught it was also able to fix it. Although I have to go for checkups twice yearly or if I have certain signs or systems."

"Are you okay now?" Harley's eyes searched hers, and she could see his concern deepen.

"I'm fine," Jennifer assured him. "I eat healthily and follow a good exercise routine. I don't miss any of my checkups."

"Good to know." Harley nodded, and Jennifer noted he still hadn't let her hand go.

"Soon after the operation, when I was recovering, my father started to be away from home for long periods," Jennifer explained. "My mother told Liam and me he was working in Boston."

"Before I went to the hospital, Liam overheard them talking to Aunt Betty about my father having to go work in Boston to pay for all my medical bills," Jennifer's heart tightened. "Andrew started staying away for extended periods, and my mother began frequent trips to Boston. One day, my mother came home, and she was so upset. But she put on a brave face for Liam and I. The next day, Andrew arrived and packed his belongings. This time, when he left, he never returned."

"But your parents never divorced?" Harley's brow furrowed.

"No, when Liam and I were cleaning up the attic a few years ago, we found all my mother's papers, but there were no divorce papers, no filing for custody of us," Jennifer shrugged. "As far as we can tell, they were still married when Mother died."

"What about her estate?" Harley asked.

"My mother didn't have anything except her share of the cottage that went to Liam and me," Jennifer told him.

Harley nodded and was quiet for a while before asking, "If that surgeon helped you, why couldn't they help your mother?"

"According to my aunt, my mother had numerous operations, and there are only so many times you can patch up the valves and other parts." Jennifer swallowed. Even after all these years, talking about her mother ripped at her soul. "She needed a heart transplant, but she never got her special heart."

Tears sprung to her eyes, and she burst into tears before she could stop herself. Harley finally let go of her hand to wrap his arms around Jennifer, pulling her to him. She pushed her face into his warm chest, clinging to his strength as she wept.

"I'm so sorry, Jennifer," Harley's voice soothed as he stroked her hair just like her mother used to when she comforted Jennifer.

"Do you want to know something really silly?" Jennifer hiccupped, resting her cheek against his chest.

"What?" Harley dipped his head slightly to look at her.

"After my operation, my mom, dad, and aunt all told me I had to take care because I had a very special heart." She drew in a shaky breath. "When my mother was in heart failure, I wondered why they couldn't find her a new one, and my aunt told me that she couldn't just have any heart. She needed a special one."

"Did your mother have a rare blood group or something?" Harley asked.

"She was O-positive," Jennifer said, "The doctors couldn't find a match for her." She closed her eyes and let the steady rhythm of Harley's heart comfort her.

"I don't see where any of that is silly," Harley stated.

"No, there's nothing silly about that," Jennifer agreed. "The silly part was that I couldn't understand why they couldn't give her my special heart." She swallowed as Harley stayed quiet, and she continued. "My aunt told me it was because it was my special heart, and my mother wouldn't take it away from me."

The tears started to fall again, and her voice wobbled. "I wondered why the lovely lady who fixed me couldn't fix my mother and thought it was my fault because I got the last of the special hearts." She swiped at her tears. "The silly part is that a part of me still thinks it was because of me that my mom died and didn't get her special heart."

"Hey." Harley gently pushed her away and held her by the top of her arms. "You were a child, and that's not silly at all."

"No, it's only silly because the first thing I felt was guilt when I saw Andrew standing there," Jennifer admitted. "Like it was my fault he'd left and my mother died."

"You went through a traumatic event watching your mother fade away," Harley's voice was filled with compassion, and his eyes resonated with understanding. "You never got a chance to speak to Andrew about what happened. No one explained that there was nothing anyone could do for your mother."

As their gazes locked, Jennifer's surroundings blurred and faded away until all she could see were Harley's piercing aquamarine eyes.

She felt her breathing quicken as his gaze intensified, and they both leaned towards each other. It was as if an invisible force was pulling them together, drawn by their shared vulnerability, unspoken longing, and the burden they'd each carried. Fate had intertwined their lives creating a powerful connection between them.

Just as their lips were about to touch, Caroline's voice shattered the bubble Jennifer had felt enveloping them, pulling them away from each other. They stood wide-eyed and blinking in confusion, trying to make sense of what had just happened. Just before Caroline rounded the corner of rocks that hid them from the rest of the cove, they quickly pulled away from each other as Caroline appeared, breathless and flushed as if she'd run a marathon.

"Oh good, you're here," she said, leaning against a rock as she caught her breath. "Betty called me to let me know that Andrew was back?"

"Uh—" Jennifer coughed nervously. "Y... Yes."

"Are you okay?" Caroline looked worriedly at Jennifer. "That must've been such a huge shock to you and Liam?"

"It was," Jennifer said, her mind still reeling from hers and Harley's almost kiss.

She glanced nervously at him. He was staring at her as if in a trance.

"Harley?" Caroline's brows shot up as she looked at him. "What are you doing here?" She glanced at Jennifer, her eyes narrowing, before looking at Harley again. "You two aren't arguing again, are you?"

"What?" Jennifer and Harley said in unison, guilt washed over Jennifer.

"No, we're not," Jennifer blurted out. "Harley came to find out if I was okay after my altercation with Andrew."

"Altercation?" Jennifer's brows furrowed, and she looked at Harley questioningly,

"What happened?"

"I got stuck in the attic," Harley explained. "The ladder fell."

"You know how sound travels up there," Jennifer reminded Caroline.

"Okay..." Caroline's brows knit more tightly together. "So... Harley overheard your argument with Andrew?"

"It was more like an attack on Andrew," Harley said and immediately looked at Jennifer. "I didn't mean that the way it sounded."

"It's okay," Jennifer said, making Caroline's eyes widen in surprise that Jennifer hadn't erupted in an angry, blazing ball of fury at Harley. "Harley's right."

"Whoa!" Caroline's chin dipped, her head drew back, and she shook it as if she'd heard things. "Did I hear right?" She pointed from Jennifer to Harley. "Did you just agree with Harley?"

"It's the truth," Jennifer admitted. "He came here looking for our help, but what he got was forty years of pent-up pain and anger from myself and Liam."

"Looking for help?" Caroline's face screwed up in confusion. "What? Does he need a kidney or a piece of your liver?"

"Close," Jennifer said with a nod. "Andrew wants mine and Liam's DNA."

"I was right then. Andrew does want an organ from you then?" Caroline pursed her lips.

"It's not for him," Harley told Caroline and looked at Jennifer to elaborate.

"No, it's for my half-sister, Molly, who has leukemia and is the same age as my niece," Jennifer stated, watching Caroline's jaw drop in disbelief.

CHAPTER 8

H arley sat on the comfortable, worn couch in the cozy living room of Beach Plum Cottage. The dim hallway lights and the glare from the television lit the house. Harley was keeping an eye on Betty while Jennifer went to Liam's home to discuss what they were going to do about Molly.

Harley stared unseeingly at the classic black-and-white Betty Davis movie playing on the screen. He couldn't get the day's events from his mind as he waited on edge for Jennifer to return. Harley rubbed a hand over his eyes before standing and quietly making his way down the hall to check on Betty.

The bedroom door groaned as he pushed it a little wider to see Betty was sleeping soundly. Like Harley, Betty worried about her niece and nephew's decision about Molly. She retold the story Jennifer had told him that afternoon about Andrew's desertion.

"I wish I could make them understand what happened back then," Betty had told Harley. *"But I made my sister promise that I'd look after Jennifer and Liam, and one day when Andrew could, he'd talk to them."*

Harley had asked her what she meant, and Betty had changed the subject, asking Harley if he'd make a cup of tea. When he'd gotten back with the tea, Betty was asleep. He sighed as he started to make his way back to the living room. The memory of Jennifer and his almost kiss flashed through his mind. His hand ran over his shirt, which he hadn't changed since that afternoon. It still had her scent and tear stains on it.

Harley was so deep in thought as he rounded the corner to step into the living room, he nearly had a heart attack when he bumped into Jennifer.

"Jennifer!" Harley breathed, reaching out to steady her and dropping her hands as he felt their warmth zing through him like an electric current. "I'm sorry, I didn't hear you come in."

"I was trying to be quiet," Jennifer told him. "I didn't know if you'd be asleep in the guest bedroom, and I didn't want to wake you or Aunt Betty."

He glanced into the living room and saw the television was off.

"Sorry, were you still watching that?" Jennifer turned toward it.

"No," Harley denied. "I was just flicking through the channels while waiting for you to come home."

They stood staring awkwardly at each other for a few moments before Betty's voice floated down the hallway.

"Jennifer?" Betty called. "Is that you?"

"Yes, Aunt Betty," Jennifer called back, giving Harley a tight smile. "Thank you for watching her for me tonight."

"You're welcome," Harley told her, stepping around Jennifer, careful not to make contact. "I think I'm going to go."

"You're not going to stay in the guest room?" Jennifer asked with a hint of disappointment, making Harley's already hammering heartbeat pick up speed.

"I have to collect Uncle Sam in the morning," Harley explained. "It's best if I'm home to put some clothes together for him."

"Oh!" Jennifer's brows shot up in surprise. "I'm glad Sam's being released from the hospital."

"He is too." Harley gave a soft laugh. "He's convinced they will give him more metal appendages if he stays longer."

"Is that because of his hip replacement?" Jennifer smiled. "What does he call it..."

"His bionic hip." Harley shook his head and rolled his eyes.

"Jennifer!" Aunt Betty called a little louder this time.

"That's my cue to leave," Harley said. "Say goodnight to Betty for me."

"I will," Jennifer promised as Harley turned to leave.

He took a few steps and stopped. Turning, Harley said softly, "Jennifer?"

She stopped walking toward Betty's room and turned toward him. "Yes?"

"What did you and Liam decide about Molly?" Harley knew he was meddling again, but he had to know.

"Yes." Jennifer nodded. "Liam and I are going to tell Andrew tomorrow."

Harley breathed a silent sigh of relief. "I'm glad. You're doing the right thing."

Jennifer nodded, and Harley smiled, giving her a pretend tip of the hat as he turned to leave.

"Harley," Jennifer's soft voice stopped him.

He looked back at her, and his heart squeezed at the look of vulnerability he'd never seen in her eyes before.

"Liam and I can't go for tests on the same day," Jennifer said hesitantly. "Would you..." She swallowed, and he could see she was struggling with her emotions. "Would you come with me?" She cleared her throat. "I... Uh, I don't like hospitals and tests."

A warmth spread through Harley's veins as the enormity of what she was asking hit him. He also knew that Jennifer hated feeling the way she was right now.

"Of course," Harley promised. "I was going to ask if you minded if I tagged along for support. I've been through this process before and can guide you and Liam through it."

He saw the gratitude shine in her eyes as her shoulders sagged in relief. "Thank you!" she whispered.

"I'll call you after I've collected Sam," Harley promised.

"You know, you should bring him here while he and Betty recover," Jennifer suggested. "We can ask Daniella if she knows of a nurse who'd like extra work."

"That's not a bad idea," Harley said. "I'll speak to Uncle Sam when I collect him."

They said goodnight, and while Harley was reluctant to leave, he forced himself to walk out the front door and get into his pickup to head home. On the drive home, he reflected on how an accident could draw people together. Since Betty's accident, he and Jennifer had gone through an entire day without fighting. Instead, they were united in their concern for Betty, their similar family history, and a family member with a debilitating disease.

The following morning, Harley collected Uncle Sam from the hospital. On the ride home, Harley decided to tell him about Jennifer's idea.

"Uncle Sam, as I told you yesterday afternoon, Betty had another fall and is bedridden for the next two weeks," Harley told him.

"I'm not going senile, son," Sam pointed out. "I do remember you telling me about Betty's fall."

"That's not where I was going with this." Harley rolled his eyes. "You must also take it easy for the next few weeks."

"I know. I was there when the doctor told you," Sam frowned at Harley. "Seriously, Lee, are you testing my mental health here?"

Harley forgot how cranky Uncle Sam was while and for at least two days after a stint in hospital.

"No, I'm trying to pitch an idea to you," Harley said, hanging onto his patience.

"Then say it," Sam's voice was laced with frustration. "You're beating around the bush like you're trying to tell me you crashed my car or something." His eyes widened, and he looked at Harley. "You didn't crash my car, did you?"

"No, I haven't touched any of your cars," Harley informed him. "And don't call me Lee. You only call me that when you're annoyed or angry at me."

"Your father used to call you that always," Sam reminded him. "Do you think he did that because he was always angry at you?"

"Where is this conversation going?" Harley was getting irritated now. "Look, Jennifer suggested that you move into Beach Plum Cottage for a few weeks while you and Betty recover."

"So you want to put the geriatrics in one ward?" Sam looked at him with raised eyebrows.

"You know what, forget I said anything." Harley sighed. Uncle Sam would be irritable until he'd gotten over what they called his hospital grouches.

"Come on, son." Sam laughed and patted Harley on the shoulder. "I'm just messing with you. I think that's a great idea."

"You do?" Harley glanced at him, surprised. "Then you should also know that Daniella is finding two or three nurses to look after you and Betty."

"Why?" Sam's brows furrowed. "I may have an injured back, but I'm not useless."

"Yes, but you're not even allowed to do any cooking for the next few days," Harley told him. "What about if you fall in the shower?"

147

He pulled into the driveway of their home. "I installed handrails in Betty's and the guest bathroom yesterday in all the necessary places."

"Did you put emergency bells in there, too?" Sam said sarcastically. "All you need to do is install a reception area, and you can rename the place Beach Plum Retirement Home."

"I give up." Harley slid out of the driver's seat of his pickup. "If you're so capable. Then get out of the pickup on your own."

He slammed his car door shut and stood back with his arms folded to watch his stubborn uncle try to get out of the pickup without help, especially with that back brace that restricted Sam's movements.

Sam jerked forward as he attempted to slide to the edge of the seat before popping the passenger open. "Dang, nab it." He hissed. "This darn shell, they've got me strapped to—"

Harley ambled around to the passenger side and looked at his uncle. "Need a hand?"

Sam glared at him. "No, I'm fine flopping around like a turtle on his back."

"Okay then." Harley shrugged, hiding a smile as he turned to walk off.

"Fine!" Sam called. "You win. Maybe we do need a nurse."

Harley grinned but straightened his face as he turned back to his uncle.

"Come on, old man, let me help you." Harley gave Sam a smug smile as his uncle muttered something that would blister a young person's ears.

"And be careful who you call old." Sam let Harley help him into the house. "I hope Daniella will get a male and female nurse."

"She said she would," Harley assured Sam. "You forget she's looked after you a few times."

"I'm fortunate to have such caring nieces, nephews, and grandbabies." Sam sat in a chair.

"I don't think Reef and Emily qualify as babies anymore, Uncle Sam," Harley pointed out. "They're teenagers now. Reef is a young adult. He'll be eighteen soon."

"You all grew up way too fast!" Sam sighed, his eyes taking on a look of nostalgia.

Harley made his uncle some tea before getting him to pack while he told Jennifer that Sam was happy with her idea. His heart did a double beat as he thought about Jennifer.

"You have to get yourself under control," Harley gave his emotions a stern talking to. "Just because Jennifer and I have had a few moments of peace and bonded a little doesn't mean anything."

"What's that?" Uncle Sam made him jump as he turned to him, standing in the kitchen doorway.

"Nothing," Harley said and moved the conversation away from Jennifer. "I've made you some tea. Are you hungry?"

"No." Sitting at the kitchen counter, Sam shook his head when Harley gave him his tea. "But I've been dying for a decent brew." He spooned sugar into the cup.

"I'm going to call Jennifer and let her know you've accepted her kind offer," Harley told him.

"Are you and Jennifer finally friends?" Sam took a sip of the tea.

"Let's just say we've called a temporary truce due to all that's happened in the past few days," Harley said.

"You mean Betty's fall?" Sam asked.

"That and Andrew Gains turning up the following day." Harley saw his uncle's eyes widen in disbelief.

"Andrew Gains is back?" Sam's eyes flashed with concern.

"Yes." Harley nodded, his brow knitting together. "Why do you look so concerned?"

"Surprised!" Sam corrected. "Just surprised."

"No, that was a look of concern." Harley wasn't letting this go. "Want to tell me why?"

"Let's just say that Andrew Gains didn't leave his family without good reason," Sam said cryptically. "I hope that he dared to show his face again because that *reason* no longer exists."

"Okay, now I'm curious," Harley told him. "And I'm not going to let this go until you tell me what you know or at least if Jennifer, Betty, or Liam are in imminent danger."

"I'll make some calls." Sam pulled out his phone.

Harley didn't miss that Sam hadn't answered his question, and it sent a cold shiver down Harley's spine.

What does Uncle Sam know? Harley wondered as he remembered Betty's words last night. *I wonder what good reason Andrew Gains had for leaving his family?*

Harley's mind started ticking over as he ran through a list of contacts he knew from his military days who could find out about the man. Those thoughts were put on hold as he dialed Jennifer's number, and they flew out of his head the moment he heard her voice when she answered.

"Hi," Jennifer greeted him. "How is Sam?"

"Surprisingly chipper, considering he was in the hospital for much longer than he was happy with," Harley answered. "But he's agreed to stay at Beach Plum Cottage while he recovers, although—" His brow creased thoughtfully. "Wouldn't it be better for Betty to move in here?"

"Are you thinking because it's closer to the clinic?" Jennifer stated.

"That and because I'll be working on the cottage, which will make it noisy and dusty," Harley pointed out. "Not a good environment for them to recover in."

"Sam's house is on the edge of town," Jennifer said. "I'll speak to Aunt Betty." She paused. "But you've already installed all the rails and made it..." Her voice trailed off.

"Injury recovery friendly." Harley offered her a choice of words.

"Yes, that!" Jennifer laughed.

The melodic tones of her laugh wrapped around Harley like a gentle caress, stirring a cascade of sensations that danced through him.

He swallowed and cleared his throat. "Talk to Betty and let me know."

Jennifer promised. "I'll call you back as soon as I've spoken to her."

The call ended, leaving Harley feeling like a teenage boy waiting for his crush to call.

Stop it, Harley. As soon as the dust has settled on all Jennifer's emotional upsets over the past few days, you'll be back at each other's throats—nemeses.

"Harley!" Sam barked from the kitchen. "Can you come here for a minute?"

Harley turned and walked back to the kitchen. "Are you okay?"

"Stop fussing!" Sam tutted. "I'm fine. But I'm worried about Jennifer and Liam."

"Because of Andrew?" Waves of shock zapped his nervous system.

"It's not Andrew I'm worried about." Sam's voice dropped. "Do you know why he's back?"

Harley told his uncle what he'd overheard while stuck in the attic. Leaving out some parts, Harley also told Sam about the conversation with Jennifer afterward.

"I thought you left being an agent behind when you retired from the US Marshals," Harley teased.

"You'll always be a soldier, son," Sam said proudly. "I'll always be a Marshal at heart."

"And will you tell me what you know about Andrew Gains leaving his family?" Harley asked, already knowing the answer.

"That's not my story to tell," Sam informed him, carefully sliding off the chair. "Now, when are we moving me?"

"About that!" Harley lifted his index finger expressively. "There may be a slight change of plans or rather residence."

"Meaning, you and Jennifer finally realized that the better option to set up a temporary care home for myself and Betty would be here," Sam guessed. "It's closer to the clinic and Daniella." He grinned at the look of surprise on Harley's face. "It is also a more sterile environment than the building work environment at Beach Plum Cottage."

"You heard me on the phone, didn't you?" Harley shook his head.

"Yup!" Sam admitted, nodding in confirmation.

"Weren't you the one that told me eavesdropping was not nice!" Harley raised an eyebrow.

"Says the man that eavesdropped on a private family matter while supposedly stuck in an attic." Sam gave him a smug look. "Betty moving here for a few weeks is a much better plan."

Harley, Liam, and Jennifer flopped onto Sam's couch three hours later. Exhausted from moving all of the items Betty insisted she needed, which included her bed and nightstand, into Sam's guest bedroom.

"You realize we have to move all that stuff back in a couple of weeks?" Liam pointed out.

"Let's not think about that right now," Jennifer suggested. "We have another appointment to get to in an hour."

"Oh, right!" Liam drawled. "Can't we just send him a text message?"

"You haven't seen Andrew to give him your reply yet?" Harley looked at the Gains siblings in disbelief.

"Nope!" Liam shook his head. "We told him we were getting Betty sorted out and could only see him this afternoon."

"And you wanted to put him through a little more torture," Harley guessed. "That's not nice."

"Neither is abandoning your eleven-year-old son and eight-year-old daughter, still recovering from heart surgery," Liam stated.

"Okay." Harley drew in a silent breath, trying to see the situation from their point of view and not Andrew, who was a father on edge because his child needed urgent help.

"We'd also like you to be there as our mediator," Liam surprised Harley by saying and glanced at Jennifer. "Jen tells me you've been through the testing and bone marrow donation before?"

Harley's head shot around and his eyes met Jennifer. They must've held a shadow of betrayal in them.

Her eyes flashed with hurt that he didn't trust her as she said. "I didn't tell him why you went through it."

"I—" Harley felt her shrink from him and knew he'd taken his first step to falling back into their old pattern of misunderstandings and goading each other. "It's okay if you did."

"It's not my story to tell," Jennifer repeated the words his uncle had said to him earlier about Andrew Gains.

Harley told Liam about Daniel and stood waiting for the look of pity that always filled the eyes of anyone who knew. Like when he told Jennifer, there was nothing but compassion in Liam's eyes.

"I'm sorry, Harley," Liam said. "If you don't want to get involved, I'll understand."

"No, this is going to sound weird," Harley told them, "but I feel it's almost as if I'm supposed to help you."

"I can understand that," Jennifer's voice was soft.

"Me too," Liam admitted and checked his watch. "Shoot, my watch has stopped."

"What time are you supposed to meet Andrew?" Harley looked at his watch.

Jennifer glanced over his shoulder. "In ten minutes."

"Let's get moving," Harley said, standing as someone knocked at the door. "Excuse me."

He opened it to find Daniella with two nurses.

"Hi," Daniella greeted him before stepping around her cousin and inviting the nurses inside to introduce them. "Are you all off somewhere?"

"Yeah, we have a meeting at the Summer Inn," Liam told her.

"What about Aunt Betty and Sam?" Jennifer reminded them.

"That's why I'm here," Daniella pointed out and brought some help. She looked at the nurses. "This is as good a time as any to get them started."

"I think you should also introduce them to Sam and Betty." Harley smiled at his cousin. "They tend to listen to you much more than they do us."

"That's because I'm a trained medical professional they trust." Daniella grinned. "Now go, get out of here."

Fifteen minutes later, they were seated in Liam's office at the Summer Inn Hotel.

"Thank you for meeting me." Andrew looked at Liam and Jennifer. "I know this isn't easy for either of you."

"We were always going to help Molly," Liam began, ignoring Andrew's attempt to smooth the path between them. "As a father, I can understand your desperation." He looked at Harley. "Harley has explained the procedure to us and the importance of getting tested as soon as possible."

"You're Sam's nephew," Andrew addressed Harley.

"That's correct," Harley confirmed.

"Are you Matilda or Mark's son?" Andrew asked.

"Mark's son," Harley answered him. "Did you know my father and Aunt Matilda?"

"I did." Andrew nodded. "Your Uncle Sam raised his younger brother and sister after their parents died in a terrible storm." His eyes filled with admiration. "Sam is a remarkable man and a pillar of strength." He looked at Jennifer and Liam. "Just like Betty. I owe them both a huge debt of gratitude I don't think I'll ever be able to repay."

"How about you start by moving this conversation forward so we can get back to them?" Jennifer's icy tones sent a cold shiver down Harley's spine.

"Of course," Andrew said, the flash of pain in the man's eyes didn't go amiss to Harley.

It did make him even more curious as to Andrew's story. Harley looked at Jennifer and Liam, wondering why neither of them had even asked Andrew to explain himself. But Harley remembered what Jennifer told him about how she and Liam had let go of their father by cremating their memories of him. As far as Liam and Jennifer were concerned, their father was dead. Andrew was no longer a part of their family, just a nameless face in the crowd. Or right now—someone else's father needing their help.

While Harley understood that Jennifer and Liam were angry and hurt at Andrew, he hoped they'd have more compassion for what the man was going through. Not rubbing salt in what Harley was starting to think was still a very raw wound for Andrew. Whatever had driven

Andrew Gains away from his family and kept him away wasn't a lack of love for his first family.

"When were you thinking of getting the tests done?" Andrew asked Jennifer and Liam. "I'll pay for all your expenses to Boston and put you up at the Langham Hotel."

"You spare no expense to help your *family*, I see," Liam sneered. "We don't need you putting us up anywhere. We've managed to pay our way to where we are now. I can assure you we can pay for our accommodation in Boston."

"I meant you no insult," Andrew told them. "I have a standing booking for a few suites at the Langham."

"Then you'd better make that three suites," Jennifer overrode her brother's comment. "Because Harley will be joining us."

"Oh!" Andrew looked from Harley to Jennifer and nodded in understanding. "I'm sorry. I should've realized you two were a couple."

"That's —" Jennifer was cut off but Liam.

"Whom my sister or I date is not your concern," Liam told Andrew. "But Jennifer would feel better if Harley was with her during the testing and through the procedure should she be a donor match."

"Of course," Andrew said, giving Jennifer a tight smile before looking at Liam. "You're welcome to bring Lila or a lady friend."

"You will leave my daughter out of this," Liam warned. "Once this is over, we don't want to see you again."

"I—" Andrew's eyes darkened with emotion again. But he quickly regained his composure. "Molly will want to know who helped her and thank them."

"Knowing she has a better chance at fighting the leukemia if we're able to help her is enough for us!" Jennifer told him. "Liam and I agree it's best for everyone to keep our worlds apart."

"If that's really what you want," Andrew's voice was thick with emotion, but he agreed to their terms. "I will not darken your lives again after you've done me this favor."

"Oh, we're not doing this for you," Liam assured him. "We're doing it for your daughter."

"I know." Andrew nodded. "I'm under no illusions that you'd do the same for me." He was quiet for a few seconds before saying. "While I understand that you'll walk away after you've helped Molly, I would ask that you at least meet my wife, Georgia, and Molly."

"I thought we already covered this?" Liam's brows raised. "Jennifer and I don't want to know the family you replaced your old one with."

A knock at the door distracted them. "Come in," Liam called.

The door opened, and Liam's assistant stuck her head in.

"Mr. Gains, a woman outside wants to see Mr. Andrew Gains," she informed Liam.

"Okay, send her in," Liam's brow furrowed.

"I'm so sorry, Andrew, but if we don't leave now, we're not going to get back to Boston in time—" The tall, elegant woman stopped talking as her eyes met Harley's. Her face paled, and her eyes widened in shock. "Mr. Donovan?"

"You two know each other?" Jennifer asked with narrowed eyes.

"Yes." Harley's tone was clipped as he fought to control the anger that ignited when he heard that woman's voice. "She's the negligent doctor responsible for my son's death."

CHAPTER 9

"**I** beg your pardon?" Andrew Gains looked at Harley in surprise. "That's quite an accusation to make, Harley."

"No, it's not!" Harley didn't take his eyes off the tall, elegant woman who had just entered Liam's office.

"I thought Daniel passed away from getting the flu," Jennifer said. She frowned, looking at the woman who'd just entered.

"Georgia, I presume?" Liam addressed the woman and stood up as everyone else was now standing.

"No," Andrew corrected him. "This is Doctor Jessica Ainsley, my sister-in-law."

"I hope *she's* not Molly's oncologist," Harley's voice was filled with disdain.

"While I was the one who diagnosed Molly's condition," Jessica's voice was frosty, "I'm not her doctor. Doctor Mulder is."

"Good call," Harley said, looking at Andrew and then at Jennifer. "I'm sorry, I have to go."

Jennifer's heart went out to Harley. These past few days, like her, he'd been confronted by his painful past, and it was all her family's fault.

"I'll come with you," Jennifer offered.

"No, stay and sort out an arrangement with your... with Andrew and his *sister-in-law*!" Harley's eyes narrowed as he gave Jessica a cold look.

"Liam will sort out the arrangements." Jennifer looked at her brother. "I have to give Harley a ride home. We brought him here in my car."

"Sure!" Liam gestured with his hand and flopped back into his chair.

"I'll leave," Jessica said, her eyes sliding to Harley. "I'm the one that interrupted the meeting."

"Why did you barge in here?" Jennifer looked at her curiously.

"Andrew and I need to get back to Boston before eight tonight," Jessica informed them, turning to Andrew. "I came to check if you're almost finished."

"As *Mr. Donovan* and I are leaving," Jennifer told her haughtily, "why don't you take a seat while Andrew and my brother sort out the last of the details."

Before anyone could speak, Jennifer ushered Harley, who looked like he wanted to throttle Jessica, out of the room. They walked toward the front sitting room where she and Harley stood staring out at the white stretch of beach. They turned and looked to the left, where Alex's superyacht bobbed in the late afternoon sunlight.

"It still puzzles me why, if Alex has all that luxury docked there, he stays in a suite in the hotel?" Jennifer sighed, making small talk while Harley gained control of his emotions.

"Because he can pretty much do what he likes!" Harriet's voice came from the side where the bar was.

Jennifer and Harley turned to see her sitting in a chair, a tall iced coffee beside her, as she flipped through a magazine.

"Hello, Harriet," Jennifer and Harley greeted.

"I'm sorry, we didn't see you sitting there," Jennifer apologized.

"I'm not surprised," Harriet said, eyeing Harley. "Harley looks like he's ready to go into battle."

"Close," Harley told her.

"Did it have anything to do with that lady doctor who went into Liam's office a few minutes ago?" Harriet enquired.

"How did you know she was a doctor?" Harley asked Harriet.

"I think everyone in the sitting area knew she was," Harriet told them. "I've been sitting here waiting for my friend for fifteen minutes. The woman received five phone calls and answered each one as Doctor Ainsley. She even had a heated conversation with someone where she reminded them that *she* was the doctor in their conversation."

"Sounds like someone we know," a deep voice had them all turn and see Alex, who sounded like he had a cold.

Jennifer frowned when she felt Harley stiffen beside her, and as the man drew closer, she noticed a scar on his left cheek. Alex didn't have a scar on his face. Her eyes widened when she realized it was the reclusive Ethan Blackwell—Alex's brother.

Harriet stood and greeted Ethan with the customary kiss on the cheek before linking her arm through his and turning to introduce them.

"Ethan, I'd like you to meet Harley Donovan and my new business partner, Jennifer Gains," Harriet made the introductions.

"It's nice to finally meet you, Miss Gains," Ethan shook Jennifer's hand. "I'm sorry we've missed each other at the various functions we were supposed to meet at."

"I understand," Jennifer assured him. *He really was incredibly handsome.*

Ethan's mysterious air and piercing blue eyes were more intense than his brother Alex's. Even Ethan's voice held a low, husky quality that seemed to caress you. Gooseflesh tickled her skin, and her breath caught when his smile broadened and touched his eyes. Alex and Ethan were classed as identical twins, and if you saw them together, it would be hard to tell them apart until you got closer and spoke to them. The difference became glaringly obvious despite the scar on Ethan's cheek.

Jennifer noticed that Harley hesitated when Ethan held his hand toward him. A muscle had ticked at the side of Harley's jaw when he'd taken Ethan's hand to shake.

What on earth is up with him today? Jennifer glanced at Harley, his fists balled at his sides while his eyes narrowed, targeting Ethan.

"We're going for cocktails and then to Newbury Port to a quaint French restaurant," Harriet told them. "Why don't the two of you join us?" she invited, giving Harley a sly look. "Maybe getting out of this environment will do you good."

"Yes, please, join us," Ethan said, smiling at Jennifer. "I'd love to talk to you about a few prospective clients and how you got Brody Croft to start in a TV series."

Harley was about to speak, but Jennifer jumped in. "Thank you, but Harley and I have to get back to our uncle and aunt, who are not well."

"Oh, how are Betty and Sam?" Harriet asked, looking disappointed at them turning down their dinner invite.

"Doing well," Jennifer answered, glancing sideways at Harley, who was still standing like a coiled spring waiting to be set free, and she had a feeling his target would be Ethan. "But they are both still in recovery, leaving Harley and me on nursing duty."

"I'm sorry to hear your families are unwell," Ethan said politely. "Maybe another time?"

"Yes, I'd like that," Jennifer told him with a smile.

Harriet and Ethan said goodbye and left.

Jennifer turned to Harley, looking at him with raised brows. "What is it with you today?" She shook her head. "Are you missing our verbal sparring matches and now looking for another person to take my place?"

"I'm sorry," Harley breathed and rubbed his hand over his eyes. "Coming face to face with Doctor Ainsley and then Ethan Blackwell got me riled up."

"I noticed!" Jennifer looked at him enquiringly. "Do you want to talk about it?"

"Not really." Harley shook his head.

"Okay!" Jennifer shrugged. "Do you want to get a coffee and something to eat before we head back to your house?" She looked toward the restaurant. "I know the owner of the second-best restaurant in town, and I get an excellent discount."

"Oh?" Harley started to relax at Jennifer's switch to a teasing mood. "I am hungry." He pursed his lips. "And if you get a good discount, we shouldn't let that opportunity go to waste."

Jennifer grinned. "Agreed." She patted her stomach, admitting, "All this tension with Betty, Sam, my... Andrew, and his sister-in-law, has worked up an appetite." She blew out a breath. "I'm starving."

She hooked her arm through his and nearly jumped away as a zap of electricity shot up her arm and jolted her heart, conjuring a picture of Cupid shooting an arrow at her. Jennifer shook away her fanciful thoughts as she and Harley entered the hotel restaurant, where the hostess immediately greeted them.

"Good afternoon, Miss Gains." The hostess smiled warmly at Jennifer. "A table for two?"

"Yes, please, Carmen." Jennifer smiled politely. Carmen always irritated Jennifer with her soft voice and sugary-sweet attitude. *No one's that sweet and friendly all the time.*

"Jennifer?" Harley's voice snapped her from her musings.

"Sorry." Jennifer followed Harley and Carmen to a secluded table always reserved for the hotel's VIP guests, top management, or their families. "The hunger has clouded my brain."

"Then let's get you something to eat," Harley suggested as they slid into their chairs.

"Yes, before I turn into a zombie!" Jennifer laughed, but her face sobered when she saw the light leave Harley's eyes and a shadow appear. "I'm not really going to become a zombie and start eating brains."

Harley laughed. "I'm sorry," he said. "It's just so many things reminding me of Daniel lately."

"Oh, of course. He was twelve!" Jennifer pulled a sorry face. "He was into zombie movies?"

"Daniel loved everything zombie, superhero, sci-fi," Harley recalled, barely noticing when a server handed him a menu. "He was a comic collector and a fantastic artist. He even started his own superhero comic books. It was his dream to be a graphic novelist or a cartoonist." He absently opened the menu. "He has a whole lot of them. He drew at least two a month."

"Did you get them published?" Jennifer asked, and Harley's head shot up to look at her.

"No." Harley shook his head, frowning. "To be honest, I never really thought about it. It was really tough packing up his room in my and my ex-wife's houses."

"You did both rooms?" Jennifer looked at him with raised brows. "I couldn't imagine how hard that must've been for you."

"Angela was having a hard time with Daniel's death," Harley explained.

"You were *both* having a hard time with it," Jennifer pointed out, feeling awful that Harley had to take all that on by himself. "Maybe it would've been good for your ex-wife to help you go through your son's room."

Harley smiled at Jennifer's protective instincts. "I pushed through each day after Daniel's death. I felt like I was walking, trying to wade through emotional quicksand. I had to drag myself through each day." He ran his hand over his chin. "My sister, cousin, and uncle rallied around me, but I hardly noticed they were there. While I was barely coping, Angela, my ex-wife, had shut down completely."

"Oh!" Jennifer suddenly felt awful for saying what she did about his ex-wife.

"The day Daniel died, we sat beside him until the nurses took him away," Harley explained. "Angela hadn't said a word, just sat holding his hand until they pulled the sheet over his head. That's when she first snapped. Angela flung herself onto the bed and wouldn't let them take him. I managed to pull her off and hold her as she broke down."

"I'm so sorry, Harley." Jennifer's voice was gruff with compassion.

Sorry seemed such an insignificant thing to say to someone who had lost a part of their heart and soul. But what else was there to say? Words couldn't heal the wound that, even after ten years, was still as raw as it had been the day Harley had lost his only child. Jennifer felt a lump form in her throat and tears stung the back of her eyes. She reached across the table and took his hand, which he clasped like a drowning man clinging to a straw.

The server interrupted them, and Jennifer ordered coffee and specialty burgers for them as Harley didn't seem to register the server's presence. He was struggling with the ghosts of the past.

"Angela didn't speak to anyone after that day. She barely moved, ate, drank, and didn't take care of herself unless her sister Clair saw to her." Harley swallowed. "At the funeral, I sat beside her, and she clung to my hand, staring at Daniel's coffin. It wasn't until everyone left that I broke down once again. She tried to jump into the grave and wanted to be buried with Daniel. She told me that I may as well bury her because she had no life without her baby."

171

Jennifer swiped a tear from her cheek and gathered her emotions. "I understand why she couldn't pack up your son's room. I'm sorry I said what I did."

"It's okay. You're not the first one to say it," Harley assured her. "Angela and I had this instant connection when we met. We married two months after meeting, and a few years later, we had Daniel. But as Daniel grew, we realized we had grown apart. Our instant spark had fizzled out as quickly as it had ignited."

"Your divorce was amicable?" Jennifer asked before she could stop herself.

When Harley spoke about Angela, she could see how much he cared for her, and it made something inside her sting. Jennifer wanted to know all she could about Angela and Harley's feelings for the woman, while on the other hand, she wanted to close her ears and pretend the woman didn't exist.

Jennifer gave herself a mental shake. *What on earth is wrong with me?*

"Yes." Harley nodded. "Well, not at first because I came home to surprise my family early from an assignment to find Daniel was with her mother, and Angela had another *guest* sleeping over."

The knot in her stomach twisted at the look of hurt and betrayal that flashed in Harley's eyes.

"I don't quite know what to say to that," Jennifer said honestly. "Although I did find one of my exes cheating on me, I caught him and his other girlfriend on a romantic picnic in Central Park in New York." She squeezed his hand. "It was nothing like your experience."

"Finding anyone cheating, no matter the circumstance is a gut-wrenching experience," Harley assured her. "For the record, that man didn't deserve you if he didn't know what he had in you."

Jennifer stared at Harley, stunned, not quite knowing what to say to his compliment, while something went wild with excitement in her stomach. Her butterflies weren't just fluttering around wildly. They were having an electrifying party.

Get a grip, Jennifer. This is Harley. We don't get along. The only reason we are right now is because of all the drama I've dragged him into.

A drama that has caused him haunting pain from memories.

She mentally flicked away her thoughts as if they were annoying ants and focused on what Harley was saying.

"How... Uh." Jennifer cleared her throat. "How long have you been divorced?"

Jennifer was trying not to think about their clasped hands or what the gentle caress of his thumb over the top of hers was doing to her nervous system.

"I've been divorced for thirteen years," Harley answered. "We were married for eleven years." He released her hand and sat back, holding her gaze. "Have you ever been married or engaged?"

Jennifer drew her hand back and clasped both hands in front of her. The one Harley had held still tingled from his touch.

"No to both questions," Jennifer told him. "I think the longest relationship I've had was two years." She took a breadstick from the basket that had magically appeared on their table. "That was the Charlie who cheated on me."

"Was his name Charlie, or are you using Charlie as an insult?" Harley asked her, the amusement back in his eyes.

"His name was Charlie." Jennifer grinned, knowing the look that was about to cross Harley's face when she told him the man's last name. "Charlie Chapman."

"Are you joking?" Harley's eyes narrowed as he looked at her suspiciously.

"Nope." Jennifer's lips curled into a full-blown smile. "His name was really Charlie Chapman."

"His parents gave him that name?" Harley asked, gaping at her. "He wasn't an actor, and that was his stage name?"

"Nope, it was the name his parents gave him." Jennifer laughed, and Harley joined her. "I didn't believe him either when I first met him. I thought it was a bad pickup line. And no, he wasn't an actor. He was a Wall Street broker."

"His name must've drawn a lot of attention on his portfolio," Harley commented, letting go of her hand to sit back in the chair.

"His name drew a lot of attention everywhere he went," Jennifer said, remembering her two years with Charlie. "Can you believe that some people believed his story when he told them Charlie Chaplin was his great-great-great-great grandfather that he was named after?"

"Wow!" Harley gave a low whistle. "Did he say Chaplin when telling that story?"

"Yup." Jennifer nodded, taking a bite of the breadstick.

"Just shows how people can selectively hear what they want in certain situations," Harley pointed out.

Their burgers arrived, and they ate silently for a while before Jennifer asked, "Why don't you like Ethan Blackwell?"

Harley looked at her in surprise, finished chewing the bit he'd taken, and wiped his mouth before replying, "What is it you like to say?" He raised his eyebrows. "That's not my story to tell. I can only say that he was instrumental in ruining the life of someone I love."

"Ah." Jennifer nodded. "So that narrows it down a bit," she teased him.

"I don't have a wide circle of people I love," Harley said, pouring milk into his coffee and stirring it. "So you could probably take a few stabs at guessing which one, but I still won't be able to confirm or deny anything."

"Noted," Jennifer said and read between the lines. *Stop prying!* "Can you tell me why you accused Andrew's sister-in-law of being responsible for what happened to Daniel?"

"You are full of questions today," Harley commented, leaning back in the chair and observing her. "If I answer your questions, but about me, you have to answer mine."

"Okay, but the same rules apply," Jennifer added. "They have to be questions about me."

"Fair enough," Harley agreed. "As you asked two questions already, I get to ask you two."

"No, that's not fair," Jennifer stated. "You get one question for answering my questions about Doctor *I love to brag about being a doctor.*"

"The woman is a narcissist," Harley told Jennifer. "She has a high opinion of herself as a doctor." He shook his head. "To be fair, Doctor Ainsley was excellent with Daniel and thorough. At least Angela and I thought she was until Daniel got the flu."

"I wanted to ask you about how Daniel got sick after the bone marrow transplant, but I thought it was rude to pry, especially when it upset you," Jennifer admitted.

"While the memories are still painful," Harley told Jennifer, "it's been good to finally talk to someone about them."

"I felt the same way about telling you about my childhood and Andrew," Jennifer admitted. "It was good to finally let all the hurt out. It was like finally facing the monsters I've hidden in the recesses of my mind."

"Life works in mysterious ways," Harley said. "Who would've thought when we met two weeks ago that we'd be sitting telling each other our deepest secrets?"

"Not me." Jennifer laughed. "Now stop hedging and tell me about Doctor Ainsley."

Harley took a deep breath and continued, "Daniel wasn't in isolation when he was recovering, but we had to be careful when we went into his room." He took a sip of coffee. "We had to disinfect our hands and put on booties, caps, gowns, masks, and gloves. We couldn't go in until a nurse ensured Daniel was wearing a mask and gloves."

"That's understandable." Jennifer nodded.

"His blood count was rising but slowly, and his immune system was weak." Harley cleared his throat as his voice became hoarse with emotion. "I told you what happened on the day the flu took him. The day he passed away when Angela had her first breakdown, Doctor Ainsley had to sedate Angela, and she'd no sooner given the sedative when she started sneezing."

"Doctor Ainsley had the flu?" Jennifer's eyes widened in disbelief. "She had the flu and still went near Daniel?"

"Yes." Harley nodded. "Although Doctor Ainsley denied she had the flu or even a cold. She said it was allergies, and she'd never go near an immune-compromised cancer patient if she were sick."

"What happened?" Jennifer poured water into a glass. "Was there an investigation?"

"Yes, but we couldn't prove anything," Harley told her. "Doctor Ainsley was found guilty of negligence, got a suspension, and gave us a payout, which we donated to the children's cancer ward."

"After her suspension, she went back to work as if nothing happened." Jennifer finished the story feeling angry for Harley.

"Doctor Ainsley tried to contact me a few times after that, but I wouldn't take her calls." A muscle ticked at the side of Harley's jaw, and his eyes flickered angrily. "I had nothing more to say to her and didn't want to hear any empty apologies."

"I don't blame you," Jennifer told him. "Now that I know what happened, I think you showed a lot of restraint when she walked into Liam's office."

"I didn't want to end up in jail." Harley laughed.

"I would've insisted Andrew get all charges dropped," Jennifer assured him.

"Andrew's an attorney?" Harley's eyebrows rose.

"He may have been a terrible parent and negligent husband," Jennifer said before grudgingly adding. "But he is one of the top defense attorneys in Massachusetts."

"I noted the grudging respect you said that with." Harley's eyes twinkled teasingly.

"Aunt Betty taught us that it doesn't matter what you think of the person. You have to give them credit where credit is due," Jennifer repeated one of her aunt's mantras. "My turn to ask another question."

"What?" Harley looked at her in confusion. "No. I haven't asked a question yet."

"You did." Jennifer gave him a smug smile. "You asked me if Andrew was an attorney."

"Oh, no, you don't." Harley's eyes narrowed. "We agreed the question has to be about us and not one of our loved ones."

"Andrew isn't one of my loved ones," Jennifer pointed out.

"That's not fair!" Harley shook his head. "I've been cheated."

"Okay, Mr. Moan and Groan," Jennifer teased. "Ask another question then."

Harley's smile faded, and his expression became serious as he watched her for a few seconds before leaning forward with his elbows on the table. "Why haven't you asked Andrew why he left and kept away for forty years?"

Jennifer was taken aback by Harley's question. Not because he'd asked it but because she didn't know how to answer it when she'd asked herself the same thing over and over since Andrew had arrived the previous day.

"I'm sorry." Harley held up his hands. "I shouldn't have asked."

"No!" Jennifer said quickly. "You've been so supportive through all my family drama, even though it opened an emotional wound for you. You've witnessed Liam and me not behaving at our best around Andrew, and demanding an explanation for his actions is what most people would've done."

"Yet you and Liam seem to have no desire to do so," Harley pointed out.

"No, we don't want to know," Jennifer told him honestly. "That would mean we still cared, and we don't." She shrugged, pushing aside the little voice in her head calling her a liar. "Andrew had forty years to explain, but he didn't, and that's not what the purpose of his visit was about either. He didn't come here to mend any bridges. He came because he needed something from us." She cleared the lump from her throat.

"I get it." Harley nodded in understanding. "Do you want to know why he left?"

"That's your third question in a row!" Jennifer pointed out.

"Okay, but I don't withdraw the questions," Harley told her, grinning.

"Fine, I'll answer that question after you answer mine." Jennifer sipped the water as she thought about her next question. "Do you have Daniel's comic books he created?"

"Yes, I do," Harley answered. "Why?" He held up a hand. "And that's not a question to you. It's included in my answer."

"Fair enough," Jennifer agreed, enjoying their getting-to-know-each-other session. "How would you feel about letting me read them?"

"Why?" Harley's eyes narrowed suspiciously.

"I'm an editor, and I know many people in the trade, including a publishing house specializing in graphic novels," Jennifer told him. "Don't answer now. Think about it. But you told me about Daniel's journal and how he feared he'd fade into nothing without leaving a mark. Maybe Daniel's mark is meant to be through his drawings."

Harley was quiet as he contemplated her offer. "I'll have to talk it over with Angela. But I think it's a great idea."

They finished their meal, got a doggy bag, and decided to go to the Beach Hut to get some takeout for Sam and Betty. They walked across the beach to the Beach Hut where Finn greeted them with a sly smile.

"Are you two here to fight again, or are the rumors true and you've called a truce?" Finn grinned.

"Funny." Jennifer pulled a face at the man who was like another brother to her. "We've come to order takeout for Aunt Betty and Sam."

"Daniella mentioned that they were living together now." Finn's smile grew.

"Daniella was here?" Harley asked. "When?"

"Oh, about an hour ago," Finn told them. "I believe she had the same idea as you."

"Are you saying Daniella already bought food for them?" Jennifer's eyes narrowed irritably at Finn. He loved to goof around.

"Yes." Finn nodded. "Can I get you two anything?" He eyed the doggy bag in Harley's hand. "Although I see you've already had something at Liam's."

"Yes, we've eaten, thanks, Finn," Harley told him and glanced at Jennifer. "We'd better stop at Liam's office on the way back to Sam's house."

"Yes, I'd almost forgotten about that." Jennifer sighed, and they were about to leave when Finn caught her hand.

"Jen, Daniella told me that Andrew is back." Finn's eyes were heavy with concern. "Are you and Liam okay?"

"Honestly," Jennifer answered, feeling the weight of his question and tired of pretending, "I'm not sure."

CHAPTER 10

H arley wasn't a very good passenger in a car. He liked to be in control of the wheel, especially along the back road where he'd met Jennifer thirteen days ago. Harley had to stop from reaching toward the dashboard or the handle above the door whenever Jennifer took a corner.

They were going to Boston and planned to stay there for three days. Or two days and three nights, as far as Jennifer was concerned. Liam and Caroline had visited him a few days ago to let him know that the day after the DNA tests, which was tomorrow, was Jennifer's birthday. They asked if Harley would give Jennifer their surprise. Since she was a young girl, Jennifer had wanted to spend a day just doing tourist things in Boston.

Harley was surprised by that and that Boston was Jennifer's favorite city. However, because she knew Andrew and his family were from there, Jennifer never stayed longer than a day or two when she traveled through Boston. But she'd always wanted to have a full tour around Boston. See the historical sights and architecture and get lost in her favorite city, then end the day dining at a restaurant on the waterfront overlooking the harbor.

Harley agreed to surprise Jennifer with her birthday gift from her aunt, brother, and best friend, who'd all bought her a ticket to something she'd always wanted to do in Boston. Now, all Harley had to figure out was how to keep Jennifer in Boston for another day and hope the front desk didn't give their surprise away when they checked in.

"Oh, look," Harley said, pointing to a spot on the opposite side of the road. "That's where we first met."

Jennifer glanced to the side and grinned. "That's right. The day you put your emergency triangle in the middle of the road and then nearly made me have an accident when you jumped in front of my car."

"The way I remember it," Harley teased, "you *did* have an accident."

"That was water!" Jennifer told him through gritted teeth. "The bottle cap popped off and fell on the floor."

185

"So you thought that instead of pulling to the side to get the lid, it was safer to reach for it while driving?" Harley looked at her in amazement.

"I was keeping an eye on the road," Jennifer defended her actions. "It's not the busiest road, which is why I take it. How was I supposed to know that a crazy person had set up a triangle on a bend?"

"It's a slight curve," Harley pointed out as they rounded the curve in the road. "You can see around it as no mountains or hills are blocking your view."

"I know," Jennifer told him. "I drive this road a *lot*."

"And my triangle, that you splintered into pieces, by the way, was *not* in the middle of the road," Harley told her. "You swerved onto the curb and rode over it."

"I didn't swerve!" Jennifer glanced at him, her violet eyes sparking angrily.

She has the most gorgeous eyes, Harley thought before giving himself a mental shake. *Good grief, man.*

"No." Harley sighed and shook his head so much for their six-day peace truce. "My triangle tried to dodge your tires by jumping into the middle of the road, but you hit it anyway."

"Wow!" Jennifer shook her head. "You're not going to let this go, are you?"

"You squashed my triangle and then gunned for me!" Harley stated, turning in the seat to look at her profile. "Oh, and after nearly killing me, you left me on the side of the road—stranded with no phone."

"I told you to always take a charger with you," Jennifer grinned, flipping out the compartment at the base of the dash. "See, there's my car charger." She glanced at him. "Besides, I called a tow truck a few minutes after leaving you at the side of the road."

"Yes, but you also tried to get the tow company to leave me there for another hour or two!" Harley looked at her in disbelief.

"Oh, they told you that, did they?" Jennifer pulled a face, her eyes sparkling with mischief. "Well, at least for this trip, you're in a *reliable* vehicle with a charged cell phone. Not your outdated pickup truck."

"It's not outdated!" Harley said defensively. "It's a classic."

Jennifer nodded. "That's what I said—outdated."

"I think you missed your calling," Harley told her, shifting position to stare out the front window again. "You'd have made a great attorney."

"It does run in the family," Jennifer agreed, grinning cheekily. "My mother was studying to be an attorney when she met my... Andrew, and Betty used to be a family attorney in Boston."

"Oh!" Harley didn't know that Betty used to be an attorney. "I did not know that about Betty or your mother."

"That's how Betty and Sam met," Jennifer told him.

"I've often wondered how those two met." Harley looked at Jennifer, intrigued. "I've never got around to asking, though. They've known each other for a long time. I assumed they'd met on Plum Island as my great-great-grandfather is from there."

"I didn't know that!" Jennifer glanced at him. "I thought Sam moved to Plum Island around forty years ago, a few years after Aunt Betty and my mother moved us back to Beach Plum Cottage after my grandfather died."

"Betty and your mother's father?" Harley asked her to clarify which grandparent.

"Yes, Carl Swan!" Jennifer said. "I don't remember him as I was two when he died. Liam remembers him better than I do."

"So you were two when you moved to Plum Island?" Harley asked.

"Yes, and Liam was five," Jennifer answered.

"How old were you when you first got sick?" Harley asked, hoping he wasn't overstepping.

"I was five." Jennifer slowed down to turn onto the main highway as they neared Boston. "I was getting short of breath, passing out, and always had bad chest pains. Andrew got a doctor from Boston to come and check me out."

"Why didn't he just take you to Boston?" Harley raised his brows.

"I don't know," Jennifer said with a shrug. "I was five, and I didn't ask. The doctor who looked at me was the one who rushed me to Newbury Port Hospital. I was in hospital for months after that, hooked onto a machine. The day before my sixth birthday, I had a heart operation and was told I had a very special heart."

"You had a heart transplant at six?" Harley's brows shot up as he looked at her in surprise.

"No, the doctor my father brought to us from Boston fixed my heart," Jennifer told him. "I don't know all the medical terms. I've always tried not to think about the fact that I nearly died at the age of five."

"I'm sorry, I didn't mean to bring it up," Harley told her.

"Oh, no." Jennifer smiled reassuringly. "I don't mind talking about it. I leave all the medical stuff to my doctors and I live my life as best I can while taking care of my heart and the rest of my body."

"And you've done a marvelous job of taking care of your body." The words slipped out of Harley's mouth before he could stop them. "Sorry, I didn't mean that to sound as lecherous as it did."

"It's okay." Jennifer laughed. "And thank you for the compliment."

"You said you go for checkups twice a year?" Harley moved the conversation away from the thoughts that had found their way to his tongue without his permission.

"I do," Jennifer confirmed. "And thank you for reminding me. I must get my records transferred to a new cardiologist in Newbury Port."

"You haven't done that yet?" Harley asked her in alarm. "Shouldn't that have been one of the first things you did when you got back to Plum Island?"

"Who died and made you my parent?" Jennifer glanced at him with a raised eyebrow.

"I'm just concerned." Harley raised his hands. "Sorry, but I know how quickly a person's health can change, and if you're able to prepare the nearest hospital, it's best to do it."

"Thank you for your concern for my health." Jennifer held up her arm where a silver bracelet slid to her wrist. "See. I have a cardiac bracelet to alert medical professionals to my condition. And *yes,* all my details are up to date. I changed my address the day before I arrived home."

"That's a good thing to have," Harley told her. "My niece Emily has one for her hearing problem and allergies."

"Emily's Daniella's daughter, right?" Jennifer enquired.

"Yes." Harley nodded. "She's fifteen going on forty. Emily is the caretaker of our family. She always ensures none of us miss a birthday or special day."

"I've only met her a few times," Jennifer told him. "I didn't know she had hearing problems."

"She lost her hearing when she was seven," Harley told her. "Emily was prone to ear infections that caused damage to the middle eardrum."

"Oh no!" Jennifer's eyes were filled with compassion as he glanced at Harley. "I'm sorry to hear that. How awful for her."

"She has partial hearing," Harley told Jennifer. "Daniella is forever researching the latest treatments for Emily."

"Your family has been through so much." Jennifer's voice was barely audible. "And now I'm dragging you into my family drama."

"You didn't drag me into anything," Harley assured her. "I'm glad I can help in any way, even if it's just for support."

"Thank you," Jennifer said, slowing down as they reached the Boston city limits. "Liam said we must go straight to the hospital when we arrive." She expertly navigated her way through the Boston streets. "Georgia and Molly want to meet us."

"I'm glad you agreed to meet them," Harley admitted. "I'm not saying anything bad will happen, and I've only got positive thoughts for Molly. But if anything did happen, you'd feel better about yourself for having met her. Even if it was just for a brief moment."

"That's deep." Jennifer smiled as she turned into the hospital parking area. "And absolutely right." She found an empty parking place and parked the car. Switching off the engine, she leaned over the steering wheel, gazing at the hospital. "I thought I'd never see this place again."

"I thought you had your operation in Newbury Port?" Harley said.

"We often came here for my mother's checkups," Jennifer told him. "The doctor who fixed my heart saw to my mother here and at Newbury Port when she could."

"Where was your mother in her final moments?" Harley's voice was soft and filled with compassion, sensing she needed to talk.

"Newbury Port," Jennifer answered, opening the car door. "I still don't see why we couldn't have this testing done at Newbury Port."

Jennifer slid out of the car and closed the door. Harley followed, and they walked into the hospital side by side.

"Andrew knows the staff here, and they want everything close to where Molly is," Harley told her.

When they entered the hospital, the familiar scent of antiseptic hit Harley. The memories of a time long past clawed at the edges of his consciousness, threatening to resurface. They walked side by side down the well-lit corridor. The sound of their footsteps ricocheting off the sterile walls was a harsh reminder of the worst time in his life. Passing the room where his son had once been, Harley's gaze involuntarily shifted towards it. The door was closed, making him sigh with relief as he managed to keep the ghostly memories of the time he'd spent there with Daniel at bay. But as Harley and Jennifer pushed on, looking for Molly's room, the whispers of his son's voice over the beeping of machines flowed through his mind.

Sensing the shift in Harley's demeanor, Jennifer glanced at him with concern. His shoulders were tense, and the lines on his forehead deepened.

"Are you okay?" Jennifer reached out and took his hand.

The soft warmth kept him grounded in the present as he nodded, and they rounded the corner, finding Molly's room.

"This is the number," Harley told her.

The blinds on the hallway window were drawn, and the door was closed. Jennifer knocked on the door, and Andrew greeted them within seconds.

"Jennifer, Harley, you made it." A look of relief flashed through Andrew's eyes, and Harley knew the man had to refrain from reaching out to hug Jennifer.

"You sound surprised." Jennifer's voice became frosty as her eyes narrowed. "Did you think I was going to change my mind?"

"Wha..." Andrew looked at her, confused. "No, that's not what I meant at all. I'm relieved that you arrived okay. I was worried about you driving here."

"I can assure you, I've driven from Plum Island to Boston many times," Jennifer told him haughtily. "Is my brother still here?"

"Yes, he went to make a phone call and should be back any minute," Andrew told them before stepping back. "Please, come in. Molly's just finished having a shower."

"We can come back," Jennifer said. Her eyes were shuttered, and the air around her felt cold.

"No, please. Molly and Georgia are so excited to meet you. They've been waiting the whole day," Andrew told them, stepping aside so they could enter. "Molly, this is Jennifer and her friend Harley."

"Hello," Molly's face was pale and drawn. She had dark circles no fifteen-year-old should have around her eyes that were the same shape and color as Jennifer's, which lit up when she saw them.

"Hello, Molly." Jennifer's shoulders relaxed, her voice and eyes warmed as she looked at Molly. "It's nice to meet you."

"We're just sorry it's under these circumstances," a soft female voice said from the opposite side of Molly's bed.

"Jennifer," Andrew said, stepping up to the woman and putting her arm around her shoulders. "This is Georgia."

"Hello!" Jennifer's eyes turned to ice, and her tone clipped as she acknowledged Georgia.

"Would you like to sit?" Molly asked Jennifer and Harley, who she had to raise her head to look at. "You're very tall."

"So I've been told." Harley grinned at the teen, his eyes seeing a pile of books on the nightstand. "I see you like to read."

"Yes." Molly nodded. "I love books. One day, I want to be an author."

The word hit Harley in the heart as Daniel's voice echoed through his mind: *I'm going to be a graphic novelist and write the most awesome superhero comics.*

Harley shook his thoughts away. "That's a good career." He looked at Jennifer, who was examining Molly like she was a foreign antibody. "Jennifer is an editor and worked at one of New York's top publishing houses."

"Realy?" Molly's eyes widened as she moved her gaze to Jennifer. "That's so cool." She smiled. "Although if I was going to guess your career, I'd say you were a supermodel."

"Don't give her a big head, Molly," Liam's voice came from the door. He walked into the room, hugging Jennifer. "Hey, sis, glad you got here safely."

"Does everyone think I'm a bad driver?" Jennifer glared warningly at Harley as she said that.

"It's not you, Jennifer," Georgia told her. "It's the other drivers on the road."

Jennifer's eyes frosted again as her gaze returned to Georgia and Andrew. But before she could say anything, Liam jumped in.

"Can we go over what happens next?" Liam asked, pointing to the hallway and grinning at Molly. "You get some rest, and I'll see you soon, okay?"

"I'll look forward to that," Molly told him with a tired smile. "And meeting Lila."

Harley saw Jennifer's eyes widen in surprise as she turned to look questioningly at her brother. Liam leaned past Molly and kissed her cheek.

"Remember, be brave, and I'll be back next week with Lila." Liam led the adults from the room.

"Harley, would you stay with me until my mom returns?" Molly asked Harley, stopping him in his tracks. For a minute, he saw Daniel lying where Molly was.

"Of course," Harley looked at Andrew and Georgia. "That's if your mom and father don't mind."

"Thank you," Georgia squeezed Harley's arm as she walked past him and whispered. "She tries to hide it but she's scared and doesn't like being left alone."

"I understand," Harley assured Georgia.

Harley sat beside Molly's bed and grabbed one of the books. "You like Shakespeare?"

"I just read that to make my parents happy." Molly laughed. "My grandmother brings me the books I really like." She pulled open the drawer of her side table. "I love young adult fantasy."

"I see that." Harley laughed, looking at the four books hidden beneath her washcloths.

"Are you named after the motorbike?" Molly asked him curiously.

"You know, I'm not sure," Harley told her truthfully. "I never thought to ask."

"Really?" Molly looked at him in disbelief. "Harley is not that common of a name, so you must've wondered why your parents gave you that name. My father named me Molly after someone he said changed his life."

"Ah!" Harley nodded before looking at her curiously. "Molly, do you know who Jennifer and Liam are?"

"Yes." Molly nodded. "They are my half-brother and sister from my father's first marriage."

"You don't think it's strange that you've never met them until today?" Harley asked her.

"My father never really spoke about his first family," Molly told Harley. "I've always known I have a brother and sister. My father always told me they were far away, but one day we'd meet."

"I'm sorry that you had to meet them like this." Harley smiled at her.

"Are you and Jennifer a couple?" Molly asked him. "You make a beautiful couple."

"Thank you," Harley said. "But Jennifer and I are just friends."

"Oh!" Molly looked disappointed, her young brow frowning as she glanced at him. "Is that why you're sad because you want to be more than friends?"

Harley was amazed at her perception. "No." He shook his head. "I'm not sad."

"Okay!" Molly didn't look convinced and asked him an unrelated question. "Do you know why my father never saw my brother and sister for so long?"

Harley's brows shot up as he looked at her, not expecting that question. "No, I'm sorry, I don't."

"Neither do I." Molly pursed her lips and shook her head before yawing and sliding down on the pillow. "But I think it had something to do with my father's father."

"Your grandfather?" Harley's brow creased.

"I never called him that. He was a mean, stern man who frightened me." Molly yawned again, and Harley saw she'd overextended her energy. He helped her pull the blankets over her shoulders. "Mommy never went to grandmother's house if she knew he'd be there." She looked at Harley. "Will you come to see me again?"

"Of course," Harley promised, ensuring she was tucked in. "Why don't you get some sleep? I'll sit here until your parents come back."

"Thank you." Molly smiled sleepily and reached through the blanket to take his hand. "Dad always holds my hand when I'm scared."

Harley smiled. She reminded him so much of Jennifer. He took her hand in his as Molly drifted off to sleep.

A few minutes later, the door opened, admitting Georgia, Andrew, and Jennifer. Harley put a finger to his lips and indicated that Molly had just fallen asleep. He saw Jennifer's eyes soften as they looked at Molly with her small hand in Harley's. He gently extracted his hand from hers and stood.

"Is everything okay?" Harley asked Jennifer, who nodded.

"Yes, Liam's on his way back to Plum Island, and we should get to the hotel," Jennifer told Harley. "I'm starving."

"Okay." Harley smiled, then looked at Andrew and Georgia. "We'll see you tomorrow."

"Yes, and thank you for watching Molly," Georgia said as she and Andrew walked them to the door.

"Of course." Harley smiled at the woman, recognizing the shadows of fear and doubt warring with hope while trying to stay positive in Georgia's eyes. He gave her an encouraging smile. "Stay strong."

"I'm trying." Georgia's eyes sparkled with unshed tears.

"Let's go, Harley." Jennifer gave Georgia a tight smile. "Say goodbye to Molly for me."

"I will." Georgia nodded.

"You were cold to Georgia and Andrew," Harley noted as they walked toward Jennifer's car.

"Do you want to drive?" Jennifer changed the subject. "I'm getting a headache."

"Sure." Harley took the keyfob she handed him. "Do you want to stop to get something for your headache?"

"No, I've got something, thanks," Jennifer told him, sliding into the passenger seat. "Do you want to eat at the hotel, order room service on your own, or go to a restaurant?"

Harley pulled away from the hospital and headed toward the Langham Hotel.

"Let's eat at the hotel tonight," Harley suggested. "We can go to a restaurant tomorrow night."

"We should've come here early with Liam," Jennifer sighed. "Then we could've been going home right now too."

"Then you wouldn't get to know Molly," Harley pointed out.

"I've met her now." Jennifer looked at him with narrowed eyes. "What did the two of you speak about while we were out of the room?"

"Mainly about you and Liam," Harley told her. "She asked me if you and I were a couple."

"Oh?" Jennifer turned to him, and something flashed in her eyes.

"I told her we were friends, and she said we'd make an awesome couple because we were beautiful." Harley laughed at the look on Jennifer's face.

"I wouldn't call you beautiful," Jennifer stated. "I'd say ruggedly handsome."

"Thank you," Harley said, trying to steady his pounding heart and stop himself from screaming, *she thinks I'm ruggedly handsome* in his head.

"She seems like a sweet kid." That was all Jennifer had to say on the subject as they neared the hotel. "What do you say we check in, get our luggage to our rooms, and meet in the dining room in forty minutes?"

"That sounds like a plan," Harley agreed. "It gives me a chance to shower."

"Yes, and me too." Jennifer nodded as Harley pulled into a parking space.

Thirty-five minutes later, Harley was on his way to the dining room. His and Jennifer's rooms were on the same floor, so he stopped by her door and knocked. When she answered it, the scent of jasmine and fresh soap tantalized his nostrils and sent a zing through his nervous system.

She looked beautiful in a sleeveless deep blue satin cowl neck top, loose flowing white cotton pants, and wedge heels that matched the color of her top. Her hair was loose and bounced straight and neat to her shoulders. She had a slight touch of mascara on her long eyelashes and a light pink gloss on her lips.

"You look lovely." Harley's voice was gruff and low.

"Thank you." Jennifer smiled, closing her room door and hooking her arm through his. "You don't look too bad yourself. I don't think I've seen you in cotton slacks, a button-down shirt, and a jacket."

"That's not true," Harley told her. "I wore something similar to Alex's dinner party."

"Sorry, I forgot." Jennifer pressed the elevator button. "How's your room?"

"Awesome," Harley replied. "And yours?"

"Very grand," Jennifer told him as they entered the elevator.

During dinner, Harley and Jennifer spoke about their careers, childhood, and what was next for them. It was great getting to know Jennifer and seeing her so relaxed. Every time she laughed, the sound seemed to warm his heart. Harley couldn't help but notice how the light danced in her eyes or glinted off her shiny hair.

He walked her to the door, feeling deflated that the night was over. When they were outside Jennifer's room, she turned to thank him for being there for a wonderful evening. Their eyes locked, and Harley didn't know who moved first, but the next thing he knew, his lips crushed hers as he pulled her against him. She wound her arms around his neck.

Harley had no idea how long they were lost in each other until the ding of the elevator down the hall dropped them back into reality. They stepped apart and stood blinking at each other in the dimly lit hallway, the air thick with unspoken emotions. The intensity of the kiss lingered between them.

Harley's voice was a low, husky murmur, breaking the charged silence. "I should go. We have to be at the hospital early tomorrow."

She nodded, her eyes reflecting a myriad of emotions. There was gratitude, desire, and vulnerability that resonated with Harley's inner turmoil. As they stood there, the distant click of the tea trolley kept them grounded in reality.

"Goodnight, Harley," Jennifer whispered, her gaze still locked with his.

Harley nodded, his chest tightening with a mixture of conflicting emotions. He knew he should turn and go, but it was like his leg had taken root on the spot, and he couldn't tear his eyes away from her.

"Good evening," the server greeted them as he passed by.

Harley looked at the man. "Good evening," he said as he heard the click of Jennifer's door unlocking.

He turned and watched her slip inside, giving him a small wave with her fingers before closing it. Harley stood alone in the dim hallway, her lips' imprint still tingling on his. He smiled as he turned and walked down the hallway to his suite. Pulling out his phone, he saw a missed call from Uncle Sam.

Harley had called him early and left a message for him to call back. He hit redial, and Sam answered after a few rings.

"Harley, son, is everything okay?" Sam asked, his voice laced with concern. "Your message said call me as soon as possible."

"Hi, Uncle Sam," Harley greeted his uncle as he let himself into his suite. "I need to know what you meant the other day when you said that it's not Andrew you're worried but what he brings with him?"

Sam went quiet before answering. "You don't want to get involved with Andrew and his family, son," he warned. "Stay out of it and keep Jennifer as far away from her father and grandparents as possible."

"Why?" Harley persisted.

"Because Andrew's father is an evil man with connections in very high places," Sam told him. "Judge Pearce Gains is not someone you want to mess with."

"Why does that name sound so familiar to me?" Harley frowned.

"Probably because he's good friends with your ex-wife, Angela Wesley's, family," Sam told him.

Suddenly, Harley knew who Sam was talking about. His eyes narrowed. "Angela's mother didn't like the man."

"No one did," Sam told him. "But they pretended to. No one wants to get on the bad side of a judge with some higher powers in his pocket."

CHAPTER 11

J ennifer checked her wristwatch. It was nearly eight in the morning. Her brow creased.

Where is Harley? Jennifer buttered a piece of toast and took a bite.

They were supposed to meet at eight in the dining room for breakfast. Jennifer wanted to go past his room on the way to breakfast but had decided not to, especially after last night's kiss. Her heart jolted.

That kiss should never have happened! Jennifer drank her coffee. *Now things are going to be awkward!*

She shifted in the chair as memories of the kiss tumbled into her thoughts, making the butterflies in her stomach go wild.

Stop it! Jennifer reprimanded her traitorous emotions. *Harley and I were just becoming good friends, and now is not the time for emotional entanglements!* She finished her toast. *Just play it cool and act normal like the kiss didn't happen.*

Jennifer rechecked her wristwatch and frowned—eight-fifteen. She looked toward the entrance of the dining room. While she'd only known Harley for a few weeks, Jennifer knew he was extremely punctual.

"I hope he's okay," Jennifer mumbled, finishing her coffee.

She signaled the server, who came right over.

"Can I get you anything else, Miss Gains?" The man smiled politely.

"No, thanks. Just charge the breakfast to my room, please," Jennifer told him.

"It's all been taken care of," the server assured her, pulling out her chair.

"Thank you." Jennifer stood.

"Have a wonderful morning," the server said.

Jennifer left the dining room and walked to the front desk.

"Good morning, Miss Gains," the front desk clerk greeted Jennifer. "Would you like me to order you a taxi?"

She and Harley had agreed they would leave her car parked at the hotel as it was easier to take a cab to the hospital and back. Besides, Andrew was paying for their expenses. A few cab rides didn't seem a high price for forty years of absence. Jennifer pushed the tiny pangs of guilt she felt aside. She was not going to feel bad for the man.

However, Jennifer did sympathize with Andrew and his wife for what they were going through, and her heart ached for poor Molly. Jennifer hoped that she or Liam were donor matches. Molly deserved every chance to beat this disease, and Jennifer would help her in any way she could. Like Aunt Betty and Harley pointed out, Andrew deserting Jennifer and Liam had nothing to do with Molly.

If she was being honest, it was nice being a big sister.

"Miss Gains?" the front desk clerk's voice broke into Jennifer's musings.

"Sorry, yes, I need a cab to take me to Boston General," She answered. "Also, would you mind ringing Mr. Donovan's room please? We were supposed to meet at eight in the dining room, and he didn't show up."

"Oh!" The clerk's brows widened. "Mr. Donovan left at seven this morning."

"Where did he go?" Jennifer asked, surprised.

"He ordered a cab to take him to Chestnut Hill," the clerk told her.

"Chestnut Hill?" Jennifer's brow knitted together in confusion.

"Do you want to leave a message for him?" the clerk asked.

"No." Jennifer shook her head. "If you'd just order a cab, please."

"It's already outside." The clerk smiled. "Have a nice day."

Jennifer nodded distractedly as she headed to the cab. On the way to the hospital, she felt like she was caught in a storm of emotions that ranged from disappointment to anger. She was disappointed because she was looking forward to spending time with Harley and angry because he'd promised to be with her for the tests.

Get a freakin' grip, Jennifer! She pinched the bridge of her nose. *You're a grown woman. You don't need someone to hold your hand.* Her brow furrowed as her mind filled with questions. *Why would Harley go to Chestnut Hill?* Her eyes widened as a thought crossed her mind—Andrew lived in Chestnut Hill!

Jennifer climbed out of the cab when it came to a stop at the hospital entrance. She was about to pay when the cab driver told her it had already been taken care of. Jennifer thanked the man and walked into the cool, sterile building. A shiver flitted up her spine as it always did when she entered a hospital. Jennifer disliked everything about them, especially that ominous feeling that shrouded a person as you walked around the place.

Jennifer announced herself at the reception and let them know she was there to have DNA testing done. A nurse suddenly appeared beside her to escort her to an examination room, where Jennifer was seated in a chair.

"Doctor Mulder will be with you shortly," the nurse told Jennifer before leaving the room.

A few minutes later, the door opened, and Andrew stepped in.

"Hello, Jennifer," Andrew greeted, glancing around the room. "Where's Harley?"

"I don't know!" Jennifer's eyes narrowed on him. "He left early this morning to go to Chestnut Hill." Her eyes searched his. "You wouldn't happen to know why Harley would be going to your neighborhood, would you?"

"No!" Andrew frowned. "Maybe to visit his ex-in-laws?"

"His ex-in-law?" It was Jennifer's turn to frown in confusion before looking at Andrew questioningly. "How would you know who his ex-in-laws are?"

"My sister-in-law, Doctor Jessica Ainsley, you met in Liam's office," Andrew explained. "She told me after I asked her why Harley would accuse her of being responsible for the death of his son."

"I know who Doctor Ainsley is!" Jennifer told him impatiently. "I'm just surprised Harley would go to his in-laws so early in the morning without telling me."

"Maybe he thought he'd be back before you left for the hospital," Andrew offered an explanation. "I can call Margaret Wesley if you'd like me to?"

"No!" Jennifer's face scrunched up as she looked at him. She craned her neck to look past Andrew at the door. "Where is this doctor?"

"Do you mind if I stay here?" Andrew asked, pointing toward the chair beside her.

"Sure," Jennifer said with a shrug.

Andrew sat beside her. "Molly enjoyed meeting you and Liam yesterday."

"Molly's a great kid," Jennifer told him. "You've done a great job raising her."

"I can't take all the credit for that," Andrew admitted. "Molly has always been an independent spirit. She reminds me of you."

"Really?" Jennifer looked at him skeptically. "And how would *you* know anything about me?"

"I know more than you think," Andrew told her, his voice low as he caught her eye again. "You may not have seen me, but I was there."

"That's just creepy!" Jennifer looked at him with raised brows and decided to change the subject. "Who did you say Harley's ex-in-laws were?"

"The Wesley family," Andrew answered. "They own Wesley Fashion and Textiles."

"Oh!" Jennifer was surprised. "Wow."

"I'm surprised that I never met Harley," Andrew said. "I know the Wesley and their two daughters."

"Harley was in the Navy and then the SEALs," Jennifer explained. "I think they lived in California until he and his ex-wife divorced."

"I believe Harley was married to Angela, the eldest of the daughters and the less troubled one," Andrew commented.

The room door opened, and the doctor walked in. He wasn't very tall but fit, had warm eyes, and a ready smile.

"Hello, Andrew," the doctor greeted and turned to smile at Jennifer. "You must be Miss Gains?"

Jennifer nodded.

"I'm Doctor Mulder," the man introduced himself.

"I figured," Jennifer said, eyeing him coolly.

A nurse walked into the room with a medical trolly.

"I see you've had heart surgery," Doctor Mulder looked at Jennifer.

"I was six at the time," Jennifer told him. "It was a hereditary disorder, not a disease. I go for checkups at least twice a year, and so far, I'm clear and in excellent health."

"Good to know." Doctor Mulder smiled. "Are you taking any medication?"

"No." Jennifer shook her head.

"Alright, let's get this done." Doctor Mulder started to put on rubber gloves. "We'll draw a bit of blood to do HLA typing." He looked at Andrew, grinning. "I've been warned that you have an aversion to needles."

"Who told you that?" Jennifer glared at Andrew.

"Andrew told me about a few of your episodes when you were a child." Doctor Mulder laughed. "Don't worry, we've had far worse than a child knocking over the medicine cart."

"So that's why you're taking my blood, not the nurse." Jennifer shook her hand, shooting Andrew another glare. "I assure you I haven't had a freak out at a blood draw in years."

"That's good to hear." Doctor Mulder turned and spoke quietly to the nurse.

The nurse pushed a small table beside Jennifer.

"Could you please put your arm on here," the nurse asked.

Jennifer complied. Her heart started to pound when the nurse put a tourniquet just above her elbow before walking back to the doctor. Jennifer turned toward the doctor, which was a big mistake when she saw the needle the doctor was readying.

She knew she should look away. It was how she coped with the regular blood tests she had to have, but it was too late. She'd seen it. Jennifer's heart thudded against her rib cage as if it was trying to bust out and run for its life, which was what she wanted to do. Her free hand clenched on the armrest when Andrew's hand covered it gently, lifting her fingers and threading them with his.

Jennifer looked at their clasped hands, and memories of how Andrew had always held her hand at a doctor's appointment, the dentist's, or when it stormed flashed through her mind.

Daddy's got you, sweetheart. Nothing's going to hurt you. Except him! Another voice screamed from the back of her mind, shattering the good memories.

"All done!" Doctor Mulder's voice pulled her back to the present.

Jennifer turned and blinked in surprise as the nurse patched the hole from the needle with a cotton ball and medical tape.

"Oh!" Jennifer looked at Doctor Mulder. "Thank you."

"Thank you for coming forward, and let's hope you or your brother are a donor match." Doctor Mulder stood and pulled off the gloves. He addressed Andrew. "I've ordered a rush on these tests, and we should have them within a few days."

"Thank you," Andrew said, standing and shaking the doctor's hand. "I appreciate that."

Doctor Mulder gave him a tight smile and turned to Jennifer. "It was nice to meet you, Miss Gains."

Jennifer nodded but stayed seated for a few minutes as her knees felt slightly shaky when she looked at the vial of blood. She could never have been a doctor. Blood and gore made her queasy. When Caroline had cut her foot open at the beach when they were young, Jennifer had nearly passed out at the sight of the blood. She still couldn't remember how she'd managed to help Caroline get home.

"Molly asked if you'd say hello before leaving," Andrew drew Jennifer from her thoughts.

"I was going to pop in and say hello," Jennifer told him, pushing herself up from the chair and forcing her legs to work. "I hope you don't mind, but I got her a little something from the hotel gift shop last night."

She pulled a few books from a famous young adult fantasy author from her purse.

Andrew's brow rose, and a small smile lifted the one side of his mouth.

"I think you and I both know you didn't get *those* from the gift shop." Andrew pointed to the books. "Molly read that author's first book that came out last year and has been waiting on tenterhooks for the next two installments of the trilogy to come out." His eyes fell to the books. "Which are not due out for another two months."

Busted! Jennifer shrugged. "You're not the only one that does their homework." She walked past him and into the corridor.

"Thank you." Andrew's words were filled with emotion that chipped away a little of the ice around Jennifer's heart.

When they stepped into Molly's room, she was watching television with Georgia, sitting and knitting beside the bed. Molly's eyes lit up, and the television was turned off when she saw Jennifer.

"Jennifer, you came!" Molly held out her arms for a hug.

Jennifer swallowed at the sight of her half-sister. Molly was going through more than someone so young should have to go through, but still, she managed to smile. Jennifer hugged her.

"Of course," Jennifer said, sitting on the edge of Molly's bed as Andrew sat beside Georgia. "Hello, Georgia."

"Hello, it's so nice to see you." Georgia's eyes brimmed with warmth and shone with unshed tears.

Jennifer couldn't help it. As much as she tried to keep a wall up, her heart went out to Georgia.

"Where's Harley?" Molly asked Jennifer. "He said he'd visit when you were done with the testing." Her smile fell as she looked worriedly at Jennifer. "Are you okay?" Her hand reached out and covered Jennifer's comfortingly. "I'm sorry you had to go through that."

Jennifer looked at Molly, startled by the teen's words, and had to fight back the tears that stung the back of her eyes.

"I'm fine," Jennifer assured Molly and had to clear her throat as her voice sounded gruff. "Goodness, I'd do it again a million times if it would help you."

Molly threw her arms around Jennifer's neck and held her tightly.

"Thank you, Jennifer," Molly whispered.

Jennifer quickly wiped the stray tear that escaped from her cheek before Molly let her go and sat back against her cushions.

"Oh. A little birdy told me you loved to read." Jennifer's hand shook as she placed it in her purse.

"I do." Molly nodded, her eyes falling on Jennifer's purse.

"I believe one of your favorite genres is young adult fantasy." Jennifer teased.

"Oh, yes." Molly's eyes lit up again. "A new author has moved into my number one favorite spot."

"It wouldn't happen to be..." Jennifer pulled the two books from her bag. "Heather Marks?"

"No way!" Molly gaped at the books in Jennifer's hands. "Are those—"

"Book 2 and Book 3 in the Fire Bird trilogy?" Jennifer grinned, handing them to her.

"How did you—" Molly looked at the books and then Jennifer in amazement.

"I'm Heather Mark's new agent," Jennifer told Molly. "I asked her if I could give you an advanced copy, and she was delighted." She smiled. "Open them."

Molly opened book one and drew in a breath as she read, "*To Molly, a brave soul who shines like a beacon of strength in the face of adversity. I hope these pages offer you moments of escape, joy, and the belief that a good book can light up the world around you, even in the darkest times. With love and admiration, Heather Marks.*"

Jennifer turned when she heard Georgia sniff and found her wiping tears from her cheeks. Her eyes caught Andrew's, and he also had tears shining in his eyes.

"I hope you don't mind, but I told Heather that I thought my little sister was the bravest person I knew," Jennifer told Molly.

"No." Molly's eyes filled with tears as she stared at Jennifer. "I don't mind at all."

Molly reached over and hugged Jennifer again as a nurse walked into the room.

"Oh, I see you have a full house here today." The nurse smiled warmly as she picked up Molly's chart.

"Nurse Brenda, this is my sister, Jennifer," Molly introduced proudly.

"Hello, Jennifer," Nurse Brenda greeted her. "It's lovely to meet you." She glanced at the books on Molly's lap. "Is that the new Heather Marks?"

"Yes, Jennifer is her agent," Molly boasted. "Look, Heather wrote a note to me."

"Oh, my word, love." Nurse Brenda looked at the message. Her eyes were filled with warmth when they glanced at Jennifer. "What a lovely gift you've given your sister."

Jennifer swallowed, finding it more and more challenging to keep the tears at bay.

"I'm sorry, family, but I have to take Molly for her treatments," Nurse Brenda told them.

Jennifer stood, and Molly grabbed her hand. "Will you visit again before you return to Plum Island?"

"Yes, of course," Jennifer promised. "If your parents don't mind." She glanced at Andrew and Georgia. "I'd like to come back this evening."

"Of course," Georgia and Andrew said in unison.

"Yay." Molly allowed Nurse Brenda to secure her books in the drawer beside Molly's bed.

"I'd better be going," Jennifer said, instinctively kissing Molly's brow. "I'll see you this evening."

Jennifer had just left the room and was ordering a cab when Georgia's voice stopped her, "Jennifer, wait."

She finished ordering the car and turned to find Georgia hurrying toward her.

"Is everything okay?" Jennifer frowned.

"I just wanted to thank you for everything you've done for Molly," Georgia said. "I know it couldn't have been easy, Andrew showing up like he did and then finding out you had a sister."

"No, it wasn't," Jennifer agreed. "But my issues with your husband are not with Molly, and I'm glad I've met her." She swallowed and cleared her throat. "And I hope either Liam or me can help her with all my heart."

Georgia's eyes misted over, and the brave mask she'd been wearing slipped, making Jennifer's heart squeeze tighter for the woman whose eyes were filled with fear and anguish.

"Thank you." She reached out and squeezed Jennifer's hand as a few tears rolled down her cheeks.

"I know it's not the same, but I know it's not easy watching someone you love suffer while you wait for a miracle to happen." Jennifer's voice trembled with empathy and capped with resolve. "If either Liam or I turn out to be a match, we'll be here for Molly and do everything we can for our little sister."

Georgia's face crumpled as she let go of Jennifer's hand and pulled a tissue from her pocket to wipe her eyes. "That means a lot."

Her phone bleeped, and she looked at it to find her cab was there. "I have to go. My cab is here." Jennifer glanced at Georgia worriedly. "Are you okay?"

Georgia nodded. "I do this every day lately." She wiped her nose. "Take these little breakdown breaks, so I don't fall to pieces in front of Molly."

"You're a good mother, Georgia," Jennifer complimented. "I'll be back this evening. Can I bring you anything?"

"I'm fine," Georgia told her. "Andrew and I take shifts, so Molly's not alone at any time during the day."

"Andrew has my number if you want me to get anything for Molly or you on my way back here this evening." Jennifer's phone beeped again, and she sent a message. *On my way.*

"I will," Georgia told her. "I hope Harley can join you tonight. Molly has taken a shine to him."

Jennifer nodded and was about to turn and go when a thought struck her. "Georgia, can I ask you something?"

"Of course." Georgia nodded.

"Molly's been sick for a while now," Jennifer commented, and Georgia nodded in confirmation. "Why did Andrew come to us last if he knew one of us would be the most likely match?"

"Because of *that man*!" Georgia's words were laced with venom, and her eyes filled with anger, surprising Jennifer. "Even on his deathbed, he made our lives hell."

"What, man?" Jennifer asked, her brows creasing.

"Georgia?" Andrew's voice reached them, and Jennifer saw him walking toward them.

"Please, don't repeat what I just said," Georgia's voice was low, her eyes pleading.

Jennifer gave her a reassuring smile and nodded.

"Jennifer, why don't you let me give you a ride back to the hotel?" Andrew offered.

"No thanks," Jennifer's tone was once again clipped as she addressed him. "My cab's here. I was just asking Georgia if Molly needed anything I could bring with me this evening."

"You've given her the most wonderful gifts already," Andrew told her. "All she wants now is for you to visit."

Jennifer nodded and smiled at Georgia. "Bye. Tell Molly I'll be here by six."

With that, she turned and headed for her cab. When she returned to the hotel, there was still no sign of Harley, and the front desk said he hadn't yet returned.

Jennifer was feeling emotionally drained by the time she got to her suite. Meeting Molly had been such a joy, and Jennifer had instantly felt a bond with her. She was Jennifer's little sister, and she was ill. Why couldn't her family catch a break?

As she entered her room, she found a note on the floor. When Jennifer opened it, her heart skipped a beat when she saw it was from Harley, and he'd written the time in the top right-hand corner—*seven am*. Jennifer must have just missed him. Unable to sleep, as she felt like she was trying to swim in a turbulent sea of emotions, Jennifer had gone for a walk just before seven. After her walk, Jennifer hadn't returned to her suite. She'd gone straight to breakfast. She read the note:

Dear Jennifer

I'm sorry I won't be able to go with you for your tests. I have some urgent family business to take care of.

I'll make it up to you, I promise.

Harley x

"Is that a kiss?" Jennifer looked at the little x next to Harley's name and couldn't contain the fluttering it caused in her stomach. "Geez, Jennifer, what are you? Sixteen!"

Jennifer rolled her eyes as she walked into the suite, kicking off her shoes. She strode through the living room and into the bedroom, where she kicked off her shoes. She needed a shower to wash the hospital off her.

As she showered, she wondered who the evil man was that had Georgia react like she had. Jennifer made a mental note to ask Aunt Betty what she knew about Georgia's and Andrew's family. As far as Jennifer knew, Andrew's father was a judge, and his mother was a nurse or something.

While Aunt Betty never said anything, Jennifer and Liam always suspected she kept apprised of what was happening in Andrews's life. No matter what she told Andrew, Jennifer had never allowed herself to Google him or his family—it was her golden rule to herself. There was no point poking at an old wound, and while she didn't look, she could keep making herself believe she didn't care.

It was seven-thirty in the evening when Jennifer returned from the hospital after visiting Molly, and Harley was still not back. Jennifer was getting worried as she checked her phone for the millionth time, but Harley still hadn't called or messaged.

Jennifer thought about going to the dining room for dinner as she was hungry but decided to have room service instead. She'd just had a shower, put on a comfortable t-shirt and sweatpants, and was about to curl up in front of the television while waiting for her dinner to arrive.

Her eyes kept going to her laptop lying on the coffee table, and she itched to break her golden rule and dig into who the evil man Georgia referred to might be. She was about to give in and do an internet search when there was a knock on the door.

"Saved by room service!" Jennifer sighed, putting her laptop on the coffee table. "I'll take that as a sign the universe doesn't want me to pry."

But as she walked to the door, Jennifer knew that as soon as she'd gotten her dinner, she would get back onto her laptop. Jennifer needed to understand why Georgia had looked so angry and then terrified that Jennifer was going to say something to Andrew. She grabbed her wallet from her purse, yanked the door open, and froze.

A petite blonde woman with uncertain hazel eyes who was at least a head shorter than Jennifer's five-foot-nine stood staring at her. The woman's hair looked like it hadn't been brushed in days and had a few twigs stuck in it. The woman's face was smeared with dirt, as was her pale yellow sweats, blue t-shirt, and hoodie. The woman looked at Jennifer nervously, fidgeting with her hands.

"You're not room service." Jennifer said the first thing that popped into her head. "Are you lost?"

"I'm looking for Lee," the woman's voice was barely audible, and Jennifer had to strain to hear her.

"I'm sorry, but I don't know a Lee," Jennifer told her.

The elevator dinged, and the woman jumped in fright and shot behind Jennifer, nearly knocking her flying. Jennifer turned to see the woman cowering in fear. Her brow creased, and alarm bells rang in Jennifer's ears. Her attention was drawn away from the woman by the clatter of dishes drawing nearer.

"It's okay," Jennifer said, giving the woman a reassuring smile. "It's just room service."

The woman moved behind the door.

"Miss Gains," the server stopped at the door. "Your room service order." He looked into the suite. "May I set your dinner out on the dining table?"

"No." Jennifer shook her head, pulling a few bills from her wallet and handing them to the man. "I'll take it from here. Thank you."

"Okay!" The server looked at her, taking the money. "Thank you."

"No problem." Jennifer took the trolley and pulled it into her suite. "I'll leave it outside when I'm done."

She stepped back and closed the door, turning to see the woman eyeing out the trolley. Jennifer wasn't sure what to do and started questioning her sanity for letting the woman into the room. Well, she pushed her way into the room after being spooked by the elevator. The woman was terrified and, by the way, she was eyeing the food trolley, starving. Jennifer found herself in a bit of a dilemma, wondering if she'd just let an axe murderer into her room and chase away her only lifeline when she sent the server on his way.

Okay, Jennifer. Look for a weapon to keep handy and stay near to a phone. She turned her head. Her cell phone was on the coffee table next to her laptop. *Shoot.*

Jennifer's eyes narrowed as she looked at the woman, wondering who she was or who Lee was that the woman was looking for and why she'd knocked on Jennifer's door. An idea popped into Jennifer's head as she edged around the food trolley, careful not to turn her back on the wild woman.

"Are you hungry?" Jennifer asked.

"Yes." The woman nodded and looked at Jennifer, her eyes wide with excitement as she asked. "Do you have pie?"

"No." Jennifer shook her head, her frown deepening as the woman's face dropped.

"I love pie." She smiled. "Cherry pie. Lee always lets me have cherry pie."

Jennifer felt concerned as she observed a sudden shift in the woman's demeanor. It became apparent that the woman was struggling with emotional instability or possibly a mental health condition. One moment, she seemed timid like a frightened mouse, and the next, she became surprisingly enthusiastic, resembling an excited teenager at the mere mention of pie. The abrupt changes raised Jennifer's awareness, leaving her uncertain about how to navigate the situation.

"I can order a pie and see if the hotel has cherry," Jennifer found herself offering.

"Really?" the woman looked at Jennifer in awe. "With ice cream and grape soda?"

"Sure..." Jennifer gestured with her hands as she started wheeling the dinner trolley to the dining table. "Why don't you sit here? I'm sure there's more than enough for an army."

"Lee was in the army," the woman told her, taking a seat at the table, patiently waiting while Jennifer put the food out.

"Oh?" Jennifer glanced at the woman's ring finger. It was bare.

The woman dived into the food as soon as Jennifer had finished putting some lasagne and salad onto a plate for her before going to the small kitchenette and getting another dinner plate. She looked like she hadn't eaten in days the way she was wolfing the food down.

"Why did you think Lee was here with me?" Jennifer asked her, sliding into a seat around the table.

"You were with him last night," the woman said, polishing off her food. "May I have some more?"

"Sure." Jennifer dished up some more for her. "I wasn't with a Lee..." Her eyes widened in realization. "Do you mean Harley?"

"Yes." The woman smiled, and Jennifer nodded.

CHAPTER 12

The front living room of the Wesley family's Chestnut Hill residence was adorned with lavish and refined decor featuring plush antique furnishings. A magnificent chandelier hung from the ceiling, casting a warm and soothing glow over the polished wooden floor. The reflection of the light through the sparkling crystals surrounding it created a tranquil ambiance, which was in contrast to the inner turmoil of each person in the room.

Harley sat in a wingback chair as he watched his ex-wife Angela's father, Randal, pace back and forth on the far side of the room as he spoke to his good friend, the Boston Police Commissioner. Margaret Wesley sat primly on the edge of one of the sofas, nursing a glass of bourbon. While her eyes were shadowed with worry, she held her head high like a queen.

Angela used to put on her mother's voice and repeat Margaret's mantra in times of crisis: A lady keeps her composure no matter what.

Harley savored a sip of his smooth bourbon from the fancy crystal goblet. His gaze shifted towards the family wall the Wesleys had assembled, displaying a collection of ancestral portraits that spanned generations. When he saw the pictures of Daniel, his heart skipped a beat. Daniel had his own special place on the wall—his timeline with photos from when he was born until just a few days before his death. Harley took another sip of his drink, but his heart was gripped with pain as he gazed at the pictures of his late son.

"Thank you, Grant," Randal ended his conversation and went to sit beside Margaret.

"Well?" Wallis Hanover the second, Clair's husband, stopped his incessant pacing, downed his third glass of bourbon, and took a seat across from Harley. "Is there any news of them?"

"No." Randal put his phone on the coffee table and ran a hand through his hair, shifting his attention to Harley. "Thank you, Harley, for helping us. We'd never have found that motel."

"It's not me you should thank," Harley told them. "Uncle Sam's contacts helped me. Lucky for us, Clair isn't a master criminal and used a credit card to rent a car."

"Have the police found Clair's car?" Wallis asked Harley.

"Yes." Harley nodded.

"Oh. Where was Clair's car found?" Wallis put the empty glass on the coaster on the coffee table.

"At the Newbury Port Hospital," Harley told him, his eyes narrowing as he looked at Margaret and Randal. "Haven't you filled him in?"

"We haven't had the time," Margaret answered before Randal could.

Something in her eyes made Harley wonder if she'd deliberately withheld information from Wallis.

While Harley hadn't been the Wesleys' first choice of a husband for their precious daughter, they had always treated Harley as part of the family. Even when he and Angela divorced, they'd invited him to all the family events—even Angela's wedding when she married Wallis.

Not wanting Daniel to think Harley was against Angela remarrying, Harley had gone to the wedding. Randal had surprised him at the reception when he'd told Harley that he and Margaret were unhappy about Angela and Harley splitting up. They were even more unhappy about her marrying Wallis Hanover.

His eyes pinned the man who was a few feet shorter than Harley. While the man was fit, he was more slender than muscular. Wallis was quite the lady's man before he started having an affair with Harley's wife. His eyes narrowed, and he watched Wallis scan his phone again. The man oozed playboy charm that went hand in hand with his family's name and money.

Harley's eyes returned to the family portrait wall and noted that his and Angela's wedding photo was still on the wall. Angela and Wallis's wedding photo was missing from their family portrait wall. Harley suspected that Margaret must've taken it down when Wallis divorced Angela and married her twin sister, Clair—another picture that was missing from the wall.

Harley was drawn from his thoughts when the clock in the hallway chimed as it hit another hour. He glanced at his wristwatch. It was nine pm. It had been fourteen and a half hours since he'd gotten Margaret's call that morning. He'd barely answered when Margaret's voice, ringing with uncustomary urgency, told him that Angela and Clair were missing.

Harley's mind was clouded in confusion as he'd only gotten a few hours of sleep the night before. Harley had been tossing and turning as

Jennifer tormented his thoughts, and the feeling of her lips still tingled on his. When Margaret called at six-thirty that morning, he felt he'd only just closed his eyes, and for a few seconds, Harley thought he was dreaming.

Until another call came through while Margaret was on the phone, and Harley saw it was the Mental Health Institute that looked after Angela. He put a panicky Margaret on hold to answer the call.

The institute was also panicked as Clair had knocked out two of the guards with tranquilizer darts to get Angela out of the facility. When he ended the call to the institute, he was surprised to find Margaret still on the line.

The Wesleys were relieved to hear that Harley was in Boston and wanted him to go to Chestnut Hill immediately to help them. Randal had put a call into his police commissioner friend, Grant Nickle, who put out a bolo for Clair's car. Clair had left her car at the Newbury Port Hospital, a block from the institute. They had walked or taken a cab to the nearest car rental company.

While Clair had used a credit card to rent a car, she hadn't used one of hers—she'd used one of Angela's that Clair had taken out in her sister's name. Which wouldn't be too hard, considering they were identical twins. Harley's eyes went to the pictures of the sisters on the wall. He could tell the difference, and so could their parents.

Uncle Sam had managed to get those details from some of his old contacts from when he was a US Marshal. That's how Harley could track Clair and Angela to a motel on the outskirts of Boston. However, Harley had no idea why they'd go there. It was in the middle of an industrial area.

Another mystery was where Angela and Clair had gone for the day. They'd left the motel at ten that morning, and according to a retired US Marshal friend of Sam, who was watching the hotel, the women had yet to return.

Wallis's phone beeped again, which made Harley suspicious. The man certainly got a lot of text messages.

"Any news?" Harley asked Wallis.

Wallis's head shot up, and something Harley thought looked a lot like guilt flashed in his eyes before he shook his. "Oh, no, this is work."

"Wallis's father has retired," Randal told Harley. "And the man announced Wallis as his successor to taking over the family business."

The look of disdain Randal shot Wallis didn't go unnoticed by Harley, although Wallis didn't see it as he was too busy on his phone.

"We were shocked at the news," Margaret told Harley. "We thought for sure Shaun would give that title to his eldest and the far better option, Wallis's older sister, Shannon." She took a sip of her drink. "Shannon has always been the apple of Shaun's eye." She gave Wallis a disgusted look. "It's no wonder though, as brother and sister are like chalk and cheese."

Wallis looked up, unphased by their remarks. "My sister didn't want the company," he informed them. "All she wanted was some obscure business my father has." He waved it off.

Harley put his unfinished drink on a coaster on the coffee table.

"It's getting late." He glanced at his wristwatch again. "I'd better get back to the hotel and apologize to my friend for letting her down today."

"Her?" Margaret looked at Harley curiously. "Someone special?"

"Just a friend," Harley said casually while his heart screamed. *Jennifer is much more than a friend, or at least you want her to be.*

"And who is this friend?" Wallis was suddenly interested in their conversation.

"Not someone you'd be interested in," Harley assured him.

"I wasn't fishing for you to set me up on a date, Harley," Wallis drawled. "I was merely asking out of interest and concern that you've not had much of a love life since you've been burdened with Angela's mental illness."

"Excuse me?" Margaret's chest puffed up, and her eyes narrowed as she turned her icy glare on Wallis. "That's *our daughter* you're talking about."

"I meant no disrespect." Wallis held up his hands. "But Harley shouldn't be the one burdened with having to take care of her like he has been doing."

"You mean, unlike her husband, who divorced her the minute things got too much for him to handle?" Harley balled his fists at his side as the anger seeped through his system.

"As I explained," Wallis said unapologetically, "Angela and I were already in the middle of getting a divorce before she had her last breakdown." He raised his eyebrows as he added to divert the attention from him having cheated on Angela with her twin. "And need I remind you that the day the divorce came through, she attacked Clair and I." He pulled his shirt sleeve up to show the jagged scar. "With a butcher's knife."

Harley noted some blood stains on the cuff of Wallis's shirt. He'd noticed a few dots of blood on the man's collar earlier but had put it down to careless shaving. Wallis wasn't looking his perfectly groomed best at the moment and his face looked like a novice had shaved it.

"Not to mention poor Clair's hand." Wallis's eyes darkened, and he shook his head. "I couldn't believe Angela would come at us with a butcher knife."

Harley knew it was no joke what Angela had done when she'd snapped after finding out that Clair and Wallis were getting engaged, but what did they expect? They knew Angela was battling with the death of their son. Two weeks after Daniel passed away, Angela came down with the flu and started to wonder if she'd been the one to pass the flu on to Daniel.

Even though Harley, her parents, and more than one doctor had told her it couldn't have been her, the seeds of doubt had been sown in Angela's mind, which was the final straw. Angela had withdrawn into her shell. Harley had been staying at Angela's house while they waited for a place for her at the mental health clinic she'd been in and out of for the year after Daniel's death. Harley had left Angela in the care of their housekeeper to run errands. While he was out, Wallis and Clair visited Angela to tell her about their engagement.

Harley had returned to flashing lights from police cars and an ambulance. His first thought was that Angela had tried to take her life again, only to find her in handcuffs. She had blood all over her clothes, hands and face. It had been Wallis's blood. He'd gotten between Angela when she went for Clair with a butcher's knife. The housekeeper had heard Angela screaming *you did this*, and by the time she got into the kitchen, Wallis was bleeding. He was also holding a manic Angela, intent on harming Clair.

After that, Angela was never the same, and she pulled away from her family. While she'd speak to her mother and father on the phone, if you mentioned Clair or Wallis, Angela would have a manic attack. The only one Angela trusted was Harley, and even though he and Angela were no longer romantically involved, she'd been the mother of his child. They shared a parental bond and a deep connection forged from grief. Angela was as much a part of his family as his sister, niece, nephew, uncle, or cousin.

"Harley?" Margaret's voice snapped him from his thoughts. "Are you okay?"

"Tired," Harley confessed. "I didn't sleep well last night. I've gotten used to my bed at Sam's house."

"Please try to get some sleep," Randal advised as they walked Harley out, and a town car pulled up. "I've asked Duncan to take you to the hotel. He's at your service while you're in town."

"Thank you," Harley said, surprised when Margaret hugged him.

"No, thank you, Harley," Margaret said in a rare emotional moment. "For everything you've done for Angie and today."

"Of course." Harley smiled. "And don't worry, we'll find them."

Harley climbed into the car, and they were just pulling out of the driveway when his phone rang. Harley's heart skipped a beat when he saw it was Jennifer. He'd wanted nothing more than to call her all day, but he didn't know what to say. This wasn't something to discuss over the phone, as he didn't want Jennifer to get the wrong impression of his relationship with Angela. Harley also wanted to apologize for letting her down in person, not over the phone, as that didn't seem right.

"Hello," Harley answered. "I know you're angry and disappointed, and I let you down—"

"Harley—" Jennifer's voice sounded frantic. "Where are you?"

"I'm on my way to the hotel." Concern rushed through him.

"Can you turn around and get to the warehouse district on the outskirts of town?" Jennifer asked.

"The warehouse district!" Harley's brow knitted tighter together, and his heart thudded against his rib cage. "Where are you?"

"At the warehouse district," Jennifer told him. "I'm at Tons and Tons of Storage."

Harley's eyes widened in disbelief. "What are you doing there?"

"I can't explain, just get here," Jennifer pleaded before the phone went dead.

Fear, like nothing he'd felt before, coursed through him. He leaned over to the front. "Duncan, please take me to the warehouse district as quickly as possible."

Duncan nodded and turned the car around to head toward the other end of town. The drive seemed to take forever as scenarios played out in Harley's mind. He'd tried calling Jennifer, but her phone went to voicemail, and the text messages weren't delivered. Which made Harley even more frantic with worry. Not only was Jennifer in that part of town, but she was there without communication. Either the phone had died, or it had been taken from her.

While he knew Jennifer kept a charger in her car, Harley clung to option A as he didn't even want to contemplate option B. At last, the car pulled up outside Tons and Tons of Storage. It was a twenty-four-hour storage facility that rented out storage space, which Harley knew well as it was where he kept a storage space filled with Daniel's things. That was why he had a keycard to get in and wondered if it was just a coincidence that Jennifer used the same storage facility. But Harley didn't believe in coincidences, and a lousy feeling crept up his spine.

"Where to, sir?" Duncan glanced at Harley in the mirror as the gates slid open, and they drove in. "This is a large place to try to find someone."

As they passed the first and second aisles of the large garage spaces, that bad feeling intensified, and Harley instinctively knew where he was going to find Jennifer.

"Take the next right," Harley instructed Duncan. "Go down to the last garage on the right."

As they neared the storage space, Harley saw the light shining from his storage garage, and he knew that was where he would find Jennifer. He held his breath as he bolted from the car the minute it stopped and dashed into the storage space.

"Jennifer!" Harley barked.

He froze when he saw a white Ford sedan parked inside. Both front doors were open, and the smell of car fumes lingered in the air. Someone was in the passenger seat of the car. Harley swallowed as his heart thudded against his chest. He stood staring at the car for a few seconds. He drew in a breath and was about to walk toward the car when a voice stopped him.

"Harley!"

Harley turned toward the voice as Andrew Gains stepped into the garage.

"Andrew?" Harley frowned; his voice dropped, and the fear clawed at his throat as he asked. "Where's Jennifer?"

"Over here," Jennifer stepped out from behind Andrew, holding her stomach and looking green.

"Are you okay?" Harley asked, relief flooding him as he walked toward her, but Andrew stepped in front of him, blocking his path to Jennifer.

"I'm fine. I'm not good with blood, gore, or—" Jennifer told him but was cut off by Andrew.

"Where have you been all day, Harley?" Andrew asked him as the man observed Harley with shrewd eyes.

"I had some family business to take care of." Harley's frown deepened as he looked at Andrew suspiciously. "Why do I get the feeling you're..." His voice trailed off, and his eyes widened.

Fear once again coursed through his veins as he spun around, and before Andrew or Jennifer could stop him, he dashed to the car. Harley's heart seemed to stop beating for a few seconds as his breath caught in his throat when he saw the lifeless figure in the driver's seat. His heart kicked into gear again, hammering uncontrollably as his eyes scanned the familiar face and standard hospital-sweat pants and shirt.

"No, no, no!" Harley's voice was barely a whisper as he fell to his knees.

As Harley's head dipped into the car, his nostrils were assaulted by the smell of bleach. But he ignored it and was about to reach out to feel for a pulse and check the back of the figure's neck for a scar, but Andrew grabbed his hand.

"I wouldn't do that if I were you," Andrew warned him, glancing around the room. "I'm sure your fingerprints are all over this place, so you don't want to touch anything else here." He pulled Harley off the floor. "You especially don't want to touch the car or the body."

"I need to see which one of the—" Harley swallowed, unable to fathom the thought.

"It's Clair," Andrew told him, his voice low and compassionate.

"Are you sure?" Harley looked at Andrew questioningly. "You can tell the difference when they are awake and talking." His head turned back to the woman in the car. "But when they're sleeping, it's more difficult."

"Harley, it's Clair." Jennifer stepped around Andrew, taking Harley's hand and pulling him away from the car. "Please do as Andrew says and move away from the crime scene."

"How can you be so sure it's Clair?" Harley's mind was reeling, his thoughts scattered, as his brain tried to make sense of it all.

"Because Angela is with Andrew's mother," Jennifer said, surprising Harley.

"How did Angela end up at Andrew's mother's place?" Harley asked, confused.

"It's a long story," Jennifer told him, turning as they heard footsteps.

Harley glanced around and saw a bottle of open bleach standing near the back wheel of the driver's door. "Were you cleaning over here?" He looked from Andrew to Jennifer.

They both shook their heads.

"No, that was there when we came in," Andrew assured Harley.

Before he could ask more questions, they were interrupted by the sound of footsteps and a voice.

"Mr. Donovan is everything all…" Duncan stopped at the garage door, his eyes widening as he took in the scene. "Is that?" He pointed at the car. "Are they…"

"Who are you?" Jennifer eyed Duncan suspiciously.

"It's Duncan," Andrew answered her question. "He drives for the Wesley family."

Before Jennifer could reply, the sound of sirens split the quiet night, and within a few minutes, they'd pulled up in front of the garage, lighting up the area with flashing lights. Medics rushed in, skirting around the two police officers who climbed out of the car. The next few minutes were a blur of questions, more police officers arriving, along with two US Marshals whom Sam had gotten to help search for Angela and Clair.

The atmosphere in the storage garage grew taut as the police meticulously combed through the scene, their focused expressions etched with determination. Harley stood watching the ME, who was carefully examining Clair. Her focus shifted from the body to items in and around the vehicle.

Jennifer stood by Harley's side, their hands clasped as they and Andrew watched the investigation unfold.

"Are you okay?" Jennifer whispered to him.

He turned and gave her a tight smile, grateful that Jennifer was by his side even though he knew her stomach was roiling, and she tried not to look at Clair's body. He'd noted Jennifer keenly observing what each part of the forensic team that had gotten there surprisingly quickly was doing.

"I know this is disturbing for you," Harley's voice was as low as hers. "But I'm glad you're here by my side."

Jennifer gave him a small smile and drew closer to his side. "Harley, I want you to know that the thought you may have done this never crossed my mind. I'm sorry Andrew went at you like he did."

"Andrew was only protecting you and surprised me with that question to see how I'd react," Harley explained. "It was a tactic."

"It was a horrible tactic," Jennifer hissed, her eyes flashing angrily. "He didn't even warn me he would attack you with it. In fact, he never even hinted at thinking you did this."

"Andrew is one of the top defense attorneys in the state," Harley reminded her. "I think with that one question, he was able to ascertain my innocence."

"I hope so." Jennifer tilted her head to where Andrew was standing with the two US Marshals. "I take it the older of the two Marshals is Sam's friend?"

"Yes, Sam trained the man," Harley told her. "I can't believe this is happening."

His eyes scanned the boxes that had been neatly stacked and were now being searched through by forensics. Harley swallowed and turned away as a sea of emotions washed over him, seeing strangers paw through Daniel's belongings.

"This is a big storage space," Jennifer commented.

"It used to have all Angela's furniture from her house in it," Harley explained. "When she asked me to sell all her things and donate the money to the children's ward, I didn't downgrade it."

"Harley!" Randal Wesley's voice interrupted their conversation.

He turned to see the man standing behind the police line with Margaret and Wallis.

"Are those Clair and Angela's parents?" Jennifer asked.

"Yes, and the man in the clean outfit is Wallis Hanover," Harley told her. "Angela's second ex-husband and now Clair's widower."

Jennifer frowned. "Oh, he divorced Angela and married Clair?"

"Yes." Harley nodded. "He'd been having an affair with Clair for about a year."

"What a jerk!" Jennifer eyed Wallis with disdain.

"Harley!" Randal called again, indicating for him to go there.

"Excuse me." Harley reluctantly let go of Jennifer's hand, but before he walked away, Jennifer stopped him.

"Harley, wait!" Jennifer stepped around him so her back faced the Wesley's. "You can't tell anyone where Angela is, not even her parents."

Harley frowned. "They need to know Angela is okay. They've just lost one daughter."

"Please, Harley." Jennifer placed a hand on his arm. Even in an emotional time like this, her touch affected him. "I made a promise to Angela."

"You still haven't told me how the two of you met," Harley reminded Jennifer.

"I'll explain later," Jennifer promised.

Harley's eyes searched hers, and what he saw in them made him fall even more in love with her—his heart jolted, and his throat went dry as realization dawned on him. Harley stared at her for a few seconds, hoping his eyes didn't mirror his thoughts or feelings. Now was the most inappropriate time for him to realize his deep feelings for Jennifer.

Not trusting his voice or what would pop out of his mouth, Harley nodded in agreement, and she moved out of his way. He made his way over to Margaret, Randal, and Wallis.

"Change of wardrobe, Wallis?" Harley noted.

"I was all sweaty from worry," Wallis told him. His shadowed eyes kept darting toward the car.

"Is that really Clair?" Wallis asked, moving the subject away from his wardrobe change. He was looking toward the car. His voice was gruff, and his eyes shone with grief. "Are they sure it's Clair?" He glanced at Harley for clarification. "Did you check? Are you sure it's not Angela?"

Harley looked toward Margaret and Randal, who were looking to him for the same confirmation Wallis was seeking. "I'm so sorry." He nodded, his heart going out to them. "It's Clair."

"No!" Wallis said breathlessly. "It can't be Clair." His eyes were glued to the car where the medics were gently lifting Clair's body. "Look!" He patted Harley's arm and pointed toward the body. "That's not Clair. That's the sweat suit from the mental health institute Angela is at." He shook his head vigorously. "It's not Clair."

Before Harley could respond, the older US Marshals stepped to one side of the room, but close enough that Harley, the Wesleys, and Wallis could hear him even though he wasn't talking loudly.

"The ME is convinced that it's not suicide but was staged to look like Clair had committed suicide," the Marshal said into the phone. "There was a suicide note found on the floor beneath the driver's seat. The ME thinks it slid there when the victim put up a fight against whoever was trying to get her into the car. There was also an open water bottle near the car, and the victim's shirt was wet. Which could mean she was drugged, and that is how the murderer eventually managed to subdue her." The man paused. "Yes. The ME says it looks like she managed to scratch whoever did this to her. She'll get the skin cells from beneath the nails when she's back in the lab."

"No!" Wallis yelled, pushing past Harley and the officers holding him back. He rushed toward Clair, who the medics were about to zip into a body bag. "I need to know!"

"Sir, you can't go there," one of the officers yelled at Wallis and started to rush after him, but Andrew stopped the man.

"Let him see her. It's his wife," Andrew told the officers.

While the police were distracted by the commotion, Randal and Marget saw an opportunity to follow Wallis. Harley went after them. When they got to where Clair's body was on a gurney, the medics were desperately trying to stop Wallis, who was standing on the car side of the gurney, from turning the body over.

"I have to prove it's not Clair!" Wallis shouted at the medics.

Wallis's eyes grew wild with determination. He pulled Clair's body toward him. It teetered at the edge of the gurney. "I'll prove to you all this is *not* Clair. It can't be!"

Wallis pulled the long strands of blond hair away from Clair's neck.

A sorrowful cry escaped through his lips when he found the scar behind her ear from a horse riding accident. "No, oh oh oh."

Wallis pulled Clair's body toward him and rolled off the gurney. Wallis grabbed her just in time but kicked over the bleach, slipped, and landed on the floor on his rump, cradling Clair on his lap. Sobs racked Wallis's body as he sat rocking back and forth with Clair clutched tightly in his arms.

"Clair!" Margaret's voice broke. She and Randal were about to move toward Wallis and Clair when the ME's voice split through the air like a gunshot.

"NO!" The ME shouted when she heard the commotion and pushed through the people gaping down at Wallis. "NO!" She growled again, jumping into action. "Quick." She instructed the Medics. "Get her hands and ensure they don't touch the bleach."

But it was too late. Clair's arms and hands had spread into the pool of bleach Wallis was sitting in. The medics managed to pry Clair from Wallis.

"Get him examined for chemical burns," the ME snapped, her eyes filled with anger as they fell on Wallis. Harley could see she was trying to contain it, but her tone was clipped as she addressed the family and Wallis. "My condolences to all of you. I know this is a difficult time for you. But I ask that you please follow the police officer's instructions and allow me to do my job." She glanced at Wallis and Clair's family. "If you would please go back behind the police line." Her eyes fell on Wallis. "A medic will examine you for any chemical burns."

Randal, Margaret, and Wallis followed the police officer while the ME called one of the forensic teams over. "Why was this left here?" She pointed to the bottle of bleach.

"We were waiting for you to finish before we took it away," the forensic officer told her.

"You could've at least put the cap back on," The ME snapped. "Get this mess cleaned up." With that, she stormed out, commanding an officer to get someone to collect everyone at the scene's DNA. "Not that it probably matters now." She muttered.

"Wow!" Jennifer gave a low whistle, stepping next to Harley. "She's fun."

Harley's eyes were fixed on the bleach as a thought kept tumbling over and over in his mind—*Why was Wallis so convinced it couldn't have been Clair's body?* His brow furrowed as a conversation from years ago drifted through his mind.

"I've been married to Angela for two years," Wallis said before joking, "and I still don't know how you can tell the twin sisters apart just by looking at them. I still have to check there's no scar behind Angela's ear to ensure I'm with the correct sister."

But what if Wallis hadn't been joking? Harley's mind brought up images of the blood stains on Wallis's collar. What if they weren't from a botched shaving job? His brow creased as he remembered there were also blotches of blood on Wallis's shirt cuff. Harley pictured the gurney and where it was positioned. Wallis had stood near the car when he could've just stood at the top of the gurney where Clair's head was.

Harley's eyes widened. *Did Wallis do this?* Bleach was an excellent way to taint evidence. He gave himself a mental shake. Harley was being paranoid. No one was as good an actor as how Wallis had reacted to finding out it was Clair. Harley had seen that same look of desperation, denial, and devastation in Angela's eyes when Daniel passed away. He'd seen it in his own eyes every time Harley had looked in a mirror for years after Daniel's death, and it reappeared each year on Daniel's birthday or when thoughts of his son crossed his mind.

"Harley?" Jennifer's soft, concerned voice broke through his thoughts, and her hand curled around his forearm. "Maybe we should go?"

"I'm sorry you and Andrew have been dragged into this," Harley's voice was gruff as he suddenly felt exhausted. However, there was still the matter of Angela to attend to. His hand covered Jennifer, and he stepped closer to her. "I know this is selfish of me. But I'm so glad you're here."

"I wouldn't be anywhere else," Jennifer assured him, their eyes locking.

The chaos around them started fading as they got lost in each other's eyes. A detective approached them just as he was about to reach and touch her face. The man had his cell phone in his hand. Harley and Jennifer turned toward him, their hands clasping.

"Mr. Donovan?" The police officer addressed Harley. "Can you confirm this is your storage garage?"

Before Harley could answer, Andrew stepped up beside them. "I'm sorry, but I'm going to have to ask my client to refrain from answering any questions."

Harley and Jennifer looked at Andrew in confusion.

"Very well," the detective said, holding up his phone and hitting play. "Mr. Donovan, in light of this video, I'm going to have to ask you to come to the police station for questioning."

Harley's brow furrowed in confusion until the detective hit play, and Harley's eyes widened in shock. He remembered that day clearly. It was near the first end of the first quarter of the year. Harley had been called to the mental health institute because Clair was demanding to see Angela. The footage showed Harley and Clair in a heated argument. His words seemed to echo through the garage.

"You won't like the consequences if you come back here without informing me first," Harley growled at her. "And don't think I don't know what you did!"

CHAPTER 13

"**W**hat just happened?" Jennifer stood blinking stupidly as she watched Harley being driven away in the back of a police car. She whirled and glared at Andrew. "Why did you let the police take Harley?"

"He's not under arrest, Miss Gains," the older US Marshal assured her.

"I'm going to meet Harley at the police station," Andrew assured her.

"Andrew?" Randal Wesley walked up to them. "Why on earth are the police taking Harley away?"

"How could they even think Harley would do this?" Margaret joined her husband.

"Because he threatened Clair," Wallis sneered as he joined them.

"You mean that petty argument you sent everyone?" Margaret turned and glared at Wallis, who looked at her in surprise. "Yes, I know it was you, Wallis."

"You should learn to edit your videos," Randal advised him. "Your class ring was showing at the end of the video."

"*You* sent that video of Harley and Clair arguing?" Jennifer's eyes narrowed on the man.

Her eyes assessed him. Wallis was a moderately good-looking man. He was about five-ten to five-eleven with sandy blond hair, brown eyes, and all the telltale signs of wealth about him, from his expensive clothes to his wristwatch that cost more than most average people made in a year or two. Jennifer couldn't see why someone like Angela would cheat on Harley with the man.

"Who are you?" Wallis looked at her down his nose.

"You must be Harley's friend?" Margaret guessed, holding out her perfectly manicured hand. "I'm Margaret Wesley, and this is my husband, Randal."

"Jennifer." She shook Margaret and then Randal's hand. "I'm very sorry about your loss."

"Thank you," Randal said before addressing Andrew. "The police took Harley in over that silly video Wallis sent them?"

"He was caught on camera threatening Clair," Andrew pointed out. "Right now, that's the police's biggest lead, so they would take him in for questioning."

"But you're going to help him, right?" Jennifer looked at Andrew.

"Of course, Jen," Andrew's voice dropped, and her nickname slipped from his lips. "I promised you I'd help."

"But you're also helping because you know Harley is innocent, right?" Jennifer looked at him questioningly.

"Yes, I believe he is innocent," Andrew assured her. "We'd better go if I'm still going to drop you off on my way."

"On your way?" Margaret frowned, looking from Jennifer to Andrew before her eyes widened. "Goodness." She put her hand to her throat. "Are you little Jenny Gains?"

"Not so little anymore, and I go by Jennifer," Jennifer gave Margaret a tight smile.

"Yes, I see it now," Randal said with a nod, looking at Jennifer. "You look just like your mother."

"Gains?" Wallis's brow crinkled before it dawned on him. "You're Andrew's eldest daughter?"

"We really have to go," Andrew broke up the conversation before once again giving his condolences to Clair's family. "I'm terribly sorry for your loss."

"Thank you," Margaret and Randal said in unison.

"Andrew, please keep us apprised of the situation with Harley," Margaret told him. "He was with us most of the day. There's no way Harley was responsible for this."

"I don't know, Margaret," Wallis said. "You know how he despised Clair."

"Oh, be quiet, Wallis," Margaret hissed at the man. "I'd suspect you of this long before thinking it was Harley."

Jennifer caught a flash of something in Wallis's eyes at Margaret's words and suppressed a shudder. There was something dark about the man. On the outside, he appeared to be grieving, but there was no depth to his grief. Even when he was putting on that magnificent display while tragically clutching Clair in his arms, Jennifer had thought it looked a bit staged.

Jennifer made a mental note to look into Wallis Hanover. Something about the man felt off to her. For a grieving widower, Wallis had gone from wailing distraughtly to cool and haughty in zero seconds.

"Let's go." Andrew steered Jennifer out of the garage, and they headed for his town car, seemingly appearing from nowhere.

"Wasn't that rude in your circles?" Jennifer asked as they slid into the back of the luxury car.

"I needed to get you out there before the police questioned you," Andrew told her.

"I don't have anything to hide," Jennifer pointed out.

"Only Angela!" Andrew reminded her. "Until we've found the evidence Angela said Clair hid, I prefer you stay on the sidelines for as long as possible."

"Isn't that some sort of aiding and abetting?" Jennifer asked.

"No." Andrew shook his head. "Right now, no one's questioned you or asked about Angela, but they will right after they've interrogated Harley."

"Why didn't the police ask what I was doing there?" Jennifer asked Andrew.

"I told them you were with me, and I was there to help Harley," Andrew answered.

"When did you call emergency services?" Jennifer hadn't seen him make the call.

"I didn't," Andrew shook his head. "I thought you did."

Andrew's brow knitted into a deep frown. "That's disturbing." He rubbed his chin thoughtfully, a gesture that Jennifer remembered well.

"What about your driver?" Jennifer suggested.

"No, James wouldn't do that unless I asked him to," Andrew assured her, pulling out his phone. "I'll ask Sam to find out where the call came from." He scrolled to Sam's number. "I need to tell him that Harley's been taken into custody."

"You've been talking to Sam?" Jennifer looked at him in surprise. "Harley's uncle?"

"Yes." Andrew nodded, hitting the dial and speaker when Sam answered.

"Andrew!" Sam answered despite it being almost three in the morning. "What's going on? I got a message from David, the US Marshal that was there with you. He tells me the police took Harley in because of a video?"

"Hello, Sam," Jennifer greeted him, letting him know she was there.

"Hello, Jen. How are you holding up?" Sam asked.

"I'll be better when Harley's been released," Jennifer told him. "Wallis Moron sent the police an anonymous video of Harley arguing with the victim."

"They took him in over an argument?" Sam asked, surprised. "If that's all they have to go on, they'll try and manipulate Harley into confessing."

"He threatened Clair in the video," Andrew told him.

"Threatened her how?" Sam asked. "Harley and Clair were always arguing. That woman had an agenda, and Harley suspected it wasn't good. Clair was trying to get control of Angela's care and estate."

"You're talking about guardianship and conservatorship of the estate due to Angela's incapacitated mental state?" Andrew's eyes narrowed thoughtfully. "Who *does* control them?"

"Harley," Sam told Andrew.

Jennifer saw Andrew nod as he stared at the phone. "Is there any proof that Clair has been trying to get control?"

"Yes." Sam was quiet for a few seconds. "Harley has gotten numerous letters, and about eight or ten months ago, Clair went to the Newbury Port Mental Health Facility with documents she wanted the facility to sign."

"What documents?" Andrew's eyes met Jennifer's.

"It was a petition to have Harley removed as guardian as he wasn't immediate family, and Clair felt that he was keeping Angela unnecessarily," Sam told them. "According to Clair, she'd had Angela assessed by a psychiatrist who'd gained access to the facility as a family friend to see Angela."

"Doesn't Angela have a strict visitors' policy?" Andrew's deep frown was back.

"Yes," Sam confirmed. "Apparently, Harley approved the visit."

"Did Harley know the man?" Jennifer asked.

"No," Sam said. "Harley also didn't approve the visit. His signature had been forged. Harley was in California on the day the visit was approved, and the doctor visited."

"Can he prove that?" Jennifer asked before Andrew could.

"I'm pretty sure," Sam said, his voice confident. "He was in Coronado."

"Coronado?" Jennifer's face scratched up in confusion.

"Naval Special Warfare Basic Training Command," Sam told them. "I'm sure they'll corroborate his whereabouts."

"Well, no one's going to doubt the Navy, are they?" Jennifer stated, her heart thudding as new hope flowed through her.

Andrew rubbed his chin once again. "Surely the institute has strict measures to prevent things like that?"

"I guess it was done the same way Clair got Angela out of the facility," Sam pointed out. "Clair has someone on the inside."

"Sam—" Andrew started to ask a favor when Sam cut him off.

"Check into any connections between Clair and staff at the institute?" Sam guessed. "I've already got someone on it."

"Great!" Jennifer sighed in relief, and a thought hit her. "Wait! Do you think that was the argument that Clair and Harley had and that Wallis recorded?

"We'd need to get the time stamp from the video," Andrew told them.

"Send it to me," Sam suggested. "I can get that information."

"Sure," Andrew agreed. "I'll send it as soon as we hang up."

"I wish I was there and could help more," Sam said frustratedly. "This darn back injury!"

"Take it easy, Sam," Jennifer advised. "You're doing a lot by using your vast tapestry of connections."

"Andrew, will you represent Harley?" Sam asked.

"He already is," Jennifer felt a moment of pride for Andrew.

"Look after him," Sam warned.

"You know I will, Sam," Andrew stated.

They said goodbye and hung up. When Jennifer looked up, she was surprised they'd pulled into the Gain's Chestnut Hill residence.

"Is your mother still going to be awake?" Jennifer asked, sliding out of the car and looking at the stately home.

A memory from her childhood flashed through her mind as they stepped inside the foyer with its elegant chandelier that greeted guests with its sparkling light that glinted off the polished tiled floors. Jennifer could remember feeling intimidated, the same feeling that had hit her the minute she'd stepped inside. She squashed the memories and refused to feel slighted by a house.

"I hope Angela's okay in this mausoleum," Jennifer drawled.

"Angela's asleep in a guest bedroom," the firm female voice addressed them.

Jennifer turned to see an elegant older woman standing in the doorway of a room resembling a home office.

"Hello, Jennifer." The woman's eyes warmed, and a smile split her lips. "Welcome, ho..." She stopped herself. "Welcome."

"And you are?" Jennifer's eyes narrowed.

She knew she was being rude, especially after the Gains family had helped her with no questions asked. But Jennifer still harbored a lot of anger toward them. Anger that spewed out in the form of barbs or rudeness that Aunt Betty would not have approved of. But Aunt Betty wasn't there to keep Jennifer's anger and retaliation in check.

"Jennifer, this is my mother, your gra..." Andrew's voice dropped off. "My mother, Davina."

"Wow!" Jennifer's brows shot up, and before she could stop it, her brain loaded the barbed arrow and shot it through her lips. "I guess one good thing from your side of the family is the excellent genes. You don't look like you're pushing a hundred."

"Thank you," Davina said, raising an eyebrow to let Jennifer know she knew it wasn't meant as a compliment. "I turn ninety-five in

November. My side of the family and Andrew's father's family tend to age more gracefully than most."

"Would you like something to drink or eat, Jennifer?" Andrew steered the conversation to a more neutral ground.

"No, thank you," Jennifer turned down the offer. "I was hoping to take Angela back to the hotel with me."

"I wouldn't advise that," Davina told her, steering them into the front living room.

It was a large room with modern decor and plush cream furniture that was complemented by heavy cream drapes woven with soft hues of rose, gold, and light green.

"Please take a seat." Davina sat in a large armchair that looked like it was made for a giant.

Jennifer sat in the second giant armchair, which was as comfortable as it looked.

"Don't be mad at me," Andrew said, sitting on the sofa between the armchairs. "But I took the liberty of having yours and Harley's things moved from the hotel here."

"You did what?" Jennifer spluttered in disbelief before anger streaked through her. "That was taking liberties."

"I was the one that suggested Andrew have you and Harley moved here." Davina's tone of voice brooked no argument. "Not only is it safer from a murderer, but Andrew can protect you from the police and press."

"Press?" Jennifer's brows knit. She hadn't thought about that.

"Oh, yes!" Davina nodded. "The Wesleys are a high-profile family. This is going to be a media frenzy when news gets out."

"I'd be surprised if it hadn't already," Andrew said, standing. "Sorry, I have to get to the police station."

"Can I come with you?" Jennifer stood with him.

Okay, so the house and Davina were intimidating! Jennifer didn't want to be left here on her own.

"It's best if you don't," Andrew told her encouragingly. "It's going to be alright. I promise you."

"You'll keep me updated?" Jennifer made Andrew promise. When she walked him to the front door, she asked. "What about Georgia?"

"I've updated her," Andrew told Jennifer. He opened the front door and turned toward her. "Oh, your car is in the garage, and later on this morning, Paul Holland will be here to see you."

"Who is Paul Holland, and why is he coming to see me?" Jennifer's head dipped back as she looked at him questioningly.

"He's the second-best defense attorney at Gains Law," Davina answered for Andrew.

"I don't need an attorney. And why do I get the second-best attorney?" Jennifer didn't know why, but that hurt, and she felt slighted. *Shouldn't I have the best attorney from Gains Law?*

"I can't defend both of you," Andrew answered her question, winking at her, before slipping through the door and gently pulling it closed behind him.

Jennifer suddenly felt cold and alone in the mausoleum with a strange old lady.

"Can I show you to your room?" Davina asked as Jennifer turned awkwardly toward her.

"Sure," Jennifer said, nodding.

While she followed Davina up the sweeping staircase that reminded Jennifer of something out of *Gone with the Wind*, her mind ticked over making plans.

"Here you are," Davina opened the door, and Jennifer stepped into a suite that, except for a kitchenette, rivaled the one she was in at the Langham. "I've put you next to Angela, and when Harley gets here, he'll be in the room on the opposite side of the hall to you."

"It's lovely," Jennifer grudgingly admitted. "All I need now is good room service."

Davina pointed to a phone beside the bed. "Star-one will get you to the kitchen."

Jennifer gaped at Davina. "You're joking?"

"No." Davina shook her head. "My late husband liked his luxuries."

"Clearly!" Jennifer said snidely as she walked further into the room.

"While you're here—" Davina stood in the doorway. "I was hoping you and I could get to know each other." She folded her hands in front of her, reminding Jennifer of a proper lady of the manor. "I'm sure you have a million questions."

Jennifer stopped, looked around the room, and looked at Davina before pursing her lips and shaking her head. "No," she denied. "Your family's absence and silence over the past forty years answered any questions my brother or I had."

Davina's mask slipped for a split second as she flinched like Jennifer had slapped her before she regained her composure.

"Fair enough." Davina put her hand on the door handle. "I'll leave you to get some sleep. Breakfast is from six to nine."

"Wow! It really is like a hotel!" Jennifer nodded.

"Goodnight, Jennifer." Davina backed out of the room and closed the door as she disappeared.

Jennifer flopped onto the amazingly comfortable king-sized bed with a white divan with lemon swirls that picked up the soft touches of lemon hues in the silver drapes and cream walls.

"The Gains family love cream," Jennifer noted.

Her eyes spotted her laptop case on the oak desk against the wall near a door that looked like it led to the bathroom. She got up and walked over to the door. Popping her head in, her eyes widened. There was a sizable dressing room on the one side and a bathroom she wanted to live in on the other side.

"Okay, Jennifer, don't get seduced by all the opulence!" Jennifer gave herself a stern talking-to. "So what if the sunken tub has jets, and the shower probably has settings ranging from a gentle rainfall to a powerful water massage." She drew in a breath and turned to her laptop. "Nope. I'm not falling for it."

Jennifer grabbed her laptop and took it to the bed. Kicking off her shoes, she bounced onto the mattress that she imagined a cloud must feel like. Jennifer pulled her laptop out of the bag and set it up when she heard a gentle whirring noise. Her head shot around the room and landed on the closet near the windows. She tilted her head as she studied it. It had two doors—top and bottom.

Jennifer bounced off the bed and walked over to it, her feet sinking into the soft carpet. She pulled the bottom door open first. Her brows shot up—it was a small refrigerator stocked with beverages, including small bottles of different types of milk, sparkling, and still water."

"Huh!" Jennifer snorted. "Look at that."

She looked at the closet above it. There was a small button in the middle near the bottom of it. Jennifer grinned, thinking how she'd always wanted to climb into the pages and tell the character *not* to push the freakin' button in the books she'd read that had mysterious buttons. Jennifer had always thought it was a little unrealistic that the character always pushed the mysterious button.

Now she knew it wasn't unrealistic because she really wanted to push the mysterious button, especially as the closet had no other handles on it. She laughed as she reached and pushed it, bracing herself in case she was transported to Narnia or some other land through a mysterious closet. It shot up, making Jennifer give a soft yelp and jump back as it opened to reveal four shelves. On the bottom shelf was a fancy coffee maker like the one Jules had mentioned she wanted to get for Caroline. Next to it was an electric kettle and a teapot. An assortment of coffees, teas, hot chocolate, and sweeteners was on the shelf above. Above that were cups, saucers, and a bowl of spoons.

"I wonder if I can sneak the coffee maker into my suitcase?" Jennifer laughed, sighing. "Good grief. I'd never want to leave my room if I lived here."

Jennifer wondered what Molly's room looked like as she remembered Molly telling her they lived with her grandmother now that she was alone. While Jennifer didn't pry, she took that to mean Molly's grandfather had either passed away or was in a home.

She toyed with the idea of making a hot chocolate but took a bottle of water instead. She figured out how to close the closet. As it turned out, she had to push the button again. The door closed slower than it shot open.

"Just as well," Jennifer said, watching the door click into place. "If it closed as fast as it opened, it could probably do some damage."

She walked back to the bed and couldn't help it. She jumped and plopped down as if she was falling onto a cloud and nearly bounced her laptop onto the floor. Jennifer sighed, sat up, opened the water, and took a few sips before putting it on the nightstand and pulling her laptop toward her.

"Time to do some research into the Wesley and Hanover families." Jennifer's fingers flew over the keyboard.

Before long, she was digging through all the information she could find on the two families. Jennifer jotted down a few notes of information she wondered if Sam could get for her. Jennifer didn't want Andrew to know that she was doing her own investigation. While Jennifer had told Andrew a general overview of what Angela had told her, Jennifer had withheld some key facts as she still didn't trust him.

"Jenny!" Warm breath tickled the side of Jennifer's cheek. "Jenny, Jenny, Jenny."

Jennifer swatted at her cheek and slowly opened her eyes as someone called her name repeatedly. She yawned and stretched, shooting into a sitting position when her foot hit something soft and warm.

"I'm so glad you're awake!" Angela sat stretched out on the bed next to Jennifer. "Thank you for coming back."

"What time is it?" Jennifer rubbed her eyes.

"I don't know." Angela frowned. "But the sun's coming up."

Jennifer turned her head and saw the day was breaking through the night. She glanced at her wristwatch—ten minutes past six.

"Let me guess!" Jennifer pushed herself into a sitting position and saw her laptop still open on the bed. Her notebook had fallen on the floor.

"I'm sorry." Angela jumped off the bed and picked up the notebook. "I might have knocked it off." Her eyes widened as she saw something on the page. "I can give you my address." She handed the book to Jennifer. "I don't live there anymore. My sister and that—" Her eyes flashed with fear. "—that horrible man live there."

"Angela is the horrible man Wallis?" Jennifer asked.

Angela's eyes widened in surprise. "No, not Wallis." She shook her head. "But he's not a nice person either." She scrambled onto the bed

273

and grabbed onto Jennifer like a frightened child. "I think he tried to make my sister do bad things."

"Bad things like what you told me last night?" Jennifer asked.

Angela nodded. "Yes." Her eyes locked with Jennifer's. "Jenny, you can't go there."

"Go where?" Jennifer asked her.

"To that house!" Angela said

Angela's fear deepened and started darkening into panic, sending alarm bells off in Jennifer's head. She'd found out where they led to the previous night, which was one reason she'd called Andrew for help. Jennifer had needed legal and medical help, which she was sure he'd be able to help with.

"It's okay, Angie!" Jennifer soothed, putting her arm around Angela's shaking shoulders. "Why don't we go have breakfast?"

Angela's shoulder relaxed as she drew away from Jennifer. "Do you think there'll be pancakes?"

"If not, I'm sure they'll make you some," Jennifer told her, closing the notebook and her laptop before sliding off the bed. "Let's get dressed and see what they have in the dining room."

"I don't have clothes!" Angela slid off the bed and looked at the pajamas she had on. "Davina lent me these last night."

"You're shorter than I am," Jennifer walked into the dressing room where she'd seen her clothes had been unpacked and slid through the few summer dresses she'd packed. "How about a dress with pink roses on?"

Jennifer held up the dress.

"That's so pretty," Angela sighed, walking toward Jennifer and taking the dress. "I haven't worn a dress in years."

Jennifer's brows shot up as she saw Angela's demeanor change from youthful innocence to mature adult when she held the dress against herself and looked in the full-length mirror.

"Angela?" Jennifer's voice was soft so as not to startle her.

Angela turned toward Jennifer. The pain, anguish, and torment that filled her eyes made Jennifer's breath catch in her throat as her heart swelled for the woman before her.

"I remember!" Angela murmured, her eyes filling with tears as she turned and looked at Jennifer. "Jennifer, I remember everything!" She sucked in a few shaky breaths as her eyes filled with tears that rolled down her cheeks. "Oh no, Clair!"

The dress fell onto the floor a few seconds before Angela collapsed bedside it, holding her stomach with one hand and the other covering her mouth.

"Angela." Jennifer scrambled onto the floor beside her, wrapping her arms around Angela as her body was wracked in sobs. "I'm sorry."

Jennifer didn't know how long they sat on the floor until Angela's sobs turned into hiccups and shaky breaths.

"What have I done?" Angela's voice was hoarse with emotion from the painful sobs that had wracked her frame. "This is all my fault."

"No, Angela," Jennifer shook her head, moving away so she could face her. "How could this possibly be your fault?"

"I brought them into our lives." Angela looked at Jennifer. "I was struggling with Daniel." She swallowed. "I didn't know how to be a mother, and Harley was gone for long periods." She closed her eyes and leaned her head back. "Daniel was my world, but I needed just a little space in it for me." Her hands shook as she crumpled the tissue. "Wallis was fun, exciting, and doted on me while being so good to Daniel."

"It's okay, Angela." Jennifer stood and got some tissues from the dresser, sitting next to Angela on the floor as she passed them to her. "You don't have to talk about this if it's too painful."

"No. None of it's okay." Angela gave a self-mocking snort as she blew her nose. "I've been selfish. I've hidden in a fantasy world for the past ten years, and now my twin sister is dead." She swiped tears from her cheeks. "She's dead, and Harley hasn't been able to move on with his life because I couldn't face reality or a life without my baby boy."

"Angela what you went through—" Jennifer grabbed a tissue as she felt her eyes misting over.

"Harley went through it, too." Angela swallowed. "And while I fell to pieces, he took his pain and turned it into strength so he could be there for me. Patiently waiting for me to put myself back together." She sniffed. "Harley never backed away when I splintered and shattered. He stood beside me, holding me together, supported me, and ensured I was safe."

"He loves you," Jennifer told her, and as the words left her lips, the truth of them was like a knife through her heart, and she felt it crack and start to splinter. She forced the pain from her voice. "He'd do anything for you."

"I know." Angela nodded. "The worst thing is I let him." She started to cry again. "Jennifer, what have I done to all the people I love?" Her chest vibrated as she sucked in breaths.

"Angela, you lost a child and were going through a divorce," Jennifer pointed out. "You did nothing wrong. Your mind did what it did to cope and help you heal."

Angela threw her arms around Jennifer's neck and hugged her. "Thank you, Jennifer. You are one of the kindest people I know."

Angela sat back, wiping her tears away and blowing her nose. Jennifer saw her eyes fall on the dress as she pushed herself into a standing position and offered Angela her hand.

"Why don't you jump in the shower and put on that dress," Jennifer suggested as she pulled Angela up. "I have some brand new underwear..." She looked around the dressing room. "They must be packed in here somewhere."

Angela helped her go through the drawers. Jennifer found the garments and gave them to Angela.

"Thank you," Angela said. "I'll go to my room and meet you in the dining room."

"Are you sure?" Jennifer's brow creased. She wasn't sure what to expect from Angela and didn't want to leave her alone.

"I'll be fine," Angela promised.

Twenty minutes later, Jennifer was ready to go for breakfast and decided to stop by and find out if Angela was ready. She knocked on Angela's door, and when there was no reply, Jennifer opened it.

"Angela?" Jennifer called, stepping into the room.

The pajamas Angela had on were on the bed. Jennifer walked through to the bathroom. The shower had recently been used.

"She must have gone down to breakfast," Jennifer mumbled.

She returned to the bedroom, and a folded note on the nightstand caught her eye. Jennifer walked over to it, unsure whether or not to open it until she got closer and saw it was addressed to her. Alarm bells started to ring in her head. As she opened the note, her heart dropped to her feet.

Jennifer,

I know how to make things right.

I also remember where Clair told me the evidence was hidden.

I'm going home to get it.

I've put my phone number on your cell phone.

This is to clear Harley's name and bring the real killer to justice.

Angela

Jennifer's hands shook as she pulled out her phone and scrolled through the number, finding Angela's. She hit dial, her eyes widening in surprise when a phone started ringing in Angela's bedroom. Jennifer followed the sound to the drawer on the far side nightstand.

Jennifer pulled it open and saw the phone flashing with her name on the screen. As Jennifer reached for it, the phone went to voicemail.

Jennifer, if this is you, and it has to be because you're the only one with the number, take the phone to Harley, and don't tell anyone you have it.

It's your special day.

Happy Birthday, Jennifer.

The message clicked off, and Jennifer stared at Angela's phone in disbelief. She clicked it on, and it was password-protected.

"Great!" Jennifer said, shaking her head. "How am I supposed to..." The voice message ran through her mind. "How did Angela know it's my birthday?"

She turned and ran back to her room. Her purse was on the dresser, and it was open. Jennifer dug into it and fished out her wallet. She opened it and saw that her driver's license had been turned upside down. Angela had gone through her wallet. She opened it to the cash compartment and found the cash she had in there missing and another note.

I'll pay you back, I promise

Angela.

"Where did she get all the paper from for a note!" Jennifer's head swiveled, and she remembered that her notebook had been on the floor when she woke up. "How long had Angela been in my room before I woke?"

A feeling of dread ran down Jennifer's spine—*Have I been played?*

She looked at Angela's phone. A thought struck her, and she clicked it on, punching in her birthdate, which unlocked the phone. Jennifer found video footage on the phone of the day Clair busted Angela from the mental institute. Clair had recorded the entire day and captured the real murderer or murderers! Her blood went cold when she saw who the male perpetrators was.

Jennifer now knew who'd called the police to the garage! She squinted at the older of the two people she'd frozen on the screen. Something about them jogged her memory, and an article she'd read while searching for information about the Hanover and Wesley families sprung into her mind.

Jennifer opened the internet search on her phone and found the article. Her eyes widened as she compared the faces —it was the same person. Jennifer's blood ran cold as her eyes scanned the old article dated a week after Andrew walked out on their family.

The Jury found Shaun Hanover not guilty, and Gloria Liddle's death was ruled an unfortunate accident thanks to his attorney, Andrew Gains. Throughout the trial, his family and friends stuck by him, insisting he was innocent. Andrew Gains wouldn't comment on his victory and left ahead of Shaun. Andrew's father, Judge Pearce Gains, was only too happy to give a statement commenting that he couldn't have been prouder of his son for ensuring Shaun wasn't jailed for a crime he didn't commit.

Gloria's younger sister, Leigh-Anne, wasn't as happy about the outcome of the trial and stated that it wasn't justice that had prevailed; it was money and a corrupt system that failed Gloria. Miss Liddle was quoted saying that she didn't care how long it took, she'd make sure that the truth came out and Gloria would finally get justice for what happened to her.

"I have to get to Harley," Jennifer murmured, her mind reeling as she grabbed her purse and car keys. "This isn't about money—it's about revenge, and he's caught in the middle!"

———

CHAPTER 14

H arley couldn't believe what was happening. It was like a bad dream.

"They have nothing on you besides your lockup and your argument with Clair," Andrew assured him. "Everyone fought with Clair. She wasn't the easiest person to get along with."

"Yes, but right now, the police only know of *my* argument with Clair," Harley pointed out.

"Leave it to me," Andrew told him, glancing toward the door. "I wonder where the detective went?"

"Not sure." Harley's eyes narrowed as he looked at the door. "The officer who came to get him told there was someone with new evidence for him."

"You heard that?"Andrew looked at him, amazed.

"No. My cousin's daughter is partly deaf, and we all learned sign language and how to read lips to help her," Harley explained.

"Good skill to have." Andrew nodded. "Sam always made sure his family was close."

"Yup!" Harley nodded. "Uncle Sam is all about family."

Andrew gave a tight smile. "Yes. Family is important."

Harley refrained from saying the first words to spring to mind about Andrew leaving his first family. Still, it wasn't Harley's business, and Andrew was his attorney, so it was best to keep on the man's good side. He'd researched Andrew before he and Jennifer came to Boston. The man had never lost a case. He was the attorney you wanted on your side in situations Harley had found himself in.

The door opened, and the detective walked back in.

"In light of new evidence brought to us, Mr. Donovan, you are free to go," the detective told them.

"What new evidence?" Andrew's eyes narrowed as he stared at the detective.

"I'm sure your daughter will enlighten you as soon as you leave," the detective told Andrew.

"My daughter?" Andrew's frown deepened.

"Yes, Miss Jennifer Gains," the detective told him. "She's waiting in the reception area for Mr. Donovan."

"Jennifer's here?" Harley's heart thudded as he stood.

The detective nodded, holding the door open. As Andrew stood up, the detective stopped him.

"While Mr. Donovan can leave," the detective stepped aside as Harley reached the door, "I have a few questions for you, Mr. Gains, about an old case of yours."

"Excuse me?" Andrew looked at the man in confusion.

"Do you want me to wait for you, Andrew?" Harley looked at him, alarmed.

"You can wait with Miss Gains," the detective told Harley. "I'm sure she'll fill you in."

With that, the detective ushered the confused Harley from the interrogation room and shut the door. Harley stood staring at the door for a few seconds before turning and walking down the hall to the reception. Although it wasn't an appropriate time, the minute Harley saw Jennifer sitting on a bench waiting for him, his heart skipped a few beats.

"Jennifer," Harley called, getting her attention.

Her head shot around, and as soon as she saw him, she stood and rushed into his arms.

"Oh, thank goodness." Jennifer hugged him.

His arm automatically enclosed her waist and pulled her against him, taking in her scent and warmth. She stepped out of his arms and looked down the corridor.

"Where's my f... Andrew?" Jennifer looked at Harley questioningly.

"The detective detained him for questioning on an old case," Harley told her with a shake of his head.

"Shoot, I didn't think of that," Jennifer said, snapping her fingers. "We'll have to wait for him as his driver, James, had to go home for a family emergency. We need to give Andrew a lift home. While we're there, we can get our clothes."

"Yes, I believe we were moved from the Langham to the Gains' Chestnut Hill residence," Harley commented.

"It may as well be the Langham," Jennifer told him. "Are you okay?"

"Tired, upset about Clair, and very confused as to what's going on." Harley's brow creased. "The detective said there was new evidence. Did you bring in new evidence?"

Jennifer grabbed his hand and dragged him to the benches where she had been sitting. When they were seated, she pulled out a phone.

"Yes, it was me." Jennifer's voice dropped to a whisper. "The police now have two new leads."

"Can you *please* tell me what's going on?" Harley rubbed his tired eyes. "I've had nothing to drink and eat since I left the Wesley's house last night right before you called me." He looked at Jennifer.

"What time did Mrs. Wesley call you yesterday to ask you to help them find Angela and Clair?" Jennifer's question made him look at her in surprise.

"Around six-thirty in the morning," Harley answered, wondering where her line of questioning was going. "I got dressed and wrote you a note. I didn't want to wake you, so I slipped it beneath your door and went to Chestnut Hill, where Margaret and Randal live." He bit his lip thoughtfully. "I left the hotel at about seven a.m."

"I was out walking," Jennifer said. "I didn't go back to my room either. I went straight to the dining room when I got back at eight and left for the hospital from there."

"According to the clerk at the motel that Angela and Clair were checked into, they left at about ten that morning," Harley told her.

"That's when they must've gone to the Langham looking for you," Jennifer guessed. "So that would be roughly fifteen to twenty minutes."

"Let's put them at the hotel around ten-twenty to ten-thirty that morning," Harley said.

"I got back to the hotel around mid-day, went shopping, returned to my room at around four, and then left to visit Molly at the hospital at six yesterday evening." Jennifer pulled out her phone and made notes.

"I spent the entire day trying to track Angela and Clair's whereabouts," Harley told Jennifer. A pang of guilt shot through him. "Maybe if I didn't go rushing off, Clair might still be alive."

"You can't blame yourself for what happened to Clair," Jennifer pointed out. "From what I've been able to piece together by what Angela told me, Clair was trying to protect Angela."

"From what?" Harley looked at Jennifer, startled by that revelation.

"The bad man?" Jennifer's brows knit together in confusion. "When Angela mentioned him, she started freaking out and hid beneath the bed. She was convinced he could hear and see everything she did."

"Angela had an episode around you?" Harley was even more startled by that. "Are you okay?"

"Why wouldn't I be?" Jennifer looked at him questioningly.

"Angela can get a bit... uh... difficult when she has one of her episodes," Harley explained. "She's been known to get aggressive as well."

"Angela?" Jennifer's eyebrows shot up in disbelief. "Aggressive?" She shook her head. "She was scared and paranoid but not at all aggressive."

"She attacked Clair and Wallis with a butcher's knife," Harley told Jennifer, his eyes narrowing when she didn't seem surprised by the information. "But you already knew that."

"Yes, Angela told me." Jennifer looked at her phone. "Let's finish this timeline."

"Okay, when did you meet Angela?" Harley asked as that was still to be explained to him.

"Angela arrived at my hotel room last night around eight. She looked like she'd crawled through a few bushes and was starving." Jennifer's eyes widened, and she shook her head.

Harley's heart lurched again as their eyes met. "Why did Angela go to your hotel room?"

"She was looking for you," Jennifer told him. "She saw us together yesterday, and when you weren't in your room, she came to mine."

"How did she get from your hotel room to Andrew's house?" Harley asked, deciding to piece things together a bit at a time.

"While Angela was wolfing down two large portions of lasagna, two slices of cherry pie with ice cream, and three grape sodas..." Jennifer frowned at the look on Harley's face. "What?"

"You gave Angela all that to eat and drink?" Harley said in disbelief. "She's on medication and shouldn't have so much sugar."

"Well, it kept her talking," Jennifer defended her actions. "Besides, she's a grown woman who wanted it, and I wasn't going to say no like she was a child."

"Never mind." Harley held up his hands. "Please continue."

"While she was wolfing down her pie, I asked her why she was looking for you, and she told me that Clair told her to find you," Jennifer told him. "To tell you that Angela was in danger and to keep her safe from the bad man."

"Bad man?" Harley squeezed the bridge of his nose. Angela had mentioned the wrong man before but could never tell him who the lousy man was. "Did she tell you who the bad man was?"

Jennifer's eyebrows rose. "Like I said, when I asked her who the bad man was, Angela started freaking out and hid under the bed, then wouldn't come out. She was convinced the bad man could hear everything as he knew all about her."

"I'm sorry." Harley felt his heart drop. "She didn't hurt you or try to ... um..."

"Attack me?" Jennifer asked. "No. She just hid under the bed." She shook her head. "When she wouldn't come out, I ordered a second slice of cherry pie, ice cream, and two grape sodas."

"Yikes!" Harley shuddered, thinking about all the sugar and how it was going to react with Angela's medication. "You lured her from beneath the bed with her favorite treats."

"Yup." Jennifer nodded. "I was sitting on the floor beside the bed with a piece of pie for myself and just chatting about random things when she slid out to get stuck into the pie." She grinned at the pained look that must've been on Harley's face. "While we were sitting on the floor, Angela told me about how she'd met a new friend at the beginning of the year."

"New friend?" Harley looked at Jennifer curiously. "What new friend? Is there a new patient at the institute Angela has befriended as she won't mix or talk to the other residents?"

"A doctor, I believe," Jennifer told him, sending a zap of shock through his system. "He only saw her as a doctor twice and then started visiting her as a friend."

"He?" Harley felt his alarm growing. "Did she mention who he was?"

"She only gave me a first name: Simon." Jennifer's words widened his eyes, and anger shot through him.

"Doctor Simon O'Neil," Harley hissed, gritting his teeth. "He's the doctor Clair and I were arguing about in that video the police have."

"That fits." Jennifer jotted notes in her timeline. "At first, he was there to assess if Angela should stay in the institute. He was convinced that if Angela went onto some new medication, she'd be able to leave the institute within a few months."

"What?" Harley spluttered. "Why wasn't I told about any of this?"

"Maybe because Clair might have thought you'd stop it," Jennifer replied. "According to Angela, Clair was furious with Simon for his evaluation, so he visited her as a friend three times a week for the past six months."

"No way!" Harley said with force, running his hand through his hair. "I would've known if Angela had other visitors. She wouldn't even take phone calls from her family without going into a melt-down."

"Phone calls from which family members?" Jennifer asked.

"Mostly her parents," Harley answered. "Clair stopped calling about a—" His eyes widened in realization. "Around the end of last year."

"Do you know that everything is recorded in the visitor lounges at the institute?" Jennifer pulled out her phone and flicked to a video clip. "Notice the dates."

Harley watched the different video clips Jennifer flicked through, which were time-stamped from January to a month ago. In them were recordings of Angela and Simon, who seemed much more intimate than friends in the past few months. But what surprised Harley the most was that Clair had visited Angela regularly for the past six months. Worse, he was never told about it.

"I'm sorry, Harley." Jennifer's eyes were filled with compassion. "I know how much Angela means to you."

"No, it's not that," Harley assured her. "I'm supposed to be her guardian. If she attacks someone I didn't approve of on the visitor's list, that doesn't look good and shows I'm not doing a good job as her guardian." He blew out a breath. "If that gets taken from me..." He shook her head. "Well, now it doesn't matter, as Clair was the one who was after Angela's money."

"I thought the Wesleys were uber rich!" Jennifer looked surprised by Harley's words.

"Yes. Margaret and Randal are," Harley told her. "But Angela and Clair each got a trust fund that was theirs when they turned twenty-five. Angela invested her money, and Clair blew through hers within a few years. Then, when Angela was committed, and Randal took over as CEO of Wesley Industries in Angela's absence, he gave Clair a job as VIP of marketing."

"So she's making good money?" Jennifer pointed out. "Why would she want to get her hand on Angela's money?"

"I have no idea," Harley stated. "What do rich people spend their money on?"

"Cars, boats, expensive clothes, holidays..." Jennifer listed.

"Gambling," Harley added. "I believe Wallis is a notorious gambler." He remembered the conversation from the previous evening. "That's why the Wesleys were so surprised that when Wallis's father retired, he appointed Wallis as the next CEO of their company."

"Why wouldn't he if Wallis is his father's heir?" Jennifer asked curiously.

"Because Wallis's father had cut Wallis off after his last multi-million dollar gambling debt nearly crippled their company," Harley told her. "I thought Mr. Hanover would've appointed his daughter, Shannon, Wallis's younger sister, the CEO instead."

"Weird, but not relevant," Jennifer said, moving the subject away from the Hanover family. "Getting back to Angela and Clair. When they couldn't reach you, Clair got them some food, and they went to the storage locker to lie low and eat."

"Angela needs to keep her blood sugar up," Harley told Jennifer. "She has to eat regularly."

"Angela said that Clair had been feeling weird the whole day and very sleepy," Jennifer continued the story. "Clair thought she just needed more water. They'd taken a few water bottles from the institute beside Angela's bed. Angela said she warned Clair not to drink it because it tasted funny, and Angela was convinced the bad man had poisoned them."

"That's why she asked me to bring her large bottles of water from the shops to last her a week every time I visited her," Harley realized. "And why wasn't she drinking the water at the institute? She thought she was being poisoned."

"Angela said they were going through the boxes and were reading some of Daniel's prized comic books when Clair suddenly collapsed," Jennifer told him. "When she couldn't wake Clair, she phoned her friends, but the bad man showed up with some bad people. Angela and her friends had to leave before they were discovered hiding at the back of the storage garage. Angela escaped out of the side door at the back."

"There are three doors into that storage garage," Harley told Jennifer. The large roll-up one opens in the front. A smaller one next to it so you don't have to open the large roll-up one and the back entrance that leads to the garbage bins."

"I saw that when we were there last night." Jennifer nodded and glanced down the hallway. "How long do you think they'll keep Andrew for?"

"They kept me for hours and hours," Harley pointed out, glancing at his wristwatch. "Wow, is it eleven a.m. already?"

"You must be starving," Jennifer said, pocketing her phone. "There's a vending machine if you want to get a snack."

"No, thank you." Harley suppressed a shudder. He didn't like vending machines, no matter how hungry he was. "How did Angela get from the storage locker to the Langham? Did she walk all that way?"

Worry coursed through him.

"No. She said a friend drove her to the hotel on their way to work," Jennifer told him. "I wasn't back at the hotel yet, and neither were you, so she waited in the bushes for one of us to arrive."

"And again, she didn't mention who the friend was," Harley guessed. "Do you think it could've been Simon?"

"I don't know." Jennifer frowned thoughtfully. "This must've been late afternoon, and Angela specifically said her friend dropped her on the way to work." She shrugged. "I guess Simon could have had a late consultation?"

"There is one way to find out," Harley pointed out. "To go to the Gains house and ask Angela."

"Yeah, about that." Jennifer pulled a face.

"Please tell me that Angela is still safely at Andrew's house." Harley was on the point of being unable to take any more surprises.

This was supposed to have been a trip that got Jennifer on the path of getting answers from her father and celebrating her birthday. His eyes widened.

"Oh no!" Harley breathed and looked at Jennifer.

"What?" Jennifer glanced at him, alarmed. "What is it?"

"With everything that's happening, I nearly forgot." Harley slapped his forehead before leaning forward and surprising Jennifer by planting a kiss on her lips. "Happy birthday, Jennifer."

"How did you know?" Jennifer's cheeks pinkened, and her hand touched her lips.

"Your brother, Caroline, and Aunt Betty," Harley told her. "They planned a surprise for you."

"Oh no!" Jennifer raised an eyebrow. "Not a surprise birthday party." She shuddered. "I hate those things, and it's not like it's a milestone birthday." She glanced around the police station. "Besides, we have a murder mystery to solve. There's no time for birthday celebrations."

"There's always time to wish a friend happy birthday, though." Harley smiled. "And, no, it's not a surprise party." He looked at his wristwatch and glanced down the hallway. "Maybe if we can get out of here soon and solve a mystery in a couple of hours, we can still have your birthday surprise."

"What is the surprise?" Jennifer asked him with narrowed eyes as if trying to read his mind.

"I can't tell you," Harley told her. "Let's get back to the mystery." He looked at the phone in her hand. "Now that we have a bit more to go on, what you haven't told me is what evidence you gave the police and where Angela is."

"Okay, let's start with Angela because it leads to the evidence," Jennifer told him. "When I got to the Gains house last night, I couldn't sleep. I went digging around for information on the family."

"Why?" Harley asked.

"I don't know." Jennifer shrugged. "I guess I wanted to know more about the Wesleys and the Hanovers, as Wallis gives me the creeps. I thought he might have been the one who killed Clair, thinking it was Angela, and that Wallis was the bad man that Angela was afraid of."

"I know. I thought that too," Harley admitted. "Especially when he destroyed evidence."

Jennifer told Harley about falling asleep and waking up with Angela waiting for her and how Angela had left while Jennifer was in the shower.

"You just let her go?" Harley said in disbelief.

"What was I supposed to do?" Jennifer looked at him with raised brows. "She took a couple of hundred from my purse and left."

"Wait!" Harley held up his hands. "She stole money from you too?"

"No!" Jennifer frowned, shaking her head. "I said Angela took it, not stole it. She left me an IOU."

"I'm sorry." Harley blew out a breath and ran a hand through his hair. "Let me know how much she took, and I'll pay you back."

"No!" Jennifer shook her head frustratedly. "I didn't tell you about the money to be paid back. I told you to let you know that Angela got a cab."

"Did you call the cab company?" Harley asked.

"I did." Jennifer nodded in confirmation. "Her note said she was going home because she remembered where Clair said the evidence was hidden."

"Where did the cab take her to?" Harley asked.

"I thought it was to her house, the one you told me that Clair and Wallis were living in while Angela was in the institute?" Jennifer said, and Harley nodded. "But it wasn't. They took her to this address."

Jennifer dug in her pocket and pulled out a piece of paper she'd written on. "It's the bus depot where she bought a ticket to Newbury Port."

"She is going home," Harley told Jennifer. "Angela calls the institute home." He looked at Jennifer in confusion. "What evidence did you have that cleared my name if she's going to Newbury Port to get it?"

Jennifer told him about the phone.

"You gave the phone to the cops with the video evidence of two people putting Clair's lifeless body into the car?" Harley asked. "Did you make a copy of the video?"

"Of course." Jennifer looked hurt that he'd even have to ask. "I read mystery novels." She dug into her purse, lowering her voice even more. "Only I gave the cops a phone I bought this morning with the video on and told them it was left for me." She grinned and pulled out a phone he recognized as Angela's old phone. "I kept the original."

"That's tampering with evidence." Harley glanced around worriedly.

"They have the video. We needed to keep the phone because there are more files on here I can't unlock," Jennifer told him. "I thought maybe you'd be able to help with that."

"I can try," Harley promised. "Show me the video you can unlock."

Jennifer unlocked the phone. "This is the evidence she left for me to clear your name."

She scrolled to a video file dated the previous day's date, typed in a password, and pressed play. The video showed two people, a woman and a man, who Harley instantly recognized. They were putting Clair's lifeless form into the car. There was a noise, and the camera shook as if it had been bumped or the person recording it had gotten a fright. The woman turned toward the camera as something banged like a door hitting a wall.

"Get out of here!" The woman told the man, turning toward the camera again, fear flashed in her eyes.

The man turned and headed straight for whoever was filming.

"What are *you doing here!*" The woman hissed, looking at the camera as a shadow fell over her and the screen went black.

"I know you know the man." Jennifer's eyes narrowed. "He must've been the one to call the cops hoping to frame you."

"Yes, that's Duncan. He's the Wesley's driver that brought me to the garage last night." Harley nodded. "He must've been the one to call the police." He shook his head. "But that video doesn't make sense because Duncan looked genuinely shocked to see Clair dead." He pinched the bridge of his nose. "And why would Annie want to hurt Angela or Clair?"

301

"Annie?"

Harley blinked in disbelief, barely hearing the catch in Jennifer's voice as his mind spun. "There must be some mistake!" He shook his head and pressed play on the video again. "There must be another explanation for this."

He took the phone and examined the footage twice after that.

"Harley, how do you know Annie?" Jennifer asked him.

He looked up from the phone and saw she had her phone in her hand.

"Annie runs the mental health institute in Newbury Port," Harley told her. "I've known her for years. She was Randal Wesley's assistant for years while getting her degree in psychology."

"Annie!" Jennifer nodded, looking past Harley, her eyes widening.

Harley turned to see Duncan being brought into the police station in handcuffs with James, Andrew's driver, rushing behind him.

"Don't worry, Duncan, I'll get Mr. Gains. He'll help you," James's voice was frantic.

"I didn't do this, Uncle James. I promise you," Duncan said, his eyes frantic. "We were helping Angela. Find Angela, and she'll tell you who the—"

"James?" Andrew's voice cut through Duncan's tirade. "What on earth is going on here?"

"The police arrested Duncan and are accusing him and my Annie of murdering Miss Clair," James told Andrew.

CHAPTER 15

"Uh-oh!" Jennifer whispered as she watched the commotion unfold in the police station. She snatched Angela's phone from Harley and shoved it into her purse. "I think it's time for us to leave."

"Wait! I'd like to talk to James about his nephew." Harley stood.

"I don't think now is a good time to talk to James," Jennifer reasoned. "And if Duncan is James's nephew, it means James is somehow connected to what happened forty years ago."

"Forty years ago?" Harley's brow furrowed as he glanced at Jennifer before his eyes widened in realization. "An old case that Andrew worked on."

"Uh-huh!" Jennifer nodded, glad that Harley caught on quick-ly. "If we exit right without getting caught up in all this," she made a circular motion with her hand toward where James was telling Andrew why Duncan was arrested, "I'll bring you up to speed."

"I thought I was already up to speed on what's happening here?" Harley shook his head.

"No." Jennifer shook her head. "You're up to speed on every-thing I know about Angela and Clair but not about how every-thing connects together."

"Jennifer!" Andrew called.

Shoot! Jennifer rolled her eyes. *This is what I get for being nice and wanting to offer the man a ride home.* "Hi!" She gave him a small wave. "I see you're busy, and now that James is here, you don't need a ride home." She tugged Harley's arm to get him to leave with her. "So we'll leave you to sort this out. We have to return to Plum Island," Jennifer said as she glanced at her wristwatch. "Oh wow," she breathed. "We'd better get going if we want to get home before dark."

"It's a two-hour drive, and it's not even midday yet!" Harley pointed out.

She shook her head at Harley, who was clearly distracted by every-thing going on as he didn't see the *get with the picture, Harley,* look that Jennifer shot him. Jennifer would've elbowed Harley to get his full attention if Andrew hadn't pinned her with his gaze.

"If you could just give me a few minutes before you rush off?" Andrew asked, his eyes darkening with emotion as his voice dropped. "Please."

"Fine!" Jennifer couldn't stop the flood of emotion that rushed through her at the look that clouded Andrew's eyes.

"Thank you." Andrew gave her a tight smile before turning his attention to James. "James, maybe you should go home, and I'll call you when I have news. This is going to take some time."

"I would rather stay here and wait, Mr. Gains," James told him.

Jennifer's eyes narrowed as she looked at James. *So James was Duncan's uncle!* Her eyebrow raised as she nodded, biting the side of her mouth. *This puts a whole new spin on things.* She rubbed her chin. *Mm. Maybe talking to James isn't such a bad idea after all. I can find out how James and Duncan are related.*

"Earth to Jennifer!" Harley's warm breath tickled her ear, making her jump. "Sorry, I didn't mean to startle you." He looked at her curiously. "What is going on in your mind with those razor-focused thoughts?"

"I was just thinking about James's connection to Duncan," Jennifer told him, watching the interaction between Andrew, James, and the detective. "And wondering how Duncan is related to James?"

"As Duncan called James his uncle, I'd say that's the relationship!" Harley commented.

"I get that, *genius!*" Jennifer mocked. "What I meant is, is Duncan James's sister's child because they had different last names? Is James an uncle by marriage?"

"Okay, I get it!" Harley told her. "Here's a thought!" He looked at Jennifer. "Why don't you ask him?"

An idea took root in Jennifer's mind. "Or..." She smiled at Harley. "While I'm talking to Andrew, *you* ask James. That way, we get out of here a lot faster, and I can fill you in with the rest of this mystery." Another idea struck her. "Oooh, I know Caroline is looking for some plots for season three of The Cobble Cove Mysteries, and I think this will be great!"

"Can you do that?" Harley asked her with a frown. "Don't you have to get everyone involved with the mystery's permission or something like that?"

"Nope!" Jennifer shook her head. "Obviously, we're going to change a few things."

Excitement flooded her. Jennifer remembered helping Caroline plot the first few mysteries for a series of Caroline's books and how much she'd loved putting it all together. While Jennifer wasn't much of a writer, she did love mysteries, and when she watched them, she always tried to solve them before the show's end.

Last year, Jennifer had lived a real mystery with Caroline on Plum Island. While it wasn't the birthday she'd planned, which was to spend the day with Harriet seeing...

"Oh no! Harriet!" Jennifer breathed.

"Harriet?" Harley turned to see if she was there.

"I'm supposed to meet her at the Langham in..." Jennifer looked at the time on the large clock on the wall. "An hour."

"Why is Harriet in Boston?" Harley looked at her curiously.

"We're supposed to spend the day doing touristy things around Boston," Jennifer told him, feeling slightly embarrassed by the absurdity of it. She practically lived on Boston's doorstep. "It's my favorite city; I've always wanted to see it like a tourist."

Harley gaped at her. "You planned to do that with Harriet?"

"Yes." Jennifer felt slightly offended by how he stared at her like she was weird. "I know it's silly. I was born here, and I've driven through Boston more times than I can remember, but I've never taken the time to *see it*."

"No, I get it!" Harley assured her, pursed his lips, and ran a hand through his hair. "I was supposed to do that with you today—that was your birthday surprise from your family and friends."

Now Jennifer was gaping at Harley. "Are you kidding me?" She couldn't believe it, and a smile split her lips. "That's so sweet of everyone."

"Obviously, none of us knew you'd planned to do that with Harriet," Harley told her. "We'd even booked an extra night at the Langham so I could take you around Boston to end the evening with dinner and a show of your choice."

"No way!" Jennifer's smile broadened. "Now I'm disappointed about the turn this trip took." A thought struck her. "But we could still do the last part. Maybe not the show but dinner at my choice of restaurant."

"Really?" Harley smiled. "How about we do lunch as well? I'm starving."

"I am, too," Jennifer admitted. "But before we do that, we have an hour to get to Chestnut Hill, get our stuff, and collect Harriet from the Langham." She paused and pulled a face. "I'm sorry, but she may have to join us for dinner."

"Sure." Harley nodded and turned when Andrew approached them. He whispered, "You talk to Andrew. I'll go speak to James."

Jennifer nodded as Harley excused himself and headed toward James.

"Thank you for waiting," Andrew said, looking awkward. "First, I wanted to say happy birthday, Jennifer." He gave her a tight smile. He reached into his jacket pocket and pulled out a small box with a gold wrapper and a small blue bow. "This is for you. I've had it since..." His eyes darkened with a flash of pain as he cleared his throat. "Since the day before your mother passed away."

Jennifer's brows shot up in shock at his words. "What is it?"

"It's a gift your mother and I picked out for you," Andrew told her.

"I don't understand," Jennifer's brows knitted together. "When did you and my mother pick a gift for me?"

"There is so much I have to tell you." Andrew sighed resignedly. "I was finally free to do so a year ago, but Molly got sick, and time passed quickly until we found ourselves at this point."

"This seems like it's going to be a *long* conversation. I don't have time or *want* to hear it." Jennifer knew she was being rude. "I really have to go, as a friend is waiting for me at the Langham."

She had given Andrew a free pass since he'd come through for her the previous night. But that was one night, helping out a friend of hers. It didn't make up for forty years of complete radio silence. She didn't care if she had him to thank for not having college debt. Jennifer and Liam needed their father, but he wasn't there for them.

Anything Andrew had to say now wouldn't change or make up for the past. Not even a brightly wrapped square box that Jennifer was sure was jewelry would make her want to hear anything Andrew had to say. Although the part he'd thrown in about choosing whatever was in that box with Jennifer's mother before she'd died had intrigued her.

"Of course!" Andrew gave her a tight smile and dug an envelope from his pocket. "It comes with this."

Jennifer took the items hesitantly, feeling like a fish about to take some juicy-looking bait even though she could see the huge hook sticking out the other end. But she couldn't resist the temptation and knew as soon as she had the items in her hand that she was being reeled in.

"Thanks!" Jennifer said, holding the items up. "Is this all you wanted to talk to me about?"

"I was hoping to get you to stay for dinner at my house," Andrew admitted. "But I can see you're in a rush to leave Boston."

"Aunt Betty has a broken leg, and I can't expect Liam to be the only one looking out for her," Jennifer explained. *Why am I looking for excuses?* "And Aunt Betty likes me to be home for my birthday."

"I understand." Andrew smiled, although his eyes flashed with disappointment. "Before you leave. Could you tell me what evidence you gave the police that cleared Harley's name?"

"Sure." Jennifer nodded, fishing her phone from her purse. She scrolled through it to find the video she sent to Andrew. "You're not going to like it, though, as it doesn't look good for your new client and his aunt."

Andrew's brows rose at the mention of Duncan and his aunt. He pulled out his phone and looked at the video Jennifer had sent him.

"No, it doesn't." Andrew's eyes narrowed at the screen. "Now I know why the police questioned me on an old case of mine."

"Old case?" Jennifer hoped she looked convincing enough.

"Nothing!" Andrew shook his head, pocketing his phone. "I'd better get into the interrogation room with Duncan." He looked at Jennifer for a few seconds as if contemplating saying something before nodding. "I'll be in touch."

"Sure," Jennifer said, nodding and holding up the items he'd given her. "Thank you for these."

"I hope you enjoy the rest of your special day," Andrew told her before walking off.

Jennifer watched him walk back down the hallway he'd come from.

"What do you have there?" Harley's voice made her jump again. "You're very jumpy today."

"Do you blame me?" Jennifer breathed out, putting the present and what felt like a heavy card in her purse. "This was supposed to be a simple trip to Boston to have a DNA test and spend some time with my new friend on my birthday."

"Instead, you got dragged further into your family and mine's drama," Harley reiterated. "With a murder thrown in and my ex-wife befriending you and pulling you even further down the rabbit hole."

"Something like that." Jennifer nodded. "Shall we get out of here? There's a burger place across the road we can stop at. I'll message Harriet and let her know I'll be late."

"She's not going to be amused by that." Harley gave a lopsided grin as they walked out of the police station. "Harriet strikes me as a person who likes punctuality."

"Nah!" Jennifer waved it off. "She'll be fine. Besides, I organized a surprise for her with compliments of Andrew Gains."

Harley frowned at Jennifer for a minute before a thought dawned on him. "You didn't!"

"If you're talking about putting five bottles of Krug Clos d'Ambonnay on Andrew's Langham Hotel tab." Jennifer smiled smugly. "Then I most certainly did."

"Well, now that his father's deceased, I believe Andrew Gains is worth a few million in pocket change," Harley informed her.

"Have you been internet searching the Gains family?" Jennifer looked at him suspiciously as they crossed the street to the diner.

"I may have looked them up," Harley shrugged. "Just like I know, through your own admission, that you internet searched the Wesley and Hanover families."

"Wow! You've been hanging out with Andrew way too long." Jennifer shook her head as they were seated at a booth near the window that looked onto the police station. "You sounded like an attorney—*by your own admission*." She put on a deep voice.

The server placed menus in front of them.

"Would you like to hear the specials?" The young woman asked them.

But the server's question was directed to Harley, who her eyes were devouring, sending a wave of an emotion Jennifer didn't quite recognize through her. It felt like a spurt of anger that made her want to slap the woman.

Whoa! What the heck is that about? Jennifer found she was gripping the paper menu so hard she'd torn a part of it. *Oops.* She put the menu on the table and straightened it.

"No, thank you," Harley answered the fawning server. "I'd like a burger, fries, and a bottle of water, please." He closed and handed the menu back to look at Jennifer. "Are you ready to order, or have you not finished murdering the menu yet."

"It's such a flimsy paper menu," Jennifer observed. "It nearly fell apart in my hands." She smiled at the server, trying not to grin.

"It's okay. It happens all the time," the server assured her. "What would you like?"

"I'll have the same as he's having, but can I have a chocolate malt and a bottle of water, please?" Jennifer ordered.

"That sounds good." Harley smiled at the server, and Jennifer thought the woman would swoon. "Make that two chocolate malts."

"Sure." The server nodded. "Do you still want the bottle of water?"

"Yes, please." Harley nodded.

The server took their menus and left with their order. Harley leaned his elbows on the table and looked at Jennifer questioningly.

"So..." Harley's eyes dropped to Jennifer's purse on the seat beside her. "Are you going to open the gift Andrew gave you?"

"I'm not sure," Jennifer admitted. "It feels like a trap."

"How so?" Harley asked.

"Andrew said that he and my mother picked it out together before she died," Jennifer told Harley what Andrew had said. "My mother died a few months before my eighth birthday."

"That's awful." Harley reached over and squeezed her hand. "Then open the present."

"I don't see how my mother could've chosen a present for me back then, as she was bedridden in the hospital," Jennifer said skeptically. "So how did my mother choose a birthday present for me, and why would Andrew have kept it for forty years?"

"You won't know unless you open the present and the card," Harley pointed out.

"If I open it, will you stop hounding me about it?" Jennifer sighed and pulled the present and the envelope from her purse to put them on the table before her and Harley.

"If you *open* it, you may find some answers," Harley told her.

Jennifer eyed the present, wondering if Andrew had re-wrapped it. There's no way the present would still look so pristine after forty years.

Did they even make those tiny royal blue bows forty years ago? Jennifer tilted her head. *Wow! I'm in my forties and not even my early forties!*

"Should I open it for you?" Harley's voice snapped her out of her thoughts.

Jennifer's *procrastination* thoughts, as Caroline called them. Whenever Jennifer tried to avoid something, she'd think of the weirdest things and then get lost in the tunnels of thoughts it would take her down. Like now!

She didn't want to open the present because it meant she was slowly being drawn back into Andrew's world. Next, Jennifer would want to find the answers to the questions she'd stopped asking years ago.

Jennifer wasn't ready to test those scars to find out how well they'd really healed after forty years. Her eyes fell on the envelope, and her heart skipped a beat when she recognized the handwriting.

How didn't I notice that before? Jennifer picked up the envelope as the server returned with their food and drinks. She put it down next to the present before sitting back.

"Oh, is it someone's birthday?" The server saw the present, and her eyes slid toward Harley.

He smiled politely and pointed to Jennifer. "Not mine. Hers."

"Happy Birthday," the server said as she handed Jennifer her food, shake, and water. "You get a free dessert for your table on your birthday if there are no more than four of you."

"Those are huge burgers!" Harley stated and looked at Jennifer. "Do you think we're going to have space for dessert after these?"

Jennifer gave him a tight smile before looking at the server. "Thank you for the birthday wishes." Then back at Harley. "There's always room for free dessert."

The server laughed and left their table, but not before another doe-eyed look at Harley, igniting that weird feeling inside Jennifer once again.

Oh no! Jennifer's eyes widened. *Am I jealous?*

"Jennifer?" Harley called. "You're doing that thing I've noticed you do when trying to put off doing something."

"What thing?" Jennifer knew exactly what he was talking about.

"You go off into deep thought," Harley told her. "Like you've retreated into yourself behind a mental wall where nothing can reach you."

"Yet here you are still talking to me," Jennifer said sarcastically, lashing out at him because she was... *No! No! Impossible. Why on earth would I be jealous of someone ogling Harley? Oops, I'm doing it again, and he's onto me.* "Sorry. That was uncalled for, and my daddy issues are not your fault."

"Are you sure it's just your daddy issues that have you so touchy?" Harley asked, putting ketchup on his plate.

"I don't have any other issues!" Jennifer said haughtily.

"Okay!" Harley held up his hands in a surrender gesture. "I just thought that you might feel guilty over playing a part in getting Duncan arrested."

"That wasn't playing a part!" Jennifer picked up the knife and fork and cut into the burger. "It was either you or him, and the way I see it, Duncan is the one that *should* be in the interrogation room, not you."

"He told James he didn't do it when James met him at the police station," Harley cut a piece of his burger. "We were both there and heard it." He took a bite, sitting back while he ate before saying, "And from where I was standing, he didn't look like a young man who had just murdered someone. He was scared."

"Of course, he was scared," Jennifer said. "He got caught after trying to frame you for the murder."

"All Duncan did was call the police," Harley pointed out. "He also looked genuinely shocked to see a dead body in that car."

Jennifer took a bite of the burger, hardly noticing how tasty it was, as she watched Harley intently. "What did you get out of James?"

"I went over there and asked him what was going on." Harley took a sip of his malt, pausing until he put the glass on the table. "James told me that his nephew called him when he saw the cops pulling up at his apartment."

"If he didn't do it, how would Duncan know the cops were there for him?" Jennifer asked. "They could've been there for another person in the apartment block."

"Duncan doesn't live in an apartment block," Harley told her. "He lives in an apartment over a garage on Angela's property."

Jennifer's eyes widened. "The property that Clair was living at?"

"Yes," Harley nodded. "The police pulled up in front of the apartment, not the main house."

'They could've still been there for the main house," Jennifer said. "But getting back to your conversation with James," she picked up a fry, "did he tell you how he and Duncan are related?"

"He did." Harley paused once again to take another bit of food.

"Are you pausing for dramatic effect or just to annoy me?" Jennifer's eyes narrowed.

"I'm trying to eat as I'm hungry." Harley wiped his mouth on a napkin and grinned. "But also for the dramatic effect."

"Well, don't do that!" Jennifer advised him. "It's annoying and the reason I don't watch game shows."

"You know, if you just opened the darn present and card, you'd be less testy," Harley advised. "While I understand you have a lot of unresolved feelings and emotions over your fath... Andrew, there's only so many knocks I'm willing to take over it."

Jennifer's heart squeezed, and guilt washed over her. It wasn't just the turmoil over her family issues or stumbling into the middle of a murder mystery. It was her mixed emotions over Harley that were adding to her testyness.

Mixed emotions? That annoying voice in her head seemed to laugh at her. *Oh, girl, you are tumbling head over heels here.* Jennifer gritted. "That's enough!"

"I beg your pardon?" Harley's brow furrowed as he looked at her in disbelief.

Shoot! Did I just say that aloud? Jennifer felt her cheeks flame. "Sorry. That wasn't meant for you. I'm at war about that," she lied, pointing to the present and card. "Part of me wants to open it so badly." She picked up the card and showed it to Harley. "This is my mother's handwriting. I know it well because I kept every note and birthday card she gave me." She looked at the envelope. "This might be the last thing she ever wrote, and it's like stepping back in time. I'm eight years old again and clinging to everything my mother touched or gave me." Jennifer held up the envelope before putting it on the table again. "I thought I had everything of my mother's neatly stacked on a shelf of memories in my heart, my mind, and a box in my closet at the cottage on Plum Island."

"Memories you'd dealt with, come to terms with, and found a way to live with," Harley added and smiled warmly, his eyes filled with compassion and another emotion that took her breath away. "This is something new that you're afraid will make you relive all that pain."

"Something like that!" Jennifer swallowed down the burning lump in her throat. "Then there's the other side of this coin—Andrew!"

Harley reached over the table and took her hand. "Whatever happens, I'll be right by your side." He gently squeezed her hand to show his support. "So don't worry about the trap doors or hidden hooks. I'll catch you before you fall or get reeled in."

"Promise?" Jennifer smiled, taking a sip of her malt to try and wash down the stubborn lump in her throat and the tears stinging her eyes.

"Promise!" Harley held her eyes briefly before they dropped to the envelope. "Do you want me to open it and read it for you?"

Jennifer looked at the letter and nodded. She knew she was being a coward, but Jennifer also knew if she saw her mother's handwriting, she would burst into a flood of tears.

Harley squeezed her hand before taking the envelope and carefully slitting it open with a clean knife from the table. He pulled out a birthday card, and when he opened it, he found a handwritten letter folded inside.

"I'll read the card first," Harley told her.

My darling Jennifer,

Happy birthday love. I'm not sure which birthday you'll get this card on, but I'm hoping it's not so far in the future that I'm just a distant memory.

I hope you like the present your father and I picked out. I couldn't make it to a store, so your father had the store brought to me. I managed to pick out two last presents, one for each of the people I love the most in this whole world.

Love

Mom

Jennifer sat staring at the card in Harley's hands. Her jaw was clenched tight as she gulped down the water, trying to keep the tears at bay. A picture of a heart-shaped gift box on the card stated: *Children are the greatest gift.*

"Jennifer?" Harley's voice was soft as he took her hand once again. "Are you okay?"

Her eyes met his, and she nodded.

"Do you want me to read the letter?" Harley asked, scanning it until the last page. His head shot up, and he looked at her. "Before I start, I must warn you that these two pages are two different letters, one from your mother and the other from your ... from Andrew."

"Read the one from my mother," Jennifer's voice was hoarse. "I'm not interested in anything Andrew has to say." She paused and wiped her eyes. "Or at least not yet, anyway."

Harley turned to the letter from Jennifer's mother.

"Oh!" Harley's brows shot up, and looked at Jennifer. "The first sentence after Darling Jennifer is: *Before you read my letter, you must read your father's so you'll understand mine.*"

"I knew this was a trap." Anger spurted through Jennifer. "It's probably not even a letter from my mother, and Andrew set all this up to reel me in so he could *explain* himself and clear his conscience."

She finished her shake and pushed aside her plate with the half-eaten burger and fries. "I've lost my appetite. Let's get the bill and leave. I need to collect Harriet soon anyway."

Jennifer made a grab for the card Harley had put on the table but he stopped her.

"Stop it!" Harley shook his head and slid the card toward himself. "You need to read these." His eyes looked suspiciously glassy, and his voice hoarse.

"You can read them to me in the car," Jennifer said, hailing the server who came right over. "Can we have the check, please?"

"You're not going to have a dessert?" The server looked disappointed.

"Maybe another time," Jennifer said, knowing full well that wouldn't happen.

"If you come back on your..." the server glanced at Jennifer's hand, "boyfriend's birthday I'll give you both double desserts."

"We'll keep that in mind," Jennifer gave her a tight smile as she paid the check while Harley continued to read the letters. "Let's go."

Harley's head snapped up and he looked around startled to see the dishes being collected. "I was going to get the check."

"Too late," Jennifer said, stuffing the present and managing to grab the card and envelope as she slid from the chair. "We have to get to Chestnut Hill and then pick up Harriet."

Harley carefully folded the letters and slipped them into the pocket of his pants when he stood. As they were walking out the door, the server stopped them.

"Wait!" she called. "I know this is probably nothing and just my overactive imagination. But there's been a man standing across the street pretending to read a newspaper, but I could swear he was watching you."

Harley and Jennifer turned to see a man dash into a store, making Jennifer's heart slammed into her chest. She turned to the server.

"Did you get a good look at him?" Jennifer asked.

"He was average height and build. I couldn't see his hair because he wore a fedora hat, dark blue jeans, and a light blue cotton shirt." The server frowned.

"Thank you," Jennifer and Harley said in unison before walking out the door.

"Should we go to the store he disappeared into?" Jennifer looked at Harley.

"No. While whoever he is is in the store, I say we head to your car and put as much distance between us as possible," Harley suggested.

"Agreed," Jennifer said as they walked to where her car was parked in front of the police station.

As Jennifer drove off, she kept an eye in the mirror but didn't see the man leave the store. They were nearing Chestnut Hill when Harley told her to pull over. She did as he asked and looked at him questioningly.

"Please open the present from your mother and Andrew," Harley insisted.

"You're not going to leave this alone, are you?" Jennifer rolled her eyes.

Harley shook his head. She reached over to the back and pulled the present from her purse. Jennifer didn't give herself a chance to ponder and ripped the wrapping off to review a blue velvet box. She opened it, and tears sprang to her eyes. It was a gold charm bracelet like she'd always wanted. Jennifer was going to travel the world and wanted to get a charm from wherever she went.

Two charms were on it: a heart to symbolize her mother's love and a butterfly, her mother's favorite creature.

I'm not leaving you, my loves. I'll always be here in your hearts, and whenever you see a butterfly, it will be me reminding you of how much I love you.

Jennifer's hand shook as she stared at it, and this time, she didn't stop the tears that rolled down her cheeks.

"Hey!" Harley's soft voice whispered as he wrapped his arms around her. "It's beautiful."

Their eyes met and locked. Harley's hands moved and cupped her face. His thumb gently wiped the tears before his lips descended and touched hers, blocking out the pain and the world around them.

CHAPTER 16

H arley sat behind the wheel of Jennifer's car with the road stretching out before him like a ribbon of asphalt winding from the heart of Boston to the quaint town of Newbury Port. The engine's purr filled the car's interior, a mechanical symphony accompanying the tension that hung in the air. A heavy silence lingered between Harley and Jennifer, the echoes of their kiss resonating like an unspoken secret.

The car glided over the road, cutting through the open spaces and stretches of tranquil green countryside while the bright blue cloudless sky formed a canopy above them. Cool air filtered through the car vents, keeping the heat that shimmied off the road outside.

Harley fixed his eyes on the road ahead, projecting an air of calm belying the turmoil within him that was only evident by the white tinge around his knuckle gripping the steering wheel. Harley felt like he was in a cocoon of unspoken words, each passing mile a reminder of the uncharted territory he and Jennifer had drifted into. Although their entire relationship so far had been uncharted territory for Harley. He'd never met anyone quite like Jennifer.

As the silence seemed to thicken around them like a heavy fog, Harley glanced toward the passenger seat to see Jennifer staring out the side window. The letters her mother and Andrew had written to her forty years ago lay on her lap, neatly folded and unread by her. As his attention returned to the road, his eyes caught the charm bracelet cradled in a center pocket between the seats.

The backseat leather squeaked, capturing Harley's attention, and he looked in the mirror to see Harriet scooching forward to lean between the seats. They had collected her on their way out of Boston. Harley had been acutely aware of Harriet's shrewd eyes observing Jennifer and him since she slid into the back of the car. She reminded him of a spectator in a theater, anticipating the next act of the drama unfolding before her.

When their trip began, Jennifer had filled Harriet in on what was happening and why Jennifer's birthday plans had changed. They were headed for Plum Island via Newbury Port to find Angela, who they believed was in danger.

"Harley, you haven't told us how James and Duncan are related," Harriet pointed out.

"That's why you've been so quiet!" Jennifer turned and looked at Harriet.

"Yes, that's why *I've* been so quiet." Harriet grinned smugly and wagged her index finger between the two of them. "I'm not too sure what's going on between you, but I have to tell you that you're not hiding whatever disagreement you've had this time too well, either." She shook her head and raised her eyebrows. "You can cut the tension in the car with a pizza cutter."

"Don't you mean knife?" Harley caught Harriet's eyes in the mirror.

"No, Harriet likes to put a new spin on old sayings." Jennifer sighed.

"You really are eccentric!" Harley laughed, looking at her in the mirror.

"Thank you." Harriet exaggerated her thanks. "It's so nice to finally be noticed for who I really am."

"And let's not forget sarcastic!" Jennifer rolled her eyes at her friend before turning to Harley. It had been the first time since their last kiss she'd made full eye contact. "Yes, you broke off from that conversation to hand me these." She pointed to the letters on her lap.

"Which escalated the tension in the car tenfold," Harriet pointed out and scooched closer to the front. "Are you going to read those?"

"It doesn't look like it," Harley answered before Jennifer could. "Jennifer won't even wear the charm bracelet from her mother."

"I don't know it's really from my mother," Jennifer defended her actions. "Andrew could be a liar, which would fit as he's a top defense attorney, so he's used to manipulating people into doing or thinking what he wants them to."

"So read them and find out," Harriet said, holding out her hand. "Or give them to me, and I'll read them for you."

"Okay," Jennifer surprised Harley by saying to Harriet, but she turned toward him. "But first, I want to know why you're hedging about telling us how James and Duncan are related."

"I'm not hedging," Harley said a little defensively because it was true he was.

He was shocked to discover who James's ex-wife was and hoped he could speak to them before pulling Jennifer further into this mess. It wasn't fair that Harley's life was whirling around her like a category five tornado pulling her into its path. This was his family's, or at least extended family, that he was technically divorced from, mess, not hers.

"Well?" Harriet prompted Harley, her eyes filled with impatience. "You are the worst at passing on information. Trying to get details from you is like streaming a movie with a bad wifi connection. The movie starts to get interesting, and wham, the picture freezes."

Harley looked into the mirror, grinning at Harriet. "The two of you are so impatient." He shook his head and sighed. There was no dodging this. "James is Duncan's uncle by marriage."

Jennifer's head shot around to look at him, her eyes wide. "James is married to Annie, as in Leigh-Ann Liddle?"

"Yes." Harley nodded. "Or rather, *was* his wife. They're divorced."

"I wonder how long they were married for?" Jennifer frowned, rubbing her top lip as she did when she was thinking.

"They were married for twenty years and have been divorced for three years," Harley told her.

"You got all that from a few minutes talking to James?" Jennifer looked at Harley, impressed.

"While I like to think I'd have made a decent detective, I know how long they were married and divorced because Annie told me a while ago," Harley explained. "I didn't know who she was married to, though, as it never came up."

"Do you know who Leigh-Ann Liddle is?" Jennifer turned toward Harley.

"Yes. I told you Annie used to work for the Wesleys until she got her psychology degree and eventually took over as head of the Newbury Port Mental Health Institute," Harley told her again.

Jennifer reached between the seats and picked up her phone, which she flipped through. "I've sent you and Harriet some articles about Leigh-Ann Liddle."

"Just tell us!" Harriet groaned, dropping her head back in frustration. "You know I get car sick reading in a car, especially in the back seat."

"I'll give you an overview," Jennifer said as she turned to face Harley and Harriet. "Leigh-Ann had an older sister, Gloria, who was Shaun Hanover's assistant forty-two years ago."

"Wallis's father?" Harley frowned at Jennifer before turning back to the road.

"Yes." Jennifer nodded. "She was the daughter of Sylvia Liddle, who was the Wesleys' housekeeper, and they lived in staff housing on the Wesleys' property."

"Okay." Harley wondered where this was going.

Annie hadn't mentioned she had a sister. But then he and Annie weren't good friends. They were more like acquaintances as Harley dealt with her over Angela's care.

"A year after she started working for Shaun Hanover, Gloria had a little boy," Jennifer told them. "In all the articles I've read about Gloria, there's been no mention of who the father was, and as far as I can gather, Gloria never married."

"You think she was having an affair with Shaun Hanover?" Harriet guessed. Excitement tinged her voice. "And that her baby was the illegitimate child of Shaun!"

"That's what I thought at first, too," Jennifer nodded. "So I sent Sam a message." She looked at Harley. "I'm so glad your uncle uses messaging, as I can't get Aunt Betty to." She flipped through some messages. "According to Sam, Gloria had opened a case of abuse against Shaun and alleged that he and two of his friends had abused her."

"Let me guess," Harley said, not able to quell the surge of anger that washed over him. "No one believed her because of who Shaun Hanover is."

"That and the other two were, as your uncle put it, even more evil than Shaun Hanover could ever be," Jennifer told him. "Luckily, the morning before she reported the incident to the police station, Gloria had gone to the hospital. She'd demanded a copy of her file before she left as a precaution. That's how scared she was."

"Were charges filed against Shaun and his friends?" Harley glanced at Jennifer.

"No." Jennifer shook her head. "Sam told me that Gloria dropped the charges a day later."

"She was paid off!" Harriet sneered in disgust.

"That's what Sam said, too," Jennifer told Harriet. "Nine months later, she had a baby boy. Shaun Hanover's wife, the doctor who delivered the baby in a private hospital, got Gloria's medical records from the hospital she went to on the day she reported the abuse."

"Uh-oh!" Harriet breathed.

"Uh-oh is the right word. Doctor Brenda Denning, Shaun's wife, ordered three paternity tests." Jennifer held up three fingers. "Doctor Denning also convinced Gloria to reopen the abuse charges."

"Wow!" Harriet said. "She must've been furious at her husband."

"Angela once told me that Doctor Denning and Shaun had been forced to marry by their parents," Harley told them. "It was to amalgamate their two companies, although Doctor Denning's family owned the majority of the joined company."

"I couldn't imagine having to marry someone, and they obviously had children," Harriet stated.

"Yes, a daughter, Shannon, and Wallis," Harley added. "Shaun and his wife live on opposite ends of their manor house. I guess now I know why they hate each other."

Jennifer nodded and continued the story, "While waiting for the paternity test results, Gloria had an accident by the Wesley's pool," Jennifer continued the story. "She slipped and hit her head, killing her instantly."

"That wasn't at all suspicious!" Harriet said sarcastically.

"Doctor Denning was the one to rule it a suspicious death," Jennifer stated. "The police arrested Shaun Hanover as some of the Wesley's staff saw him climbing over the far wall that divides their two properties."

"They arrested him on that?" Harley said in disbelief.

"No. The police arrested Shaun because his shirt and hands were covered in Gloria's blood," Jennifer informed them. "The ME found that Gloria had been drugged, and there was evidence that she'd struggled with someone before she was hit in the head."

"Because of the abuse charges and paternity tests, it would also probably cost him a fortune as I'm guessing Doctor Denning's family would've had an airtight prenup." Harriet held up her phone. "This article you sent me says that Shaun Hanover was acquitted of all charges, and Gloria's death was ruled an accident after a quick trial.

Shaun was supported by his good friends Randal Wesley and Judge Pearce Gains who, although not the judge presiding over the case, kept a close watch over it. At the end of the trial, he proclaimed Shaun's innocence throughout the trial." She gave a low whistle. "His defense attorney, ... OH!"

"Who was the defense attorney?" Harley looked into the mirror and saw Harriet look at Jennifer wide-eyed.

"He's going to find out when he reads the article." Jennifer shrugged, sighing. "It was Andrew Gains."

"Your fa... Andrew was the attorney that defended Shaun Hanover?" Harley looked at Jennifer and frowned. "Wait! Did you say forty years ago?"

Jennifer nodded. "I know what you're thinking. It was around the time he'd left us."

"No!" Harley lied. "I..." He didn't know what to say. "Everyone deserves a fair trial, right?"

"I guess." Jennifer shrugged. "But I doubt this was anything but fair."

"Did the paternity tests ever show results?" Harriet asked.

"Sam said that they all came back as not a match," Jennifer turned toward Harriet.

"Who were the other two that took the paternity tests?" Harley wanted to know.

Jennifer snorted. "Randal Wesley and Judge Pearce Gains."

The car went quiet for a few seconds as Harley absorbed the information.

"And all three tests came back negative?" Harriet said in disbelief. "That sounds like a cover-up to me."

"I agree," Harley said.

"Sam agrees, too," Jennifer told them. "He said that during the trial, even Doctor Denning switched sides and said that it's her opinion that Gloria had them all fooled. She was a gold digger out to get what she could from their family."

"That's odd." Harriet and Harley said in unison.

"That's what Leigh-Ann Liddle said to the press," Jennifer said, looking at the article on her phone. "As well as how she'd do whatever it took to get justice for her sister."

"And you think that Clair's murder is somehow connected to that forty-year-old case?" Harriet asked.

"That's my gut feeling, yes." Jennifer nodded.

"But why go after the Wesleys's daughter?" Harriet looked at Jennifer, confusion lacing her voice.

"That's what we need to figure out," Jennifer said, turning to Harley. "We're almost there."

"Yup." Harley nodded. "I hope this is where Angela went."

As they drove into Newbury Port, Harley turned onto the road that led to the institute.

"And you didn't get a look at the man the server said had been watching you at the diner?" Harriet asked.

"No," Harley and Jennifer said in unison.

Harley entered the institute's parking lot, found a space, and parked. "I'm going to have to go in alone."

"Seriously?" Jennifer and Harriet looked at him in disbelief.

"No way!" Jennifer shook her head. "We want to come with you."

"I'll call you when I've ensured Angela is here," Harley promised. "So please, stay here."

"Fine!" Jennifer folded her arms over her chest.

"Why don't you read the letters while you wait?" Harley suggested as he slid out of the car, handing Jennifer the keys. "Don't leave without me."

"Don't tempt me," Jennifer muttered, taking the keys.

Harley walked into the center, greeted by a familiar face at the reception desk.

"Mr. Donovan." The nurse smiled at him. "We weren't expecting you today."

"Is that because Angela isn't back, or she is back but I don't usually visit until Monday?" Harley put on his most engaging charm, trying to keep images of kissing Jennifer from his mind.

"Thankfully, Angela was found and brought back to the institute," the nurse told him, making him frown.

"Found?" Harley looked at the woman. "Please don't make Angela sound like a dog." He bristled. "And who brought her back?"

"I'm sorry," the nurse instantly apologized. "I didn't mean it to sound the way it came out."

Harley nodded, accepting her apology. "Who brought her back?" He asked again.

"Mrs. Montgomery," the nurse told him, sending shock waves down his spine.

"Annie brought her back?" Harley felt his heart jolt as fear pumped through his veins. "I need to see for myself that Angela is safe."

"Of course, Mr. Donovan" The nurse picked up a visitor pass and handed it to him. "Angela is back in her room."

"Thank you," Harley walked through the security doors.

He stepped through the X-ray machine and strode down the corridor leading to Angela's room. He knocked on the door and listened. There was no sound. Harley frowned.

Maybe she's sleeping or has gone to the lounge, Harley thought, gently pushing the handle down and calling as he put his head through the door, "Angela?"

He peeked around the door, but the room appeared to be empty. Harley stepped inside and looked around. The bed was rumpled where he could see she'd been sitting. Muddy footprints on the floor led from the glass door that went into a small private garden area.

Harley walked to the glass doors and slid them open. His gaze assessed the neatly cut hedge and bright patches of flowers Angela had planted under the watchful eye of the nurses. But there was no sign of Angela. Harley stood still, cocking his head to hear if she was in the bathroom, but the room was quiet. Turning to close the door, he saw a flash of red and white beneath a low-lying bush.

Harley frowned and walked into the garden to see what it was and was surprised to see it was Daniel's superhero lunch box. He reached down and picked it up, hearing there was something inside it.

"What on earth?" Harley said, walking back into Angela's room.

He sat at the small desk, putting the lunch box before him. Memories of Daniel proudly taking it to school when he was six flashed through Harley's mind, and tears stung his eyes. He was amazed to see Angela had kept it.

"She must've brought it with her when she was transferred here," Harley told himself.

As Harley looked at the security lock on the box, he remembered how Daniel loved the fact that it had a secret code to unlock it. However, they all knew the code, so Harley hoped it was still the same. He punched in the month of each of their birthdays, and the box popped open. As he opened it, he couldn't help but tear up. He could still hear the echoes of Daniel's delighted laugh every time the box dramatically popped open.

Only there wasn't a hidden stash of sweets or baseball cards in the box. There was a thumb drive and a note.

Harley,

The BAD MAN killed Annie's sister and Clair, and now they are coming for me.

Take the drive to Uncle Sam and ONLY Uncle Sam.

Be careful, as the BAD MAN has eyes and ears everywhere.

He's framing Duncan for Clair's murder because we know the truth.

Angela

Harley stared at the note in disbelief for a few seconds before reaching into the box and taking the thumb drive, which he pocketed along with Angela's note. He felt like he was in a video game where you had to find objects and rescue people. Only Harley had missed or overlooked a whole lot of pieces along the way.

He looked down at the lunch box, and something made him take a felt pen and some paper. Harley scribbled a note on it, put it in the box, locked it, and placed it back beneath the bush as close to how Harley found it as he could remember. He'd just pushed it into place when the room door slammed open. Harley was still crouched down as he turned and saw who it was.

"What are you doing..." Harley didn't get a chance to finish as things happened so fast.

"I'll take that!"

That was the last thing Harley heard before something stung his shoulder, and the world around him went black.

"Harley!" A female voice called to him from behind a thick foggy veil. "Wake up!"

Harley tried to open his eyes, but they felt so heavy because he was so tired.

"HARLEY!"

Something thumped painfully into his shoulder, making him pry his eyes open. The world around him was fuzzy. All of a sudden, a face appeared in front of him.

"Oh, good, you're awake!" The face and voice were familiar, but he couldn't quite capture them through his fuzzy brain. "Now get us the heck out of here!"

"Where am I?" Harley squeezed his eyes shut and tried to lift his arm to rub them but couldn't. Frowning, he looked down as the fuzz started to clear and he looked at the ropes secured around his body. "I'm tied to a chair?"

"Oh great! His brain's fried!"

Harley shook the last of the fog away, which left him with a dull headache and a dry mouth.

"What did he drug me with?" Harley tried to wet his mouth and lips.

"Probably a dart from that tranquilizer gun."

He turned his head. "Oh, you are here."

"Wow! That's nice."

"I'm sorry," Harley said. "But it's not every day someone gets the drop on me and ties me to a chair."

"Oh, and this isn't new for me?"

"Again, Harriet, I apologize," Harley said, his eyes widening as reality rushed back in, and his head swiveled toward her. "Harriet?"

"Seriously, I think you must've hit your head when you were tran-qed," Harriet reasoned. "You are kind of big, so I reckon when you crumple to the ground, you hit it with quite a force."

"No!" Harley shook his head. "I was crouching down putting the lunch box..." His eyes widened. "Oh no, the thumb drive."

"What?" Harriet gave him a weird look.

"Angela left a thumb drive for me to find," Harley explained.

"How would she know you'd find it?" Harriet asked.

"I guess she knows me well enough to know I'd find her, and I'd thoroughly search her room if she wasn't in it," Harley told her.

"Nice!" Harriet gave him a disgusted look. "You're saying that you search Angela's room when she's not around."

"No!" Harley shook his head, getting irritated by Harriet's snappy assumptions. "Well, yes, I occasionally look around the room."

"Uh-huh!" Harriet nodded. "I get it. Your ex has issues, and you're trying to look out for her and make sure she doesn't stab you when you visit."

"Something like that." Harley shook his head, looking around the room, his eyes fixed on the camera. "He covered the camera."

"Yup!" Harriet nodded.

"Wait!" Harley looked at Harriet curiously. "How are you ..." His face dropped as realization dawned on him.

"How am I here in your ex-wife's room?" Harriet looked at him with raised brows, her voice dripped with sarcasm. "Or how did I get tied to a chair by a rambling *crazy person?*"

"Both of those, but more importantly, where is Jennifer?" Harley looked at her, fear slowly meandering through his system.

"Well, we came to find you when Jennifer received a text message from Angela telling her they're at Beach Plum Cottage and need her help because the 'BAD MAN' is after them," Harriet explained. "But that terrible half-nurse security guard hybrid at the front desk wouldn't let us through. Jennifer messaged Angela to tell her our situation, and she kindly gave us a way into her room."

"Angela helped you break into a high-security mental health institute?" Harley stared at Harriet in amazement.

"It isn't so high security if we managed to scale the wall over there, and they let a crazy person just walk in here." Harriet paused for a moment, and her eyes narrowed. "Wait, maybe he was already in here."

"Harriet, you can't go around calling people crazy. Especially not in here," Harley pointed out.

"Uh-huh!" Harriet gave him a hooded look. "Who's housed in the basement floor of this building?"

"The criminally insane!" Harley realized what he'd said too late.

"So I can call them insane rather than crazy?" Harriet stated. "That's actually better as that man was freakin' insane mumbling to himself about people blaming him, and it's not his fault. He hasn't hurt anyone, and that it was unfair that Clair blamed him for Daniel..."

"What did you say?" Harley's heart froze in his chest, and he felt the blood drain from his face.

"Which part do you want me to repeat?" Harriet asked. "Because I was just getting to the part where he tied me to a chair with his belt and then my wrists behind my back with cable ties." She shook her head as her voice raised. "Who carries cable ties in their pocket?"

"The part about Daniel." Harley's voice was harsh.

"He said that it was unfair of Clair to blame him for Daniel. He had his flu shot, but she didn't. She only pretended to so she could see the doctor she was having an affair with," Harriet repeated. "He was rambling about Daniel was like his son too, that he'd never do anything to hurt Daniel, just like he'd never hurt Gloria. He was trying to protect her and his baby brother."

"He said this while he was tying you to a chair?" Harley had to move the conversation away from the revelation about Daniel. His mind was reeling as he asked Harriet. "Do you know who the man was that tied you up?"

"Probably the same man that got the drop on a Navy SEAL and tied them to a chair?" Harriet pursed her lips and looked at him smugly.

"I'm an ex-Navy SEAL, and I was distracted, and that's the only reason that old man got the drop on me," Harley hissed defensively.

"Wait!" Harriet looked at him. "Old man?" Harley nodded, and he could see a dash of humor spark in her eyes for a few seconds. "If I wasn't tied to a chair and worried sick about the cra... sorry, insane person that has Jennifer and is heading to Beach Plum Cottage, I'd be laughing that you got taken down by an old man."

"Noted!" Harley said, watching Harriet hop the chair over to the wall. "Hold on." His brow creased. "You keep referring to the man who tied you up and took Jennifer as a cra... insane person. Was he old?"

"Nope!" Harriet pushed herself to her feet. She stopped and twisted her mouth thoughtfully. "I'd say he was about our age."

"He didn't give you his name?" Harley knew it was a long shot, but he was pretty sure it was Wallis!

"Oh, yes." Harriet looked at him. "He introduced himself right before he produced a gun and tied me to a chair!" Her voice raised near the end.

Harley's brow was knit and lifted as he watched her, wondering what she was doing. The chair curled over her butt and back, looking like a deformed Ninja Turtle.

"What on earth are you doing?" Harley looked at her in confusion.

"I'm going to hit the chair against the wall to break it and get free," Harriet explained. "What did you think I was doing? Chair yoga?"

Harley knew it wasn't appropriate, but it had been a stressful two days, and the sight of Harriet standing looking like a butterfly without wings as her arms were tied behind her with the chair, making her hunched over as she hit it against the wall stuck a funny bone. He burst out laughing.

"Well, that's just great!" Harriet said. "You sit there laughing at me doing nothing, the big Navy SEAL who got taken down by a geriatric. At least I'm trying to get myself free."

Harley sobered and cleared his throat. "He wasn't exactly a geriatric and rather fit for an older man."

"Okay, how old was he?" Harriet asked, swinging against the wall and nearly bouncing herself over.

"I think mid... Uh..." Harley cleared his throat. "I don't know."

"Okay!" Harriet said, about to take another run at the wall.

"You do know that's a metal chair, and you're not going to break it like that," Harley pointed out.

Harriet stopped, blinked, and glared at him. "You should've said that before I looked like a baby rhino trying to knock down a cement tree!"

"I'd say you looked more like a square Ninja Turtle." Harley bit back a smile. "We could call you Square-O-Chair."

"That's not even funny," Harriet hissed, bobbing along with the chair on her back, making her way back to him. "Then tell me, Mr. ex-Navy SEAL, with *ex* being the operative word, how the heck are we going to get out of here to save Jennifer and your ex-wife?"

"I'm going to just..." Harley fiddled with the knot, and it finally came loose and he undid the one around his chest. "Finish untying myself and think about freeing you while I check for the..." He fished in his secret pocket and found the thumb drive. "Phew. I still have it."

"Great, now untie me, and I'll tell you where he took Jennifer," Harriet bargained.

"You already told me." Harley stared at her smugly. "You'll be safer here."

"And how are you going to get to Plum Island?" Harriet pursed her lips and raised her eyebrows.

"Did they take Jennifer's car?" Harley's brain was in such a spin he wasn't thinking straight he had to focus.

"Nope." Harriet shook her head.

"Good, then I'll take her car," Harley told her.

"Good luck getting into or hot wiring the Subaru." It was Harriet's turn to smile smugly.

"You have the keys, don't you?" Harley shook his head.

Harriet nodded. "I do, and I just happen to be sitting on them."

"Ouch, that must be uncomfortable as Jennifer has a big ring of keys," Harley stated, walking toward her to untie her.

"You have no idea," Harriet said.

Harley untied Harriet, and she stood rubbing her wrists and loosening her arms.

"Come on, let's get out of here," Harley said, pulling the door open and stepping out into the quiet hallway. "That's strange. It's never this quiet."

"That's because everyone's at dinner," Harriet whispered, pointing to the dining room.

"Great, come on." Harley and Harriet rushed into the reception area.

They were surprised to see no guards there.

"I wonder where the..." Harley's eyes widened when he saw Harriet pointing to the reception desk.

"I hope they're sleeping like you were and not dead!" Harriet said, looking a little green.

Harley stepped around and felt for a pulse. "They're sleeping." His eyes narrowed. "The geriatric did this."

"Ah-ha!" Harriet pointed at him. "It was a geriatric that took you down."

"No, he took me by surprise," Harley growled. "Come on. We don't have time for this."

"Sure." Harriet ran behind him as they dashed through the front door. "That's disturbing that we could just run right out the front door without getting stopped."

"I had a key card that opened the door," Harley told her, showing her his visitor's pass.

"Shouldn't you have left it at the reception desk?" Harriet asked as they got to Jennifer's car.

"Keys." Harley held out his hand and raised an eyebrow when she fished them out of the front pocket of her designer jeans. "I thought you had them in your back pocket."

"I'm from New York!" Harriet pointed out. "Putting anything in your back pocket is like handing someone what you've put in there with all the pickpockets."

"Good to know." Harley unlocked the car, and they climbed in.

"I hope you're going to return the pass eventually," Harriet said, sliding the safety belt on.

"Of course." Harley started the car and backed out of the parking lot. "Let's hope there's no cops on the road."

As they sped toward Plum Island, he asked Harriet to explain the man who had taken Jennifer.

"A few inches taller than me, moderately handsome, deep voice although he was muttering a lot," Harriet's brow creased thoughtfully. "Oh, and his one eye had a spot of yellow in it."

Harley's eyes widened. Now, the Daniel and Clair comment made sense. He hit the steering wheel. "I knew it!"

"Are you going to tell me how an older man got the drop on you?" Harriet asked him again.

"You're not going to leave this alone, are you?" Harley looked at her, and she shook her head.

"I've seen how you automatically scan your surroundings," Harriet told him. "So, I'm thinking there's only a few ways someone would get the drop on you. You were drugged or surprised to see them, which meant you knew them and probably trusted them."

"Wow!" Harley breathed as they drove into Plum Island. "You're quite the detective." He sighed and ran a hand through his hair. "Yes, the man surprised me, I knew him, and he's someone I'd usually trust with my life."

353

"But he knocked you out and tied you to a chair," Harriet pointed out. "Who was he? So I know if I ever meet this man, I should be very wary of them."

"You already have met him," Harley told her. "It was my Uncle Sam."

CHAPTER 17

J ennifer's heart was beating like a wild bird trapped in a cage, but she refused to let fear rule her. She looked at the man driving beside her. While Jennifer could see he wasn't emotionally stable and he'd kidnapped her at gunpoint, she wasn't afraid of him. As soon as he'd locked her in the car and taken off, he'd started to explain to her why he'd kidnapped her. He'd even dropped the gun on the back floor, telling her it wasn't loaded.

"I don't want to hurt anyone," he told her again, glancing at her as they headed through the streets of Plum Island. "I'm sorry I scared you like this. But I can't let another person I care about get hurt because I've been a scared little boy for the past forty years, but no more."

"I know it's probably in a different way," Jennifer sympathized. "I can understand how you feel. You think you have control of your own life and can push the fear, anger, and frustration aside and ignore it because acknowledging it means they've won."

"That's right, you're Andrew Gains's daughter." He nodded. "We call him the white knight in dark armor."

"I don't think there's any white knight in Andrew," Jennifer disagreed and moved the subject back toward him. "Who's made you feel like a scared little boy?"

"Like you, I have father issues," he admitted. "I've tried to cling to the time when he was my hero. I used to think he was the greatest father and such a caring human being." He snorted. "I was ten when I found out who my father really was!" He shook his head. "He's a brilliant man. Scarily so and can turn any situation into one favoring him even if he has to lie and cheat to do it."

"Sounds like we have the same kind of fathers," Jennifer commented.

"Andrew?" His brows shot up in surprise. "Andrew is *nothing* like my father. Growing up, I used to wish Andrew was my father. He was always kind to me and never believed my father's lies." Pain shadowed his eyes, and he shook his. "Even my own mother believed my father over me." He glanced at her. "She believed a man she hates over the son she professes to love more than life itself."

"How can you say that about Andrew?" Jennifer looked at him, shocked. "Didn't Andrew defend your father and destroy a family's life by getting your father acquitted? Andrew got in that family's way of getting justice for what your father did."

"No, you have it all wrong." He shook his head. "What Andrew did was ensure that his family were safe and well looked after for the rest of their lives."

"He got a settlement for them?" Jennifer frowned. "I never read anything about that."

"Of course not." His eyes narrowed. "It wouldn't have looked good for my father or his buddies if that came to light."

"Your father should never have gotten off like that." Jennifer wasn't apologetic for her statement about Andrew.

"I can't agree with you more about my father," he told her. "We finally got the evidence we needed to prove he was guilty, and now Clair's dead."

His eyes misted, and knuckles whitened on the steering wheel.

"So you didn't kill Clair?" Jennifer knew that wasn't the most intelligent question to ask.

He turned his head to look at her with pain searing through his eyes.

"No. I loved Clair." His voice was gravely. "Even after everything she'd done, I loved her."

Jennifer wanted to believe him, and her gut told her he didn't kill her, but her mind was on the fence about it.

"Turn here," Jennifer said, pointing at the turn-off to Beach Plum Cottage. She looked at the man. "Seriously, you'd better be telling me the truth because I *do* have a loaded gun at my house."

He gave a soft snort. "If it makes you feel better, get your gun when we get to your house." Sadness and a look of resignation clouded his eyes. "In fact, we may need it if *they've* got here first."

"Who?" Jennifer frowned. It was the second time he'd mentioned them, or them getting to Angela first. "When you first dragged me to your car, you kept saying you couldn't let them get to Angela first."

He slowed down as they neared the gates to the property. Jennifer's heart started thudding again when she saw a strange car in the driveway.

"Do you recognize that car?" Jennifer asked, and he nodded. "Is it a good sign or a bad sign?"

"Good." He looked around. "Are those garages?" He pointed.

"Yes." Jennifer nodded. "The remote for them is inside, though." She looked at him as realization dawned. "You want to hide the cars in the garage?"

"I think that would be best, don't you?" He looked at her questioningly.

"Yes." Jennifer nodded and tried the door handle as he slowed to a stop. "I can't get out."

"Sorry." He took the child lock off, and Jennifer jumped out of the car.

She rushed toward the front door, remembering she didn't have her keys, and turned to go back to the old beach plum tree. Jennifer cringed, looking at the knot where her aunt had left the spare key.

Please don't be any creepy critters in there. Don't be a baby, Jennifer. In the past two days, you've found a dead body, met Andrew and his family, and got entangled in a dangerous mess, but you're scared of a few small tree critters. Jennifer still shuddered at the thought of sticking her hand into that little dark hole in the tree.

She turned her face slightly and was about to reach into the tree when she was stopped.

"I can do that for you," her kidnapper said, reaching in and finding the key. He dusted it off and handed it to Jennifer. "Here you go."

He stood behind the large tree, his eyes scanning the area.

"Thank you," Jennifer hurried to the front door and unlocked it, wondering where the other car's occupants were.

She didn't have long to wait to get her answer. As she pushed the door open, Angela called her.

"Jennifer!"

Jennifer turned to see her and Annie Liddle, or rather Montgomery, running toward them. Before they reached the front door, the man who'd kidnapped her stepped out from behind the tree, making the two women skid to a halt as they stared at him in shock.

Oh no! Jennifer's pulse began to race in fear as she saw the expression of fright on the woman's face and was about to doubt her judgment of him when the situation did an about-turn.

"Wallis!" Angela's fear faded, and she flung herself into his arms, tears springing. "I thought you were dead." She pushed herself back for a few seconds, looking at him, and her voice became frantic. "Clair! They got Clair."

While the scene unfolding was emotionally charged, Jennifer couldn't help sighing in relief that her kidnapper had been telling the truth. Her eyes widened as his words about his father and mother rushed through her mind: *Even my own mother believed my father's lies.* Her brow creased as she watched the exchange between Wallis and Angela. Annie stood to one side, keeping a careful eye out.

What did your father lie about, Wallis? Jennifer's frown deepened. Wallis said he was ten when he found out who his father really was.

How old is Wallis? She reviewed everything he'd rambled about in the car on their way to Beach Plum Cottage.

"I know," Wallis told Angela, pulling her to him again. His voice was hoarse with emotion. "I know."

"I knew you'd find us," Angela told Wallis and then looked toward Jennifer with a watery smile. "I knew you'd come too."

"Who can ignore a text message: *At Beach Plum Cottage, we need help. The BAD MAN is after us*?" Jennifer recounted the message Angela had sent her. *And here I am, following two crazy people down yet another adrenaline-fueling, terror-invoking adventure!* She gave herself a mental shake. *Not crazy people, Jennifer. Emotionally unstable people!* She corrected herself.

"Jennifer?" Annie's voice snapped her from her thoughts.

Jennifer stepped back when she realized Annie had moved and was standing right before her.

"You need to wear a bell," Jennifer told Annie.

"We need to get inside," Annie said.

"Not before you tell me why you and your nephew were moving Clair's body into that car?" Jennifer's pulse started racing as she faced the older woman with shrewd eyes.

"I'll tell you once we're inside and safe," Annie bargained.

"Why are you at *my* house?" Jennifer suddenly asked. "How did you know where I lived?"

The thought finally occurred to her. With everything that had happened, Jennifer hadn't realized she'd never told Angela where she lived, yet Angela somehow knew.

"We were told to come here," Angela told Jennifer, moving beside Annie. "We'd be safer here."

"Who told you to come here?" Jennifer's eyes narrowed as she slightly turned her face as she asked.

"Betty!" Annie replied, her words sending shock waves down Jennifer's spine.

"My Aunt Betty!" Jennifer pointed at her chest, and confusion rushed through her.

"Do you know any other Bettys?" Annie looked at her with raised brows.

"Please, Jennifer," Angela implored. "Give Wallis the garage remote so he can hide the cars."

Jennifer's confusion had escalated. This was all getting too much, and she realized it was way more complex than just a simple out-for-revenge or avenge plot. This mystery had more twists and turns than the gnarled oak tree out the back of her house that looked like all its branches had been twisted in a heavy wind.

Jennifer gritted her teeth ruing the day she'd agreed to go for a freakin' DNA test in Boston. Which was no longer her favorite city! Jennifer stepped back her mind, finding alternate routes to fly to New York rather than through Boston.

Good grief! Jennifer walked to the key hook on the wall a few feet from the door and got the garage remote she handed to Wallis. *This is what I get for wanting to talk Harriet into doing one of those escape rooms with me for my birthday because I needed some action and adventure in my life.* Her eyes narrowed, and she shook her head. *You have a sick sense of humor, universe!*

"Do you have something to eat?" Angela asked, eyeing the kitchen.

"Help yourself." Jennifer pointed toward the kitchen. "I'm sure Aunt Betty has a kitchen full of food. Her housekeeper comes twice a week and stocks up."

"Thank you." Angela dashed into the kitchen.

Annie watched her go, and Jennifer noted how fond Annie was of Angela. She frowned, tilting her head.

"You really care about her, don't you?" Jennifer asked Annie.

Annie looked at Jennifer and nodded. "The poor woman has been through so much thanks to her family." She shook her head, her eyes narrowed, and her voice filled with venom. "Especially that no good sister of hers. I never trusted Clair."

That alarmed Jennifer, whose pulse again started racing as nervous thoughts tumbled into her head. "You disliked Clair?" Her eyes narrowed. She knew she should stop asking, but she couldn't help herself. Jennifer needed to put the pieces together. "Enough to kill her?"

"What?" Annie looked at her in horror. "You think I killed Clair?"

"Annie didn't kill Clair," Angela walked through with a box of cherry Pop-Tarts under her arm and munching on some chocolate chip cookies.

Where on earth does that slip of a woman put all the junk food she eats? Jennifer gave herself another mental shake. *Now is not the time to drift into procrastination thoughts.*

"Then who did?" Jennifer asked as Wallis walked inside.

Jennifer stepped back toward the glass sliding door on the far side of the living room as she heard him close and lock the front door. Her eyes scanned the three people, who were really strangers to her, standing in her house. Three strangers were involved in a murder, and Jennifer had just left them in the house. She went from feeling like Alice falling through a rabbit hole to the little pig who'd just left three big bad wolves in its brick house.

Before anyone could answer, someone banged on the front door. The moment had gotten so tense in the living room that Jennifer nearly had a heart attack as the first thump hit the oak door.

"Jennifer!" A male voice was muffled and undistinguishable through the thick door. "Jennifer. Are you in there?"

The four people in the house went deathly quiet, looking at each other in wide-eyed fear. The thumping stopped, and there was silence for a few moments.

"Jennifer!" The male voice bellowed from the glass door, making her yelp and spin around. "Let me in."

Her hand covered her heart as it nearly shot out her chest. Jennifer's breath came out in a pant as the fear slowly subsided, and she rushed toward the door, glad to see someone she trusted standing there.

"Sam!" Jennifer was still trying to regulate her breath as she slid the door open and threw herself into his arms. "Oh, thank goodness it's you."

"Are you okay, honey?" Sam squeezed her before stepping back.

Her eyes narrowed at him. "But announce yourself next time." Jennifer hissed. "You know I have a genetic heart condition, and you nearly gave me heart failure."

"I'm sorry," Sam apologized before stepping around her and walking into the house. "Are you all okay?"

The other three occupants of the living room all greeted Sam the same way Jennifer had. With relief! She closed the glass door, locked it, and drew the curtains.

"Now that we're all here," Jennifer indicated to the chairs. "In *my* house. Why don't you all take a seat and tell me *what the heck is going on!*" She plonked down in her aunt's favorite wingback chair, eyeing her *guests*.

Sam sat next to Annie on the small sofa while Wallis and Angela sat on the larger sofa with Angela's pile of snacks between them.

"Can I make you a sandwich or get you an apple?" Jennifer asked Angela, who'd nearly polished off an entire box of choc-chip cookies.

"Oh no," Angela declined. "I'm fine with these snacks."

Jennifer looked at her, feeling ill at the amount of sugar and empty carbs Angela was consuming, before moving her attention to Annie.

"You can start by telling me what you and your nephew Duncan were doing in Harley's garage lockup," Jennifer looked at Annie.

"Can I answer?" Angela raised her arm.

Jennifer's gaze honed in on Angela as she tried to gauge the woman's state of mind. Other than feeding her addiction to sugar, Angela seemed lucid.

"Sure, why not?" Jennifer shrugged.

"About a year ago, Clair came to see me," Angela explained and glanced at Annie. "I allowed her to only if Annie stayed with us."

"Angela has always been convinced that Clair was trying to... harm her," Wallis filled Jennifer in. He turned and smiled warmly at Angela.

"I'm sorry I never believed you." His eyes darkened with sorrow once again. "I should've believed you, as I know what it's like when people don't."

Angela reached over and squeezed his hand compassionately before turning back to Jennifer. "Clair told me that Harley and my parents were keeping me locked in the institute and being fed drugs that weren't helping me but hindering my recovery."

"I told Clair to stop lying as I know exactly what medication Angela is on," Annie added.

"Clair was furious when I believed Annie over her," Angela continued. "Annie made her leave after Clair accused Annie, Harley, and my parents of manipulating me so they could keep control of the company and my money."

"Wait!" Jennifer stopped her. "What do you mean keep control of the company and your money?" Before Wallis could launch into an explanation, she held up her hand. "Let me rephrase that. Why would your family need to keep you locked away to control the company, and why would they need *your* money?"

"My grandfather and my father never got along," Angela explained. "Especially after my grandad found out my father was mixing with what gramps called the wrong crowd."

"Her grandfather meant my father and your..." Wallis pursed his lips. "Pearce Gains, Andrew's father."

"No matter what my father tried, Gramps held onto control of the company until I was old enough to take over," Angela said. The information made Jennifer's eyes widen as she nodded.

"Angela's grandfather, Harrold, left the company, all his estates, and the entire family fortune to Angela," Sam finished for Angela.

"What about Clair?" Jennifer asked. "She's your twin. Didn't your grandfather leave her anything?'

"Gramps left me in charge of the trust fund he'd set up for Clair," Angela informed Jennifer.

"Clair has never been happy about that," Wallis said. "That and how Angela warned Clair that the only way she'd ever see any of the money was for her to clean herself up and take a job at the company."

"Clair did clean up her act," Angela told Jennifer. "And she worked really hard in the marketing department. I even promoted her to VP of it."

"Where does your relationship fit into all this?" Jennifer asked Angela and Wallis.

"I cheated on Harley with Wallis. Harley and I got divorced. I married Wallis," Angela told her.

"And I cheated on Angela with Clair and fell for her." Wallis sent an apologetic look to Angela.

"We knew a few months after we got married it was a mistake," Angela admitted, and Wallis nodded. "I was lonely with Harley being gone all the time, running a company, and being a mom took its toll, and Wallis was there for me."

"We grew up together," Wallis explained. "I was always envious of how close their family seemed." He shook his head. "I used to think of Randal and Margaret Wesley as my parents. Marrying Angela made it seem official." He looked at his hands. "My father and sister always tried to push Angela and me together in our early twenties."

"You married Angela because you wanted her parents to be yours?" Jennifer looked at him in disbelief.

"No!" Wallis looked at her as if she was crazy. "I married Angela because I thought I was in love with her."

"We loved each other, but we weren't in love with each other," Angela told Jennifer. "By the time I realized I still loved Harley..." She sighed. "It was too late. I'd ruined any chance I'd had with him." She smiled. "Then Daniel got sick. Mine and Harley's lives changed so drastically. My sole focus became Daniel and doing whatever it took to get him better."

"Angela even made me temporary CEO of Wesley Industries," Wallis surprised Jennifer. "That did not sit well with Angela's parents, but it drew Clair and me closer." His eyes narrowed and flashed with an emotion Jennifer couldn't define. "It also made my father proud, and he tried to talk me out of divorcing Angela. He said that Angela would make the position permanent if I stayed married to her."

"You were so besotted with Clair that you didn't realize that she was using your feelings to get what she wanted," Annie's eyes flashed angrily at Wallis. "She wanted control of Wesley Industries."

"So why did Clair end up dead?" Jennifer asked, moving the conversation away from the family drama.

"Because she finally grew a conscience when she realized what the people actually meant when they said Angela needed to be more permanently moved out of the way," Annie answered.

"And not *only* Angela," Sam added.

Jennifer's heart slammed into her rib cage when she realized that Sam was talking about Harley as he was the one who had control of Angela's entire life, including control over Wesley Industries and what Jennifer thought must be a sizable amount of money.

"Angela and Harley are in great danger, aren't they?" The words tumbled from Jennifer's lips. "And all because of money?"

"Especially now they know Clair was the one that died and not Angela," Annie pointed out.

"Clair!" Wallis's words were ragged, and his eyes haunted. "I should've got her to understand who she worked for a lot sooner."

"This isn't your fault, Wallis," Angela soothed.

"Yes, it is!" Annie and Sam said in unison.

"You should've spoken up years ago, you coward!" Annie sneered at him.

"Annie, please," Angela implored her. "You don't know what it's like to live in fear like Wallis has since he was ten years old."

"Ten years old!" Jennifer looked at Wallis. "How old are you?"

"Fifty." Wallis looked at her curiously.

Jennifer's eyes widened as it suddenly dawned on her. "The night you found out who your father really was was the night of Gloria Liddle's death."

"Yes." Wallis nodded.

Her eyes narrowed. "Your mother was trying to get your father and his friends arrested for abusing Gloria and was trying to figure out who fathered Duncan." Her eyes darted from Annie to Wallis. "Why did your mother suddenly swap sides during your father's trial and support him, changing her statement about Gloria?"

"Because my father told her I killed Gloria." Wallis's words had Jennifer's jaw-dropping.

I did not see that coming! Jennifer stared at Wallis. "She changed her mind because of you."

"She changed her mind because she believed my father's lies," Wallis corrected Jennifer. "I was playing video games in the Wesley's pool house when I heard Gloria and someone arguing by the pool. They were shouting and made baby Duncan cry."

"I was sleeping on the sofa then," Angela told Jennifer. "I didn't hear a thing until Shannon rushed into the pool house with Wallis and shoved him in the shower."

"You were there?" Jennifer asked Angela, amazed.

"I didn't see anything because Shannon wouldn't let us out of the pool house until Gloria had been taken away and Sylvia, Gloria's mother, took Duncan," Angela told her.

"Where was Clair?" Jennifer asked.

"She'd gone to her room long before that," Wallis told her. "Clair hardly ever socialized with us."

"Was Shannon with you?" Jennifer looked from Wallis to Angela.

"Yes, she was looking after us while my parents were out," Angela answered.

"What happened, Wallis?" Jennifer looked at him.

"I rushed out when I heard Gloria scream, and Duncan's cries got louder," Wallis continued to tell Jennifer the story. "I saw a dark shadow rush off to one side, but I ignored it when I saw Gloria lying on the ground bleeding." He stared into the distance, taken by the memory. "I yelled, Glory, and dropped down beside her. There was so much blood. I remembered our lesson during a school camping trip: you had to try and stop the bleeding. I took a towel and pressed it to her head."

"That's when Shaun appeared and got his daughter to take Wallis inside and clean him up," Sam finished the story. "Shaun told his wife and close circle of friends," he looked at Jennifer, "which included Pearce Gains that Wallis had killed Gloria because he thought she was trying to break their family up by having his father's baby."

"Is Duncan your father's child?" Jennifer felt her heart lurch.

"No!" Angela, Sam, Annie, and Wallis said in unison and looked at Jennifer.

"Do you know whose child he is?" Jennifer asked, warning bells going off in her head at how they looked at her. "Is he Andrew's child?"

"He's my half-brother," Angela told her. "That night, while my parents were out celebrating their anniversary, Shaun was tasked with taking care of the *Gloria* problem."

"So your father did kill Angela?" Jennifer's head shot toward Wallis, who nodded. She looked at Angela. "Do both of your parents know who Duncan is?"

"Yes." Angela nodded. "When my mother discovered the truth about Duncan, she demanded that my father look after him."

"I was given a position at the Wesley's company while I worked through college," Annie told her. "Between Margaret and Harrold Wesley, they saw that my family was cared for. Randal was rather off to me after the trial but I needed the work so it was water off a duck's back."

"I thought Andrew took care of that," Jennifer said.

"Andrew ensured that my family was never harmed," Annie told Jennifer, "and my mother was given a hefty settlement to ensure we could take care of Duncan."

"Andrew has information that could destroy the Wesleys, Hanovers, and a whole lot of other powerful people in and around Boston," Sam explained to Jennifer.

"What a hero!" Jennifer stated sarcastically. A pain shot through her chest, and she flinched.

"Are you okay?" Sam's eyes widened with concern.

"Just pangs," Jennifer told him. "I've had too much excitement over the past few days."

"Is it your heart?" Angela's eyes widened worriedly. "Davina told me about your heart."

"That was gossipy of her," Jennifer stated. "No. It's just a stitch or something. I always get them when I get upset, over excited, or in any tense situation."

"I didn't think it would be your heart," Sam said. "Davina made sure she fixed it permanently for you."

Sam's words made Jennifer freeze as she looked at Sam. "What did you say?"

Sam's expression showed he hadn't meant to give that information away. "You didn't speak to Davina while you were in Boston? Or Andrew?"

"I spoke to them both," Jennifer's eyes narrowed suspiciously as she spoke to Sam. "But I kept it as polite as I could, not because of them but because I promised Molly I wouldn't upset her father or grandmother any more than they were with her in the hospital."

"Ah!" Sam nodded. "So, you never asked Andrew or Davina why Andrew left forty years ago?"

"No!" Jennifer shook her head. "I wasn't going to ask because I hoped to salvage a bit of my trip to Boston."

"Of course!" Sam said. "I know it's not ideal, but happy birthday, Jennifer."

"Oh!" Annie's eyes widened, and she turned to Jennifer. "Happy birthday."

Wallis wished her well and apologized again for kidnapping her on her birthday. Jennifer looked at him and saw who he was for the first time since meeting him—a boy looking for love and acceptance.

Someone to believe in him. Her eyes traveled to Angela, and instead of seeing animosity between them, she noticed a bond of friendship. Angela was the one person who accepted Wallis and believed in him, or she wouldn't have put him temporarily in charge of Wesley Industries. A thought struck Jennifer.

"Who's the current CEO of Wesley Industries?" Jennifer saw their startled looks at her sudden conversation change from her birthday.

"I am," Wallis told her.

"You're CEO of both Hanover and Wesley industries?" Jennifer asked him to clarify.

"Yes." Wallis nodded.

"And Harley is okay with that?" Jennifer remembered that Harley didn't have a very high opinion of Wallis.

"He's never tried to get me to step down," Wallis told her.

"I wouldn't let him," Angela said.

"Didn't you try to kill Wallis and Clair when they came to tell you they were engaged?" Jennifer remembered Angela telling her a bit of the story.

"Angela didn't attack Clair over our engagement," Wallis told Jennifer.

Wallis looked at Angela, whose eyes had darkened with emotion; her face paled, and she swiped at a few stray tears. Angela took Wallis's hand and turned to Jennifer. Her eyes were hooded, and she struggled to control her emotions.

"Clair came to apologize to me," Angela's voice was low and hoarse with pain.

"For stealing your husband?" Jennifer guessed.

"No." Angela's face started to crumple, and she sucked in a shaky breath as the tears rolled down her cheeks. "For giving Daniel the flu."

"WHAT?" Harley's voice boomed from the front door.

CHAPTER 18

H arley stood glued to the spot, gaping at Angela before she dashed off the sofa and rushed into his arms.

"I'm sorry, Harley," Angela sobbed. "I'm so, so, sorry. I couldn't tell you. I wanted to tell you, but I couldn't."

Harley stiffened, although his arms automatically went around Angela's tiny waist.

"You couldn't or wouldn't?" Anger, hurt, and betrayal made him feel like he'd run through a brick wall.

The world felt like it wobbled beneath his feet while his head felt like it was vibrating.

"I'm just going to move over here," Harriet said, popping out from behind Harley and walking to where Sam was.

"I couldn't," Angela sobbed.

"I thought there was more to the story about you attacking Clair like you did," Harley told her, stepping away from her. "You let me almost destroy an innocent doctor's career."

"I was protecting you," Angela reasoned. "I knew if you knew it was Clair... You already disliked her so much."

"I don't know what to say to this," Harley said honestly. "You let me believe that our son died because of a negligent doctor when all along you were protecting your sister. A woman who was so jealous of you that she wanted to take everything from you by whatever means necessary."

"She's telling the truth," Wallis said, sticking up for Angela.

"I don't remember including you in this conversation." Harley glared at Wallis. "What are you even doing here?" His gaze had swung toward Jennifer. He pushed past Angela and went to Jennifer's side. "Are you okay?" His eyes traveled over her. "Did Wallis hurt you?"

"No," Jennifer stood, and his heart skipped a beat as their eyes met. "I'm fine. Wallis just wanted to find Angela and Annie."

"So he kidnapped you at gunpoint?" He turned and glared at Wallis. "It was you that has been following us since the diner, wasn't it?"

"Yes," Wallis admitted. "I knew you'd lead me to Angela, and I needed to know she was alright and that BAD MAN hadn't gotten to her like they'd gotten to Clair."

"Who is this bad man?" Harley and Jennifer uttered at the same time.

"Not who," Annie said. "What!"

"Are you talking about the BAD MAN club?" Harriet asked, frowning. "That club is so exclusive that it hand-picks and invites members to join."

"The Bad Man you've been talking about is a club?" Harley addressed Angela.

"Yes," Wallis answered for Angela and looked at Harriet. "It only *invites* members that can serve its purpose, and turning down the invitation is *not* an option when you're invited."

"They are rumored to be a criminal organization that's taken over Boston's underworld trades," Annie added.

"But underworld trades, you mean..." Jennifer prompted.

"Getting corrupt officials to do what they want them to do," Annie told her. "Like judges throwing cases out of court, getting senators to pass various bills, and so on."

"Oh, so not drugs or any old-time criminal activity," Harriet said.

"They don't run the drugs themselves," Wallis said. "But they help the head of the cartels by opening up their distribution centers for a price."

"Like money?" Jennifer asked.

"No favors," Annie answered. "They get protection for their members."

"Like getting them off for murder?" Jennifer realized.

"Why is this club after Angela?" Harley asked.

He glanced at Angela standing between Annie and Wallis, who had his arm protectively around her, making his fists clench at his sides. Harley's mind still hadn't processed the information about Clair's part in his son's death. Whenever the thought popped into his head, he felt the world tilt, and he was drawn back to relive the worst day of his life.

"Because Clair managed to get invited into it. But she didn't like how they did things and started working for me," Andrew's voice filled the living room, making all eyes turn toward him.

"Doesn't anyone knock anymore?" Jennifer hissed. "There's also a bell!"

"I'm sorry," Andrew apologized to Jennifer. "I did knock, and the bell isn't working."

"Sorry, I disconnected it to fix it before my accident," Sam told Jennifer.

"Wait!" Jennifer looked at Wallis. "I thought you locked the door when you came inside?"

"I did," Wallis confirmed.

"I have a key," Harley told her.

"Awesome," Jennifer said, rolling her eyes before turning to Andrew. "Are you here alone, or is someone going to pop out from behind you too?"

"No, but I'm afraid I was being followed, and I don't think they're far behind me," Andrew admitted.

"This just gets better and better," Jennifer said sarcastically. "Now you're luring bad people right to my doorstep."

"Do you have any idea who's following you?" Sam asked, and Harley's eyes narrowed in on his uncle.

"I do. It seems we've managed to spook BAD MAN enough that we have the organization's new head on our tail." Andrew informed them. His eyes narrowed as he looked at Sam. "You were supposed to get Jennifer, Harley, and Harriet out of the way."

"He tried!" Harley snarled, glaring at his uncle.

"Seems I underestimated the dosage of the tranquilizer dart," Sam said.

"You and I are going to have words about this," Harley warned Sam as Andrew interrupted them.

"And Wallis, you were supposed to stay in Boston and keep an eye on James," Andrew's eyes flashed angrily. "Luckily, Sam was able to arrange someone to keep an eye on him and Duncan."

"I needed to ensure Angela was okay," Wallis snapped back. "I couldn't lose her too."

Andrew pinched the bridge of his nose. "I'm really sorry about Clair." He blew out a breath. "It seems Angela was right about someone poisoning her water."

"What?" Annie breathed in shock. "How would anyone poison Angela's water at the institute?"

"One of the nurses," Sam informed her. "Don't worry, he's taken care of."

"Clair took the water that Angela refused to drink when she busted Angela out of the institute after we got information that BAD MAN wanted her out of the way," Andrew explained. "We told Clair that we'd get Angela out of harm's way, but she panicked and took it into her own hands to save Angela."

"I'm confused," Harriet said, shaking her head. "Is Clair the bad person in this story or a good person? Who the heck side was she on?"

"Clair was only ever on Clair's side," Harley assured Harriet.

"That's not true," Wallis instantly defended her. "She didn't harm Daniel deliberately. She didn't realize she had the flu until it was too late."

"Clair was misunderstood," Angela defended her sister. "While she may have been selfish and angry at the world, she gave her life to save mine."

"And she did the right thing, even though she knew she was in danger," Andrew backed up Angela's statement. "I've spent forty years trying to bring this organization to its knees. It has destroyed families and communities and worked above the law for too long." He looked around the room. "Good people have lost their lives and sacrificed their souls to end their reign of terror. Now, thanks to Clair, Annie, and Angela, we've finally got the evidence to do so, along with everyone connected to it."

"I think what Andrew is trying to say is, we need to move out, now!" Sam ordered. "I have the evidence." He smiled at Angela.

"No, you don't!" Harley held up the thumb drive as all eyes turned to him. "You've got Daniel's lunch box with a note from me saying I love you, son, and a Sharpie in."

"May I have that?" Andrew held out his hand.

"I want to give it to you," Harley told him. "But I look around the room, and apart from Jennifer, Harriet, and me, I don't trust any of you. You've done nothing but lie to us." He glared at Sam. "And you betrayed my trust to get close to me so you could steal this."

"That's not why I did what I did," Sam told him. "I was trying to…"

"Protect me!" Harley nodded. "Like you were protecting Jennifer by not telling her about Andrew?" He glanced around the cottage. "Is Betty in on this too?"

"Is she?" Jennifer gasped, looking from Andrew to Sam.

"I've been in contact with Betty at least once a week for the past forty years," Andrew admitted. "My weekly updates about you and Liam."

Harley felt Jennifer stiffen beside him. "You're right, Harley. Everyone in this room is a liar; we can't trust them."

"Jennifer, please," Andrew implored her. "We don't have time for this. You have no idea what the people whose empire we're about to crumble are capable of."

"I think we've all been victims of them," Jennifer told him. "Harley lost his wife and child."

"That wasn't them," Andrew told her.

"No, Andrew, she's right," Wallis said. "My sister and father encouraged me to pursue Angela even though she was married to Harley." He looked apologetically toward Harley. "I never meant for Daniel or Angela to get hurt."

Harley nodded, his fists balling, and he gritted his teeth.

"I never meant to keep Clair's flu a secret from you, Harley," Angela's voice was soft, her eyes puffy from crying. "The news has broken me. While you were being strong for me while trying to keep your life together, I wasn't going to throw the straw that would break you, too."

Harley stared at her with mixed emotions coursing through him. He knew that she was telling the truth, and in her own twisted way, she thought she was protecting him. But Harley couldn't get over the fact that Angela had let him go on a witch hunt when he was looking for someone to blame for Daniel. The one thing that had always been glaringly obvious to Harley was that even though they were dysfunctional, the Wesleys had each other's back at whatever cost.

"Is this why you left us?" Jennifer's eyes were fixed on Andrew, and Harley stepped closer to her side.

He knew how hard that question had been for Jennifer to ask, and he stepped closer to her side and took her hand.

"Jennifer, is now the time to be asking this?" Sam was the one to step forward. "We need to get you all out of here as fast as possible."

"I think now's the perfect time," Jennifer stated, her eyes never leaving Andrew.

"We'd all like to know." Harriet stood on Jennifer's other side and glanced around the room. "At least the three of us would, as I'm betting the rest of you already know."

"Yes!" Andrew nodded. "My mother needed help as she'd gotten an invitation to BAD MAN. I'd only ever heard rumors about the club. That's when you were so ill."

"So what?" Jennifer's voice became low and was filled with anger. "You traded an operation to help her?"

"No." Andrew shook his head. "My mother was always going to perform the operation. My father found out and was the one that extended the invitation to my mother."

"You don't turn down an invitation from BAD MAN." Jennifer nodded.

"No, you don't, but someone of equal value can take your place," Andrew stated.

"And that was you!" Jennifer guessed.

"Your fa..." Sam stopped. "Andrew is the best defense attorney in the state, if not the USA, and his father knew that. A judge can only do so much and needed someone like Andrew in the club."

"I'd left my family law firm a month after I met your mother," Andrew smiled as his eyes took on a faraway look. "She was clerking with Betty at a family law firm. Sam and I were working a case together and Betty was on the other side of it."

"That's how you and Betty met," Harley realized.

"Yes," Sam confirmed. "The moment I saw the fire in her eyes when Andrew walked into her office, I knew—" He stopped talking and laughed. "She stood up to Andrew and put him in his place."

"It was that case that made me realize just how naive I'd been and how much my father had manipulated me and hidden the truth of our family legacy from me," Andrew said in disgust. "I eloped with your mother, and as soon as we'd saved enough money, Betty and I were going to start our own law firm, and your mother was going to manage it."

"But your mother's father fell ill and passed away so suddenly. Betty returned to Plum Island and took over the family business. Your mother and I followed her." Andrew told her. "She and Betty had this wonderful childhood here, and we wanted that for you and Liam."

"Andrew gave up everything, and his father was furious," Sam continued. "Andrew and I were friends back then, as were Betty and me, so I bought a place in town to keep an eye on them."

"My father threatened me often," Andrew told her. "But he knew Sam and I hadn't left Boston empty-handed, and we could sink him at any time."

"But when you got ill, and Andrew needed Davina's help to save your life, Pearce had found the perfect way to get Andrew back into the fold," Sam picked up the story.

"So you took your mother's place in the BAD MAN club?" Jennifer's eyes widened.

"I had to," Andrew nodded. "There's no way my mother would've joined that club. She and my father were pushed together by their parents. While my father had wanted to marry my mother, all she'd wanted was her career. Until I came along, her life was about protecting me while still forging an awe-inspiring career despite who my father was."

"Your mother fixed my heart?" It was a rhetorical question from Jennifer. "Why couldn't she help my mother?"

"Oh, honey..." Andrew stopped himself. "Sorry, Jennifer. Your mother's heart was too damaged, and she was too weak for a transplant." He ran a hand through his hair. "My mother adored you, Liam, and your mother. She was devastated when she realized she couldn't help your mother."

"You took your mother's place in the club, and then what?" Jennifer said. "You had to pledge to leave your family behind?"

"No." Andrew shook his head. "That's not how the club works. Once you're in the club, they keep an eye on your immediate family and will pull them in should they feel they'd benefit the club."

"Or, like with Davina, can manipulate their members," Sam elaborated.

"My father wanted me in the club at any cost. My cost was that my family was looked after financially but were left alone by the club," Andrew told her. "If ever any of you or anyone remotely close to you were approached, I, along with my family and mother, would disappear, and information about my father and his two disciples would find its way into hands that were itching to find dirt on them."

"And that's why Sam was always near," Jennifer put the pieces together. "He was ready to pack us up and disappear us?"

"Yes," Sam admitted.

"So all these years, you've been stationed here standing guard over the Gains family?" Harley shook his head in disbelief. A thought struck him. "So that's how you knew the Wesley family?"

"Yes." Sam nodded. "And before you ask, I had nothing to do with you and Angela falling in love. I didn't even know she would be at the function I took you to."

Harley turned toward Andrew, looking at him accusingly. "The club wasn't trying to manipulate me by pushing Angela and me together."

"No, Harley, I can assure you we had nothing to do with that," Andrew promised. "But it did cause waves in the club as Angela was supposed to marry Wallis."

"People just manipulated like puppets by these people?" Jennifer said in disgust.

"Pretty much." Andrew nodded. "But they did as I asked and left you, Betty, and Liam alone." He looked at Harley. "They also left your family alone."

"You knew who I was when you met me the other day!" Harley accused.

"I did." Andrew nodded. "But I thought it best not to mention it." He looked at Jennifer. "You, Liam, and Harley were never supposed to get caught up in this."

"That's why I kept encouraging you to get Angela's parents to take control of her guardianship," Sam told him.

"Are you such a good attorney that the club bowed to your stipulations?" Jennifer watched Andrew intently.

"The reason they stuck to my stipulations is because my grandfather started the club," Andrew's words shocked the room into silence. "And I'm the one that's going to shut it down."

"Oh, Andrew, you disappoint me," A woman's voice came from the front door.

They'd all been so engrossed in Andrew's story that no one had heard her and her heavily armed goons walk into the cottage. Jennifer's hand instantly tightened in Harley's, and he moved into a position to shield her and Harriet as best he could.

"Hello, Shannon," Andrew greeted the tall, well-dressed woman who reminded Harley of Cruella deVille. All she needed was the multi-toned hair.

Shannon? Harley's eyes widened as he realized she was Wallis's sister. His first thought was that Wallis had doubled-crossed them and let her know where they were until he remembered Andrew said he was being followed, and she must've been who was following him. Harley snuck the drive back into the secret pocket in his jeans as she assessed the situation.

"Oh, hello, little brother," Shannon's eyes flicked over Wallis.

"What are you doing here, Shannon?" Wallis squared his shoulders.

"I want to say looking for you, but that would be a lie," Shannon drawled. "I was following Andrew to stop him from making the worst mistake of his life." She raised her eyebrows. "And look, I have all the leverage to get him to do what I say."

"Here," Sam threw his keys on the floor at her feet. "What you're looking for is hidden in a kid's lunch box beneath my car seat. Take it and leave."

"Do you think me a fool?" Shannon eyed Sam like he was a piece of dirt. She asked one of her goons to get the keys and check. "We'll see if you're telling the truth and then decide what to do with all of you."

Harley caught Sam's eye as the man left, and a silent message passed between them.

"Jennifer, when I say go, run to your aunt's bedroom and collect Annie, Angela, and Wallis along the way," Harley instructed. "Aunt Betty's room turns into a panic room. And now I know why."

"What?" Jennifer whispered and spluttered before asking. "What are you going to do?" she looked up at him with wide, worried eyes.

"Get rid of the threat," he told her.

He could see she was reluctant to do what he asked but nodded.

Harley caught his uncle's eye before saying. "Go!" he hissed and sprung as fast as a striking snake, taking down the remaining guard.

Sam came up behind him and managed to detain Shannon as Harley went after the second guard, who he took down with the tranquilizer gun his uncle threw at him as he rushed out the door.

When they'd all been detained. Harley saw Jennifer coming down the hallway. He rushed toward her.

"Why aren't you in the room?" Harley asked, his voice filled with panic. "I haven't had a look around the property yet. There may be more guards."

"I was worried about you," Jennifer told him. "And..." Her eyes went toward the living. "Sam and Andrew."

"They're fine," Harley assured her. "But I need you to get into Aunt Betty's room, or I won't be fine worrying about you."

Jennifer nodded as their eyes met and locked. Harley didn't know who made the first move, but they were locked into each other's arms for a deep, searing kiss the next minute.

"Uh-um!" coming from Betty's room, drew them apart, and Harley lifted his head to see Harriet looking at them knowingly. "Sorry to interrupt. But I have a room of people wondering what's happening out here. And I don't want to go in there and tell them their fearless leader is a bit busy interrogating a witness with his lips!"

"Uh... Harley... um," Jennifer looked at him, her cheeks flaming. "He was just telling me to be careful."

"Is that what they call sneaking in a secret smooch these days?" Harriet nodded.

"Just get inside and lock the door," Harley ordered Harriet, who saluted him and slipped inside.

"We'll talk when this is over," Harley promised, stealing one more kiss before turning her toward the door. He watched her slip into the room and waited until he heard the safe door slide shut.

Once Jennifer was safe, Harley went to check out the property only to find the glass door open and Andrew lying unconscious on the floor. "Uncle Sam."

Harley rushed outside, nearly knocking Sam off his feet.

"My bad back!" Sam grumbled. "Good grief, where's the fire?"

"Where's Shannon, and what happened to Andrew?"

"He'll be okay," Sam assured him. "But Shannon's disappeared into the cove."

As he spoke, the distinct sound of helicopter blades could be heard.

"Good. Reinforcements are here, and so is Andrew's transport," Sam informed him. "As soon as we've got Andrew and the rest of you out of here, I'll lead a search for Shannon."

"I'm not going anywhere," Harley told him. "I'm going to help look for Shannon. Especially if she was the one that killed Clair."

"Clair was already dead from the poisoned water," Sam told him. "James, who is Shannon's spy and right-hand man, set the scene up to look like Clair had committed suicide."

"James?" Harley had heard Andrew mention James earlier. "James, Andrew's driver?"

"Yep. He worked for Pearce, too, remember," Sam pointed out. "The man comes off all nice, but he's as cold as ice and loyal to whoever runs BAD MAN."

"What a stupid name!" Harley commented as he helped Sam get Andrew up.

"When it started with Andrew's grandfather, he was known as the bad man whom no one messed with," Sam explained. "The name stuck."

Within a few minutes a dozen US Marshals and FBI agents invaded Beach Plum Cottage. Sam took over the operation, and Harley handed the disk to Andrew before they went to get everyone locked in Betty's room.

As soon as the door opened, Angela burst through it and rushed into Harley's arms.

"Harley, I'm so glad you're alright. I was so scared something had happened to you," Angela wailed, her eyes filled with tears. "I don't know what I'd do if anything happened to you. I love you."

"I love you too, Ange," Harley's voice softened. He couldn't stay mad at her.

"Do you mind? You're blocking the hallway." Harriet's voice was laced with disdain, and when he lifted his head, his eyes widened when they met Jennifer's stricken ones.

By the time Harley had untangled himself from Angela, Jennifer, and Harriet were nowhere to be seen. Before Harley could find them, Andrew approached him.

"I'm going to need you to come with me to Boston to deliver the evidence and get Angela, Wallis, Annie, and Duncan to safety," Andrew told him. "I'll need you to sign guardianship for Angela over to me. While you hold that title, you or anyone around you, including my daughter, aren't safe."

"I thought you were about to crumble this organization," Harley pointed out.

"You know these things don't happen overnight, and there's always a loose end," Andrew reminded him.

Harley understood, and the last thing he wanted was to put Jennifer in danger. So he agreed. He looked for Jennifer as they were getting into the helicopter. Still, it wasn't until Angela grabbed his hand and pulled him inside that he turned to see her staring after them. It wasn't until the door was closed and he looked down to see he was holding Angela's hand that he realized how it must've looked to her.

But it was too late to get out of the helicopter and explain as the bird lifted into the air.

CHAPTER 19

The sun dipped low on the horizon, casting long shadows across the coastal landscape. Waves crashed against the rugged cliffs, their rhythmic symphony filling the air. The Cove, a secluded haven tucked away from prying eyes, seemed to hold its breath as tension crackled in the sea breeze.

Jennifer stood at the cliff's edge, the salty air stinging her face as she and Harriet peered over the side to the cove below. They could see Sam, alongside a team of US Marshals and FBI, descend on it.

"Aunt Betty's gun," Jennifer turned to Harriet. "Get it from the safe in her room. The code is my birthdate."

Harriet hesitated. "Jen, I'm not letting you go down there alone." She shook her head stubbornly. "Let Sam and his heavily armed team get her."

"They'll take too long to find her." Jennifer looked down at the cove. "I think I know where she'll head to." Her eyes met Harriet's concerned ones. "I know the cove better than anyone. Get the gun. Head down the stone stairs, and right behind the last one, a small opening becomes a cave."

"What about a flashlight," Harriet tried to stall Jennifer.

"I have my phone." Jennifer patted the pockets of her jeans. "Get the gun and hurry."

Jennifer slipped past her before Harriet could slow her down with more arguments. She headed down the stone stairs, hopping behind the last one and freezing as the barrel of a gun was pointed at her. Shannon emerged from the shadows, a sinister smirk playing on her lips.

"I was hoping it was you rushing down the stairs," Shannon taunted. "The little golden child. You'll be my bargaining chip to get out of here unscathed."

While her heart beat frantically, Jennifer was determined not to let Shannon get the better of her.

"You're wasting your time. Harley and Angela are on their way with my father and all the evidence. Only this time, they're going to someone not indebted to BAD MAN." Jennifer kept her voice level and eyes narrowed. "Your legacy of tyranny is about to crumble. Just give yourself up."

Shannon laughed as she spun Jennifer around and dug the cold steep of the barrel into her back. "Do you think there isn't a contingency plan for this sort of thing happening?" Her voice was close to Jennifer's ear. "Don't you get it? BAD MAN is like a hydra. You cut the head off one part. There are still others to take over."

"Not this time," Jennifer informed her. "Didn't my father tell you?"

"That's the second time you've referred to Andrew as your father," Shannon pointed out. "Have you suddenly gotten over your abandonment issues with him?"

"I now understand *why* he *had* to leave us," Jennifer hissed. "It's you and your family I now have an issue with. Who do you think you are? You can't mess with people's lives the way you have."

"You're so innocent, Jennifer." Shannon pushed her forward. "It's a dog-eat-dog world, and I prefer being *the* apex of apex predators."

"No, you don't understand," Jennifer pointed out. "An apex predator is only apex while his prey fear him. But not when they realize there's strength in unity."

"Whatever," Shannon fobbed Jennifer's wisdom off. "Move." She shoved Jennifer forward again, out of the cave. "Stand down." She addressed Sam and his men. "You all know by now what I'm capable of."

"Back off!" Sam commanded, his authoritative voice slicing through the air.

As the men moved back, Shannon, undeterred, ascended the stone stairs, using Jennifer as a human shield. At the top of the stairs, she pushed Jennifer towards her bulletproof SUV, intending to make a hasty escape.

"Don't try anything while I open the car," Shannon warned. "I'd hate for you never to get the warm fuzzy family reunion your little heart has been secretly yearning for, for forty years."

As Shannon reached the car door, Harriet's voice rang out like a warning shot.

"Stop, or I'll shoot!"

Shannon grabbed Jennifer's hair to use her as a human shield again. Her hair was released when Shannon slid her arm around Jennifer's neck. She saw Harriet wielding Aunt Betty's large six-shooter pistol and pointing it at Shannon with deadly precision. The atmosphere crackled with tension as Harriet, determined and unyielding, questioned Shannon's fate.

"Oh, look, it's the faithful friend!" Shannon sneered. "What are you going to do?" She laughed. "Shoot me through your friend?" She cocked her head. "I guess that gun's probably powerful enough to go through both of us."

"I've been shooting since I was old enough to walk," Harriet warned Shannon. "Tilt your head again, and I'll show just how good I am."

"Are you sure that thing still fires?" Shannon snorted. "It looks like it's from the Wild West. I doubt the bullets in it are even real as they probably haven't made them since then either."

"Maybe." Harriet's hand didn't shake, nor did her voice falter as she inched closer. "But let me ask you this." She raised an eyebrow. "Are you willing to find out if this pistol still works? Do you feel lucky, Shannon?"

"Seriously?" Jennifer hissed at Harriet, who loved Clint Eastwood movies and was probably trying to find a way to say that.

"I think you have your movies muddled up," Shannon pointed out. "Dirty Harry's gun wasn't as ancient as that thing."

"If you don't release Jennifer and give yourself up, I guess we'll find out if it fires," Harriet said, her voice and aim still not faltering as she addressed Jennifer. "Jen, what animals freak you out? Remember you told me they're the one creature you probably wouldn't have a conscience about learning to hunt?"

"D..." Jennifer's eyes widened even more as she realized what Harriet was telling her to do. *Is she crazy?*

But the slight movement of Harriet's finger on the trigger and shoulders told Jennifer Harriet was deadly serious. Jennifer knew that Aunt Betty would frown on what she was about to do, but it was the only way to get out of Shannon's grip. She bit down hard on Shannon's arm.

"Cow!" Shannon grunted and released the grip on Jennifer's neck.

Jennifer took the gap and slipped out of Shannon's grip. She dodged sideways and knocked Shannon's weapon out of her hand, sending it flying to the ground. Jennifer jumped to the side, but Shannon managed to grab her arm as the gunshot exploded through the air. The world seemed to slow, and something hot stung the top of Jennifers' arm as she heard Shannon grunt, and the next thing Jennifer was being pulled down to the ground, landing beside Shannon.

Pain seared through Jennifer's arm once the world sped up, making her squeeze her eyes shut. Her hand shot up to grip the painful area and encountered sticky liquid. Her eyes opened as she brought her hand toward her face.

Is that blood?

"Jennifer, are you okay?" Harriet appeared above her.

"You shot me!" Jennifer accused, holding up her bloody fingers. "I can't believe you actually shot me!" All the fear, anger, and anxiety of the day tumbled to the surface. "It's my birthday. You're not supposed to shoot me!"

"I'm sorry!" Harriet's brows knitted together, and she held the gun up. "But in my defense, when you told me that Aunt Betty had a gun. I thought it was a cute automatic that a woman carries in her purse, not something out of a Clint Eastwood movie."

"Jennifer!" Sam's voice alerted them to the team swarming towards them. He reached them, and his eyes fell on Jennifer's bloody arm. "Oh, no. You were shot!" He looked at Harriet. His eyes were wide with concern.

"Um..." Harriet handed him the gun. "It wasn't my fault that Aunt Betty doubles as Dirty Harry, and I didn't realize the kick on this relic from the Dirty Harry museum."

"You have Betty's gun?" Sam took the weapon and slid the safety on before sliding it into the waistband of his pants. "What's Betty's gun got to do with..." Sam's eyes turned toward an unconscious Shannon." He looked at Harriet in amazement. "You shot her?"

"*She* shot me as well," Jennifer pushed herself into a sitting position, tired of staring up at them from the ground.

"*I didn't mean to*," Harriet growled, rubbing her shoulder. "Besides, that relic nearly took me out as well. I'm sure I dislocated my shoulder."

"I thought you knew how to shoot?" Jennifer said.

"A normal gun!" Harriet stated. "Not that thing!" She pointed to the gun. "Shannon was right about it being from the Wild West."

Sirens suddenly erupted around them as the police and an ambulance arrived. Harriet had shot Shannon through the shoulder, and when she'd fallen, Shannon had hit her head, knocking herself unconscious.

After the medic had patched Jennifer's arm up and the sea of police, US Marshals, and the FBI left, Jennifer turned to Harriet with a grin. She couldn't resist saying, "I guess Shannon wasn't lucky after all."

"That's what you get for playing the odds against Dirty Harriet!" Sam laughed. "Are you ladies going to be okay?"

"We're fine, Sam," Jennifer assured him. "Have you heard from Harley and my fa... Andrew?"

"Yes, they managed to get to Andrew's contact at the FBI, and the information is in the right hands," Sam told them. "It looks like the three of you just took down an organization akin to a mafia one."

Harriet and Jennifer watched Sam leave before heading inside. Jennifer went to her aunt's wine cabinet and pulled out a bottle of merlot.

"I'm going to order takeout and drink wine," Jennifer told Harriet. "Do you want to join me?"

She nodded. "Of course." Harriet glanced at her wristwatch. "It's only just gone nine. Why don't we go out for dinner and try to salvage the last few hours of your birthday?"

"No. Let's order in because I'm exhausted," Jennifer said, pointing to her arm. "And I was shot."

"Is this going to be a thing?" Harriet sighed. "Hello, I'm Jennifer, and this is Harriet. She shot me."

"I like that." Jennifer grinned, handing Harriet a glass of wine. "As it's my birthday, you can order the takeout."

"Fair enough," Harriet agreed.

An hour later, they were eating dinner and going over the past few days' events when Harriet pulled out two folded pieces of paper. "Now that you and Andrew are on the way to patching up your relationship," she held up the letters, "are you ready to read these?"

Jennifer sighed. Those letters had been haunting her the whole day. She took a big sip of wine and nodded. "Why don't I pour us some more wine, and you read them to me."

"Are you sure?" Harriet looked at her questioningly.

"It's not like you haven't already read them," Jennifer pointed out.

"I haven't," Harriet surprised Jennifer by saying.

"Really?" Jennifer looked at her, amazed. "You've had them since our botched break-in at the Newbury Port mental health facility."

"I haven't really had the time to read them," Harriet pointed out. "And I wouldn't have because they are not mine to read."

"You are such a weird combination of sophistication, sarcasm, eccentricity, and decency." Jennifer shook her head and then frowned when a thought struck her. "Why don't you ever talk about your family?"

"I talk about my family." Harriet took a sip of her wine. "But they're not as interesting as yours and everyone else's on this island." She opened the letters. "Shall I read?"

"Sure," Jennifer nodded, her eyes narrowing as she decided the next mystery to solve was why Harriet avoided talking about her family at all costs.

Dearest Jennifer, Nothing I can say or do will ever excuse the way I left your and Liam's life. But it was a choice I had to make, and even though it nearly killed me, it is one I'd make again if I had to.

"Okay, stop!" Jennifer blew out a breath. "Maybe don't read it. Rather rip it up and throw it away."

"I haven't even gotten to the good part yet!" Harriet looked at her in disappointment.

"Andrew has already explained himself," Jennifer told her. "I know there is a lot we need to work through. But I'd rather we did it face to face than through a letter."

"Okay, then." Harriet started folding Andrew's letter. "If you're sure."

"No. Read it!" Jennifer changed her mind.

Harriet grinned and continued.

While I can't go into great detail, know that I didn't leave because I no longer wanted to be with my family. I left because I wanted them to be safe. I wanted to be able to watch you grow up and spoil my grandkids.

The only way for me to ensure you got the operation you needed and Liam went to the school for gifted children so he could reach his full potential, was to walk away.

I could only ensure your and your brother's safety if I walked away.

I would rather have you both angry and disappointed in me and know that you were safe even if I die a little each day inside not being with you.

You may not understand now, but one day, when all this is over, I can explain it to you. You'll read and hear things about me that you won't like, but sometimes you must get your hands dirty to clean house. And that is what I'm doing—cleaning a corrupt house.

I hope one day you'll allow me to explain everything to you and be able to find it in your hearts to forgive me.

Love always.

Dad

Jennifer sipped her wine as she absorbed what Andrew had written.

"I thought you said there was a good part?" Jennifer glared at Harriet.

"There wasn't," Harriet admitted. "I just wanted an excuse to finish it."

"Nice!" Jennifer shook her head.

"Are you ready to hear your mother's letter now?" Harriet asked.

Jennifer nodded and poured herself some more wine. "Start after the part where my mother instructs me to read my father's letter first."

Harriet nodded and opened the letter.

I want you and Liam to know that your father didn't leave us because he didn't love us. Your father left because of how much he loved us. While you might think he's abandoned us, he hasn't. Your father had to sacrifice his family to ensure our safety and that you get all the medical care you need.

"So now it's my fault Andrew left us?" Jennifer's brows knit together. "Because I had a heart condition that needed an expensive operation that I've recently found out was done by Davina."

"No!" Harriet shook her head. "Andrew left to protect all of you." She sighed. "And, like Andrew told you, Davina was the best cardiothoracic surgeon of her time who did groundbreaking procedures."

"Yeah, I'm one of those groundbreaking surgeries," Jennifer noted.

"I thought you and Andrew were getting past all this animosity you have toward him," Harriet commented and held up the letter. "May I continue?"

Jennifer nodded.

Your grandfather is not the greatest person, but he needs your father's help to pull him out of a really bad situation. Your father's not doing this for your grandfather. He's doing it for us and his mother. In exchange for his help, your grandfather agreed to support us and put you and Liam through college. He also promised that our family would be protected from the danger that seemed to follow your grandfather around.

The only problem is that your father has to cut all ties with us to ensure our safety. To save your grandmother, who had been drawn into danger because of your grandfather, your father has to cut all ties to us. Due to the nature of the work your father has to do, this is a good thing as we don't want to be drawn into the dark world of the rich circles the Gains family moves in.

One day, when it's finally over, I hope you do me one small favor: give your father a fair chance to explain everything before you judge him.

Love you,

Mom.

"Well, that told me nothing," Jennifer said, raising her glass in a mock salute.

"It was your mother's last wish," Harriet pointed out.

"Thank you for that!" Jennifer shook her head. "Not only did you shoot me today, but you also made me feel like a lousy daughter for not granting my mother her final wish."

"Again, with the shooting!" Harriet exclaimed.

Jennifer looked at the bandage on her arm. "You're lucky I don't press charges."

"For saving your life?" Harriet stared at her in disbelief before her eyes narrowed. "I know what this is really about."

"My friend shooting me on my birthday and then making me feel guilty for not rushing into Andrew's arms and forgiving him?" Jennifer rubbed it in. "I told him I'm open to talking and working things out." She plonked the wine on the table, and the contents nearly sloshed out the glass. "That's sort of forgiving him."

"No." Harriet shook her head. "This is about Harley choosing to go off with Angela and not staying here with you."

"What?" Jennifer spluttered. "No!" She denied it vehemently. "Harley and I are just friends."

"Uh-huh!" Harriet nodded. "I saw the look on your face when they ran into each other's arms before they left."

"They've been together for a long time," Jennifer said, trying to sound like she didn't care. "Angela needed him, and Harley's always been there for her."

"But you wanted him to be here for you and choose you." Harriet pressed. "I saw the two of you kissing, remember."

"That wasn't a kiss, kiss!" Jennifer said. "It was a be careful kiss."

"He didn't kiss me like that when he told me to be careful." Harriet gave Jennifer a smug grin. "Then there was the whole tension between the two of you on the ride between Boston and Newbury Port." She sipped her wine.

"That was because of the kiss we shared an hour before we left," Jennifer admitted.

"Ah-ha!" Harriet snapped her fingers. "I knew something was brewing between the two of you."

"Something was starting between us," Jennifer corrected Harriet. "That was before Angela admitted that she'd never stopped loving Harley, and he hopped on the first vehicle out of here to go with her."

"Jennifer, Harley went with Angela because—" Harriet couldn't finish her sentence because Jennifer cut her off.

She already knew how Harley felt. It was made very clear to her in the way that he'd nearly knocked her flying to get to Angela after they'd shared an intimate moment and then decided to go to Boston with Angela and Andrew. Leaving her here with a dangerous criminal. Everyone she loved seemed to have a habit of running off to Boston.

It was official: Boston was no longer her favorite city. Her eyes widened as she realized she'd just admitted to being in love with Harley.

"I know why he went, Harriet," Jennifer's voice wobbled with emotions.

She was finding it hard to control them as she'd never felt like this about anyone before. *Trust me to fall for someone who wasn't emo-*

tionally available. Jennifer's heart ached and started to crack. *Touché, Karma!*

Harriet's eyes narrowed as she studied Jennifer. "Oh, my word." She looked at Jennifer in amazement. "You've fallen for Harley."

"It doesn't matter what I feel." Jennifer shrugged, feeling the cracks start to splinter. "As long as Angela's in his life, Harley has no place for anyone else."

<hr />

EPILOGUE

Two weeks had slipped away since the last time she saw Harley. Harriet inadvertently revealed that he'd be returning from Boston later that day. Not that Jennifer sought out this information; she had come to terms with the realization that Harley wasn't destined to be hers. A handful of kisses was the extent of their connection.

Glancing at her wristwatch, panic surged through her. "Shoot! I'm going to be late." Hastily, Jennifer slipped into the stunning pair of high heels, yet another thoughtful gift from Harriet. The shoes arrived as a belated birthday present after Harriet caught sight of the elegant dress Jennifer had chosen for Caroline's rehearsal dinner—or rather, the extravagant rehearsal dinner ball insisted upon by Alex Blackwell in his cliffside mansion, the Glass Palace, perched above Cobble Beach.

Caroline's imminent wedding day left Jennifer in a whirlwind of emotions. It felt like just yesterday when her best friend got engaged to Brad Danes. While joy for Caroline's happiness coursed through her, it served as a bittersweet salve for Jennifer's heartbreak. Falling for someone emotionally unavailable was a painful lesson that seemed like karma's ironic payback for the hearts she had unintentionally broken in the same way.

Examining herself in the full-length mirror, Jennifer marveled at the floor-length blue satin gown. Its soft flow accentuated her long, lithe frame, with delicate shoestring straps gracefully tapering over her shoulders. The front of the dress rippled gently while the daring open V-back plunged just above her waist. Complementing the ensemble were matching blue high-heel pumps, elongating her legs, and a tasteful slit revealing a glimpse of her tanned, toned calf.

Her hair, elegantly swept into a soft bun with tendrils framing her neck and caressing her cheeks, added a touch of allure. Opting for a light touch of makeup, Jennifer applied an extra layer of mascara, eyeliner, and a pink-tinged gloss to enhance her natural radiance. Her phone buzzed, and she looked to see their car had arrived. Jennifer gave herself a last look over her eye, landing on the pink scar where Harriet had shot her before dashing out of her room.

"Aunt Betty," Jennifer hollered. "The car is here. Are you ready?"

When there was no answer, Jennifer went to Betty's room, but she wasn't there. Frowning, Jennifer went to the front of the house and nearly died of fright when she saw Harley standing in the kitchen with a single red rose.

"Harley?" Jennifer breathed, her heart beating from fright and excitement at seeing him.

"Hello, Jennifer." Harley's eyes held hers, and his voice was low. "Betty said I was to tell you she'll meet you at the ball and instructed me to escort you there."

"Oh!" Jennifer felt the excitement shatter when she realized her aunt had forced Harley to be her escort. Her pride made her lift her chin as anger washed over her. "I don't need an escort to the ball. In case you haven't noticed, this is the twenty-first century, and women go to places all on their own now."

"But what if I need an escort because I don't like attending functions alone?" Harley asked.

"I'm sure Angela will go with you," Jennifer said because she couldn't stop herself.

"I don't want to go with Angela," Harley told her, moving closer to her and handing her the rose. "I want to go with you."

"Why?" *What the heck, Jennifer? Where is my freaking mute button?*

"Because since the day I met you, there hasn't been a day when you haven't occupied my thoughts." Harley stepped closer, still holding the rose out to her. "We started off at each other's throats, banded together to help our loved ones, and went on a big dangerous adventure together." He lifted his hand and gently touched the scar on her arm. "The past three weeks while I've been away, I found myself counting the minutes until I could get back here to you."

Jennifer's heart felt like it was trying to ram through her ribs to get to him. It was thumping so hard. Her stomach fluttered uncontrollably, and her breath caught in her throat at the emotion shining in his eyes.

"But what about Angela?" *Stop talking!* Jennifer swallowed. "I heard you telling her you loved her, and then you left, leaving us here with a dangerous criminal."

"I do love Angela." Harley's reply made her heart squeeze. "But like a sister. I'm not in love with Angela."

"Oh!" Jennifer's brows rose, and the tightness around her heart eased.

"Uncle Sam told me how you and Harriet took Shannon down," Harley said, and Jennifer thought she saw pride flicker in his eyes. "That was incredibly reckless and dangerous of you but also incredibly brave."

"It was Harriet who shot her," Jennifer told him.

"And you, I believe." Harley looked at her scar once again.

"She told you that, didn't she?" Jennifer shook her head.

"Yup!" Harley's smile took her breath away. "She wanted to tell me before you did so she could explain it wasn't her fault."

Jennifer gave a snort. "Harriet was really brave." Her brows rose as she said. "I believe you helped Andrew round up the BAD MAN club members."

"Nearly all of them," Harley nodded. "And I believe you donated bone marrow for Molly a week ago." His eyes flashed with worry. "Are you sure you're up for a ball?"

"I'm fine," Jennifer assured him. "And so's Molly. Georgia and Molly have told me that her blood count is up, and so far, she's had no signs of rejection."

"That's good news," Harley said. "It's nice to know that you and Liam are rebuilding your relationship with Andrew and your new family."

"We still have a long road ahead. But we like Georgia and Molly's great. She and Lila are already best friends." Jennifer smiled. "Lila thinks it's great that she has an aunt the same age as her."

"Andrew is now Angela's guardian and is looking after her affairs," Harley caught Jennifer up on his news. "Angela is doing great and is in a mental health facility in Boston. She and Wallis are getting close again. Annie is working with Andrew's mother, Wallis's mother, and Margaret Wesley to open a cancer hospital for children."

"That's great," Jennifer said, swallowing as Harley took the final step, bringing them toe to toe.

"I've missed you," Harley's voice dropped and became hoarse as he put the rose in her hand. "I'm really hoping you missed me too, or it's going to make what I have to say rather awkward for me."

"I did miss you," Jennifer was done trying to keep her thoughts from dodging her common sense barriers and slipping through her lips. Her voice dipped as her breath caught in her throat. "What did you want to say?"

"That I've fallen head over heels in love with you," Harley told her. "That I did the day you knocked me flying with your car door and stepped out with your blazing violet eyes."

Jennifer's heart felt like it would explode with joy at his words as she stood staring at him at a loss for words. *Sure, now you lose the ability to speak!* She admonished herself.

"I'm starting to feel a little uncomfortable here," Harley's head lowered, and his lips drew closer to hers.

"Don't," Jennifer's voice was barely a whisper as her arms reached up and wound around his neck, and his clamped around her waist.

"Because I fell for you on the same day. I'm head over heels in love with you, too."

"I don't know if I'm disappointed or relieved to hear that," Harley startled her by saying.

"What?" Jennifer looked at him, astounded.

"Alex offered me his yacht in case you didn't feel the same way about me," Harley explained. "The plan was to take you out into the middle of nowhere and make you fall in love with me."

"After you kidnapped me and stranded us in the middle of the ocean, you thought I'd fall for you?" Jennifer snorted. "That definitely sounds like an Alex Blackwell plan. The man is a Neanderthal!"

Harley nodded. "I'm so glad I don't have to use it, though. Because I'd much rather swoop you into my arms and kiss you until you realized you felt the same way about me."

Before Jennifer could say another word, his lips crushed hers as the world around them faded. Jennifer knew she was where she wanted to be for the rest of her life—held in Harley's arms and cradled in his heart.

CONTINUE READING

THE CAFE ON PLUM ISLAND - COBBLE COVE ROMANCE - BOOK 3

CHAPTER 1

Carly Donovan moved gracefully through the dazzling extravagance of the Summer Inn's executive ballroom, where a fairytale wedding reception for Caroline Shaw and Brad Danes unfolded in a splash of celebrity splendor. The room radiated grandeur, from the crystal chandeliers casting a soft glow to the carefully arranged floral center-pieces. The glass front of the room opened onto a patio, seamlessly blending the celebration with the moonlit beach beyond.

Carly sought refuge in the shadows of the room as she observed the lively dance floor and skillfully avoided the many guests, both famous and Plum Island locals. She glanced at her wristwatch, wondering if two hours was long enough for her to have been there before using her excuse to make a quick escape.

Carly could slink into only so many corners, and she'd nearly bumped into one of the Blackwell brothers, who was also trying to disappear into the shadows. Which was not good as they were the main people Carly was trying to avoid.

Her eyes scanned the room, finding the bride. Caroline was talking to Jennifer Gains. Now would be the perfect time to approach her, make an excuse, and leave. Carly looked toward the dance floor, where Reef, her seventeen-year-old son, reveled in the festivities with his friends, injecting youthful energy into the elegant affair. He didn't look like he was ready to leave, so Carly sought out her brother, Harley, whom she found at the bar.

"Harley," she greeted him with a subtle smile.

"Hey, Carly," Harley replied, returning her smile. "Not enjoying the festivities, I see."

"No, I am not!" Carly's eyes slid toward where she'd seen Ethan Blackwell last, but he was no longer there. She turned back to Harley. "I want to go. I have a headache."

"Of course you do." Harly winked and followed her gaze to where Reef was dancing with Caroline's daughter, Jules. "Ah!" He nodded in realization. "Reef's not ready to leave."

"No, he is not." Carly sighed and looked at her older brother. "Would you be able to give him a lift home and keep an eye on him?"

"Of course," Harley said, turning to get his ordered drinks and glancing to where his new girlfriend Jennifer and the bride were talking. "Do you want me to make your excuses to Caroline and Brad?"

"No." Carly shook her head. "If you'll let Reef know I said goodbye, I love him, and he must behave himself."

"And that I'm now in charge, and I'm his ride home!" Harley looked at his nephew.

"Please." Carly nodded. "I'll go and say thank you, congratulations, and goodnight to Caroline." Before she turned away, she looked at her older brother. "I'm really happy you've found love again, Harley. I like Jennifer. She's lovely."

"Thank you, little sister." Harley leaned forward and kissed her cheek. "You'll find love again too."

"No!" Carly exaggerated the word emphatically and shook her head. "I'm done with that and all the drama that comes with it."

"Carly, that was a different time, as you were literally someone else back then," Harley pointed out. "

"If I agree with you, can we change the subject and say goodnight?" Carly looked at him with a pained expression. "I know that you're deeply in love and extremely happy, but for me, my son is the love of my life and the most important person to me."

"Yes, but soon he's going to be moving on to find the most important person in the world to him," Harley pointed out. "I don't want you to end up alone."

"You mean like Uncle Sam?" Carly raised an eyebrow at the reference to their bachelor uncle, who'd raised them when their parents died. "He's always seemed really happy being single and relationship drama-free."

"No, little sister, that's where you're wrong," Harley corrected her. "Uncle Sam has been secretly in love with my new girlfriend." He grinned. "I love saying that." He drew a breath before continuing as Carly rolled her eyes. "Aunt Betty."

"Betty Swan?" Carly's brows rose. "I always thought something was going on between them." She looked at Harley questioningly. "Have they finally admitted it?"

"Not in so many words," Harley admitted. "But close."

"Or, you're just in love and want everyone else to be in love," Carly told him, shaking her head. "Now, I'd better go before more guests surround Caroline."

Before Carly could wish her brother goodnight, the hair on her arms prickled as tension straightened her spine when the voice of Alex Blackwell came from behind Harley.

"Harley, there you are!" Ethan exclaimed, clapping Harley on the back, making him turn. Carly saw her brother have the same spine-stiffening reaction when he saw Alex's brother, Ethan, with him. "I'm not sure if you've met my brother, Ethan."

"Yes, we met a few weeks ago. Harriet introduced us," Harley said, and Carly saw him force a smile as he reluctantly offered Ethan his hand.

"Good to see you again," Ethan remarked, taking Harley's hand.

Carly wondered if she could slip unnoticed past the three men who towered over the petite five-foot-five figure. But before she could make a move, Alex spotted her.

"Hi. I don't believe we've met." Alex caught her with his gaze and charming smile. "I'm Alex."

"Oh, sorry," Harley said, stepping aside to bring Carly out of his shadow. "This is my sister, Carly Donovan."

"Ethan." Ethan stepped forward before Alex could shake Carly's hand. His eyes narrowed, and his brow creased. "Have we met before?"

"If you've eaten at Cobble Point Restaurant, you've probably seen my sister there," Harley replied. "Carly owns it."

Oh, great, big brother. Carly sighed inwardly. She'd been avoiding having a meeting with Ethan about her restaurant being used as a possible location for a series of Cobble Cove Mysteries.

"You're the elusive owner of that gorgeous restaurant on Lookout Point!" Ethan explained. "I've been trying to get hold of you for two weeks to discuss it being used as a possible location for Caroline's series."

"Yes, that's right." Carly's discomfort was growing from the piercing blue scrutiny of Ethan Blackwell's gaze. She offered a polite smile. "I'm sorry I have yet to get back to you, but it's been hectic lately, being summer and peak season."

"I understand," Ethan told her. "But I need to sort out all the locations by the end of next week. Would it be possible to give me thirty minutes of your time tomorrow morning?" He raised his brows questioningly. "I'll meet you at the restaurant, and I don't mind if you have to carry on working while we talk."

Carly glanced at her brother and Alex. They were staring at her expectantly. She felt like a deer caught in the headlights of an oncoming twenty-four-wheeler. Carly was trapped.

"Sure. I can meet you at ten thirty tomorrow morning at the restaurant." Carly nodded and glanced at her wristwatch. "Oh. Is that the time?" She looked up at the three men. "Please excuse me, but I have to go."

"Of course," Ethan said, stepping aside.

Carly gave him and Alex, who was staring at her as if he were trying to piece together a puzzle, a tight smile before turning to her brother.

"Thank you for looking after Reef," Carly told him. "I'll speak to you tomorrow."

Harley nodded, and Carly made her escape, heading for Caroline and Jennifer.

"Hi, Carly," Caroline, and Jennifer greeted her with warm smiles.

"Hi," Carly replied. "Congratulations." She hugged Caroline. "You look beautiful."

"Thank you." Caroline's smile broadened. "I never thought I would have a big wedding if I got married a second time."

"Well, it's a great wedding," Carly told her. "But I'm afraid I'm going to have to leave."

"Oh, no!" Caroline's face fell. "Is everything okay?"

"I have a big catering order tomorrow, and I still have a few things to sort out," Carly told her. It wasn't exactly a lie.

"I understand," Caroline said. "Thank you for coming."

"Of course." Carly smiled and hugged her again. "I hope you and Brad have a wonderful honeymoon, and I know you're going to have a happy life together."

"That's sweet of you to say." Caroline smiled.

Carly said her goodbyes and decided to find Reef to let him know she was going. Carly had already run into Ethan Blackwell, so not much else could go wrong. As she pushed her way onto the dance floor, she bumped into a tall woman who was about to storm off the dance floor with her phone plastered to her ear.

"Sorry..." Carly's voice faded as she came face-to-face with none other than Daphne Rose.

"No, it was my fault," Daphne acknowledged without a flicker of recognition for Carly in her eyes. "I'm sorry." With that, she turned and stalked away.

Carly stood staring after the woman, amazed that Daphne hadn't recognized her.

"Mom!" Reef's voice made her look away from the disappearing Daphne Rose. "Are you okay?"

"I'm fine, sweetheart," Carly assured him as she turned toward him. "I came to find you to let you know I'm going home."

"Do you want me to come with you?" Reef asked without hesitation.

"No, sweetheart, you stay and have fun. Harley said he'd give you a ride home," Carly told him.

"Mom, I can walk home because we live just across the road in the nature reserve." Reef rolled his eyes.

"You know I don't like you walking through the reserve at night," Carly told him.

"Mom, the place is lit up so brightly they can see it from space," Reef pointed out.

"Harley's will give you a lift home, and that's the end of this conversation." Carly's voice brooked no argument.

"Fine!" Reef shook his head. "Do you want me to walk you to the car in case you get..." He looked around the room. "You know..."

"No, I'll be fine." Carly smiled, and her heart swelled.

Reef was so protective of her. Her baby boy was not such a baby anymore and had towered over her since age fifteen.

"Okay." Reef hugged her and kissed her on the cheek. "Drive safely, and I love you."

"I love you too, sweetheart." Carly gave him an extra squeeze. "Please be good, and I'll see you later."

Carly hurried from the ballroom, stopping to get her purse and shawl. She hurried to her car and nearly stumbled over a young girl hiding beside it, dropping her purse and keys.

"Oh, I'm so sorry," Carly said to the teen as she bent down to retrieve her things. "Are you okay?"

"I... I... I'm fine." The young girl jumped to her feet, grabbing the book she'd been reading. "I was in your way." She pushed her round tortoiseshell glasses up her nose.

Carly was captivated by how large and blue her eyes were, wondering why she did not wear contacts since the glasses did nothing for her. Geez, Carly. How nice. You were in the company of A-listers for three hours, and already you're sinking into old habits.

Her eyes assessed the young girl's expensive attire and knew she wasn't homeless, nor did she seem to be a runaway. She was also dressed like she was attending a formal gathering. Carly's eyes narrowed. She must be the daughter of one of the wedding guests.

"Are you hiding from the wedding reception?" Carly asked her.

The girl nodded and clutched her book as if it were a shield. "Yes. I don't like parties and crowds."

"I don't either," Carly told her, smiling warmly. "Why don't you rather sit in the hotel foyer or lounge area instead of out here in the car park on the tar?"

"I was tired of my b..." She stopped what she was about to say. "The person who takes care of me when my father's busy keeps finding me in there and dragging me back to the wedding."

"Ah!" Carly nodded. "I know a place in the hotel safer than the car park where you can hide."

"Thanks, but I'd rather just go home," she said.

"Can I give you a lift?" Carly offered. "I'm heading home myself, and I can take you home."

"I can walk," the girl told her. "I live across the road in Nature Valley Estate."

"Oh!" Carly's eyes widened. "I live there too."

"Really?" The girl looked at her in surprise. "We moved in last week to number five."

"No way! I live in number three." Carly's heart slammed into her rib cage as she hoped the girl and her family were friends or relatives of the bride, not A-listers on the groom's side.

"You're Reef's mom?" The teen asked.

"Yes, that's me." Carly smiled and held out her hand. "I'm Carly Donovan."

"I'm Shay," the girl introduced herself.

"It's nice to meet you, Shay." Carly frowned thoughtfully. "If you like, I can give you a lift home if your parents allow me to."

"It's just my father," Shay told her, a shadow darkening her beautiful blue eyes. "My mother passed away seven years ago."

"I'm sorry." Carly's heart went out to her. "Should we go find him and ask him?"

"It's okay. I'll go ask my dad. If I can find him," Shay said. "If you don't mind waiting for a few minutes,"

As the teen ran into the Summer Inn, Carly started following her. She knew if Reef was going to get a lift with a stranger, Carly would like to meet them. Shay met Harriet Joyce at the entrance, where Harriet stopped her as she approached. Harriet was the groom's best friend, Harley's new girlfriend, Jennifer's good friend, and her business partner. Carly watched the two of them talk as she approached.

"Hello, Carly," Harriet greeted her warmly. "I believe you and Shay are making a break for it."

"Yes," Carly confirmed. "I have a bit of a headache." She lied.

"Are you sure it's okay for Shay to go home with you?" Harriet's eyes filled with concern. She looked at Shay. "Honey, you can go to my hotel room if you like."

"No, I want to go home," Shay told her, and she turned to look hopefully at Carly. "Would you mind if I stayed with you until my father came home?"

"I'm sure that won't be a problem if your father's okay with it," Carly said, frowning as she glanced at Harriet.

"He'll be fine," Harriet assured Carly. "I'll let him know as soon as he finishes another business call."

"My dad lives on his phone." Shay's voice dropped.

"Shay, you know he loves you more than life itself." Harriet hugged the girl and frowned. "Where is Oz?"

"I escaped him hours ago." Shay grinned. "He's probably sitting outside your hotel room door, where he thinks I am."

"You're a sneaky rascal." Harriet laughed and looked at Carly. "Thank you for looking after my girl here."

"No problem," Carly told her with a smile. "I remember being just like Shay at her age. I'd take curling up with a good book over having to go to a big gathering."

They said goodbye to Harriet and went to Carly's car.

"Is Harriet the person who looks after you when your father's busy?" Carly asked as they buckled up, and she started the car.

Carly pulled out of the Summer Inn and drove a few meters down the road before turning into the drive that ended with large cast iron electric gates. The scanner scanned her license plate, and the gates slid open.

"Yes." Shay nodded. "Well, sort of." She looked at Carly. "Harriet's my godmother."

"Oh!" Carly's eyebrows rose, and her heart sank. Her neighbors were A-listers. *There goes my quiet hide-away bungalow in a nature reserve.* "Harriet is lovely."

"Yeah, she's the best." Shay smiled. "When my mom died, she was there for me and my dad."

Carly turned into her driveway and opened her automatic garage door so she could drive in and park her car. She let them into the small outer room where hers and Reef's coats, shoes, umbrellas, and hats were. Carly kicked off her heels and hooked her shawl over a hook on the wall.

"Must I take off my shoes?" Shay asked, eyeing the room.

"No, you don't have to," Carly told her. "I needed to remove those heels, as they were killing me."

"My dad won't let me wear heels yet," Shay told her. "He said maybe he'd think about it when I'm eighteen."

"Trust me," Carly assured her. "Your feet will be better off until then."

"I love shoes, though," Shay chatted with Carly as they entered the kitchen.

"I think most women do," Carly informed her with a laugh. "Would you like some hot chocolate or herbal tea?"

"Just some water, please," Shay said.

Carly nodded and took two bottles from the refrigerator, handing one to Shay. "Would you like to watch TV?"

"Sure." Shay nodded and followed Carly into the living room, where she sat on the large sofa while Carly sat on the giant armchair. "I like old-fashioned movies."

"Oh, really?" Carly pulled a face, impressed. "Well, I just happened to have a collection of them if you'd like to choose one."

Shay flicked through the movies. "You own the restaurant at the top of Midpoint, right?"

"I do." Carly nodded, taking a sip of water.

"I believe you make the best malts around there." Shay clicked on a movie. "Oh. I love this one."

"Me too," Carly agreed, pulling her feet up next to her as she noticed the title of Shay's book. It was about archeology. "Do you like archeology?"

"Yes, I want to be an archeologist," Shay told her.

"That's awesome," Carly told her. "I wish Reef would decide what he wants to study."

"Isn't he going to college next year?" Shay asked.

"He is." Carly nodded. "But he doesn't know what he wants to study, though. He is undecided about doing computer science or engineering."

"My grandmother was an archeologist," Shay told her. "Then she met my grandfather, and after they were married, she gave it up. Gran has told me stories about her digs since I was very young. Gran still has contacts in the field and goes on the odd dig. She's taken me on a few over the years."

"How wonderful," Carly said. "You and your grandmother sound close."

"We are," Shay confirmed. "Even before my mother passed away, I spent most of my time with my grandparents. They raised me, and I saw my parents on the weekends or during school holidays. After my parents got divorced, my father had full custody of me because my mom—" She glanced at her hands and fiddled with the remote. "My mom wasn't well. So I only saw her on weekends on supervised visits."

"I'm sorry," Carly's voice dropped and was filled with compassion. "Where did you live before you moved here?"

"My family's home is in the Hamptons, but their business is in New York," Shay told her. "My father has a townhouse in New York where he would spend most of the week if he wasn't on a job."

Carly was about to ask Shay about her father when there was a knock at the door.

"Excuse me." Carly smiled at Shay as she got up and walked to the front door.

Carly pulled the front door open and froze when she saw one of the Blackwell brothers standing there. She didn't know which one, as she could never tell them apart.

"Hello, again,"

"Hi," Carly greeted him, her eyes narrowing as her brow creased as she tried to figure out which brother he was. I should've paid more attention to what they were wearing.

"It's Ethan," he said, and her heart dropped.

Great, the brother I didn't want it to be! Carly forced a smile. "How did you get my address?"

"Harriet told me where you lived." Ethan frowned at her, craning his neck to see inside her house.

"Oh?" Carly's brows knitted tighter together. "I thought we were meeting tomorrow morning."

"I hope we still are," Ethan told her, his eyes lighting with realization. "She didn't tell you, did she?" He sighed and shook his head.

"Who didn't tell me?" Carly was feeling really confused.

"My daughter!" Ethan said as Shay dashed to the front door and said. "Dad!"

Oh, great! Carly gritted her teeth. Not only does Ethan want to use my restaurant as a filming location, but he's also my next-door neighbor!

COBBLE BEACH ROMANCE SERIES

Series Books:

The Lighthouse on Plum Island – Book 1

The Cottage on Plum Island – Book 2

The Restaurant on Plum Island – Book 3

The Library on Plum Island – Book 4

The Beach Hut on Plum Island – Book 5

The Summer Inn on Plum Island – Book 6

AVAILABLE SOON ON **AMAZON**

MORE BOOKS BY AMY RAFFERTY

SERIES

Christmas at Mistletoe Lodge ~ *A Feel Good Holiday Romance*

New Year at Mistletoe Lodge ~ *A Feel Good Holiday Romance*

Reunion at Mistletoe Lodge ~ *A Feel Good Holiday Romance*

The Bakery in Bar Harbor ~ *Secrets in Maine Series*

Cupids Bow Ranch ~ *Montana Country Inn Romance Series*

Starting Over in Nantucket ~ *Cody Bay Inn Series*

Leave a Rose in the Sand ~ *Starting Over in Key West Series*

A Mystery at Summer Lodge ~ *A Coastal Vineyard Series*

Charming Bookshop Mysteries ~ *Small Town Beach Romance*

Moonlight Dream ~ *Honey Bay Cafe Series*

Nantucket Christmas Escape ~ *Second Chance Holiday Romance*

Retreat ~ *Manatee Bay Series*

Secrets of White Sands Cove ~ *A San Diego Sunset Series*

The Seabreeze Cottage ~ *La Jolla Cove Series*

STANDALONE NOVELS

The McCaid Sisters ~ *A Second Chance Romance Mystery Novel*

BOX SETS

Montana Country Inn: The Complete Collection ~ *Montana Country Inn Romance Series*

Cody Bay Inn: The Complete Collection ~ *Nantucket Romance Series*

Starting Over in Key West: The Complete Collection ~ *A Florida Keys Romance Series*

A Mystery at Summer Lodge: The Complete Collection ~ *A Coastal Vineyard Series*

Charming Bookshop Mysteries: The Complete Collection ~ *Small Town Beach Romance*

Honey Bay Cafe Series: The Complete Collection ~ *Second Chance Beach Mystery Romance*

Nantucket Christmas Escape: The Complete Collection ~ *Second Chance Holiday Romance*

Manatee Bay: The Complete Collection ~ *Treasure Seekers Beach Romance Series*

Secrets of White Sands Cove: The Complete Collection ~ *A San Diego Sunset Series*

The Seabreeze Cottage: The Complete Collection ~ *La Jolla Cove Series*

THREE IN ONE

Coastal Collection: Sea Breeze Cottage, Mystery at Summer Lodge, Secrets of White Sands Cove ~ *Three Series in One Book*

SPANISH VERSION

El Café de Bahía Honey ~ *Honey Bay Cafe (Spanish)*

Escapada Navideña a Nantucket ~ *Nantucket Christmas Escape (Spanish)*

Bahía de Manatee ~ *Manatee Bay (Spanish)*

La Posada de la Bahía Cody — *Cody Bay Inn (Spanish)*

AMY RAFFERTY VIP READERS

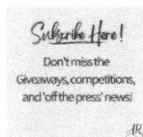

Don't want to miss out on my giveaways, competitions,

and 'hot off the press' news?

Subscribe to my email list.

It is FREE!

Click Here!

CONNECT WITH AMY RAFFERTY

Not only can you check out the latest news and deals there,

you can also get an email alert each time I release my next book.

Follow me on BookBub

I always love to hear from you and get your feedback.

Email me at ~ books@amyraffertyauthor.com

Follow on Amazon ~ Amy Rafferty

Sign up for my newsletter and free gift, Here

Join my 'Amy's Friends' group on Facebook

A NOTE FROM AMY RAFFERTY

Hi, wonderful people,

Having been described as "The Queen of Gorgeous Clean Mystery Romance," I am delighted that you are here.

I write sweet women's romance fiction for ages 20 and upwards. I bring you heartwarming, page-turning fiction featuring unforgettable families and friends and the ups and downs they face.

My mission is to bring you beach reads and feel-good fiction that fills your heart with emotion and love. You will find comfort in my strong female lead role models, along with the men who love them. Fill your hearts with family saga, the power of friendship, second chances, and later-in-life romance.

I write books you cannot put down, bringing sunshine to your days and nights.

Thank you for being here and reading my books x

Made in the USA
Las Vegas, NV
11 September 2024

95096320R00267